GOMEZ

A Novel

by

Bill Pieper

Pacific Slope Press
2005

GOMEZ

C. 2005 by **Bill Pieper**, All Rights Reserved

Except for incidental quotation in reviews or promotional materials, no part of this publication may be reproduced, stored in a retrieval system, or transmitted, in any form or by any means, electronic, mechanical, photocopying, recording, or otherwise, without the written prior permission of the author.

Cover art by **David Post**
    Claudio's Wedding Jacket, 2001 (detail)
Cover design by **Gail Segerstrom**

US Edition
Published by **Pacific Slope Press**
Printed by   LightningSource Inc.
                LaVergne, TN, USA

Pieper, Bill
    Gomez / Bill Pieper.
ISBN 0-9740215-1-2
    1. Title
Library of Congress Control Number: 2005906400

Trade distribution is through **Ingram Book Company**

Retail copies available at **http://stores.ebay.com/bpbooks**, in bookstores or with a shopping cart at **www.amazon.com** or **www.bn.com**

For information, or to arrange author interviews and appearances at stores, events or book clubs contact:

Pacific Slope Press
c/o Holden Research & Marketing
P.O. Box 254733, Sacramento, CA 95865-4733

GOMEZ

• • •

The characters, locations and situations described herein
are entirely fiction or used fictionally, and do not portray any real
persons or events.

• • •

Other Titles by This Author

So Trust Me (novellas)
Fool Me Once (novel)

GOMEZ

His many years of providing inspiration for characters and concept make the late Marc Frauenfelder all but co-author of this book. No Marc, no *Gomez*; it's that simple.

Additional Acknowledgements

As with all my work, *Gomez* has benefited immeasurably from the generous support of family, friends and fellow writers.

Here, in alphabetical order within groups intended to recognize the quantity of time and effort exacted from them, is what I hope comprises a full list. Sincere thanks for their patience, perseverance and good will on this project go to:

My dear wife Cathy Holden; my endlessly helpful friends Harvey Schwartz, Kit Snyder and Claudia Viek; the writers Gail Hensley and Persia Woolley; reader/commentators Glenn Durfee, Diane Durrett and Paul Samuelson; the writers Bill Breault, Pat Henshaw, Nan Mahon and Naida West; cover artist David Post; other readers Muriel Brennan and Sidney Hollister; and for technical assistance, James Brady, Michelle Capor, Jorge Chavarro, Brad Dowden, Dawn Morely and Jon Sole.

A further debt is owed to Professor Charles Bankowsky of the Sacramento State University Creative Writing Program and to my Fall 2001 classmates in English 230A. Nor could I have done without two other institutions that foster creative endeavors of many kinds: the California State Library and the Sacramento Public Library, particularly in the person of Janet Wininger.

Finally, my thanks along with a *mea maxima culpa* to anyone forgotten above.

GOMEZ

GOMEZ

PART I

...relativity makes many people fearful — the idea that you are one person with me today and another person with someone else later.

>Anaïs Nin
>*New Woman*, Vol. 1,
>No. III, Dec. 1971

GOMEZ

CHAPTER 1

When Gomez was in his Henry Miller period he lived off Valencia Street near 22nd in a one-room, back-alley apartment. It was San Francisco, of course, not Paris, but the Mission District of 1978 seemed gritty enough to suggest Place de Clichy in the 1930s, especially if you hadn't been to Paris, which Gomez hadn't.

He was no writer, either, but he owned all of Miller's books—the two *Tropics*, *Sexus*, *Nexus* and so on, plus obscure ones like *Air Conditioned Nightmare*. He even had his version of Anaïs Nin, an artsy banker's wife from Piedmont named Madeline Klein, who for a while there couldn't get enough of him. She was my age, 33, while Gomez said he was 38. In fact, like Miller, Gomez had a June in his past, but he was the only one of us who knew it then.

Mad and Gomez always denied a resemblance to the famous literary pair, so I finally stopped bringing it up. But if they didn't want people making the connection, why were copies of *Plexus* or Nin's *Diary* always lying around while Gomez's other books, of which he had a lot, were lined up on his wall of sagging board-and-brick shelves? The strangest part, though, is that Gomez was an alias, and that he'd looked far more Hispanic the year before, when I met him in Berkeley under different name.

In both cases he was brash, brown-eyed and swarthy, but as Gomez he'd buzz-cut his unruly mane to quarter-inch length, shaved off his Zapata-style mustache, and gone from contact lenses to a pair of round, silver, wire-rim glasses. He'd also Europeanized his wardrobe and changed the way he walked, although I couldn't swear to the last of those details. Talking to him, you knew he'd been through other transitions, but I somehow expected the Gomez one, because I'd witnessed it, to be the last.

As for Madeline, I thought she was a major babe: strawberry blonde, with long, slightly wavy hair, which she liked to tie up or accent with scarves. No one would dispute that her hair and her wide-gauge mouth were her best features or that she knew how to play them for maximum effect. Given Mad's coloring, she'd have

GOMEZ

freckles if she were Irish, but as a Pole she was blessed with clear, wrinkle-free skin, hazel eyes, breasts not so large that they sagged at all, and everything from there down was just right as well. Her face bones were maybe a little pinched, and she'd had a nose-job she assumed people noticed, but the braces her family paid for when she was a kid had given her a memorable smile.

Still, it would have remained another example of the unfulfilled longing I was used to if Gomez hadn't so pointedly drawn Mad and me together. I was shocked to be made his proxy, but with Mad corroborating his intent, that seemed the only logical explanation. It went with the Henry Miller thing, and never before had a woman pursued me. Nor am I such a moralist that I think bad consequences were inevitable.

There are always multiple turning points in life, and a key one for me was what happened at Mad's that May. I don't mean the sex. I mean afterward, which I certainly hadn't planned. How much of it she planned I've never known, but obviously some, since I was told in advance where and when to appear. Had I been less nervous and less consumed with carnal thoughts while driving across the bay and while Mad's maid, Graciela, was letting me in, I might have wondered if I was following a script.

Φ Φ Φ

"Geez," I mumbled disorientedly, "what time is it?" Something had made my eyes flutter open, and I rotated my head in Mad's direction, stretching myself under the light blanket she'd pulled over us.

Like an odalisque, she was propped on one elbow, with her hair cascading along her arm and her teeth visible in an amused smile. "Well, we're making progress," she said. "This time you even let yourself conk out. You were so skittish when you arrived, I didn't know what to expect."

It came to me where I was—in the guest cottage, behind Mad and her husband's house, on the bare wooden floor on a mattress surrounded by the glow of a half-dozen paper bags, each containing a few inches of sand and a lit candle. They were a means of illumination learned from Graciela, and they had a Spanish name Mad told me and I'd forgotten. The room was otherwise sparsely furnished, with the few chairs and the desk lost in shadows against the walls. We had left the French doors onto the small patio ajar, and the sweet odor of lemon blossom drifted in whenever the air moved.

I had my watch on, so checking the time was easy, but while leaning toward one of the lighted bags for visibility I nearly knocked over our bottle of cabernet and the wineglass we'd been sharing. "Quarter to twelve," I said, relieved. "Not too bad."

"You can stay, you know. Clark is in Borneo the rest of the week."

"Yeah, but it's a workday and I don't want to hassle the commute...not to mention trying to dodge your neighbors on my way out."

Mad gave a languorous laugh. "The driveway has tons of privacy, Paul, and you could be one of Graciela's friends for all anybody cares."

"I still ought to leave." Actually, I was still seared from a prior cycle of approach and avoidance on her part and didn't want to risk morning-after awkwardness.

"Fine," she nodded, rolling toward me, "if that's what you want." We kissed with real intimacy, as though it was the most natural thing in the world. Gently, she pulled back. "Now, I've got abluting to do while you get dressed. My new lover had DSB."

"I need vocabulary help with that one."

She laughed again. "Deep sperm buildup."

"Oh," I said, embarrassed, as she had probably intended.

Mad quietly retrieved the camisole she'd been wearing beforehand and wadded it into a makeshift towel, which she pressed against herself under the blanket when she sat up. Letting the blanket fall away, she turned and stood, holding the camisole in place. I saw her graceful back and the twin mounds of her rear, their whiteness exaggerated in the candle-glow, move toward the dark rectangle of the bathroom door. She closed it, I heard the switch click, and a crack of light showed at floor level.

I became aware, too, that my groin was radiating a form of satiated pleasure I had barely realized it was capable of. I was supposed to get dressed, but all I did was lie there. Until Mad it had never been my experience that there were women who would pantingly say while they were wrapped around you that they wanted all you had and wouldn't stop until they got it. Even if your genital endowments were modest, these same women also seemed to enjoy performing oral sex.

Like a teenager after a heavy date, I smelled my fingers to verify that what I was remembering had been real. You'd think that having gone to college in the Sixties and the eight years of my former marriage would have taught me those things, but that's not how it ever was for me, or for me and Jenny either.

Discomfiting as this is to admit, Mad was rewriting my sexual profile, leaving me to cope with the idea that a rewrite was what Gomez had in mind. No one wants to be a charity case, but resisting was impossible when she was the alm and my other options were so few. To salvage a vestige of pride, however, I was happy to pretend — outwardly, and inwardly as best I could — that having his permission wasn't really unusual, or of great importance, which appeared to suit all of our purposes.

I talked as little as possible to either of them about the other, and Gomez, who typically loved the big-brother role, showed decreased interest in talking to me about Mad. It mirrored his strategy regarding her husband, whose existence Gomez assiduously minimized. Since Gomez himself seemed to need — or prefer — the illusion in order to play, he would realize that I did too. And to whatever extent he and Mad talked about me, a thought I truly hated, I was counting on it to be minor.

Sigmund, Mad's cat, a fluffy gray tabby, nosed in through the French doors and padded over to sniff the roach-clip and stubbed-out leavings in the ashtray on her side of the mattress. He then stepped onto it opposite me and flopped down. I heard water running, and knew I needed to rouse myself. Time to file the barely believable mental images of the past hour-and-a-half, which were like starring in my own porn film without the bother of lights, camera or retakes.

I poured more wine, slid the bottle to a safer place, gathered my clothes and sat on what had been my pillow. Mad's tape deck, whose click must have awakened me when it automatically rewound, clicked again to launch a low-volume repeat of our earlier music, a dreamy flute album called *Midnight at the Taj Mahal*. I had

GOMEZ

worn only underwear, khakis, socks, running shoes, an Alligator shirt, and a velour sweatsuit jacket, but putting them on amounted to an IQ test.

The bathroom door swung open and Mad emerged wearing a short, jade-green satin robe. She left the light on behind her so we could see as she went around extinguishing the…the…*luminaria*…that was the word.

"I'll have more, too," she said, pointing at the wine bottle. With a contrived pout in her voice, she added, "But you were *mean* not to smoke with me before."

"Something for the future," I answered. "You say I did OK without it." I had been too concerned about how I would behave my first time on her turf, and I'm not really a doper. I also wanted to think she and I had a future, if only nights like this. Taking another small swallow of wine, I handed her the glass.

She sat between Sigmund and me, idly petting him, her legs folded beneath her. "What if I'd had cocaine?" she teased.

"I'm not really into that." The fact was, I'd never done it, which she probably knew, but I didn't want to confess.

She gave a sweetly skeptical smile. "Gomez says cocaine is for dancing and grass is for sex. Maybe he's right, maybe not."

OK, there he was. You never knew when he would pop up, and in this setting my least-favorite topic. "Freely asserted, freely denied, my ex-wife likes to say."

"Oh, yeah, the scientist," Mad replied, drinking some wine. Mad is also the type who lightly touches or grasps your forearm off and on while she talks, which she now did to mine with her free hand. "I'm blanking on her name," she continued. "Sorry."

"Jenny," I replied, having blundered into my other least-favorite topic. It was usually easy to divert Mad onto her childhood or the inner workings of her job. Why hadn't I done that? Even discussing her husband would be preferable to Gomez or Jenny.

"She's a Brit, you said?" Mad asked.

"Uh-huh," I answered reluctantly.

"Well," Mad shrugged, returning to her earlier thought, "Gomez is a fantastic character, but he can sure be dogmatic about things."

If Gomez was the only way to avoid Jenny, so be it. I'd blown the chance for a more benign segue, and didn't want Mad probing how my marriage had ended. Whatever she already knew was bad enough. "He can," I agreed. "That's a lot of what makes him fantastic. His lack of self doubt."

"Ever wonder if he's too fantastic?" With or without the arm-touching, Mad is big on eye contact, and she accompanied her question with an extra dose of both.

"What do you mean?"

"His whole bio," she laughed. "The Henry Miller business is an open charade, but Buenos Aires? Yale? The Black Panther Party...? Dubious at best. Of course, Miller was quite a fabulist concerning himself, too, you know."

My expression remained casual, but a chill down the backs of my arms said that she was right; and those implausibilities were just a partial list. Not only did Gomez's alleged persona strain belief, I wondered where my blind acceptance of it had come from. "He makes the pieces all fit," I said. "Or always has."

"Till now." She coyly rolled her eyes. "But I caught him in something."

"What?"

"Graciela. I only took her in because of Gomez. She's the niece of somebody he works with at the Centro, some big cheese it sounds like. I've gotten very close with her these last months, and she wanted to clear her conscience."

Gomez was a language teacher at something called the *Centro Social de los Obreros*, a labor-union funded training and job development agency, but I still didn't see what Mad was driving at. "Why is that catching him?"

"I wasn't looking for a maid. I had a biweekly cleaning service, all I needed. Clark didn't want to pay for more. I put up the money out of my trust fund when Gomez said she was a political refugee from Guatemala...that she'd be deported to face the death squads."

"And she wouldn't?"

"She's Mexican. A standard illegal from Puebla. She's a lovely person, and I'm glad to have her, but he didn't level with me."

"Probably for a good cause." Defending him had become virtually a reflex for me.

"The cause of Gomez doing her uncle a favor. I asked Graciela another thing, too. What country she thought Gomez's Spanish came from."

GOMEZ

"Oooh...she didn't pick Argentina?" This was beginning to get serious.

"She says he's an odd mix, but not Mexican, or from Spain itself...and not Guatemalan or Salvadoran."

"But it *could* be Argentine. Did you and Gomez have some kind of fight?"

"No, I haven't told him a thing. And like you say, he might still be from Buenos Aires. It's not that big a deal. I just don't like being manipulated."

"Wait a minute. He told you he was from Argentina? He only told me he'd lived there a while."

"Maybe he didn't say born, but he sure gives that impression, the way he talks about the place. Remember that first night we had dinner at his apartment, he and I were doing the tango? Gomez is the only guy I've ever known who actually can."

"He's the only guy I've met who would try."

"You must've noticed other things that don't add up." One of Mad's hands rested briefly on my wrist for emphasis. "You've been around him longer than I."

It was a remark that I should have and could have deflected, but my response was, "You know Gomez isn't his real name, don't you?"

"What!" The wineglass stopped midway to her mouth.

"He's from the US, same as we are, and his name is Andrew Steentofter." The rush with which the words came out hid how appalled I was at speaking them. And driven by what? Mindless coveting of Mad? Or misguided revenge against Gomez for holding so much power over me? I've dissected it many times. "He used to do house painting and repair work in Berkeley. That's how I met him."

"No!"

The genuineness of her surprise gave me guilty pleasure. "Come on," I said. "He has to have told you."

"Paul, really, you're kidding!"

"I'm not. Check at the Centro. Unless he's done a legal change, he'll be on the payroll as Steentofter."

"I can't believe it."

"You're the one who's doubting everything."

"But his name? I never doubted that. With his coloring, the Steen one is more of a stretch. And to me, family names are sacred

...they're your heritage. Why do you think I didn't change mine to Clark's, or Anaïs kept hers through two marriages?"

Marriages, I subsequently learned, which had involved bigamy on Nin's part, but that didn't entirely alter Mad's point. "So this means you've caught him twice. Isn't unpredictability his big attraction? I thought you two got together because he lives in the moment and is nothing like Clark. Ditto for me. He's been a personal turbocharger." Then, perhaps to punish myself for betraying a secret I'd committed to keep, I resignedly added, "Why else are you and I even sitting here?"

"You're right...to an extent." Her mouth softened into a smile that became rueful before disappearing. "But it still makes me want to hire a detective."

"Why? To throw things in his face? What harm has any of this done?" Without thinking, I was defending him again.

"No, not that. Just to know. Like a treasure hunt. If...if whoever he is...is half as cool as we give him credit for, he'll appreciate the chase."

"In a way, he might." I let the idea settle in. "Do you really see yourself visiting Sam Spade in some seedy office and having him follow Gomez around?"

"Guess not. More a wild thought. I don't know any detectives, and I'm already paying for Graciela."

"You're keeping her?"

"I promised when she told me. It's what Anaïs would do. Besides, Clark loves her cooking."

I began to envision a less tenuous future for Mad and me, still based on Gomez, but with a different center of gravity. "Some things about him we could check on our own."

"We?" She cocked her head.

"Yeah. I like the game aspect, too." Or was it mainly the psychological plus I knew I'd get from debunking him a bit?

Mad finally raised the wine to her lips, finished it, and put the glass aside.

"The easiest place to start is Yale," I continued. "The guy in the condo next to mine went there. He's older, but he's an active alum. What makes you think Gomez is faking? He couldn't have gotten so many smarts, from science to opera, by hanging around on Telegraph Avenue."

GOMEZ

"I have cousins and high school friends who were Yalies," Mad responded. "They all came back with mugs, sweatshirts, you name it. Or their diplomas are on the wall, like Clark's from Stanford. Have you ever seen a Yale magazine or any mail from there at Gomez's place? Or his office? I haven't, and that's fishy. After I learned about Graciela, it kind of jumped out at me."

"Hard to say. I don't own a college sweatshirt, and my diploma's in storage."

"So's mine. But I get mail and quarterly magazines that end up in the living room whether I read them or not."

"Right. Magazines and solicitations I do get, piles of them. My neighbor has Yale stuff in his kitchen, which is how the subject came up."

"So you'll ask him?" Mad pressed. "About Gomez?"

"No," I laughed, feeling almost cocky. "About Steentofter. I'll pass along what I find."

She seemed uncertain. "When will that be?"

"Who knows? Why?" It registered on me that another of the recorded flute ragas was playing in the background. I'd been so absorbed by the evolution of what Mad had discovered from Graciela, the music had temporarily ceased to exist.

"Better that you not phone here while Clark's home. Let me handle the keeping in touch."

"Fine. But I'll leave a call-back message at your office if something pops." But she *had* offered to stay in contact, which itself broke new ground.

Mad dropped her gaze to the purring Sigmund. "Will you be seeing Gomez?" she asked.

"Sure. For a movie, or racquetball and a few beers. I can't start avoiding him for no reason." In fact, I didn't want to avoid him. He was too much fun, and mining the details of his life would now be more interesting than ever. "I'm also not giving up on the math puzzle. He bet us a free dinner, remember?"

"Oh yeah, that." Her eyebrows flitted up, then down. "But it could play into our new plan. You know…keep him on the line till we make progress."

"What about you? You'll be seeing him too, right?" I knew her answer would be yes, but for the first time, didn't care.

GOMEZ

"We're dancing to Viva Brazil this Thursday," Mad replied. "Just don't say anything to him, OK? About us…what we're doing?"

"Of course not. You won't, either, I hope."

"Don't worry. I never tell Gomez what's not his business. He's a great dancer, we like what we have together, but he knows he's not my whole life and I'm not his." Back she came with the eye contact and arm-touching. "I like what you and I are starting to have, too."

GOMEZ

CHAPTER 2

Driving home felt almost as though I'd smoked some of Mad's Thai weed after all. Traffic was so thin, even by late night standards, I had whole pockets of freeway and the Bay Bridge to myself, and when the occasional vehicle shot by, its taillights seemed to leave tracer streaks. I'm the kind of guy who unthinkingly goes as fast as the surrounding cars, but if there aren't any, I slow down, especially when I have a lot on my mind.

Mad had described me as her "new lover," we'd clearly continue to see each other, and now had our sub-rosa investigation of Gomez to counterbalance my unease at his sharing her with me. And maybe that we were both sharing Mad with her husband supplied additional parity. But even a more typical affair would have been well beyond my norm. Although my ex-wife and I rarely had sex, I was faithful to her the nine years of our courtship and marriage, and prior to that, my dating history was scant. Technically, in terms of penetration, until Mad, and for reasons I can't explain, I had also been faithful to Jenny all the months since she moved out.

I'd always rationalized it as having been born with a low libido, and figured it made my life simpler compared to most guys I've known. Then, without warning, my libido started making up for lost time, and the more stimulation I got, the more I wanted. As my car arrived at the Treasure Island tunnel, a strange oasis of light in the middle of the bridge, I began to regret that I hadn't stayed longer with Mad and wondered what else we would have done if I had.

My name, by the way, is Paul Stiles and I'm from Kansas. I was raised in Topeka and went to college twenty miles down I-70 in Lawrence, where I started in engineering before switching to graphic design. I had a slight heart murmur from rheumatic fever as a kid that kept me out of the draft but hasn't much affected my life otherwise. Still, I got a bye on Vietnam, and also managed to miss the sexual revolution and all the other revolutions of the time, so

GOMEZ

things have been pretty unexciting for me. Until recently, in fact, I'd thought of myself as lucky.

This chain of random musing was forcibly overridden by my nose. Though out of view, the big coffee plant abutting the SF end of the bridge was now right below. They were roasting, and the acrid stink of the hulls brought me back to Gomez. On his example I don't use supermarket blends anymore, I grind my own from Graffeo in North Beach. Yet everything I knew about him, or thought I knew, had been laid open to question.

It shouldn't have taken Mad to point that out, either, and a number of things she hadn't mentioned were weighing on me as heavily as those she had. Eventually we'd have to agree on the full scope of what we were doing and on who would take the lead. She already assumed that more than Gomez's name would be proven false, while I was trying to reserve judgment. I also didn't know if I wanted her to be right or wrong, or what we'd do with the information after we had it.

Then, as I swung onto the double-decked Embarcadero Freeway, my mind began a wide-screen, Technicolor replay of how I'd come to know Gomez and his alleged biography in the first place. Seen through new eyes, my own credulousness was every bit as improbable as the rest.

Φ Φ Φ

September 1977 represented in many ways the low point of my life. Jenny was gone, along with her furniture and possessions, while I used our house as a campsite, awaiting completion of the fix-up items required by the new owners before escrow could close. I'd been living on take-out pizza and Chinese, putting in weekends at work as a refuge from everything else. What I actually was, I later learned, was clinically depressed, but the psychotherapy revolution was one more I'd let pass me by.

Jenny had arranged for a handyman, somebody recommended by her boss, so I wasn't surprised to find a layer of tarps along the front foundation and an exoskeleton of scaffolds against the wall when I returned from the BART connector bus one Monday. I was tired and down, my usual state, and took no real note of the dented, gray Volkswagen pickup parked across the mouth of my driveway except for the crude lettering on the doors identifying Handy Andy Painting and Repair.

It was twilight, closer to seven than six-thirty, but Andy or someone associated with him was still on the job. The house was of white stucco, built into the uphill side of Arch Street, with a garage below and a two-bedroom, two-bath layout above, topped by a red tile roof. The sloping yard contained century plants and dense tangles of pittosporum and pyracantha that looped over the stepped walkway and hid the structure from the street. I retrieved a folded *Berkeley Gazette* tossed near the mailbox, started up the steps, and heard music, not extremely loud, but loud.

A forced, falsetto tenor was singing harmony with the already off-key Grateful Dead. The song was *Truckin'*, so much a part of Berkeley culture that even I knew it: "…oth-er times I can ha-ardly see-ee…what a looong, strange trip it's be-en." The recorded sound emanated from a boom-box deeply layered with colored paint drips, bringing to mind the Chianti-bottle candle holders you see in Italian restaurants. A smirched, orange extension cord ran from it along the brick path and into one of my opened garage windows. The live voice, winding down as the guitars and recorded voices faded, came from the higher of two paint-spattered platforms, under whose knobby metal supports I and the radio shared the available space.

After pronouncing the call letters, the DJ cut to another Dead song, but the person on the scaffold didn't join in. Instead I heard a grunted exhortation, no longer falsetto or tenor, "Oh, kiss my royal po-po!," accompanied by the plop of a heavy paint brush burying itself in the overgrown vinca to my left.

"Bombs away!" I replied on a whim.

"What?" The face of a mustachioed Balkan or Latin American guerrilla, topped by a painter's white hat, thrust over the edge of the upper platform. "Sorry, never knew anybody was there. You the husband?"

"The *ex*-husband," I stated. "You're stuck with me for quality control, but the ex-wife is your employer."

"Yeah, I met her. Wait a minute, I'm coming down."

"Part way's fine. I'll grab the brush." Keeping it well clear of my body, I picked it up.

"Thanks, but watch yourself. Wouldn't wanna' drip on those nice threads."

Following an interval of creaking and thumping, the lower platform, which was about shoulder-high to me, contained the mustached face and painter's hat attached to a crouching, bare-chested body encased in paint-splattered white coveralls and equally splattered combat boots. He had garlic breath, crooked teeth, blazing brown eyes, loose ringlets of black hair down to his collar, a formidable nose, dark skin and a damn-the-torpedoes smile set off by a well-chewed toothpick at its corner. With some care, however, he reached and took the brush.

"Don't worry," he affirmed. "I'm not clumsy and I do good work."

"Does that mean you're Handy Andy himself?"

"In this case, yeah. Just call me Andy. I'd shake, but believe me, you'd rather I didn't."

"Right," I nodded in reply.

"What do *you* go by?"

"Oh…call me Paul. Paul Stiles."

"I thought the missus said Cullom was the family name."

"Her name. She never changed it."

"No big deal," he said. "Names are arbitrary anyway."

Without responding, I stepped back.

"Look," Andy went on, "since you're home, I'll knock off. You don't need the uproar and I'm losing the light. Thought I'd work extra, because I got a late start and this mica paint is hell on wheels to apply."

"So it goes," I told him, reflecting on the dropped brush, the battered truck, and whether the guy actually did know what he was doing.

"I never run my radio so loud it'll bother your neighbors," he added, seeming to sense my disapproval. "Got to have company on jobs like this. Giants won, by the way. On the road, 5-4." Andy hopped down from the scaffold and turned the music off.

He was in good shape, broader-shouldered than I am, maybe a little older, but about my height, just under six feet. I could see he was appraising me, too. With my dimpled chin, light brown hair, and blue eyes, I was his opposite in coloring, and was wearing a tan,

Palm Beach blazer with tie and slacks. He also assumed I knew who the Giants were playing and that I'd care who won, both untrue.

"I'm heading inside," I said. "See you in the morning...maybe."

"Depends on how early you leave," he answered, turning away to stash the brush in a tub near the hose bib with his other equipment.

I didn't think about him the rest of the night or the next day, other than to register the scaffolding when I left for work. He hadn't been around then, but he was back that evening, complete with truck blocking the driveway and music. This time, however, I was regaled with the *Liebestod* from *Tristan und Isolde*, which I recognized right away because it was a favorite of my mother's and I'd once bought her the LP. The volume easily equaled that of the day before, but Andy himself was silent. I stood listening intently to the ethereal passion of Isolde's singing herself to death without revealing my presence.

It was warm and fogless, as Berkeley September evenings often are, the sun still up and glinting across the bay at a low angle above the Golden Gate. When the music concluded, the boom-box surprised me by turning itself off. Andy had been listening to a tape. The contrast with the Grateful Dead was no accident of the FM dial; he'd made it happen.

"Beautiful," I called up to him. He continued to work at the top level, but had moved along the wall and was about to reach the corner. "My mom loves that one."

"Hey," Andy replied without interrupting himself or looking down. "The quality inspector's here. Must be quitting time. My mother loved it, too." I heard a laugh. "Expresses all the emotions she hid from my dad."

"What's the tape?"

"Birgit Nilsson. I have boxed sets of both *Tristan* and *Tannhauser*." Dressed, coifed and paint-smeared as I'd previously seen him, Andy came to the edge of the platform and began climbing down. Over-educated handymen are common in Berkeley, but reconciling Wagner with Andy's appearance confounded me.

"You get great sound out of that thing," I said, pointing to his boom-box.

"Don't let the paint slops fool you," he nodded. "That's a high-end unit. Since I work alone, I need company. Oh, guess I told you that. But I mean *good* company. Giants were idle today, besides." He stood in front of me, his mouth below his bushy mustache stocked with a fresher looking toothpick than the one I'd noted yesterday.

"Opera fills the void left by baseball?"

"Sometimes, yeah, but could be Commander Cody or Keith Jarrett. Weekdays, there are no rules."

"Listen, would you not park blocking the drive tomorrow? I'm taking my car so I can run errands after work."

"Sure, no problem. I just needed that spot to unload scaffolding. With the yard so brushy, it's the only way in." Andy worked the toothpick with his tongue, expertly flipping its former inside end out.

"True."

"That's a nice set of wheels you've got." He jerked a thumb toward the garage.

"You're kidding," I said. "It's slated for trade-in and I'm counting the days." He meant the blue 1970 Ford Ranchero I'd ended up with on a swap to benefit Jenny's new love interest. I despised the thing and was angry at myself for consenting to take it.

Andy smiled. "Pretty cherry, to my eye. I was surprised, dual pipes and all. You don't look the type."

"I'm not."

"Neither does your wife...I mean ex. Why's it even here?"

"Long story, as they say. Too long."

"OK...well, I need to clean up." He pulled a rag from his coveralls pocket and turned away.

"I'm sending out for pizza. Want to stay and eat?" The words left my mouth before I had a chance to veto them.

He briefly studied me over his shoulder. My sport coat was slung on my forearm, my collar was open and my tie loose. "Could," he said. "Sure, why not? You like anchovies?"

"Sort of. Been a long time, but I used to order them as a kid to gross out my sister."

Andy's eyes twinkled. "There are no bad reasons to like anchovies," he said.

"I'll phone Round Table from upstairs. Anything else you like or don't?"

"That deluxe veggie of theirs is good. Start with one of those."

"Anchovies aren't vegetables."

"I'm not a vegetarian," he shrugged. The toothpick danced against his lip.

"There's a bathroom off the kitchen. Shower if you want. Knock and I'll let you in around back."

"Don't have to."

"Oh?"

"Your ex gave me a key so I could do my business during the day."

"Thinks of everything, she does," I said. Everything but informing me, that was, and she knew how I felt about privacy.

"OK, see you up there," Andy replied. "I need to check my brushes and make sure I've got clean hands before I come in."

The pizza girl I called described the order as a "large *veg*, with fish" and said it would be delivered in half an hour. Since the place was only four blocks away and she knew me, she questioned my venturesome choice. "Oh, something different," I told her.

I changed into an Alligator shirt and jeans, sorted through the mail, and read the evening paper in a kitchen chair dragged into the empty living room for that purpose. Within two weeks, I'd be moved out, and knew I'd miss the view. In fact, Arch was a classy street, and I'd miss that too. Andy's scaffolds interfered with what was visible above the neighboring roofs and trees, but I could still make out open water and the tip of the Berkeley pier, like a compass-needle, falsely marking Angel Island as north.

There was bustling at the rear door as Andy came in and made his way to the shower. A few minutes later he padded through the empty dining room carrying a jug of wine by the glass ring below its cap. He was scrubbed and had donned old tennies with no socks, jeans, a striped French fisherman's shirt, and had tied his damp black locks behind his head with a rubber band.

"Thought I'd contribute," he announced, flourishing the bottle.

"I've got wine open," I said. "Thanks, though."

"Nah, try this stuff." He returned to the kitchen and I got up to follow.

"Don't need a corkscrew, but where do you keep glasses?" He was randomly flipping the cupboard doors. "God, this place is decimated. Aha!" He pulled two tumblers from the dish drainer near the sink. "These'll do."

GOMEZ

"I'm out of here at the end of the month," I said. "Pretty much everything's packed...or already gone with Jenny."

He broke the bottle's perforated seal and filled the tumblers with slurping glugs of red wine. "Here," Andy said, handing me one. "Let's see," he mused, "Jenny would be Dr. Jennifer Cullom. I returned her call when she first got in touch with me, and it was a lab at UC. Microbiology, as I remember."

"That's the basic story. She's seriously into chickens and eggs and which came first, but her checks don't bounce."

"Glad to hear it," he nodded, now toothpick-less. "Never a problem with my kind of customers anyway. Let's try the living room to see how bad I screwed up your view."

When I caught up with him Andy had his back to me and was standing in the picture window haloed by the sun's last rays. His voice echoed off the bare walls. "I could tell this was a nice room. Sorry the scaffolds are in the way." He leaned around and raised his glass. "Cheers. Thanks for the invite."

"You're welcome." We drank, then he parked his wine on the fireplace mantel and checked the sight lines from different positions on the expanse of hardwood floor. I waited nearby, wondering what to say. I'd asked him in because I was lonely, but I've never felt comfortable with strangers.

"I dig these old Berkeley places," Andy said. "It's a joy working on them in many ways. Where you headed next?"

"SF. I bought a condo in one of the Golden Gateway towers."

"Woah," he laughed. "The lion's mouth of Manhattanization. Bet they've got dynamite views there."

"They do, but views like this one cost more than I can pay. I'll be six floors up, looking at a shoulder of Telegraph Hill and the Transamerica building."

"Could be worse. You a science type like your ex?"

"No. I do graphic design in the city. I'll be able to walk to work."

"There's your silver lining. I'd like to live in SF myself sometime. You at Landau-Walters by any chance?"

I was amazed he knew enough to guess, much less be right. "Yeah, I am. Why?"

"It's a big name in the field. The place with the floating office. They did the Giants logo. Niners, too, I think."

GOMEZ

"Right, L-W did both. And the *As*. But not me. I wasn't on those jobs."

"Which ones were you on? Any I might know?"

"Almost everything for Anchor Steam beer. The label, the coasters, the mugs, the tour handouts at the brewery."

"Hey, I love that shit. Best brew around."

"Too bitter for me," I said.

"I've even met that guy, the owner, Matts Freytag."

"Really? How?" My housepainter turned out to know my biggest client. Could be he'd painted Freytag's house, wherever Freytag lived.

"Went to college with him at Yale."

"Back east?" I asked, not hiding my surprise.

"Yeah, *that* Yale," Andy grinned. "Guess I don't seem buttoned down enough."

"What would I know, really?"

"Don't worry. I never wanted to be that buttoned down. I went there on a football scholarship...and for the English department. How about you?"

"I'm a Kansas boy, including KU."

"Like a lot of places, just a name to me. You meet the ex in Kansas?" He took a big swallow of wine.

"As a matter of fact, I did. Then she landed a research slot here."

The doorbell rang and Andy retreated to the kitchen while the pizza kid handed me a flat, warm cardboard box. I put it on the floor to have my hands free to pay him. "Did you guys order fish on that?" he asked.

"Absolutely."

"Good. I'd hate to stink up my car by mistake."

I gave him an extra dollar as tip and rejoined Andy. He'd found paper towels and folded a couple for napkins, laid out forks and plates from the dish drainer, refilled his wine, and left the jug in the middle of the table. I lowered the box and he grabbed my glass from where I'd balanced it on top, pouring me a refill as well.

"Goddamn, smells great!" he said when I flipped back the lid. "I'm starved as hell."

It smelled less great to me, but I certainly planned to eat. Andy was busy helping himself. "So," I asked, "do you keep a half-gallon of burgundy in your truck, just in case?" I sat opposite him, then forked up a slice.

He had opened one of the little pouches of dried red pepper you always get with take-out orders and was liberally dusting his plate. I never used them, and must have had twenty piled in the cupboard by the stove. Something else to get tossed when my final moving day came around.

"I try," he answered before taking his first bite. "In a way, it's a totem. I believe nothing bad can happen if there's a full jug of wine around. And you're not the only guy who's invited me in at the end of the day. Women, too. The handyman mystique, I guess. Still, better to contribute. Avoids complications. I never snoop in people's houses, either, in case you were wondering."

Conversation came to a halt as we both ate. I didn't know how to restart it, but Andy did. "Why don't one of you just keep living in this place?"

"Jenny has other ideas, and I can't afford to cash her out." I looked at the tangled trunks of the wisteria arbor, the only thing visible in the descending darkness through the dining nook window. "Besides, there's a lot of memories I'd rather escape."

"That part I understand," he said, lifting his glass. "But you must've made a killing at today's prices. When'd you buy?"

"1971, including the foundation cracks."

"My god, you couldn't have timed it better if you were a speculator."

"We did alright, but it'll get eaten up funding two new households. You have to live somewhere."

"I'm in a commune," Andy said. "Big old Victorian on Alcatraz Ave. All the amenities, and way cheaper than one address per head. Even if it gets claustrophobic at times, people don't *need* half what they think they need."

By then we'd done real damage to the pizza, and Andy was wiping his mouth and hands on his folded paper towel preparatory to pulling a toothpick from his shirt pocket. "Where's your ex going?" he added, after I failed to pick up on his previous remark.

"She's already there," I answered evasively.

"Local area?"

"Yes." My voice was dull.

"What happened? Or shouldn't I ask?"

GOMEZ

I'd been consistently stonewalling that question at work or in the neighborhood, from the few people who showed interest. That so few had was a relief, yet it underscored my total lack of friends. Only Jenny had friends. Our social life, such as it was, had revolved around her colleagues or former colleagues. Now, though, for no known reason, I had a strong feeling of owing Andy a truthful reply. So I gave one — truthful but incomplete.

"She ran off with her lab assistant. Probably easier to tell you than somebody I actually know."

"Is easier. You'd be amazed what people tell me." He leaned back in his chair and clasped his hands behind his neck. "And one look says you're in a big hurt. Always better to be the dump-*er* than the dump-*ee*."

"I can't even claim I didn't see it coming."

"No great loss in the looks department, if that helps. Some faces need a cosmetic surgeon to launch a thousand ships." The toothpick, clearly a fixture of Andy's persona, pointed straight at me from his slightly pursed mouth.

"You're right, but it doesn't help."

"Of course," he said drolly, "women like that can be really hot. Or that was Henry Miller's theory...I've been rereading him lately. Maybe you had living proof."

I understood his remark as well intentioned, and was probably supposed to laugh. He couldn't have guessed how wrong he was. Nothing in my life would ever have been compared to Henry Miller, from what little I knew of Miller then. To cover my silence, I got up and started straightening the kitchen, though not much by way of straightening was required.

Andy excused himself and took off minutes later. I remember that my mouth was parched from the wine and the salty anchovies, but what I mainly remember was somehow feeling better — much better — than I had in months.

CHAPTER 3

The following day it was dark by the time I got home and Andy was gone. It seemed pathetic to be counting on my handyman—no, my ex-wife's handyman—for companionship, so I suppressed my disappointment and ate a slice of leftover pizza and the dregs of some take-out Mexican that were lingering in the fridge. His wine bottle was still on the counter, but I drank from my own supply, cleaned up, and went to bed.

Thursday I left work earlier than usual to be sure I caught him, and stopped trying to pretend otherwise. Having finished in front except for the trim, he was working on the sides by then, and his music was the oddest yet. Shivery bonging and gonging counterpoint over sustained electronic chords that rattled the windows without seeming loud—like a symphony, but with less structure. It was called *Tubular Bells*, Andy told me around his toothpick, and was going to be "hugely influential."

"Hungry?" I asked. "Tonight I'm ordering Chinese."

"Make one of the dishes moo shi pork, and you're on."

I didn't know what that was, but the heavily accented telephone voice at the restaurant did, and it duly arrived along with some chop suey, broccoli beef, and three fortune cookies. Andy insisted on doing all the kitchen setup and cleanup, and we polished off the last of his wine along the way. He deftly prepared a couple of the papery moo shi burritos for me, which were surprisingly good, but we saved the cookies till he sat down from the sink, where he'd already worn out and discarded a new toothpick.

"Another contribution," he said, unbuttoning the pocket of the blue workshirt he'd worn to dinner. "How 'bout a little Panama Gold at the end of a long day?" He put a wrinkled cigarette and a book of matches on the table. "I only chew wood when there's not good smoke."

"You go ahead," I told him.

"I will," he answered. "Why not you?"

"Not my thing."

GOMEZ

"One toke," he said. "Extremely fine stuff."

"OK, what the hell."

Andy lit the joint, drew on it, passed it to allow my modest drag, took an additional hit, then extinguished it against the outside of the matchbook. "I should've brought more wine," he observed. "I have a case at home."

We sat quietly for an interval. I didn't feel anything from the dope and didn't expect to. "Let's try the cookies," I finally said. They were between us, lying on the surface of the small paper sack they had come in.

"Alright, you choose."

I did, stroking my chin and pretending it was a weighty decision. He casually prodded one of the remaining two toward him, then grasped the third, and strode to the sink.

"What…?" I started to ask, but before I could he dropped the cookie into the garbage disposal and turned it on. There was an instant of savage grinding succeeded by a contented whir. Andy released the switch. "The road not taken," he intoned, with an abbreviated bow and his palms pressed together at his chest.

I erupted in laughter, a sound those walls hadn't heard in quite some time. "Come on, guru-man, open yours."

He broke the baked shell, extracted the paper and read aloud, "Help! I'm a hostage…"

I interrupted to finish the joke, "…in a fortune cookie factory."

"OK," he laughed, "they even had that one in Kansas. But *this* could apply to you."

He passed it over and I spoke as I read, "Change for the better is in the wind." I handed it back. "I like the thought, but you picked it."

"I could use a little positive change myself," he stated. "What's yours say?"

I twisted until the shell crumbled to reveal "The **truth shall set you free**," which I read to him.

"There's an old standard," Andy said. "Does it apply?"

"I don't know, but the lab assistant my wife ran off with was a woman."

He was the first and only person I've told and he handled it well. Out of nowhere my pulse began pounding, so I had certainly shocked myself. My dread was that he'd laugh, though he didn't. A slight twitch of his mustache was all I saw, followed by a pause, his hand gently resting on the back of mine as I put down the little rectangle of paper, then his emphatic words, "Now that'll really fry your po-po."

Releasing my hand after another pause, he went on in a deliberately measured tone, "But it's the 70s, and this *is* Berkeley."

"Not inside my head."

"Look, while you're going through this, it's the shits, but you might have a harder time if she'd found another guy. There's the whole *What's he got that I don't?* angle."

"That's what you'd think." At least I'd answered him. I was talking about it. Why that was supposed to be so great I didn't know, but it made me feel less of a freak.

"It's what I do think!" Andy insisted. "And what you *should* think. I mean, Jenny, if she wants pussy, what can you do? That's how she's wired. You don't have that on offer, and short of surgery, you aren't going to. Am I wrong?"

I always knew I'd be on the defensive if I raised this topic. The plus with Andy was that I didn't expect to see him after the painting was done, which freed me to hold my ground. "You think I haven't plowed all through that? Show half an ounce of understanding."

"What's to understand?"

"How hopelessly damn dumb I feel!"

"Dumb? Why?"

"The only woman who wants to marry me, who's ever been interested in me, turns out to be…gay!"

"How were you supposed to know? She might not've known herself."

"That's what she says. But Christ, where were my eyes? All those years, how she held back, how I never once felt accepted, physically accepted…or desired. Who cares if she didn't know!"

"She married you. There had to be something in it for her."

"Yeah, to hide from what she really was, from what she didn't want to face. To have the status of a married woman for her parents' sake, for her career."

"OK, maybe that, or maybe she's bi, but probably something more."

"Like what?"

"You seem a decent enough guy, you're successful, nice looking, you apparently treated her well. Plenty of men don't measure up on those terms."

"You're trying to say she loved me?"

"Possible. Remember, I don't know the woman. Hell, I barely know you."

"Well, if it *was* love, it was damn well concealed. You should hear the bubbly, snookums crap between her and Barbara. Makes me want to puke! I can't stand to see them together. They're starting to dress alike, for Christ sake!"

"Look, man, you're angry, you should be, and maybe now you'll direct it at the right person...Jenny. There's no percentage in being pissed at yourself."

"Maybe...but why did I accept zero for a marriage all those years? Why was I so passive!"

"There might not be an answer except to learn from your mistakes."

"I wish I'd never brought it up."

"One thing for sure, you'll get through this. You're plenty young enough to regroup and do what you want with your life. You don't have kids, right? That makes everything easier."

"Three cheers for conventional wisdom."

"Doesn't mean it's wrong," Andy shrugged. "And you'll get through faster and better if you let the anger out. Stifling's not the way to go."

"Fine. Now can we drop it?"

"Your choice. You bring it up, we'll talk about it. If you don't, we won't."

"Of course you're going home to your commune or whatever it is to entertain people with this guy you met whose lesbian wife finally ditched him."

"Nah...wouldn't be right. But believe me, nobody there would find the story that notable or that entertaining. All kinds of weird shit happens in life."

"OK, thanks," I said, letting out a deep breath and feeling less aghast at what I'd done. Andy sounded sincere, and I wanted to believe him. "Sorry I got so touchy."

"I don't mind. It was good for you. I'm tough, and you're tougher than you think."

GOMEZ

He popped in another toothpick and looked as though he might leave, which I didn't want him to on that note. "What about a Mrs. ..." I realized I didn't know his name, "...Handy Andy? Is there one?"

"It would be Mrs. Steentofter," he answered matter-of-factly, "and there was until five years ago."

"Unusual name. Where is she now?"

"New York. We met in Greenwich Village. The name is Dutch. She took it because her own was Smith, and she wanted unusual."

"Any kids?"

"Ah...no."

"You from New York yourself?" There was nothing about Andy's coloring or features I could construe as Dutch, nor did he have any trace of New York accent.

"No, no. I grew up in Vermont. My mother was French. She and my dad met in Holland and came to the US in the 30s."

"They still living?"

"Oh yeah, retired to Florida, a place I hate."

"What'd he do? Before retirement, I mean."

"Organic chem. Right there in Bennington. Follow the polymer chain," he laughed, "from him, Lord of the Laboratory, to me, Lord of the Paint Can."

"My ex thrived on organic chem."

"Means she's screwed up in more ways than one," Andy joked, toothpick and mustache bouncing.

"Well, I'm in Berkeley because of Jenny. What brought you?"

"G-school. I got a doctorate in Renaissance lit."

"Oh...wow. There's a subject I know nothing about. But look at your job. Should have been Renaissance art."

Andy sighed. "I get the same dumb remark from everybody. But compared to non-stop ass-kissing in academia, painting is honest, useful work, and the results are plain to see. Especially outdoors, which I prefer. And I'm good at it. I've done it since summer jobs when I was a kid, all through college, and when I was teaching. You're the artist."

"You can't call what I do art."

"Good. We're agreed." He threw me a wolfish grin and gathered himself to stand.

"OK, but where'd you teach?" I still didn't want him to leave.

"Stillman." Andy's chair scraped as he got to his feet. "It was my response to their shooting Bobby Kennedy...after they'd just shot Martin Luther King."

"I don't follow. What's Stillman?"

"A black college in Alabama."

"Double wow. Must have been quite an experience. And a year I sure remember." Not that I'd forget the assassinations, but it was also the year Jenny and I met, when I was 23.

Andy moved toward the dining room on his way to the front door. "An experience, alright. I was there till '71. And catch this," he laughed, "I ran for Congress...on the Black Panther ticket."

I followed him across the bare dining room floor and into the living room, where the only furniture was the kitchen chair I'd left there a few days earlier. Andy's scaffolds looked eerie outside the big front windows, with the glittering fretwork of the Berkeley power grid as backdrop. I lit the porch light, the only source of illumination in that part of the house, everything mobile having already been packed or taken by Jenny. "You...? A Black Panther? Free Huey and all that?" I guess the idea seemed incongruous to me even then, but somehow didn't raise suspicions.

"In Alabama," he replied tolerantly, "kind of a different scene."

"Obviously you lost. How old were you?"

"Let's see...ah...28. Yeah, I lost, but it was damn close. I'm as proud of that as anything I've done." He grasped the door handle.

"Sounds like you should be." I wondered if Andy looked like a revolutionary in those days, too. The late 60s were a wild time, but I'd heard Southern blacks were pretty conservative. "See you tomorrow, I suppose."

The door swung open and cool night air tinged with fog moved across my skin. "I'll be here," he answered. "Oh, I should let you know I'm also working the weekend. Hope you don't mind. I'm way behind because of this new paint. I've never used it before, and it's so thick it's more like redoing the stucco. I haven't even started the trim."

"No problem." A weekend with Handy Andy sounded fine to me. My plan had been to get a head start on some projects at the office, the one place where I still felt competent—and knew that I was—or go to a movie by myself. "Why are you using this paint?"

"My own damn fault," he said, making a suicide pistol above his ear with his thumb and forefinger. "The supplier I go to recommended it. Your ex said match the existing colors and use top of the line."

"The new owners made us leave money in escrow for paint and for replacing a toilet. *They* wanted top of the line." I couldn't see his face clearly, but I was pleased we were wrapping all this up on a neutral topic.

"I should've bid 25% higher, tell you that. Handy Andy's taking a bath on this job. I'm glad we got to know each other better, though." He stepped onto the lighted porch.

I advanced to the threshold. "What other things do you do...besides painting, that is?"

He stood in profile, looking as much at the house as at me. "Oh...light carpentry, patching roofs...usually ancillary to painting. I'm good at electrical, too, but plumbing I avoid if I can. And no ditch digging, so don't ask." He waved, turned and headed down the stairs.

CHAPTER 4

By Saturday Andy was further behind than he'd thought and I was on a ladder slinging paint. Like anybody, of course, I'd had some experience and knew the basics. Jenny and I teamed up to do the interior in an off-white the year before, and we'd done a good enough job that the new owners intended to stay with it. The outside, however, we hadn't gotten to, and there were sections of the walls and trim that looked pretty tired.

Andy was reluctant to involve me in such a hands-on way, while I was completely willing. Friday, the evening after my embarrassing revelation about Jenny, he hadn't been around, which frankly came as a reprieve. I'd been tense all day, knowing that I had more to tell him, and especially tense because I knew, given the chance, that I'd be powerless not to.

But circumstance intervened, at least in the short run. He'd left before I got home, though a fresh jug of burgundy with note attached was sitting on the porch. The note said, "Here's some vino. Looks like I have a chance to get laid, so I'd better go for it. See you in the a.m." I took for granted that he was the kind of guy who got laid and I wasn't, but I had myself a few raunchy moments at bedtime considering the idea.

When I awoke, Andy was already working, so he must have arrived at first light. I hadn't heard him or his truck, and he'd kept the radio off and positioned himself as far from my room as he could. But he didn't refuse coffee once I'd made it, or muffins, and the next thing I knew I was at the foot of his ladder in my bathrobe reading to him from the morning *Chronicle*.

He had me begin with National League baseball scores, groaning around his toothpick when I reported the Giants on the wrong end of a 7-5 game with the Dodgers, and booing or cheering when I ran through other results. We then ascertained the Giants' weekend broadcast times, and he checked his watch while urging me to help him remember.

"Do you want times for the *A*s, too?" I asked.

"No. The American League isn't baseball."

"What do you mean? It's right here under Major League Roundup."

"Only N.L. ball's the real thing. Listen to the radio with me later, and I'll explain."

"OK, maybe. What if I get dressed and help?"

"Nah. I mean...thanks for the offer, but it's my problem."

I didn't argue, I went inside, got on my grubbiest clothes, came out again, scrounged a rag, brush and hat from Andy's supplies, grabbed an extra ladder, and moved it downstream of his along the back wall. Due to the hill, the front and north sides were more than two stories high and required scaffolds, while the back and south could be reached with ladders. The important thing was to keep them level, which was easy where we were, but would be a challenge on the south slope around the corner.

"This would sure go faster if we both had paint," I said, climbing a couple of steps.

He'd put on a tape during my absence, meditational but rhythmic piano music ideally suited to a sunny morning, and hadn't been aware of my return. "You what...?" he asked.

"Paint...you know, the stuff painters use."

"Come on, man. Seriously, it's my problem."

I climbed down, got a screwdriver and threatened to open my own drum of Mica Shield before he finally acceded. The stuff in the pail I was given looked like ricotta cheese and went on like sludge. "Jeez, I see what you mean," I told him. "The brush weighs a ton. I've already nearly dropped it."

"They said one coat," Andy grumbled. "They didn't say it would take longer than two."

We decided that I would tackle the unobstructed wall areas while Andy outlined the windows and got going on the trim. He'd washed all the mildewed spots with bleach and done the necessary scraping earlier in the week. The music, I learned, was Keith Jarrett, who until then had been just a name I'd heard somewhere.

"His *Lausanne Concerts*," Andy explained, when we were close enough to talk. "Recorded there a couple of years ago. Good stuff, huh?"

"Terrific," I agreed. "What's the encore?"

"Saturday a.m. means jazz," he declared. "Pop I can't stand lately, except the Dead and Steely Dan. I dig Bob Marley, too, but disco drives me nuts. At one, before the ballgame, there's the weekly Latin music show on KPFA. Sundays I do Bach."

Other than Latin, I vaguely knew everything he'd mentioned, but I wasn't oriented to any of it. I was happy with Barry Manilow, Abba or Neal Diamond on my car radio, and Jenny had taken the household stereo. I normally watched a little TV, mostly PBS, read, and did crossword puzzles when I wasn't working. Andy stayed with KJAZ the rest of the morning, and after lunch his KPFA show came on.

It was wild, wilder than Santana, with horns, congas, maracas, swinging piano and bold vocals. I studied Spanish in high school, but deciphering the lyrics would have been just as impossible back then. A couple of times I thought Andy would knock his ladder over bopping around on it, letting loose tongue-rolling *"A-rr-ibas"* and chanting *"Soy un salsero! Soy un salsero!"* during the instrumental riffs. If he was within range on weekends, he never missed that show, he said, even in preference to the Giants.

By then the gyrations of his omnipresent toothpicks had largely ceased attracting my attention, but I found that Andy drank nothing but water or coffee during the day, and that the wine and the few hits of dope he smoked at night were essentially rituals. Despite his flamboyance, he was a creature of moderation. While we were taking a break under a big Monterey pine behind the house, I asked about his chants. I vaguely remembered that *soy* meant I am, not a Midwest food crop, and that *un* was a, the indefinite article, but they made no sense as lead-ins to the word for condiment.

"No," Andy laughed, sitting like a cross-legged Buddha on the patchy lawn. "*Salsero*...a man who loves salsa music. You would have seen salsa dancing, too, if I'd been on the scaffolds. Means *Picante*...hot, like a spicy sauce."

"How'd you get exposed to *that*?" I settled my back against the tree.

"The first stuff, not counting Miles Davis, to ever really turn me on. Freed my dancing genes, and man, I love to dance. Because of all the Puerto Ricans, salsa was the big thing in New York when I lived in the Village. Down in Argentina we had a form of it, too."

"Argentina? What about Tango?"

GOMEZ

"Yeah, plenty of that. Mostly that."

"Long way for a vacation trip."

"No, no, I taught there. Didn't I tell you the other night?

"Alabama is all I remember."

"Well, Argentina's the other place, plus TA duty at UC. I dig teaching."

We'd become two paint-speckled *compadres* by then, so I was a ready audience for further exotica. "Did you minor in Spanish at Yale or something?"

"No," he laughed, "French, which was cheating, in a way, since it's my mother's first language. Till the day my plane landed in Buenos Aires, I'd never spoken Spanish in my life. All I knew were maybe ten words from being around New York."

"How the hell could you teach? Why would they hire you?"

"Well, English is what I taught, which was supposed to be full immersion for the students. The rule was never to help them in their own language. A gig my dad lined up…through American Field Service. A total surprise."

"Why'd he do it?" The more I kept Andy talking, the more I could postpone the topic I planned to bring up, and the regrets that I knew would follow.

"He thought I was a bum, hanging around the Village like Borowski in *Tropic of Cancer*, working odd-job construction, boffing any chicks I could. And he was partly right, but I'd been making G-school plans he didn't know about. Where he was really right was figuring I couldn't turn down Buenos Aires."

"How long'd you stay?"

"Almost three years. It was a royal bitch at first, not knowing the language. Later on I had a ball. The music and the food you wouldn't believe…or the women, and how they dug making the teacher their student. The first Spanish I picked up was in bed. Then I really got into it and learned all I could. At the end I was reading Borges untranslated."

"Ever see Peron or Evita?" They were the only names I could think of to ask about, although I recognized Borges, and had a book of his stories that I'd never gotten around to reading.

"No, no," Andy replied. "That was before Peron's comeback. He was exiled in Spain and she was dead. But a fabulous place. Too bad it's so screwed up. And the Spanish turned out to be a big boon."

"Yeah, I guess, living in California. I had some in high school, but there was no language requirement for my BA. Now I'm kind of sorry."

"Where it really saved my ass was G-school."

"Renaissance lit, you said?"

"Right, but I honed in on the Spanish Renaissance…Lope de Vega to Cervantes, which nobody was doing then. My dissertation proved who wrote *The Celestina*."

"Sounds arcane, whatever it is."

"A big thing…for hispanophiles. Like Chaucer and *The Canterbury Tales*, or Francis Bacon versus Shakespeare."

"How long did that take?"

Andy looked tentative about something for the first time since I'd known him. "Forever…with my marriage and the civil rights thing. But putting a wrap on it after Alabama was toughest." He gave a slight grunt deep in his throat, exchanged his previous toothpick for a fresh one, and stood.

"OK," he said, "back to the ladders. There's no jobs for eggheads now anyway."

We made good progress, but it ended up being a damned hard day and I'd used lots of muscles I normally didn't. My hands and clothes were a mess, too, yet I noticed when we quit that I cleaned up fine in the shower while Andy had pigment ingrained in his cuticles shower or not. As for baseball, he'd spent a little time trying to educate me, but could tell I wasn't interested. Besides, the Giants downed the Dodgers 2-1 in a late-inning squeaker, which kept him so engaged that my presence became irrelevant.

It had reminded me of summer afternoons in Topeka, when my dad would have the Royals game blaring on the garage radio while he did yard work. He, however, was so imperturbable you wouldn't have guessed he was a fan, while Andy virtually took the field himself. A low-level bureaucrat with the State Department of Tax Control, my dad had no real interests or hobbies outside his work that I remember except playing bridge and watching TV. Somehow, though, he married a woman who loved opera and who never missed a chance to hear the Saturday broadcasts of the Met from New York.

GOMEZ

If he was home when the opera came on, he'd go to the garage and smoke. My only sib is an older sister, Christine, who was the apple of everyone's eye, leaving me pretty much ignored. I don't think I resented the attention she got, but I do remember trying on her makeup a few times when nobody was around, and then going crazy being sure I washed it all off. She's married now, has kids, and lives in a Kansas City suburb.

As the Berkeley Hills and the rest of the Pacific Time Zone lost the light, I phoned for another "large veg pizza with fish" to ensure that I'd have his company later.

"Thanks, man, for the food *and* the help," he said, while we were sharing some of his Panama Gold for dessert. "I really mean it. Looks now like I'll be done Monday, if you're on for tomorrow. Otherwise I'd have been lucky to finish Wednesday, when my next job's supposed to start." The tip of a newly lit joint glowed as he inhaled.

"Sure, glad to. I'd probably just be at the office if I wasn't helping here. This way you might get Tuesday off." Without hesitating, I took a hit when Andy passed the joint my way.

"Hope so," he said, slowly releasing smoke from his lips. "I always try for flex between gigs. No rest for the wicked is too much of a grind. But I can't afford to drop your price, especially since it's not a part-cash deal like most I do."

"Don't worry about it." I didn't say that I'd had fun, and that he'd improved my weekend to the point where I should be thanking him. Both were true, but too corny. I was still holding the joint.

Andy interlaced his fingers and pushed his hands away from his chest to stretch. "My brushes must be a hell of a lot bigger than your ones at work."

"Yeah," I nodded, taking a second hit and returning the joint to him, "but brushes aren't what I use. Mostly I conceptualize, then sketch with colored pencils. That paint you've got is pretty mean, though."

"Thing is, it does a fantastic job. Sets up like rock." Andy laughed and swung his sockless, tennis-shoe-clad feet onto a corner of the table. Jenny would have died to see him. "If termites ever eat the frame, Mica-Shield'll keep the place standing."

I laughed, too. "After October 1, not my problem. You mind if I ask something personal?" I'd delayed this as long as I could.

GOMEZ

He smiled confidently beneath his mustache. "Fire away."

I'd thought about asking if he actually had gotten laid the previous night, but that would have been the wrong lead-in to what I was steeling myself for. "What happened with your marriage? You know," I joked, "assuming she wasn't gay." It felt liberating to say it and still be casual.

His smile stayed but it's tone changed, in recognition that I'd crossed what was for me, a boundary. "Oh," he shrugged, "the regular kinds of things. We grew apart, as the song goes. She was fairly OK with Berkeley, but hated Alabama. It's funny we didn't split till I was ready to come back."

"So…here you are." I waved Andy off on refilling my wine, and he'd already extinguished the joint.

He poured wine for himself. "Better off, too, for the most part. I don't know what the term was in Kansas, but Donna's 'from a socially prominent family.' I was her bohemian dream…if you get the idea…or…nightmare. There was still never anything she didn't know she was signing up for."

"Like what?"

"We moved around a lot. The Village, Berkeley, Alabama. And never had any money. So? I'm the one who got things I didn't sign up for."

"Such as?"

"Her depressions, mainly. I second-guess myself now, because there are starting to be treatments, but that kind of stay-in-bed for days, I-want-to-die shit really gets old. No matter how many times you tell yourself it's not your fault, it *feels* like your fault."

"There weren't other women?"

"Jeez, you're a nosey bastard! OK, one. In Alabama, a honey-haired Atlanta gal loaded with liberal guilt who thought that boffing me was the answer. She was a campus librarian, and I couldn't resist."

"Well, goddamn! My mother was a librarian."

"Two examples," Andy nodded, taking a swig of wine, "to prove they do have sex…under the right circumstances."

"How come you and Donna didn't have kids?"

"Ah…ah…luck," he answered. "Along with having no money. But wait…marriage does mean something. If you do it, you ought to honor it. I didn't, with the librarian chick, and your ex didn't, but that's not something I condone. I could be married now, if I wanted, but it's a step I won't take till I know I'm not looking anywhere else."

"I buy the argument." Or, I thought, I had bought the argument, and what did I have to show for it?

"Oh, no. Not so fast. How come you and Jenny didn't have kids?"

"You mean beyond the fact that we never had sex?" It was my turn to smile.

"I don't believe never, whether she's gay or not."

"And you're right, although since 1976, never."

"Jesus!"

"The real reason for no kids is Jenny was absolutely opposed. Cell division in a petri dish is one thing, inside her, no way. She had her tubes tied years ago."

"Before or after the marriage?"

"Oh, after. When we first got to Berkeley. I didn't want her to, but she did and told me later."

"What a bitch. And you're saying no other women on your part, regardless?

"None. I've been thinking about that a lot lately. Especially since you and I talked the other night. I figured out what drew Jenny and me together. We had the perfect neurotic balance. Fear on my end, safety on hers." I was so nervous, I didn't know how the words could have emerged that smoothly.

"I'm not sure I follow," Andy said.

"Remember my asking why I was so passive? Why I lived with no sex and no physical acceptance, why I looked the other way when Jenny started wearing muscle shirts and meeting Barbara after work?"

"I remember."

"Well the answer...the answer is...that's who I am. Passive. Who I've always been. And that's what Jenny saw in me. She's three years older, she knew right away she could push me around, I'd roll with it, and never do anything to threaten her."

"You sure you're not over-intellectualizing here?"

"Damn right I'm sure. A guy like you couldn't understand anyway."

"A guy like me? What does that mean?"

GOMEZ

I'd already told Andy one of the things in my life I never, never talked about, and was determined to tell him another. "A guy whose father didn't put all the focus on what it means to have a small dick when they discussed the birds and the bees."

"Oh, come on!"

"I'm serious."

"Your father…your own father…told you that you have a small dick?" A strangled laugh spilled from Andy in spite of his effort to control it. "Sorry," he said. "Well, you know…"

"I got past my first big secret without having you laugh."

"Hey, I said I was sorry. But that's unbelievable. Cruel. Why did he do it?"

"He thought it was true."

"What did he say…I mean the exact words, if you remember?"

"I remember, alright. He said some of it more than once."

"Yeah, but what?"

"'You know where babies come from, don't you son?' and I said 'Yes.' Then he said, 'It's important for babies to have a mama and a papa all their lives, do you understand that?' I said 'Yes' again. He went on, 'I'm telling you because I've seen you in the bath, boy, and I've got a small one myself. If you're ever lucky enough to get a woman, hang on to what you've got. Our kind of men can't be picky.' That's the part he'd repeat, 'Our kind of men.'"

"Holy Christ! Right out of Faulkner!"

"Well, it *has* felt like a family curse."

"But do you…you know…is it actually small?"

"I think so. By the time my dad told me, I'd already noticed that other boys had bigger ones, or most of them did."

"Yeah, but you're not freak-show small, are you?"

"No, not really."

"Well, the hell with it!" Andy had lowered his feet from the table and was leaning across fifteen inches from my face. "Women don't care about that. It doesn't mean shit. I've never gone around measuring, but I'm probably smaller than average myself."

"You?" I was astounded.

"What do you want?" he demanded. "We stand in front of the bathroom mirror and drop our pants?"

"No, no, of course not."

GOMEZ

"Good," he grinned, leaning back to increase the distance between us. "Neither do I. But damn it, I would."

"What an image," I laughed.

"Did Jenny ever act like it mattered or say anything?"

"No, she didn't."

"OK," Andy jumped in. "Your father was full of..."

I cut him off. "Forget my father a minute. You're saying Jenny's a typical woman, but for obvious reasons, she's not. That I'm small would be attractive to her, make me safer. It goes right along with being passive."

"Short guys like Napoleon are supposed to be more aggressive," he shot back. "Hell, I've seen it. You'd think small dicks would have the same effect."

"Not on me."

"Maybe with a different father it would have. Ever see his weenie?"

"Yeah, a few times. By accident. You know...when I was little. This is one weird conversation."

"True, but did it look small?"

"No, at the time it looked huge."

"What was he talking about, then?"

"I don't know, but I could tell he meant it."

"Still full of shit. However big your dick is...or isn't, you can't do anything about that. Being passive you *can* do something about."

"Maybe. We'll see."

"I *hope* we do," Andy affirmed. "If your dad had said you were lucky, and were slated to be a lady killer, it could have made all the difference."

"I don't know. Jenny thinks nature's turning out to be way more important than nurture. Being gay is like being left-handed, she says, with about the same incidence in the population."

"I'd have enjoyed talking to her about that," he replied. "Makes me wish I'd done the house last year while she was still around."

"Might not have mattered. She wasn't home much."

"Well, that new selfish gene theory is interesting as hell. The idea that only genes evolve, and organisms like us are strictly for their convenience."

Andy had astounded me again. "You're right," I said. "That's just what she's been working on."

GOMEZ

"Genes determine the size of our dicks," he went on, "but unless it confers a reproductive advantage or disadvantage, which I can't see how it could, the genes in question are unaffected. In the range we're talking about, it's random variation and nothing more."

"Hold on," I said. "I meant that nature…genes…determine how passive we are, too, regardless of what our fathers say. And let's say genes do determine if we're straight or gay. Believe me, being passive and having a gay wife *are* reproductive disadvantages."

"Then you and Jenny each get revenge by taking those genes down with you."

"Or in my case, if I refuse to be passive, and avoid carrying out their program, the very damn genes I'm fighting against enjoy the win."

"Not with contraception," Andy declared, waving a forefinger at me. "But if the gay thing *is* genetic, which I've been reading up on, it would explain a lot. Jenny's point about right- and left-handedness covers being ambidextrous or semi-ambidextrous too. There's a continuum. Sex or baseball, some players are natural switch hitters and some can learn…but most can't."

It was a long time, however, before I understood that his interest in this topic wasn't merely academic, and that his excitement at expanding on Jenny's analogy related to a part of his life beyond sports.

CHAPTER 5

When the phone finally rang about 10 a.m. on Sunday, I was leveling a ladder with bricks and blocks in the vinca on the south side. I'd delayed my start till then because I was nervous about climbing with nobody around. At least I'd thought to stick the handset on a window ledge so I didn't have to run my aching butt and legs into the house.

"Paul," came Andy's voice, "it's me. I'm really sorry, but my truck blew up. Or damn near."

"You OK?"

"Yeah, other than being late for work and royally pissed. I had to tow the fucking thing from Shattuck and Adeline."

"What happened?"

"Engine caught fire. In VWs it's underneath the bed. Solvent I was carrying must've leaked onto the exhaust manifold. There was black smoke and stink like you wouldn't believe. The wiring is fried, along with everything plastic or rubber back there. I mean totaled. Not worth fixing."

"Geez, it could have exploded!"

"I nearly shit when the gas in the carburetor went. Lucky it never got to the tank. The fire department was close by and knew what to do."

"Where does that leave our job?"

"Hang on, somebody here will give me a ride. Most of what we need is at your place already."

"No, I can come down. I have that funky Ranchero. We'll throw your stuff in the back."

"Well, OK…if you're sure you don't mind."

"I don't. Where are you?"

"Oh, yeah, I never gave you a business card. Look for 2331 Alcatraz, just west of Telegraph. Here's the phone if you get lost."

"See you in twenty minutes," I said, jotting the information down.

GOMEZ

Andy's commune was an imposing, slate-blue Victorian, needing paint and repair, with a wrap-around porch and nothing except the perfectly tended vegetable garden in back to signal that it wasn't an ordinary rooming house. In far worse shape than my imagination had pictured, his truck sat among a tumble of used tires in a weed patch next to the garage. The smell alone confirmed that its days were over. The blackened tailgate had warped permanently open, the rear of the bed was heaved up, and the engine cover looked like a badly scorched toaster waffle. The residue of fire-extinguisher foam even suggested whipped cream topping.

"All my rebuild work down the drain," Andy lamented. "Couldn't have scored a bigger wipe-out if I'd rigged a bomb."

We cleared out the few items he had managed to save—tarps, clothing, pails, specialized brushes and tools—and deposited them in the Ranchero. I met a pasty-faced guy named Howard who came out to help, while a cute, willowy young woman, bra-less in a T-shirt and shorts, watched from the porch. To break Andy's brooding silence on our way across town I asked about her, learning that her name was Melissa. She was new there, Andy said woodenly, and was very sweet. I sensed that Melissa might have been his Friday night hostess, but he didn't elaborate.

"Tell me about Howard," I pressed, still hoping to distract him from his trouble. "I'm remembering you guys work together sometimes. He a painter, too?"

"He's mainly a potter, a good one. Has a kiln in our garage. But he's flexible to help when I need him. Shit! I still owe Howard for half a day. I ought to be paying you, too."

"Forget it. I'm a volunteer. I might be hurting in other ways, but I'm not hurting for money."

"That makes one of us."

At Arch Street Andy's down mood continued, and he threw himself into painting with minimal conversation, though he did play Bach's *St. Matthew Passion* on the tape deck. Apparently he alternated *St. Matthew* with the *D Minor Mass* on a weekly basis, another of his rituals, this one to honor the Sabbath.

I finished the entire south wall on my own, struggling with ladders and the mica paint, leaving Andy to work his way in the other direction, doing windows and trim from the scaffolds. By the time the Giants double-header came on, he was so far away I couldn't separate the sportscaster's voice from other happenings in the neighborhood. I never even found out who won. Andy uncharacteristically didn't say, and it didn't occur to me to ask.

He declined my offer of dinner and gloomily inquired if I could run him home after we cleaned up. He also began fretting about how to return an extra drum of Mica-Shield for credit because he didn't have enough enamel to complete the trim.

"The damn warehouse is out in east Oakland," Andy complained. "That teal blue your ex ordered up is a custom color, and they're the only place that has it."

"Take the Ranchero," I told him. "Drive yourself home. I'd rather walk to BART tomorrow anyway. In fact, screw it. I'm so sore I'm taking the day off. Run your paint errands and I'll be here to help when you show up."

"I don't want your wheels. I wasn't angling for that. Go to the office for Christ sake. Have a normal day."

"Who needs normal?" I replied. "I have plenty of those."

"So have another one."

"No," I insisted. "Take the Ranchero and do what you need to."

It was a harder sell than getting him to let me paint. His latest bad luck had made his pride more prickly, not less, but eventually I prevailed. Even so, he was too preoccupied to guess what I really had in mind. I wasn't through with Andrew Steentofter, and I definitely didn't want him to be through with me.

÷ ÷ ÷

"No shit, Paul," Andy exulted, "you've got to see this. Unbelievable!"

It was 8:45 Monday morning. He and the Ranchero had just gotten back from the warehouse, and he was bounding up the front stairs from the driveway as though yesterday's transportation disaster never happened. I'd called in sick an hour before and was sitting on the edge of the porch in my sweatsuit watching the fog drift across the bay in the distance and drinking coffee. In fact, I was so sore from two days of ladders and Mica-Shield I could legitimately claim to be sick. "What's so unbelievable?"

"This." Andy wore a canary yellow T-shirt under his coveralls. From its pocket he drew a folded scrap of paper.

GOMEZ

I opened what appeared to be a painters' price-list and found a scribbled note on the back. It took several tries to interpret the writing, and I heard Andy laughing softly in the background.

> Gomez,
> Cool truck, *vato*. Long time no see. We should get together. I was ready to roll when I spotted you going inside and didn't have time to wait. Call me.
>   Mario

"Who's Gomez?" I ventured, openly baffled.

"Me," Andy replied. "That's what's funny." He jauntily tipped his painter's cap, drawing my eyes to his swarthy face and black hair as his toothpick did another of those mustache-avoiding end-to-end moves.

"What do you mean?"

"The note was tucked under your wiper blade when I came out of the paint place."

"Who's Mario?"

"I have no idea. But whoever he is, he thinks I'm his old buddy Gomez. Too much, huh? Gomez!"

"Well, you do look the part." I still didn't see why it was so funny.

"Here's the thing, I am Hispanic. In a weird way, that is."

"With a name like Steentofter, it would have to be weird."

"Your truck was the key. My half-assed VW shouts Berkeley longhair to anybody who looks. With the Ranchero, I'm a hundred-percent *La Raza*. What a kick!"

"Come on, a Dutch father and French mother? How are you Hispanic?"

"Any of that coffee left?"

"Sure."

"Get me a cup and I'll tell you while we do the rest of the trim. You did a hell of a job on the south wall, by the way. Ready to turn pro. We finish today for sure, especially if you help tear down the scaffolds."

"Why not?" I responded. "Couldn't make me more sore than I already am. Coffee, coming right up." I arose gingerly, groaned, and went inside.

"Ladders are a bitch, aren't they?" he called after me.

"*That* you've got right."

We worked in tandem along the platforms, with Andy in the lead painting and me behind doing touch up and scraping with a razor blade where paint had encroached on the glass. He tuned the radio to KJAZ again but kept the volume down. It was sunny, a beautiful day, with just a hint of breeze.

"I'm Hispanic," Andy said over his shoulder from a few feet away, "because my mother is from southwestern France, along the Pyrenees, where nationalities are mixed, and my father is descended from conversos."

"Whatever that means."

"Portuguese and Spanish Jews who fled the Inquisition in the 1500s and settled in Holland. Some became Christians in Spain but were driven out anyway, some converted later due to intermarriage or social pressure."

"On top of it all, you're Jewish?" This seemed completely amazing to me.

"If you believe it's in the blood and want to go back three hundred years. In current generations, the family's been a-religious. And get this…I'm related to Spinoza."

"The philosopher guy?"

"Nooo, the rookie shortstop for the Cincinnati Reds." Andy had finished the window closest to me and had to project his voice as he moved toward the big ones at the front corner. Since they were metal-framed with lots of cross-hatching, he'd be there a while. "Of course, the philosopher," he went on. "The most famous Dutch Jew of all."

"I suppose you've checked the family tree."

"Not really, with everything being overseas. I'll tell you more when you get closer."

To the accompaniment of birds chirping in a neighbor's holly bush and mellow Wes Montgomery guitar licks on the radio, I put the final touches on the window I'd been occupied with and stepped to my right.

"Spinoza," Andy explained, "who was excommunicated by the Jews but never embraced any other religion, also never married and left no heirs. That much I learned in college. But he had a sister, and she married into a converso line and raised Christian children. I'm their direct kin, the story goes."

"Since when do Jews excommunicate?"

"Almost never, but Spinoza they did. He questioned everything, wouldn't recant, and had the Christians down on him, too. Afterward, at age 25, he shunned academia, became a grinder of lenses, and did his intellectual work on the side."

"There is a family resemblance, at least in temperament."

"Oh?" Andy laughed, turning toward me and deliberately painting, like some insane Celtic warrior, a vertical blue stripe beneath each of his bugged-out eyes. Over my own laughter, he continued in a tone that became serious, "I've never thought about it that way, but old Baruch…or Benedict…Spinoza…he changed his name in midlife…has always been one of my heroes."

"I doubt it would be mutual if he saw your face right now."

"Probably right," Andy agreed, laughing again. "Besides, I don't want to carry things too far. He died young, which is definitely not my plan."

"Ever been there? France or Holland, I mean. You must have family."

"None who survived the war…that I know of. My grandparents are dead, my mother's brother was killed in the Resistance, and my dad was an only child. Anyway, I never had the time or money, so I never went."

"Too bad."

"My brother has, but my parents won't. They're so appalled at the way their governments accommodated the Nazis, they've refused to go back."

"How did they meet?"

"In the 30s my mother guided a group of refugees from the Spanish Civil War to Amsterdam to get them resettled. My father helped on the Dutch end. He's older, and was working as an industrial chemist. Since they both spoke some English, they decided to cut out for the US because they saw the handwriting on the wall."

"Smart," I said, again having to raise my voice because he'd moved away.

"Especially in hindsight," he called back, louder yet. "They were Communists and would have been hunted down."

"Communists!" Now I was bug-eyed, not just at what he'd said, but at his having let fly for all of Arch Street to hear.

"Sure. It wasn't so unusual back then. In the US they were never Party members that I know of, just left-leaning, Henry Wallace liberals like the rest of Bennington. Nobody sicced McCarthy on them. But I think they fudged the facts on their entry visas. Another reason they haven't traveled is they're nervous about applying for passports. And like me, no money."

"Organic chemists make damn good money around here," I responded.

"For my folks, it was always kind of hand-to-mouth. They're doing a better lately, but in the 40s and 50s, times were tough."

"I thought they retired to Florida." I had gotten a bit closer to him, but still needed to speak out.

"Not on some cushy pension," Andy replied at similar volume. "That's because my old man invented Teflon, and eventually got royalties. But why don't you field questions for a change. How about Europe? Ever been?"

"Yeah, England and France a few years ago. Jenny's a Brit, remember, so I went to meet her mother and we crossed the Channel for a week while we were at it. Her dad was killed in the war. She has step brothers and sisters from her mom's remarriage, but she's not close with any of them."

"What about your parents? And the sister you mentioned? All we've spent time on is your dad's penis envy."

I blanched, wondering how far those words had carried, but fortunately for Stiles family propriety they'd been spoken as normal conversation because we were now side-by-side. And once I'd weathered his sardonic lead-in, it was a lifetime first to feel comfortable—actually to enjoy—telling someone about growing up in Topeka. I omitted the part about trying my sister's makeup, of course, but he probed for nuance and detail, and took no note of how paltry or unadventurous my circumstances had been compared to his. Although he'd earlier piqued my curiosity by saying that his father had invented Teflon, I got so diverted it slipped my mind.

But he hadn't been kidding when he said he was good with a brush. There was hardly a new drip or slop for me to deal with, and almost nothing to touch up. Whatever gaffes he'd made over the weekend because he was upset about his truck, today was all business. The only things left after lunch would be the front door and two south-side windows.

When we stopped to eat, I found that he'd hit Ratto's Deli on the way from the paint store and gotten monster submarine sandwiches for both of us. By 2:30, with KJAZ still our soundtrack, we were done and taking a break on a low retaining wall outside the garage before disassembling the scaffolds.

We'd been silent a while, then Andy said matter-of-factly, "This Gomez thing fascinates me. I think I'm going to go with it."

"Huh?"

"You know…*be* Gomez. Express my Hispanic heritage." By now he'd wiped the blue paint off his face and looked his standard Che Guevara self.

"You mean, change your name?"

"Yeah. How does Andrés Gomez strike you?"

"Nut-case, if you really want to know."

"Good," he laughed. "That cinches it. From here on call me Gomez."

"Legally? Not just a nickname?"

"Maybe. Or Andrés G. something…Miller, say…with the G for you-know-what. The process is easy enough."

"Why?"

"Because it's fate. It's far out. I need a change, I really do. A big change, and for more reasons than you know. Remember how sore you are? I can't be climbing ladders forever."

"But Gomez *is* a painter. Why else would he be at the paint store?"

"That's the other Gomez. He can go on painting. I'm not bound to that, not long-term."

"But this Gomez, A.K.A. Handy Andy, has a painting gig on Wednesday, and he'll probably need his scaffolds."

"True, he will. I will. Howard's going to borrow a truck from a buddy of his to haul them for me. I have time to do the tear-down on my own, by the way, if you want to knock off. Putting them up's a two-man deal, and Howard usually helps. He did with these," Andy gestured toward the house.

GOMEZ

"No, no," I countered. "I'll help. I want to see how it's done. But call Howard and have him forget the truck, because you're keeping the Ranchero."

"I am not." He chomped down hard on his toothpick.

"Look, I don't need it, I don't want it, and for Gomez it's essential."

"They're your only wheels. I'll stack the scaffolds by the sidewalk and be back for them tomorrow. You want to help, have that ex of yours pay me right away. I agreed to a check, but I'm in too big a bind to wait for the escrow company. Have them reimburse her."

"Don't be such a hardhead. *I'll* write your check...*today*. Jenny and I can work it out later. But take the Ranchero. You'd be doing me a favor."

"Bullshit."

"Our year-old Volvo was a community asset, the only car we had. She insisted on cashing out my half, then I'd buy something else. This Gomez machine you think is so cool belonged to girlfriend Barbara's brother. He's in the Army and she was supposed to sell it for him. For some stupid reason I let Jenny fob it off on me in lieu of cash. So I could drive places in the meantime, she said. Of course, poor old Paul would also have to remember where the goddamn thing came from whenever he saw it!"

"Why the hell'd you roll over for that?" Andy said. "It's not worth half of any new Volvo."

"You know why!" I burst out, as openly angry as I've ever let myself get. "What have we been talking about these past nights?"

"I know your *theory* on why. I'm not sure I really know."

"Stop splitting hairs. Ignore why I have the thing. You need it, I don't."

"Thanks," Andy nodded, regrouping. "I appreciate the offer, but I'm flat not letting you give me a truck because you're pissed at your wife. End of subject." He softly spat a partially broken toothpick into the vinca, where it disappeared among the leaves.

"I don't mean as a gift. I want a thousand bucks, which is what the dealer's offering in trade. Pay me in installments. I'm buying an Audi, picking it up next week."

"Audi. Nice, nice machine," he said in a completely different tone. "What are you getting, the GTE sedan they just came out with?"

"As a matter of fact, yes. Is there anything, any possible information on any topic, you're not carrying around in that head of yours?"

"I hope not. I try like hell for there not to be. But…you might be on to something. Here's a concept that could work for both of us."

"Yeah?" I'd moved him off plain no, which was an improvement.

"I just sunk a bunch of time and money into my old truck, which is why I'm so bummed. Even doing your own fix-ups, parts aren't cheap. I can't pay anything right now, but I know how to get some cash up front. The rest I'll swing later on."

"Sure," I said, "if you want." Money-wise, I could have given him the Ranchero, but I'd known all along he wouldn't accept. Beyond that, installments would make him stay in touch.

"OK," he went on. "We swap pink slips. Take my old hulk and trade that in. Tell them you had a fire and you're sorry for the mix-up. They'll give you something, scrap value at least. Let me know how much short of $1,000 it turns out to be. No later than January, I'll cover your loss, lump-sum cash. Everybody comes out even, and it gets rid of your problem truck and my problem truck on the same pass."

"Sounds edgy by my standards, but I guess we could." I was imagining myself at the Audi showroom with a burned-out wreck instead of the Ranchero, and wondered if I could bring it off. Still, that seemed as much of a ticket to future contact with Andy as I was going to get.

"Piece of cake," he assured me. "Say the word on what day. Howard and I'll tow the VW to the dealer's just before they open. You go in with the pink slip and the deal is done. They're not going to risk losing a sale once your trade-in's sitting in the lot. Any trade-in. Believe me."

"OK, sure, I'll give it a try." I hoped I sounded more confident than I felt.

"You want a promissory note? I can write one up."

GOMEZ

"No, a handshake's fine. I know where to find you." Those imprudent words actually came out of my mouth. I heard them. Andy stood, extended his arm, I stood, and we shook.

"Thanks, man," he said. "Come on, let's get those scaffolds down and into the Ranchero. My next job's near home, so I'd rather store things there. It'll take two trips. We can trade pink slips at my place. When you help me load for the second trip, you're off duty."

"OK. And if we stop at a B of A, I'll move money around so I can pay for the job. Jenny said $2,400, right?"

"Right." He was slowly backing away from me as we spoke.

I followed, saying, "Just thought of something. You'll need signs for the cab doors. I'll work up a logo and text at Landau-Walters and put it on for free. Part of the deal." Since he'd bitten on the Ranchero, this would be a further way to keep him in my orbit.

"What a hell-of an offer," he said warmly. "You're on, but let's wait till I pay up. I have to figure out what you should say. Won't be Handy Andy any more, remember? I'm not sure what line of work Gomez will be in by then." He equipped himself with a new toothpick.

"Yeah, I forgot. Big changes afoot." My apprehension showed, despite my efforts to conceal it.

"Don't worry," he laughed. "You'll get your cash. Handy Andy never stiffed anybody in his life, a tradition Gomez plans to continue. How do I find you when the time comes?"

"Call the office. I don't have my new home phone yet." Of course I already had a new home address, but I wanted him to call, not just mail me a check. "You don't have to wait either. We can go out in the Audi for anchovy pizza."

"Maybe," he said. "Tell you what, though. Let's pick up some beer after we hit the bank and toast a job well done while we load the last scaffolds."

PART II

Friendship is no less a mystery than love or any other
aspect of this confusion we call life.

> Jorge Luis Borges
> *The Unworthy Friend*
> Translation: Norman Thomas
> di Giovanni, 1970

GOMEZ

CHAPTER 6

With no real word from Andy by year-end, I initially blamed myself for being too pushy about the Ranchero. Not only was he beholden to me in a way he probably didn't like, I'd felt leery about contacting him because I didn't want to seem like a dunning creditor. Or was that just my passivity reasserting itself?

Certainly I'd been passive in letting him badger me into a six-pack of the mouth-puckering Anchor Steam beer for our end-of-job celebration, and even more so regarding the switcheroo with his truck. On my own, I'd have never have come up with such a plan, much less done it. I had to admit, though, everything went as predicted. The sales manager was perturbed at first, and went to see his boss, but they ended up giving me $200 on Andy's hulk and it added only a few extra minutes to the transaction.

Whatever its genesis, my new Audi was a big success. It's an elegant yellowish-beige with leather seats that smell better than any car I've ever been in. I don't smoke, and nobody else is going to be smoking in it, either. From the showroom I drove immediately to Andy's place, where I left a friendly note confirming how things had gone, how much of the $1,000 he had left to pay, my office phone, and my interest in getting together. The Ranchero wasn't there, and Melissa said he was working, as one would expect on a weekday.

Escrow closed on the Arch Street house shortly after that, so my life got pretty frantic. By the end of the month I had moved into my SF condo, taken delivery of the furniture I'd ordered, and was mastering the logistics of city living. I felt freer of Jenny than I'd imagined, but regrets and second thoughts still assailed me at odd times, generally at night. Almost the first piece of mail I received was from Andy, forwarded via my Berkeley address.

The envelope contained a single Handy Andy business card, neatly corrected in ink to read Andrés. Modifying or replacing Steentofter would have been much harder, but no surname appeared in the original text. On the back, with the same pen, was written, "IOU $800, payable circa January 31, 1978," and signed, "Gomez."

That was it. Nothing resembling a message, greeting, or good wishes, and quite a letdown, compared to what I'd hoped for. The IOU itself was immaterial. Nursing my disappointment as the weeks went by, I tried to stop thinking about him, and figured a similarly impersonal check would show up in due course.

He'd been a sympathetic ear when I'd needed one, we'd had some laughs, but a guy like that wouldn't want to hang out with Paul Stiles. I'd been stupid to think otherwise. Yet gradually resentment set in, too. If I was going to be discarded, why had he bothered to string me along?

Walking to work, on the other hand, was every bit the plus I'd been aiming for, and I still don't see myself tiring of it. After leaving the elevator I traverse a delightful green-lawned plaza with a vertical metal Bufano sculpture in the middle, and head up Battery Street in the lee of Telegraph Hill all the way to the north waterfront, near the last of the operating passenger docks.

Other than the new tourist trap being developed at Pier 39 and the converted ferry that houses Landau-Walters, the area is what the city defines as blighted, but to me the rows of disused brick warehouses and peeling gray terminals are a source of charm. Our floating quarters, jokingly called the *SS Bauhaus*, are painted the bright white of a breaking wave and held in place by special pilings that allow us to rise and fall with the tide, while hinged gangways adjust to compensate.

My office is on a middle-deck corner facing the shore, so I have a city view framed at the bottom by the rooflines of the terminals along the Embarcadero. It's small, but nice, and I coveted it for a long time before I became senior enough to lay claim. The furnishings include a Mies van der Rohe chair, an L-shaped mahogany desk built-in below the windows, and an oversized drafting table against the interior bulkhead. A Persian rug covers most of the umber steel deck, and there are framed Calder prints on the walls, potted plants, and several stylish, flex-arm lamps. Squawking gulls and Muzac are the standard aural background, along with sloshing swells whenever boat wakes or other disturbances rile the harbor.

I've always worked a lot, but when I was hiding from the obvious fact of what was going on with Jenny, I put in such long hours my boss started requiring me to go home by 10 p.m. Since then I'd been spending less time on the job and accomplishing just as much, so we were all happy—or happier. Finally, in the middle of the following January, Ivy, our department secretary, buzzed to say, "An Andrés Gomez is on the line."

I tried to damp back my elation, to summon anger instead at how long he'd ignored me. A check had apparently been mailed and this would be the kiss-off. "OK, ring him through."

"Paul," came a familiar voice. "I've got your money."

"Oh, yeah? I figured it would just arrive in an envelope. How's the Ranchero?"

"Runs like a champ."

"Where are you? Alcatraz Ave.?"

"No, those days are gone. I'm in SF, same as you. At my office."

"Office?"

"Your friend Gomez teaches English at *Centro Social de los Obreros* in the Mission, and his office hours are late afternoon Monday through Friday."

"Wow," I said. "No more painting?" I didn't remember Andy's referring to himself in the third person, but for Gomez it became a distinguishing trait.

"Not since October."

"I'll be damned. Are you living on this side of the bay, too?"

"Yeah. Hole-in-the-wall at 22nd and Valencia."

"I've wondered why we lost touch." Weak stuff, but all I had the nerve to say. Nearly four months had gone by, and he'd known we were in the same city.

"I said I'd call when I could pay. Besides, I've been busy as hell. You know what moving and getting settled are like."

"Yes, very fresh in my mind."

"How about we meet for dinner tomorrow?"

Now elation surged full force. "Great. Where?"

"Hayes Street Grill. You know it?"

"I know *of* it. What time?"

"Let's say 7. Gomez's treat. Interest on your loan."

"You don't have to do that."

"Which is why I'm doing it. Don't argue."

"OK, I'm wowed. See you there. Now fill me in on all this."

"Sure, at dinner. Glad you can make it." He hung up.

GOMEZ

It strikes me that another Gomez trait was to never say hello or goodbye. In person or on the phone, he plugged straight into his topic and unplugged at a self-designated concluding point. Andy may have been somewhat similar, but far less extreme. At the time, though, the new name was the only discontinuity I expected between the two.

I put a fair amount of thought into how I'd dress, especially after Ivy said the restaurant was a block or so behind the opera house and favored by its patrons. I couldn't imagine Andy—I mean Gomez—in a tie, so I went with a tab-collar shirt, a sweater vest, an olive scarf, and an Italian-cut tweed jacket I'd bought at Union Square since my move. I drove the Audi, because I wanted him to see it.

With a little map work I got my bearings. The neighborhood seemed basically safe, but was tattier than one would expect for a high-end eatery. Still, if opera season hadn't ended, parking would probably have been nonexistent and a seven o'clock table impossible to obtain. I squeezed between two driveways about a block to the west, and when I walked back toward the entrance saw the Ranchero parked across the way. It looked right at home, although Andy—dammit, Gomez—had bought new tires, whitewalls, no less, replaced some missing chrome, and added a **Viva Sandino!** bumper strip. Jenny and Barbara had shafted me, I'd done a good deed, and there stood the result.

No lighted signage announced our destination, but the words Hayes Street Grill were shown in gilded Times Roman characters four inches high at the lower right of each window. The windows themselves were steamy and protected from above by smart, silver-gray awnings on black metal frames. I did my best to scan the room before pushing against the glass-paneled door to go in. Since only half the tables were taken and I'd seen his car, I should have been able to spot him, but didn't.

While I was removing my scarf, the maitre d' approached and said, "You'll be joining Mr. Gomez?"

"Yes," I answered, mildly surprised, until I noticed a dark-complected man with wire-rim glasses and very short black hair partially standing from a back table near the hallway to the kitchen. He was waving and had a broad, crooked-toothed smile.

"This way, sir," the maitre d' said.

GOMEZ

"Andy," I extended my hand and it was quickly wrapped in two of his.

He glared, then let his smile return. "Andrés," he emphasized.

"Oh, yeah, sorry."

"But call me Gomez. Everybody does, and it's what I want." He sat and I followed.

"Here," he continued, "have some wine." Gomez poured from a bottle on the table into a tumbler at my place, yet the other tables I'd seen were set with stemware. "And there's bread." He slid a low wicker basket into the center of the white cloth. "I've already ordered our salads. Hope you don't mind."

"We'll find out." For something to do, I swirled the red liquid in my glass while Gomez refilled his own.

"Be the best damn salad you ever ate," he affirmed. "Ingredients change with the season."

Now that I was closer, his voice, jaw, nose and eyes were decidedly familiar, but everything else had been transformed. With radically shorter hair, glasses, and no mustache, his mouth, ears and forehead were unrecognizable, and his wardrobe made the changes more pronounced. Shiny, black, mid-heel shoes made him taller, above which were pressed, straight-legged jeans, and a tight-fitting black sweater, mock-turtle at the neck. I struggled to adjust to the new reality, including an absence of toothpicks, but assumed that would prove temporary.

"Good wine," I said, drinking some and looking around. With its gray walls, gold-framed mirrors and vases of fresh flowers, the room was unpretentiously stylish.

"Cotes du Rhone," he replied. "*Vin ordinaire*. In Spanish, *vino del pais*." He drank with me.

I tore off a piece of bread, which I could tell from its texture was going to be top-notch. "How do you...how does Gomez...afford this place? It has quite a rep."

He laughed, leaned forward and lowered his voice. "Gomez doesn't. He only has to pay for yours. This wine isn't even on the list. It's what the help drink."

"You know the owner?" I asked, surprised yet again. Was this another Yale connection, like Anchor Steam Beer?

"I do now," he answered. "Nearly everybody they hire comes from the Centro. The waiter over there is Salvadoran, and a former student. Carlos, tonight's sous-chef, I taught last fall. Off-season, January to May, anybody from the Centro eats free as long as they sit here." He jabbed a finger at our table.

"Pretty sweet."

"Listen, it's good business. A bow to the Culinary Union. They help sponsor the Centro."

"Sweet anyway, especially for you."

"That part's true. Most of the Centro folks would be uncomfortable here. I only heard about it by accident."

Gomez gestured at the waiter, calling him Roberto, and when the man arrived, launched into a volley of Spanish, although at low volume and in a pleasant tone. I picked up one word, *ensalada*, but Roberto was almost cringing, as though he'd been reprimanded.

"Please, Mr. Gomez," Roberto said. "I speak English."

"I'm worried you'll forget your native tongue," Gomez teased.

"There is no danger of that," Roberto stated, now smiling. He turned and disappeared into the kitchen.

"They're not supposed to speak *Español* here," Gomez told me, conspiratorially, using his hand to shield his mouth. "The owners think their customers will freak. It doesn't go with nouvelle cuisine. I give everybody a hard time."

"This Centro thing, what hat did that rabbit jump out of?"

"Told you I needed a change. I knew about them, had seen their ads in the *Chron* for substitute teachers. I started subbing right after I painted your place, and by November, bang, I was full-time. Gomez was, I mean. As soon as they heard his Spanish, he made the short list. That's the only name they use for me, which I need you to respect."

"OK, sure," I said. "Strange, though. To teach English in Buenos Aires, you don't need Spanish, but in California, you do."

"Nothing strange about it. The objectives are like night and day. The idea here is to be completely bilingual in an English-dominant society…something they expect all of us to model."

Our salads came, with additional bread and a pair of menus. Roberto poured us more wine. "Many thanks," Gomez said to him pointedly.

"*De nada,*" he stage-whispered in reply.

If not the best I'd eaten, the salad was still terrific, and it certainly looked like no other I'd seen. At the center of a large, deep plate sat a mix of lightly dressed endive and escarole around which were arranged little mounds of marinated white beans, mushrooms and artichoke hearts alternating with little stacks of julienned carrots, zucchini and red pepper. Feeling wildly adventurous, I ordered herb-roasted lamb with ratatouille, while Gomez requested broiled monkfish, whatever that was, from the specials board.

"*Salade composé*," he informed me, energetically forking bites of marinated goodies onto his bread and dispatching them between mouthfuls of greens. "My sainted mother is the only other source this side of the Atlantic, as far as I know."

"But darn, no anchovies." I laughed.

"They're in the marinade," he stated.

"Aren't you ordering white wine to go with your fish?"

"Hell, no. Wine is red. White wine isn't wine, it's…

"Like American League baseball," I interrupted.

Gomez made the OK sign with his thumb and forefinger. "Couldn't be put better… even if you don't know what you're talking about."

"No problem," I joked. "Images are my game, the very nature of commercial art."

My remark must have been funnier than I'd thought, because he gave a hooting laugh. I took the opportunity to ask what I'd been wanting to all along. "How come you looked more like Gomez when you were Andy and more like Camus now?"

"Not quite the comparison I had in mind," he nodded, "but good question. Keeping the *Viva la Revolución* look would've been a cliché. It made Andy more interesting, but Gomez is better this way. Give me credit. With a new name, I had to have a new look."

"Complete with fake glasses."

"They're prescription. Oldies but goodies. Handy Andy went for contacts."

Our dinners came and we talked about my new condo and car while we ate. I didn't even have to start those topics, he asked. We finished the Cotes du Rhone, and Gomez ordered us brandy, coffee and flan for desert. The latter was so sweet it made my teeth hurt and I never drink caffeine that late at night, but I was too glad to see him to object.

"A meal like this calls for cigars," he said. "Too bad Gomez doesn't smoke."

GOMEZ

"Since when?" I asked. "Although your usual after dinner ciggies wouldn't go well here."

"No, no," he waved dismissively with his right palm. "That was Berkeley schtick. Gomez uses the sacred weed only for making love. And no more toothpicks, either. It's little things as well as big that define identity."

"Speaking of Berkeley, do you still see Howard and Melissa and those folks?"

"Not really. Too many changes all around. They don't care for Gomez, just like my Berkeley friends didn't dig Alabama, and my Alabama friends never dug Berkeley. But no problem if you stick. I figure I can trust you with my past, from the way you've trusted me with yours."

"Which reminds me," he went on. "I have a couple of things here." He extracted a slim, white envelope from a rear pocket of his jeans. "Business before pleasure."

His fingers burrowed inside to hand me a crisp sheaf of new $100 bills. I absently curled them against my thumb at the edge of the table. "Count 'em if you like," he said. "Eight big ones."

"Thanks," I answered. Without counting, I pulled my wallet from my coat pocket and slid the money into it. "We're square. Want your IOU? I even brought it." The idea that he wanted me in his life carried a lot more importance than the money, but I was glad for both.

"Go on, tear it up while I watch. That's the traditional. You told me not to send one, but you didn't sound too sure."

I ripped the card into fragments and put them on his saucer. "Done," I said.

"Now for thing two," Gomez replied, placing the envelope on the table within my reach, but weighting a corner of it with our crystal candle holder. "Any women in your life yet, by the way?"

"No. I'm officially divorced, but I haven't had time."

"Yeah, sure," he scoffed. "The city is crawling with chicks, you and I are probably the only non-gay men to move here this decade, and you hide behind too busy? It was easier to get laid in Berkeley than not. San Francisco's easier yet."

"What is this, a pep talk?"

"Of sorts. If I can create a whole life for Gomez since you last saw me, you can at least put yourself in play. I'm not saying to go hustle at Henry Africa's seven nights a week. I don't dig that myself. Anyway, the rest of what I brought," he pointed at the envelope, "is to convince you that your so-called impediment is a crock of crap."

I lifted the flap, trying to guess what I'd find: the phone number of a blind date he planned to line me up with? A photo of a recently divorced female friend? Or something dumb, like personal ads clipped from the *Bay Guardian*? By touch I could tell the photograph idea had been correct, but it turned out to be vastly different than I'd imagined. While Gomez laughed freely, I blurted, "Oh, for god's sake!"

"Where...where did this...come from?" I then stammered, feeling myself blush. The photo showed Gomez and a raffish guy in a leather vest, both naked below the waist, standing shoulder-to-shoulder in front of a worn couch on the wooden floor of a typical Victorian row house. The other guy was shorter than Gomez, and therefore me, but his circumcised penis was not only two inches longer than Gomez's, it was bigger around. Gomez was uncircumcised, the first such example I'd ever seen in the flesh, and not all that large, just as he'd claimed during one of our Arch Street conversations.

"My screen test," he responded with mock pride.

"Screen test?"

"Yeah. Last month I answered an ad in the back of the *Guardian* for porno actors. Said no experience necessary. A guy at work dared me. I talked them into taking an extra Polaroid so I could prove I went. Look at the other side."

I flipped it over. Written in ball-point was, "23-A and 23-B, Dec. 10, '77, Property of Mitchell Bros. Enterprises."

"Mitchell Brothers? I can't believe it."

"No shit. I went *Behind the Green Door*. Literally."

"Yeah, right. You and Marilyn Chambers."

"Sounds like you know the territory," he grinned.

"Nobody could miss those newspaper ads," I said noncommittally. "Where are you saying this was? Their Polk Street movie palace?"

"No, out in the Haight. Hole in the wall called G. D. Productions. I only did it on a lark, remember. But the door *was* green and the Mitchells are who it turned out to be."

"The other guy? Who's he?"

"Some biker named Clay. Never saw him before. You log in, sign a release, then they pair you up at random, and have you drop your pants in another room in front of the cameras. The idea is to put you with strangers to be sure you're not inhibited…you know, that you can basically function."

"That's probably all I need to know." In fact, for reasons of my own, I wanted to downplay this whole conversation.

"Not much else you can know, not from me anyway. They posed us for a few shots to check our looks and how big our dongs are. Then had us read some lines. Said they'd call back if they were interested. I assume there'd be chicks involved and having to get it up if you made the first cut."

"Which you didn't?"

"Hell, no. They never called. I didn't expect it."

"Would you have gone?"

"Sure," Gomez laughed. "Out of curiosity. But how far beyond just showing up would depend on the vibes…you know, how I felt about the general scene. I mean, you could catch some weird diseases."

"Exactly what I was thinking. And if they'd shot some footage, would you really want to have it in circulation?"

"Probably not, but Clay was hot to trot, I'll tell you. His old lady had tried out earlier in the week and they'd given her a dildo, which is supposed to be a good sign."

"Do you think they called him?"

"Who cares? The point is, I'm no long-dong, and there's proof. And count yourself lucky. If yours was micro-small, your parents might have taken you to Johns Hopkins as an infant, where this surgeon…Monney, his name is…has turned that kind of case into girls, hormones and all."

"You're kidding, right? Where do you even get this stuff?"

"*The Journal of Bio-Medicine*. I told you I've read up on it, and no joke. They can build dicks for guys, too, and for renegade females…a whole new line of plastic surgery. But if I don't worry about mine, don't be worrying about yours. Go forth and get a woman."

"Thanks for the…ah…vote of confidence," I said, returning the photo to its envelope. "Do I keep this for inspiration?"

GOMEZ

"Sorry, no. It's for the souvenir box. In there with Handy Andy's misdemeanor citation for nude sunbathing at Lake Temescal. But I had to play show and tell, after what you said about your dad."

I returned the envelope. "The fact that Gomez auditioned at all must do wonders for him in the world of macho."

"Doesn't hurt," he laughed. "Horacio, the guy at the Centro who dared me, has kind of talked it up. I should have bet him ten bucks. Of course, I don't say anything about not being called back. He likes to think I already boffed some porno babe."

After glancing at his watch, Gomez signaled for our check and went through the drill of paying and tipping. "Thanks very much," I said to him on the way to the door. "It was super."

"Totally deserved. Gomez would be nowhere without his Ranchero." He waved to a petite, graying woman who was standing with some other customers in the opposite corner. "Mimi Yost," he told me. "One of the owners."

"Don't forget," I replied, "to walk me down the block so you can see the Audi."

"I'll go one better. We walk there and I drive us to the Ranchero. I want to check out your new machine from behind the wheel." He held open the restaurant's door.

"Yeah, OK, I guess." It would be the first time anyone had driven it but me. "The Ranchero looks good, by the way, with the tires and chrome you put on. I guess you've been under the hood tuning it up, too."

"No, that's not Gomez. I knew a guy named Andy who was pretty ambitious as a shade-tree mechanic, but there's a shop in my neighborhood I go to now.

"And another new development," he continued, as we stepped onto the sidewalk. "You play racquetball?"

"Sort of. Jenny did for a while and used to drag me along."

"How about a little competition? Gomez has a line on a free court."

GOMEZ

CHAPTER 7

Gomez loved the Audi and we ended up joyriding out to the panhandle of Golden Gate Park and back before he surrendered the driver's seat. He then offered me a turn in the revitalized Ranchero, though he must have known I'd refuse. Also, since language teachers don't need door signs on their vehicles, I was off the hook on fulfilling that part of our bargain. Racquetball was apparently a go, however, and he promised to call. He got my home number and gave me his at work. To keep expenses low, Gomez said, he had no phone at his apartment.

Later, as I eased into the echoing garage beneath my building and waited for the security gate to close, I felt certain he and I had broken new ground. Wherever things went between us, the stage of my having to connive at ways to maintain the tie was over. Gomez needed friends to bolster his new identity and his new situation, and I'd been dealt in.

I was the elevator's only occupant up to the sixth floor, but had company the minute I stepped out. Waiting with linked arms in the hall were my neighbor Jordan Mackay and another of his dishy dates. I may have seen her with him before, but wasn't sure. She was nonetheless a serious inciter of lustful thoughts, and they had the smug, slightly flushed look of a couple who'd spent the previous hours in bed.

With her dark, bobbed hair, pouty lips and heart-shaped face, all nicely framed by the spreading collar of her iridescent charcoal trenchcoat, she'd have drawn my eyes no matter where we were. I put her age at thirty or so, close to my own, making Jordan her senior by a good two decades.

"Paul, hello," he said. "Your ride up is ours down. Eve wants a nightcap at Henry Africa's."

Trim and handsome in his double-breasted navy blazer, Jordan was a corporate attorney whose silver hair completed the image. I'd gotten to know him well enough since moving in to learn that he was divorced and had two grown children. Whether we would become friends, and to what degree, or remain merely neighbors, were at that point open questions.

I nodded to each of them, saying, "Henry's is quite the place these days. Have a nice time."

They replied with banal genialities of their own and disappeared into the elevator. I walked to my unit. Jordan's was around the corner, in a dead-end spur which gave him double my view, but which often caused his guests, some even dishier than Eve, to ring my doorbell by mistake. Would that they were looking for me.

I let myself in without turning on the lights and advanced to stand at my picture window. Sterile as it was, I liked the Golden Gateway complex and spent much more time surveying my rather diminished view here than I ever had enjoying the nighttime panorama I'd left in Berkeley.

The sheer rock cliffs at Telegraph Hill's base and the lighted crown of buildings cantilevered across its brow made the foreground look like a travel poster of an Italian fishing village at night. Of course the floodlit column of Coit Tower protruding from its top could also suggest a funny hat from *Beach Blanket Babylon*. One of Herb Caen's standard jabs was to speculate on what part of our brave firemen's anatomy Lily Coit had meant to memorialize by erecting that particular structure.

Then, away to my left, the lights of Broadway and Chinatown were arrayed against the slopes of Nob Hill. Tonight I felt safe from their energy, but many other times they had led me on quests for sexual pleasures that were seemingly on offer but never really there. If I thought about it, I realized that no places with neon marquees ever would or could deliver what I craved—yet the pull persisted.

When Gomez asked about my sex life, I'd been less than honest. Not that I was dating, which is what he'd specifically asked, but I'd become obsessed with sex and was pursuing it in ways he would surely disdain. Having moved to the city and begun to frequent the porn movie houses, clubs and massage parlors that were so conspicuous, I imagined that I would build confidence by interacting with women in openly sexual ways and progress to using that confidence in personal relationships.

In fact, the reverse happened. I became more withdrawn, because I couldn't reconcile the carnality in my mind with the increasingly important roles in which I encountered women at work, nor with the issues of motherhood and feminism they constantly talked about. And in terms of carnality, the North Beach topless places where I started were tame compared to the Tenderloin below Union Square.

Once I'd sat through incredible flicks like *Pretty Peaches* at Alex de Renzy's Screening Room, go-go dancing seemed passé. Then I discovered the Mitchell Brothers' Kopenhagen Lounge, where the best-looking females I'd ever exchanged words with would finish their performances on stage, get back into their bras and panties, and squirm in my lap for tips. The stage shows, meanwhile, were *Penthouse* or *Hustler* brought to life.

Tenderloin massage parlors offered a wider range of sexual favors, but they were sleazy and expensive, and the women were rarely as foxy as the ones de Renzy and the Mitchells lined up. Besides, the parlors weren't dark or anonymous like the Kopenhagen. The few times I went, real desire faded almost as soon as I was paired with a masseuse, and I felt compelled to offer lame justifications for why I was there. In turn, the women would claim to be college students, which hardly seemed believable given their vocabularies and cool-eyed maturity.

On one occasion I even became impotent. The woman, a thirty-something Asian with downcast eyes, was understanding and fairly attractive, so she wasn't the problem. What ruined things was hearing spontaneous-sounding male and female voices and laughter through the partition from a neighboring booth and realizing that I had nothing whatever to say to the person who was trying to fellate me. I'd paid in advance and knew better than to expect a refund, but after that I confined myself to the Kopenhagen and to movies.

What a shock it would have been to walk in and find Gomez on the screen. Even knowing about his screen test, I'd be lucky not to swallow my teeth. He had doubted he'd go through with it, but could always change his mind. As it was, I'd been relieved at dinner when we moved to another topic fairly quickly, and I didn't have to worry about betraying greater knowledge of the fleshpot scene than a normal *Chronicle* reader would possess. Of course the guys who were my fellow customers all looked normal enough, but I assumed they weren't regulars — once a week, or more — like I was.

I didn't talk to them, nor they to me. We were there to ogle women; to each other we were backdrop. But I never quite managed to feel normal about my behavior, and that led to something really weird. Since all of this, and my marriage as well, seemed so unfulfilling, I began to wonder if I was gay. There was clearly a physical aspect to the attraction I'd felt toward Andy—I mean Gomez—in Berkeley, and thinking back to high school and college, I recalled having a similar sense with male friends on a few other occasions.

One night I put the idea to a test by cruising the Castro about 11 p.m. The atmosphere was as heavily sexual as the hottest Friday at Henry Africa's, but I was still very alienated from it. Gays say the thing they most have in common is that their childhood and teen years were spent feeling that they never fit in. But I fit no better outside a bar called Toad Hall as a hapless object of desire than I would at Henry's as a hapless pursuer. Who were these legions of men—eyeing me and one another—with their short hair, mustaches, tight jeans and tank-top shirts under their leather jackets?

I kept wondering, and the following week ended up at the all-male Nob Hill Cinema to see a flick called *El Paso Trucking Company*. I'd been nervous somebody I knew would spot me on Castro Street, but at the Nob Hill I was terrified. I headed for the darkest, emptiest corner, which was a mistake because right away guys moved in to see if I was looking for action. Fortunately they took no for an answer, and I migrated to another seat where there was too much light to permit extracurricular activities. Plenty of light, though, for someone to recognize me.

No one did, as far as I know, and I wasn't around all that long. The previews were pretty explicit, with hard pects, hard cocks, tight butts, threesomes, and lakes of sperm. The feature took it from there. The thing is, I was repelled—not just unmoved—repelled. I told myself I was being scientific and I'd see what the hype was about, but it was no more sexy and much less interesting than watching neighborhood dogs go at it when I was a kid. There's kissing, of course, the hands of the fuck-*er* take care of the cock of the fuck-*ee*, and there are mutually equivalent possibilities for sixty-nine. But why would they want to? And for a guy like me, worried about the size of his member, no place could have been worse. Here was an audience that worshipped bigness and didn't pretend otherwise.

Within thirty minutes I was out the door, and none of it stayed in my mind to fuel erotic dreams. For a while afterward I even swore off the Kopenhagen, but when my level of self-disgust dropped, I restored it by slinking off to watch more dildo-aided dance routines followed by Terri, or Kitten, or Misty, or whoever, rocking their lovely behinds on my lap.

And by then I'd only lived in SF four months. I never let myself tally the money I spent. I wanted to snap out of it, get on track with a real relationship, but I felt less and less as though I knew how. Could Gomez point me in the right direction? When I was with him, the answer always seemed to be yes. Or maybe Jordan Mackay? He certainly wasn't having the problems I was.

I turned away from the cityscape out the window, crossed my condo's unlit dining area, slid out of my shoes near the entryway, and padded in my socks down the dim parquetry of the hall to the bedroom.

÷ ÷ ÷

"OK," said Gomez. "These stairs are narrow. Keep it quiet and wait at the top till I flip the lights. Might take a minute."

He was ahead of me in the dark and I heard wooden steps creak as he descended. We were at the North End Rowing Club on a late-January weeknight for the first of our racquetball dates. In fact, I could hear the whole tilted, clapboard building creak as people trod the floors above us, along with a murmur of sound from the TV room, the slosh of breaking wavelets against the pilings below, the drone of the pipes feeding the showers, and the gurgle of wastewater draining away.

Located on the Hyde Street Pier near Fisherman's Wharf, the North End was mainly for folks who liked swimming year-round in the bay at water temperatures low enough to qualify them as eccentric or worse. Also among the members were dorymen and sea-kayakers who built and maintained their vessels in the deserted ground-floor boatworks Gomez and I had just traversed. The dank half-basement, which for some reason housed a racquetball court, added a fungal scent all its own to the predominant atmosphere of wood shavings and drying varnish.

I was cold in my shorts and eager to get started so I could warm up. "Hah!" came Gomez's voice, followed by a loud clack and a basso hum. Gray-brown dimness began to replace the dark.

GOMEZ

"Old-style lights," he stage-whispered. "They don't come full-on right away. Be sure you can see before trying the stairs."

I started slowly down what were ladder-like steps at the back of a spectators' gallery featuring two rows of crude wooden benches. The light got brighter and brighter as the hum decreased. Gomez, also in shorts and a sweatshirt, extracted a can of balls and two beaten-up, ovoid rackets from a cardboard box in the corner.

"Told you equipment was no problem," he said, handing me one of the rackets. I hadn't noticed in the cab of the Ranchero when he'd picked me up, nor during our stealthy entrance, but Gomez's left knee was wrapped in a heavy, hinged brace. He'd always moved so freely climbing ladders, I was surprised. He saw me looking at it.

"Football," he shrugged. "I was a pass-catching halfback. Fucked me over pretty good at the time. I only wear the brace for sports…just in case."

Gesturing at the court, I said, "Strange setup."

"Kind of a dump, but can't beat the price. Free, if I'm careful." Gomez pressed a blue rubber ball into his shorts pocket and tossed the can back into the box.

Dump might have been an understatement. The court's Plexiglas back wall was so scratched and bowed it was more translucent than clear, mildew had splotched the ceiling, the floor was tracked with scuff marks, and other marks ran up the side walls in a crazed, ascending pattern that turned to random dots across the front. None of it had seen paint or varnish in recent memory.

Gomez propped a heel on the nearest bench, bending forward to stretch his hamstring, switching after some number of deep breaths to stretch the other. Aping him, I did the same. "Free how?" I asked. "Centro deal again?"

"Yeah. One of the union honchos on our board has a membership he doesn't use, so I sign his name. There's a fee for guests, but nobody's ever on duty to check after seven. And heisting a key was easy." Gomez entered the court and worked his achilles tendons by leaning exaggeratedly into a side wall. "OK," he said, showing me the ball when he was done. "A couple of practice rallies, then we let 'er rip." His voice echoed strangely as I latched the Plexiglas door in the now brilliant light.

GOMEZ

I had more or less expected Gomez to be a slasher, and he didn't disappoint. I'm not a natural at any sport, but I'd played enough racquetball to learn the basics and had also bought a how-to paperback the day after he confirmed that we had the court. It was clear he knew the rules, and he was absolutely dogged about controlling the centerline. And from there, he never thought to spare his body if a spectacular lunge or flop could bring the ball within reach.

Those factors would all have been to his advantage if he hadn't consistently overhit. So many of his shots came off the back wall and sat up like marshmallows, I could place my returns anywhere I wanted. He scored a lot of points with tight backhand drives down the side, and he had a feathery lob serve that gave me fits. But if I kept the ball to his forehand, we had long rallies I could win because he'd finally sprawl so far making a save that I'd have an easy bunt in the opposite direction. And with Gomez always facing away from me, spread-legged and eager at mid-court, I benefited from lets by accidentally hitting him with shots he would otherwise have jumped on for winners.

It was tremendous fun. We sweat like brutes, there was side-out after side-out, the loud thwack of the caroming ball became the only sound I was conscious of, and we had more tie scores than not. I didn't notice that he was slowed by his bum knee, nor did he seem to favor it, but I began outlasting him a bit in stamina during the latter stages of a come-from-behind, 21-19 win to even the games at 1-1.

"Jesus!" he exclaimed, gasping as he hauled himself from the floor at the service line to give me a drippy bear-hug. "I should've found a guy I could beat."

It had occurred to me earlier that he was deliberately holding back to keep things close, but by then I didn't think so. I also didn't know what to do about having so much of him pressed against and around me. I put my free arm over his shoulders, rotating us apart without actually breaking contact. "Let's call intermission," I said, flushed and happy. He was now to my side, and I shifted slightly to ensure that there was a gap at our hips.

"Right," he responded, "unless you want a dead Gomez on your hands." Maintaining his own embrace after I dropped my arm, he led us to and through the Plexiglas, not releasing me until we dropped onto a bench.

GOMEZ

"You're in damn good shape, I'll give you that," he continued. Sweat poured from his face and showed in broad patches on his shirt, though his breathing had already quieted.

"Lately, yeah. I've been pounding out ten or fifteen miles a week since moving to the city. My parents even laid *The Complete Book of Running* on me for Christmas."

"For running, I rely on instinct...especially for running." His face held the same expression of wry cockiness I'd seen in my Berkeley kitchen.

"Book or not, knowing the technique helps." As it did in racquetball, notwithstanding that I made no mention of my newly acquired primer.

"Helps the author's bank account," Gomez acknowledged. "I should have guessed when you showed up in those geeky two-tone shoes. Marathons are so *in* nowadays."

"I don't own regular tennies. They're nowhere near as comfortable."

"Lucky we play here. A racquet club wouldn't let those knobby soles on the floor. Mine either, I guess." Gomez wagged one of his worn, black high-tops at me. I'd noticed them before and assumed they'd come from a thrift store, along with his red, none-too-new Oberlin sweatshirt.

"Trendy clubs I can do without," I assured him. "But this place is a real hole-in-the-wall."

"Built years ago for handball. Some of the old timers still have a go. The flooring and wall panels were made in the boat shop."

"Handball? Gomez is wimping out with a racket when he could use his fist?" I'd finally begun to feel sure enough of him and of the locale that I could tease back.

"Gomez played squash long before racquetball came along. He values his hands for other things."

"I barely know what squash is. You'd have won for sure."

"This is the wrong size court for it. I'll win plenty anyway. Had your blow?"

"Pretty much. Is there water?"

Gomez went upstairs and returned with paper cups, a large mason jar of eau-de-tap, and a pair of towels. I drank eagerly, but he poured his first cupful over his head, then toweled off. The towels, however, implied that we might be showering together later on, not a comfortable thought, and that made me observe him more closely.

"Where are Gomez's glasses?" I asked. "Or is he wearing Andy's contacts?"

"There is no Andy," he answered, showing irritation. "Get that straight."

"Sorry."

"Anyway, Gomez doesn't need glasses for sports."

"Good. Hey, I'm also sorry about hitting you with the ball. My backhand is wild, and you kept forcing yourself to the center."

"Part of the game. They were mostly dubs with no zing."

"What do you mean? One drilled you right in the po-po. Had to hurt."

He walked away and stood in the court door. "Po-po isn't a Gomez word," he stated with finality. "You nailed me in the butt, and yeah, that hurt. But give the Andy shit a rest. He and Gomez share the objective facts of their lives...the bad knee, where they went to school, and so on...but they're different people. From now on, shut up about it...or we won't be friends. You never know if somebody's listening."

"Yeah, OK. I get the picture."

"Besides, *real* name only means somebody's parents thought it up before they did."

The next games unfolded like the first two—hard-fought, close and split 1-1. We started on a tie-breaker, but gave up at 3 points each because we were too wiped out. I received another lengthy bear hug, and the friction over my references to Andy seemed forgotten. He'd made his point, though.

I was relieved, too, that his bootleg membership status and my lack of a guest pass meant he wanted to avoid unnecessary questions by skipping the showers and locker room altogether. While I'd brought clean clothes and a nylon jacket in my gym bag, I hadn't been looking forward to the penis-comparisons he was bound to make. And I'd been right. That night established our pattern of bundling up and heading for beers at the Buena Vista in all our sweaty glory, but he was unable to resist a joking reminder:

"Can't have everything. The court doesn't cost, but we lose out on weenie sightings and a chance to play drop the soap. You want to show me yours, bring a photo."

GOMEZ

"I might cheat with a below-the-waist snap of Long John Holmes." That earned me a decent laugh, and porn stars had become sufficiently mainstream that Gomez didn't inquire how I knew who Holmes was.

I put the rackets and the ball in the cardboard box, slipped on my jacket, and waited while Gomez stood with the sole of his foot resting on a bench to remove his knee brace. "Feels good to get that damn thing off," he said.

As he was horsing the cuffs of some gray sweats over his shoe I had a clear view of his leg and was shocked. He didn't see me and made no comment, but his knee was concave at the inside rear, a third of his calf muscle seemed to be missing, and there were suture marks and linear scars above and below the kneecap. A gunshot or explosion would have been as plausible a cause, if not more so, than what he'd said about football.

In seconds Gomez had the sweatpants on and was gathering his gear. The fabric above one ankle carried a washed-out, though still-visible, paint smear that had to date from the Andy era. I couldn't help noticing, but I began the habit of suppressing all remarks to that effect, though not always the thoughts themselves.

GOMEZ

CHAPTER 8

"Wow," I said, "what a knockout. Sausalito to Berkeley, with Angel Island smack in the middle."

Because we had chanced to ride up in the elevator together after work, I'd been invited to Jordan's for a glass of wine. It was the end one of those false-spring February days the Bay Area is known for. Though the sun was gone and the fog-less sky was rapidly losing the light, for the moment, visibility remained good.

I stood at the north window with my back to the living room while Jordan played bartender. Big in- and outbound freighters crossed wakes on the bay amid their usual retinues of tugboats. About the time I located the winking lights of the Richmond-San Rafael Bridge in the distance I heard footsteps behind me.

"Here," he said, "Clos-du-Val Chardonnay. Have you had it?"

"No, but I'm a willing guinea pig."

"Cheers." He pushed his glass against mine to produce a muted *ting* and we both drank. It was deliciously cold with fruit and tobacco aftertastes.

"Great," I told him.

"Hmm," he said, joining my survey, "your living room would have about the same cityscape as my bedroom, which is quite nice itself. Here you'd be staring at Landau-Walters all the time. Doesn't bother me. I don't spend my days there." Jordan turned to light a sleek pole-lamp in the corner.

"I'd still trade. If L-W floats away on the tide some night, I want to know without walking four blocks to find out."

"See it in the foreground?" Jordan pointed. "Looks like you're safe."

I hadn't till then, but he was right. There was no sight-line to my office window, but the retired ferry's top deck, with the railing lights being turned off as I watched, showed in a notch between two darkened warehouses.

"Decent outfit to work for?" he asked, feeding me a comfortable topic. "Come on, let's sit."

GOMEZ

I followed him to a cream-colored leather couch placed mid-room at the edge of a lush, blue-green rug. I, too, had a leather couch, in gray, but my other new furniture was mostly chrome and glass. His was oiled Scandinavian wood. Back when he was married it would have been the height of contemporary style, and probably represented everything his wife never allowed him to buy.

The Italian-modern pieces at my place, by contrast, were what Jenny had unsuccessfully lobbied for prior to the advent of Barbara. It gave a certain satisfaction to know that I now had them and she still didn't.

Jordan put the wine bottle, sweating a single rivulet down its neck, on a stone tile at one end of a low, trapezoidal table in front of the couch. As we settled ourselves, I saw that a book he must have been reading lay facedown on the table as well. On the nearest wall was a large, framed Miró — a print, I assumed.

"Landau-Walters *is* a good place to work," I answered. "I don't see myself leaving unless I'm fired."

"Not much danger, I hope."

"None that I know of."

"Milt Landau and Roy Walters are a couple of pistols, aren't they? I used to do most of their legal work...or my firm did."

"It's Herrick, Orrington these days...I think."

"Yes. *Brand X* we call them. The hated competition. There was a bit of a flap in the early 70s and they won out."

"I vaguely remember, but I was pretty junior then. Who's we? In your case, I mean."

"Marbury, Morrison and Carswell. I'm a senior partner." He took another swallow of wine, his raised glass emphasizing the contrast between the straw-yellow liquid and the urgent white of his monogrammed shirt.

By this point Jordan had shed his coat and tie, though I continued to wear mine. He also put his feet on the table-edge, something no one would be permitted at my place, showing the perfectly creased trousers of his brown mohair-tweed suit. The sheen of his matching pebbled oxfords said he'd stopped today at the shoe-stand in the lobby of the Shell Building, where I knew without knowing how I knew, that Marbury, Morrison's offices claimed the topmost floors.

Nor could I remember what the flap had been that caused L-W to change law firms, but in trying I must have created an awkward silence, because Jordan launched a distraction. "Pardon my shirking the host's duty. You can reach more easily, so refill your glass and top me up."

"Gladly." I did as requested.

"Didn't you mention Angel Island a minute ago?" he asked.

"Just that I could see it…which I can't any more."

"Well, I often don't see it even when I can. Perhaps I don't want to."

"Why?"

"Reminds me of my daughter. It was a magical place for her…as a tyke and early teen. For years I kept a Lightning Class sloop at the yacht basin. What she always wanted was to sail there."

"Did you?" I experienced a sharp mental image of the bay dotted with sailboats as it so frequently is in good weather.

"Of course, many times. There's an anchorage on the Tiburon side. Then we'd go ashore to nose around. Looking for angels, she called it."

"They sound like happy memories."

"You'd think."

"What's her name?"

"Good question," he shrugged exasperatedly. "There's Gwen, the name we gave her. And Kestrel, her *tribal* identity, which she insists we use."

"Not uncommon, I guess, for California."

"For what California's become. You don't have children? Am I right?"

"Right. No marriage anymore, either."

"Consider yourself lucky on both counts," Jordan grunted. "What do you make of this?" He dislodged his feet from the table and retrieved the book, a glossy paperback, flipping it over into my hand.

"*Ecotopia*," I read aloud, "by Ernest Callenbach. Never heard of it."

"Look inside."

The book readily parted at the title page. "First edition. Published in Berkeley, 1975."

"No, go back to the flyleaf."

GOMEZ

There was an inscription, a loose triangle of lilac ink at the upper left, consisting of carefully rounded letters with small, open-centered circles to serve as periods and as dots over the *is*. I assumed Jordan wanted me to, so I again read aloud. "'Daddy— This is the <u>one</u> book you and your rich friends <u>need</u> to understand …really understand. Until you do, we'll <u>never</u> have any more to talk about than we did last summer. —Kes.'

"What do I make of the inscription," I continued, "or the book?"

"Both. It came in yesterday's mail."

"Well, she really wants you to read it."

"I did, last night. Or tried. Total poppycock. It posits a female-run, ecologically benign, economically self-sufficient nation, thirty years into the future, comprised of Washington, Oregon and Northern California, which have liberated themselves from the US by threatening nuclear terrorism. Of course, peace and harmony prevail in this new utopia, and there are no lawyers."

This was said in such a wearily dismissive tone I knew he was trying for humor, but a note of pain intruded as well. To be polite, I laughed.

"How old is she?" I went on.

"Thirty-two. Close to your own age, I imagine."

"True. Where does she live?"

"The heart of Ecotopia, where else? In the redwoods, just outside Occidental."

"Not a place I know."

"Sonoma County. A few miles from the coast. An *organic nuts and berries* commune on a disused apple ranch," Jordan said with increasing bitterness. "Free love, drugs, bastard children running all over, and nobody there who's had a bath or haircut that they can remember. Don't get me started."

"Do you see each other?"

"Not on her initiative. I usually manage one visit a year, summers when I'm at the Bohemian Club compound."

"I've read about that in Herb Caen. Never knew where it was."

"Five miles from Kes and her tribe. Might as well be five light years. The reason I drop in then is they clean the place up and have an open-house. It's a ploy to keep the sheriff off their necks. And my god, if that's clean, forget any other time."

GOMEZ

I nodded sympathetically, drank wine, and he continued.

"But last summer, she stonewalled me. A cold nod when I arrived, a grudging 'Hello, daddy,' that was it. I was there less than half-an-hour, and the tone was so negative I let one of the so-called men show me around without her."

"Must have been hard to take."

"Don't worry," he affirmed, "I'm tough." It registered on me that Jordan's eyes were steel-blue, and his chiseled features and strong jaw were further evidence that he'd been one of the charmed ones, the tall, good-looking ones, long before his full head of hair went silver. Most men would like to age as well as he had, but the examples I saw daily made me realize that few did.

"And since then," I added, "you're cut out of her life?"

"Nothing new, but I thought we had already reached the irreducible minimum. I just can't shake the idea that Shaman Farm…that's what they call it…had another bastard in the works, this one my grandson or granddaughter. Kes couldn't bring herself to tell me, and was afraid somebody else would. I admit, I wouldn't take it well. Or maybe I'm off base."

"She's got to be on the pill. It would've happened years ago if she wanted a kid."

"Ah, the ray of hope. Plus she was never a Weatherman kook…or one of Patty Hearst's kidnappers. But I've lost faith that it's a phase, that she'll have a normal life, or that I'll ever be part of it."

"Actually, a grandchild might lead to rapprochement."

He pointed to *Ecotopia* lying on the couch between us. "Not according to what's in there."

"Would you mind if I borrowed it?"

"No," he said, with a surprised laugh, "be my guest. Tell me, do you get on with your parents?"

"They're back in Kansas. We have almost nothing in common, feels like we never did, but sure, we're civil. They hate California, but I was home four days at Christmas."

"Normal, in other words. That's all I really had in mind. With my son, too."

"Is he older or younger than Kes?" I asked.

"Younger…by five years. I lost them both to the 60s. My daughter to the Haight-Ashbury and James to Vietnam."

"He's dead? Terrible. I didn't know."

"I shouldn't be so melodramatic. He's in perfect health. In Canada...Vancouver. He went underground and fled when his draft number came up."

"He'll be home once he sees it's safe. The President's amnesty just started last year."

"James doesn't intend to come back. He's living with an Asian woman; he drives a cab in the winter and works summers as a fishing guide."

"On those facts, maybe you or I wouldn't either."

"Not much return on investment for three years at Stanford. Of course, it wasn't his investment."

"Was he a traitor in your opinion? I mean at the time?"

"We had harsh words. I'm a former Air Force officer. But I came to hate the US role in Vietnam and the underhanded way our last two presidents behaved. What Carter did was right."

"Does your son...James...know that?"

"Yes. We speak by phone. It's not as bad as with Kes. And he hasn't changed his name...his first name. Only his last and middle. A further consolation is that neither of them has any better relationship with their mother than they do me."

"Where did they grow up?"

"Hillsborough. My ex still lives there, but poky old Joe Shumate of Fairchild Semiconductor was dumb enough to marry her and relieve me of alimony."

"You divorced each other...and your kids divorced you."

"That's how things turned out. Frustrating that they're both so ideological. I'm no caveman! I'm a *liberal* Republican and proud of it. I despised Ronald Reagan, which cost me a judgeship. My remaining hope was Joe Alioto. If he'd been Governor after Ronnie instead of Moonbeam Brown, I'd be on the bench right now."

"Wouldn't it be a pay cut?"

"I'm past the point of having to worry about that, and I'd enjoy the challenge." He drew a breath. "Oh, hell. Sorry to be grousing. Compared to somebody with real problems, mine are nothing. Hearing from Kes unnerved me a bit."

"Where's Eve these days?" I inquired, seeking a fresh subject.

He brightened. "In Hawaii, actually. She'll be back Sunday. Quite the decorative item, isn't she?"

"Hard not to notice."

Jordan laughed. "I was afraid your eyes would drill laser holes in her the night we saw you getting out of the elevator."

"I didn't realize I was so obvious."

He laughed again. "No women in your life, I take it."

"Not at the moment, no."

"But you're single only a few months as I remember."

"Right."

"Well, men at that stage either rush right out and screw everything that moves, or they go to ground for a while, rally, then screw everything that moves. You're apparently on the latter path. Nothing to worry about."

More than he knew, I thought, again changing the subject. "You must miss her… Eve, I mean."

"Yes, but I make a point of not having all my eggs in one basket. She's the best of the lot, though."

"How did you meet?"

"Through…through an introduction service. I'm also using them to audition for a second Eve. Tara, my other steady date, moved to Miami to shack up with someone."

"It happens," I shrugged. This was the kind of problem Jordan was used to, where being rich and handsome guaranteed a solution. With his kids there was more to the story. "Is that why I've had so many lost females knocking on my door lately."

"Sorry for the bother," he quipped. "But you seem to give good directions."

"I try."

"If you're interested, Eve has friends she could fix you up with." He glanced at me with raised eyebrows.

"Think they'd be my type? I doubt that women in the market for you," I pointedly met his glance, "would be keen on substituting me."

"There's a…shall we say…*means test*, true enough, and an introduction fee, but nothing you'd likely find disqualifying. And being under forty could make you quite a hit."

"Thanks, I'll consider it." I had implied that net worth was my only handicap, but there was inevitably another I would worry about. And my youth might be no advantage. The kind of women

Jordan must be referring to would want to think you'd die well ahead of them before they'd be inclined to get serious.

"Let me know. No sense sitting home deprived when the world beckons."

"Speaking of home, I ought to get going. Next time we do this, I'll host."

"That would be delightful." We both stood up. "I have so little contact with people your age…my children's age…I like the idea of getting together."

"Me, too."

"I can't imagine an invitation to either of their homes…even if I brought the wine."

"Show up empty-handed at my door. Let me repay in full."

"I accept," he said. "Here, take a piece of this notepaper. My phone is on it. Oh, and remember Kes's book."

÷ ÷ ÷

As February proceeded, my social calendar actually began to have entries. Gomez and I went to a new foreign intrigue movie starring Jane Fonda and set in pre-war Europe, which we followed with an hour of animated conversation at a Union Street bar. I then called Jordan to arrange another evening of wine and tête-à-tête, and he responded by inviting me to join Eve and him for part of this year's Erotic Film Festival at the Presidio Theater. I was tempted, flattered, in fact, but declined.

I hadn't decided yet if I would have Eve fix me up with one of her friends, though Jordan had also suggested that as an option to my merely tagging along. But for some reason I was more interested in sex if it was illicit, or slightly illicit, and a film, however horny, attended by a roomful of couples in the name of art, sounded hygienic. Besides, if my date liked me, I'd absolutely be expected to perform afterwards, and I wasn't sure I could. The whole thing had gotten stupidly and ridiculously complicated.

Instead I read *Ecotopia*, which was much better and more thought provoking than Jordan had led me to believe. The writing was clumsy, but the idea of a society devoted to harmony with the earth rather than all-out consumption had appeal. Who could say that in thirty years things wouldn't evolve in that direction? With

GOMEZ

Jerry Brown and Jimmy Carter preaching the need to recognize limits, maybe Ecotopian roots were already taking hold.

But the real surprise was the sexual attitude of Ecotopian women. Jordan hadn't alluded to it in his synopsis, and the author was no D. H. Lawrence, but sex was an important theme. And feminism, though a societal given, wasn't anti-male or anti-sex, as had been my experience. Ecotopian women liked men, liked sex, and pursued pleasure in straightforward, balanced and non-possessive ways. As long as I didn't reflect on how hygienic, or even intimidating, that could be in practice, it was exciting.

The week after our movie Gomez and I played another round of racquetball, featuring more hammer-and-tongs competition and games running into extra points. He got the best of me 3-1, but I was beginning to decipher his lob serve, so I wouldn't be permanently out of the running. Over our now traditional beers at the Buena Vista, with Eric Clapton's *Lay Down Sally* blaring from the jukebox, we sat in our sweats toasting the amazing peace deal between Egypt and Israel, and generally shot the shit about everything, including how many women I wasn't going out with.

Finally, as we were about to leave, Gomez said, "Got anything doing Friday night? How about dinner at my place?"

"Sure," I answered, "sounds fine."

"Good. There's someone I want you to meet. But remember," he added with emphasis, "no comments about drippy faucets or the interior needing new paint. That stuff's not on my beat anymore."

PART III

Have you understood me, or must I repeat that I was virtually a novice in all that has to do with love?

> André Gide
> *The Immoralist*
> Translation: Richard Howard, 1970

CHAPTER 9

The someone Gomez wanted me to meet was Madeline Klein. Driving over, I knew only that he'd been seeing her since just before Christmas and that she had caused him to violate a stricture long lived by: not getting involved with married women. There wasn't even a pending divorce or any formal separation. Her husband was a bank exec who spent months at a time in Indonesia on an oil and natural gas project his office had sunk money into. While the cat was away, the mouse apparently played.

Compared to Mission Street, one block east, with its teeming sidewalks, Latino murals, glitzy neon, and cheek-by-jowl restaurants, Valencia was dark and quiet. I saw the Ranchero near Gomez's corner in front of a storefront ravioli factory with a **CLOSED** sign in the window. Most of the other buildings were dingy two- and-three-story apartments with garages at street level and quasi-Victorian exteriors. Adjacent to a laundromat on 22nd I squeezed into a spot and mentally rehearsed the directions I'd been given. The glimmering patches of broken windshield glass along the curb would alone have made me uneasy, without factoring in a terrified child shrieking somewhere up the block, and the sudden shouts of an argument from a nearby doorway. This was what you got for the $90-a-month rent Gomez liked to brag about.

His place was tiny, he said, way in back and hard to find. I guided myself to the intersection, crossed, turned at a dimly lit corner market — or **Tienda**, according to the lettering on the window behind the anti-burglary bars — and found a wooden gate between the wall of Gomez's building and the one next-door. As he'd described, the gate didn't yield to my push and a steel key-slot gave the impression that it was locked. Not so, however, if you stood on tiptoe and reached carefully above to catch a looped wire with your finger. Once in, I re-latched the gate and let my eyes adjust. The night was overcast and cold.

A narrow, unlit concrete passage paralleled the sides of the buildings, along which I felt my way, trailing one hand on the rough stucco to my right, occasionally bumping it across vertical pipes and conduit. From the left, through an arbor bridging the passage's end, came a soft glow, and as I got closer, faint voices and music. Looming ahead was a new-looking cyclone fence topped with razor-wire, which demarcated this property from the jumbled wrecking yard behind an auto shop on 22nd. Not quite to the fence, a short weathered stairway barely wide enough to accommodate me led up the back of the building toward the light. Visible below the landing were the shapes of several garbage cans whose sour smell I had already noted.

It was exactly the kind of alley—and neighborhood—that anybody with sense avoids, but Gomez had insisted I'd be safe. I twisted the handle of a worn mechanical doorbell to produce a clanging rattle. The voices inside said something unintelligible, although one was clearly male and the other female. Somebody opened the door.

Framed against the softly illuminated room she was a blur to begin with, while I was lit by the spill from Gomez's front windows. I'd been worried that the slacks and cardigan under my unzipped mackinaw might be too straight-arrow for the setting, and now I was not only sure of it, they were the first things on which I was judged.

"Hello, you must be Paul. Come in."

Although my ears processed those words, I was so fixated by the allure of the smile from which they emerged, it seemed I had read her lips. "Thanks," I heard myself reply, stepping across the threshold. "You must be Madeline."

She forthrightly took my hand, not to shake as I first thought, but to hold and press momentarily in a more intimate greeting. "Yes, but please call me Mad...implying," she added with a breathy laugh, "mad-*cap*, not...mad-*ness*, or...*anger*."

A practiced remark, no doubt, but I liked it anyway. "I'm to look after you," she went on. "Gomez is cooking."

I let Mad hang my coat on a clothes tree opposite the door, taking full opportunity to look as she turned her attention away. Her hair, a burnished golden-red, was pulled loosely back from her face into a sort of ponytail with lavender and green chenille cording braided into it. She was graceful and slender, wore a black leotard under a pleated, ankle-length batik skirt, and a pair of pointed

GOMEZ

Capezio flats in which her height was perhaps two inches short of mine. Her hazel eyes and creamy skin I had already appraised, along with the fact that she wore no makeup other than a liberal use of kohl eye pencil.

She faced me again and smiled. The sleeves of her leotard were pulled partly up to reveal her forearms, a simple, fish-shaped gold pin was positioned below her left collarbone, and bits of polished shell, held there in some invisible way, adorned her ears.

"Hey, man," called Gomez, separated from us by the kitchen counter, on which he was furiously stirring something with a wire whisk. "Glad you found me OK. Rest your bones. Mad'll serve up wine."

She sidestepped toward him and I studied the room to keep my eyes from tracking her. Gomez's quarters ran less than the width of the building, a single cramped, low-ceilinged rectangle with windows on two sides and books on makeshift brick-and-board shelves covering most of the other two. The entryway took up the inner front corner, and the cooking area the rear corner diagonally across from it, while a combined living/sleeping area followed the L of the outer walls. In the crook of the L his bed, fortified with oversized pillows, doubled as a couch. The only breaks in the rows of books were the doors to the bathroom and closet, and the floor held a threadbare Chinese rug, centered on which were an oak dining table and four straight-backed chairs, no two alike.

I took an end seat and continued my survey. His limited wall space held a pair of Cézanne prints, a black-and-white portrait photo of Martin Luther King, a poster reproduction of Diego Rivera's famous flower vendor, and near the kitchen, an illustrated calendar from the Restaurante Las Pampas on 18th Street. A dozen candles arrayed on various surfaces supplied light, augmented by a single bare bulb above the stove.

"How about the flip side of the tango record?" I heard Mad ask.

"No, try Jacques Brel, but drop the volume a bit," Gomez answered.

Accordion, guitar and baritone singing began in the background. "If you'd been five minutes earlier," Mad said, "you'd have caught Gaucho Gomez strutting his stuff. We even had the rug folded back." She stood at my elbow, giving off a faint scent of gardenia.

GOMEZ

"Which is why the sauce boiled over," Gomez put in.

A light *thunk* from the table meant the arrival of a tumbler for my wine. A heavier *thunk* accompanied Mad's putting down a jug of burgundy. Gomez might claim there was no more Andy, but some things didn't change. Mad's nearly empty tumbler was on the table already, along with three of the candles and several books, one splayed open, spine up.

"Here," Mad said, "blood of the grape." She poured wine for both of us.

We touched glasses and drank. Still standing, she gathered the books and found an extinguished match to serve as a bookmark in *The Diary of* Anaïs *Nin, Volume II,* the one that had been open. Mad hummed along with Brel's chorus while portaging the books to Gomez's bed and dropping them there. She returned and sat to my left.

"Sorry for the clutter," she said. "Gomez and I are having a textual dispute."

"I saw the Nin diary. What were the others?"

"More Nin," she answered. "*Volumes I* and *III*...plus a feverishly thumbed *Tropic of Capricorn.*"

"Henry Miller I read years ago in college. Both *Tropics,* but not Nin."

"No wonder Gomez likes you," Mad teased. "He's read all of Miller, and thinks the man is god. The Nins were gifts from me that he never finds time for." She looked over her shoulder but Gomez was apparently too preoccupied to respond. She returned her gaze to me and smiled.

"What's the dispute?" I automatically, unthinkingly smiled back, her teeth and lips filling my entire field of vision.

"I'm proving that she had more influence on *Capricorn* than on *Cancer.*"

"But *Cancer* was dedicated to her. I remember my prof making a to-do of it."

"No, she wrote the preface. *Cancer* was largely complete before she and Miller became lovers."

"Bullshit!" Gomez challenged from across the room, grinning broadly. I saw that he was in the same outfit of mid-heel shoes, pressed jeans, and tight-fitting black sweater that he'd worn for our dinner at the Hayes Street Grill. It was his standard uniform I learned in the months ahead.

"Another thing," Mad laughed, "Gomez is a bad loser."

"Bullshit again," he said.

"Oh, not so bad when I beat him at racquetball," I replied, letting my voice carry.

"Which is not very damn often," he shot back. "Aaak, the bread. Where the hell did I put it?" I heard him rummaging on the counter.

"He tells me you're a graphic artist," Mad said, "and that you knew one another in Berkeley."

"Right...on both counts," I replied, going on to summarize my life from Kansas to SF in response to her diplomatically phrased questions. She let me brush by the divorce with only an acknowledging nod that it had occurred, and didn't probe how Gomez and I had become friends. Although she clearly thought the University was our connection, she provided no specifics on what he may have told her. Then she rose and began setting the table.

"Did you do a thesis on Nin or something?" I asked.

"I wish. But I did meet her...at my parents' place when I was fifteen."

"No kidding? Where was that?"

"Beverly Hills. My dad's a film producer and promoter. Not a mogul. Small-time, really. He had an option on one of her novels called..."

"*A Spy in the House of Love*," Gomez interrupted, leaning over the counter. "So Mad knows I'm paying attention," he informed me, "even if her theory doesn't wash."

"Anaïs Nin came to your house?" I asked, fascinated.

"Yes. Twice, I think, but I met her only once. She was magnificent. A primitive turban for a hat, long strands of Haitian beads, and a way of locking on to what you said as though you were the world's most interesting person. She's been a hero of mine ever since. Later I found out where she and her West Coast husband lived, then drove by a lot trying to catch glimpses."

Mad glided back and forth with Gomez's mismatched china, napkins and silver, which I helped her distribute, saying, "I thought Nin lived in Paris or New York."

GOMEZ

"She did…earlier on. But her last years, mainly in LA. She led sort of a double life."

"Does '*last years,*' mean she's dead?"

Mad regarded me with disappointment. "Anaïs joined the spirit world thirteen months ago, in January of '77."

"What happened?"

"Cancer…ironically," Mad shuddered. "But she put her stamp on a whole artistic era. Born in 1903, and a Pisces, like I am. Her ashes were scattered in the ocean off Santa Monica…as mine will be."

"For Mad's birthday last week," Gomez said, arriving with a pot of what looked to be stew, "I took her to Hayes Street Grill, but this'll be as good or better." He dropped a wicker pad onto the table from under his arm and put the pot on it.

"Promises, promises," Mad responded in a disbelieving tone, though she stroked his arm with her hand at the same time.

"OK," he announced, bringing more items. "But scoot around one spot so Mad's at the end. Food won't be served till the seating is boy-girl-boy. A strict Gomez tradition."

Mad and I resettled ourselves while he poured wine. "Here's to The Three Musketeers," he said, still standing, tilting his glass toward me, then toward Mad, and finally, himself. The wire frames of his glasses glinted in the candlelight.

"*And* to the memory of Anaïs," Mad put in.

"Including her fan club, The Ninnies," he added, with a chuckle. We all drank and Gomez sat down.

"Keep in mind," Mad said archly, "there never *will* be a Gomez fan club."

"Touché," he laughed. "Unless it's for my cooking. Tonight we have beef bourguignonne, Brussels sprouts with lemon zest, hearts of romaine salad, and real French bread smuggled out the back door of a frou-frou bakery Gomez chooses not to name. For dessert, apples with blue cheese and coffee."

If what I ate was typical, his cooking deserved a fan club. Moreover, although combative repartee was obviously a constant of their relationship, when Gomez was present it struck me as incomprehensible that she could have a husband somewhere in Java or Borneo who also had a claim on her loyalties. Yet she didn't shy away from mentioning the husband.

GOMEZ

His name, I eventually learned, was Clark Thayer. He was in his late forties, well-off, a Bank of America vice-president, and descended from Southern California pioneers. Mad was his second marriage, he, her first. They had no children and lived in Piedmont, a posh East Bay suburb, in a big house. How he felt about Mad's keeping Klein as a surname instead of taking his I never heard discussed.

"Four stars," she told Gomez as we concluded our entrees and began on salad. "Give me the recipe so I can teach Graciela."

"Direct from Gomez's sainted mother," he nodded, tapping his forehead. "Lives in here, but he'll dictate if you play scribe."

"At breakfast tomorrow," Mad replied. "Let's not forget."

"Who's Graciela," I asked.

"Our new maid," she answered. "Clark's and mine. Most of her dishes are from Guatemala, but she's dying to run a *gringa* kitchen. Clark hasn't met her yet, and I really want it to go well."

"Had his fill of exotic food in the Far East, I suppose," Gomez remarked disparagingly. I came to notice over time that he never uttered the man's name.

"To an extent," Mad replied. "He has a...a native housekeeper...who cooks."

"How did you and Gomez meet?" For his sake, it was a topic I assumed would be unrelated to her marital status.

"Whose version?" she answered, and they both laughed.

"Start with yours," I said, laughing a bit as well.

She looked at Gomez. "No, I'll start with his...my version of his, if he can *bear* not to interrupt."

"Doubtful," Gomez grunted.

"He *says*," Mad emphasized, "he remembers me from EST last year. You know ...one of those Werner Ehrhard seminars. Clark and I did it together, evenings and weekends at the downtown Hilton. Not only that, Gomez insists he and I spoke, but I don't remember him at all. Of course, there were hundreds of us."

Gomez got up to clear away our plates and bring dessert. While Mad poured coffee, my mind went to work on this latest tidbit. The whole EST self-improvement phenomenon left me cold, although I knew a number of people among the tens of thousands who had joined the fold. In fact, I'd have bet my lawyer neighbor Jordan

GOMEZ

Mackay was one of them. But Gomez? He seemed the least likely ESTie I could imagine.

Moreover, last year Gomez was still Andy, so if he had approached her, and now triggered a name to go with that memory, it could blow his cover. Edgy, even by Gomez's standards. Unless Mad already knew, which would mean they were *both* playing me. But why did I care? They'd reveal the joke sooner or later, and my lack of surprise would give me one back on them. Gomez caught my eye when he sat down again, and sent a look of such total insouciance I'd swear he knew what I was thinking.

"Ah, yes, Werner Ehrhard," Gomez sighed. "Also known as John Paul Rosenberg, Jack Frost or Werner von Savage…take your pick. A guy with multiple names, it's hard to know where the bullshit ends and the horse shit begins."

"I've never understood why you signed up," Mad said. "Pricey, too."

"Intellectual curiosity, pure and simple. I ran a little con to swing the money."

"Now that must be a story," I said, having both read and heard that Werner whatever-his-real-name was a tough cookie.

"It is," Gomez acknowledged, "but one I can't tell due to…shall we say…a pledge of confidentiality. Mad thinks EST was a crock, too."

She nodded. "I was really into it at the time, but I look back on how oversimplified everything was and I'm embarrassed."

"Not to mention all their buzz words," Gomez added. "'*Truth Process,*' and '*Get off your Game!*'…god, it was endless."

"They claim they're being scientific," Mad said, "but scream '*Asshole!*' to describe non-ESTies, or any ESTie who won't roll over for them. I hated that part."

"It's like the army charging tuition for boot camp," Gomez agreed. "And I thought colleges were bad."

"But some people do benefit," Mad went on. "I know Clark did. He's better at standing up to his family and his ex-wife. It probably made me more assertive, too."

"Assertiveness," I deadpanned. "Such a critical need for Gomez."

GOMEZ

"How Mad and I got together," he declared, cutting me off, "is that I saw her again as part of a Mime Troupe show at the Centro in December."

"No, *I* saw you."

"Alright," Gomez went on, "we saw each other. The next day it was lunch at Las Pampas, and now I can't stay away from the woman."

"I ensorceled him," Mad said smugly.

"Ugh, that word!" Gomez erupted. "And you wonder why I have trouble reading Nin? Be happy that I know her brother and might get us invited to one of his parties."

"Well, I did ensorcel you," she protested, smiling. "And it's a perfectly good word."

"Hold on," I said. "Mad's in the Mime Troupe?"

"She works there, yeah, but backstage," Gomez answered.

"I'm the development director," she said. "And office factotum. I volunteered to help raise funds, but they've piled on lots more because they don't have to pay me."

"Must be a colorful place," I said. "Or is that too polite a term?"

"Extremely colorful," Mad laughed. "I love it, but I'm not sure they trust me yet. It's only been the last few years they've accepted grant money. They're very anti-establishment, very cutting-edge."

"And she's the rich suburban bitch," Gomez added.

"I'm winning them over. They like having the lights and phone stay on. I got the Hess Foundation to renew, and the Arts Council. And finally, we're getting some city hotel tax. That's my biggest coup. Thank god for Mayor Moscone."

"Hell of a guy," Gomez said. "The Centro would be nowhere without him."

"Anyway," Mad continued, "we perform at senior centers and adult schools a lot, and we've worked up bilingual versions of *Meter Maid*, *Phone Booth*, and *Red Santa*."

"Everybody howls their heads off," Gomez nodded.

"Those are our most popular skits. And the Centro's only two blocks away, so the cast parades there in costume. I tag along to help with props whenever I can."

"Ties in perfectly," Gomez told me as an aside. "Street theater and puppets are big in Latino culture."

GOMEZ

"Speaking of which," Mad said, "why don't we walk down to El Gallito for some booty-shaking?"

Minutes later we were out the door and descending the stairs to the entry-passage. I was zipped tightly into my mackinaw trying to keep warm, while Mad wore a long cape of black velour, her arms wrapped inside it, with the collar up. Gomez had wound a maroon scarf around his neck and donned a beret. Saying he knew the route best, he took the lead. Our breath hung as steam in the chill air.

Hoarse voices came from the wrecking yard beyond the cyclone fence. "*Chingase ustedes!*" said one. "*Cabron!*" said another. "*Da me lo!*" a third voice demanded. "*Ahorita!*"

Gomez stopped on the second-to-last step. "*Senores,*" he called. "*Soy Gomez, y quiero que hablen decentemente por favor...que tengan respecto para mi mujer.*"

"*Hola,* Gomez. *Buenas noches.* Sorry, man. You seen Armando lately?"

"Not since I first moved in. You know that."

"Yeah, but word is he still noses around...the *joto* scumbag." Three forms too distant to have faces in their hooded sweatshirts emerged to accompany the voices.

"Stay cool, *muchachos,*" Gomez concluded. "Come see me at the Centro. I can do you more good there than here." He turned to us, put his finger to his lips, then reached to take Mad's arm beneath her cape as we resumed our progress.

No one spoke until we neared the gate onto Valencia. "What was that about?" I asked in a low voice.

"A long-time neighborhood gang hangs out in those junked cars," Gomez replied in similar fashion. "Call themselves *Los Chingados*...The Fucker Boys. That's why my landlord put up the big fence."

Out on the sidewalk, we headed south, walking three abreast with Gomez in the middle and his arms hung over Mad's and my shoulders.

"Who's Armando?" she said, still in a constrained tone.

"Remember, I told you a speed-freak lived in my place? How ungodly a mess it was? Well, that's Armando. He dealt for the Hell's Angels to feed his habit. Was in and out of jail. He's gay, too, from what I hear. His mother lived upstairs for twenty years, but when she died he got kicked out."

GOMEZ

"You know this guy?" I asked.

"Saw him a few times while I was hauling shit from Berkeley up the stairs. Wasted, hanging on the fence like he couldn't believe what was happening. I figure he's in the Castro now. The gang goes up there to beat on gays sometimes, so he'd better be careful. He grew up as a *Chingado*, but he stiffed them for cash when he left."

"Are you absolutely *sure* you want to live in the Mission?" I asked, again wondering if my car was OK.

"Relax," Gomez laughed. "There's a good chance Mad is packing heat."

"I am not," she said indignantly, "and you know it. But I was nervous myself when I started my job. And that alley of yours isn't the greatest."

"Her so-called husband" Gomez continued, "bought Mad a snub-nosed .32 before he went to Asia this time. In case horny Mime Troupers get out of line."

"It's not them he's worried about. Alabama Street is rougher than Valencia on nights I work late. Think of the Zebra killings. Anonymous…right on the sidewalk."

"Should have been a little Beretta, then," Gomez said, displaying his endless command of stray facts. "Lighter and gets rounds off much quicker."

"So where is the thing," I pressed.

"Clark took me to an indoor range, but I'm not certified, and I didn't like carrying it. Bad karma. Besides, it got stolen."

"On our first big date, no less," Gomez put in.

"Huh?" I said, confused.

"Gomez won't come to my place, and I refused to go to his until I'd seen it in the daylight, so I got us a room at the Claremont for the weekend. The gun was in my suitcase and disappeared when we accidentally left our luggage in the hall. Filing a complaint would just make things worse, but Clark will be angry. It was registered to him."

"You mean he doesn't know?" I asked.

"There's plenty Clark doesn't know. He didn't come home for Christmas, I went there. No way was I bringing a gun through customs. I'll dream up a story to explain it if I need one. Meanwhile, as Anaïs says, '*Live* the dream.'"

"Do you keep a journal or diary of your own on all this?"

GOMEZ

"Of course, but it's private...very private. It rarely leaves home and isn't for publication while certain people are alive."

"What a relief," Gomez remarked. "And to defeat prying eyes, she writes everything in French." He threw me a puckish glance.

Judging from our earlier conversation, he'd given her an edited version of his past, so apparently she didn't realize he knew that language too. We had crossed 23rd Street by then and were about to cross 24th. A bar with a flashing rooster and the name El Gallito in red and green neon stood on the opposite corner.

"As for guns," Gomez said, having scooted ahead to grandly wave his arms as he walked backwards facing us, "I've seen all I want. I hate the damn things...not to mention bombs. But if anybody shoots me...kills me...I hope it's for the stewpot. Ending up as food, I can relate to. That's the way of nature. Ridiculous to be killed because of your race or your ideas."

Inside, the jukebox was loud and Gomez's odd take on death was the last of any substantive topic for the night. We drank bottles of Dos Equis in a wildly smoky den of bellowed Spanish, mostly male, where Gomez seemed to know about every third person. The routine was a circumspect "*Que tal, Gomez, como esta?*" Then in reply, "*Que hubo*, Rinaldo" — or Matias, or Joaquin, or Jorge — followed by a brief mutual touching of the back or shoulder. Jeans, pastel rayon shirts and the occasional broad-brimmed hat were the predominant dress, with blouses and skirts of brighter rayon for the women.

Thankfully, the music wasn't mariachis, though Mad quickly gave up trying to teach me salsa steps. She and Gomez were terrific together, subtle, not flashy, and completely in synch. But when Santana came on, things like *Evil Ways* and *Black Magic Woman*, Mad left him, pushed me out there and said they were as close to standard rock as we were going to get. You can picture how out of place I felt — and was.

It seemed absurd during a break to have Gomez discourage me from approaching the Latino women, but I realized he was serious and actually thought I might. "A cultural thing," he said in my ear. "Fastest way in the world to start trouble. Notice how these guys drool over Mad but don't go near her? That's because it would disrespect me, and thanks to the Centro, I have power. Or," he laughed, "they think I do. But I don't have power enough to protect you."

"Don't worry," I said. "Never crossed my mind."

"Good." He turned toward Mad and drummed a snatch of conga rhythm on the bar.

What he didn't grasp was that it took my entire wherewithal to receive Mad's attentions in the same friendly spirit in which I imagined they were offered. If I did anything stupid, which I wasn't going to, I would rather it be with her than any of the admittedly attractive Latinas. Gomez had long since pocketed his beret and draped his scarf over the barstool he'd been sitting on. While he and Mad danced another number, I idly noticed a cluster of moth holes in the scarf's center, as though a marksman had once used it for target practice.

After they returned Mad swallowed thirstily from her beer and poked Gomez in the ribs. "Let's take Paul out next week, too," she said. "Someplace with music he knows, where he'll have a chance with the women."

"Or," he joked, drumming again, "like the old army song, 'Get a woman, get a woman, get a woman if you can. If you can't get a woman, get a nice clean man.'"

CHAPTER 10

"My, my," Jordan said, "what a lovely little white. Not chardonnay...beyond that, I can't guess." He'd sniffed and sipped and was now holding the glass between his eye and the globe of the frosted sconce in my dining area.

It was the date for me to host, and there he was, in khakis and a lightweight plum sweater, acting like we'd been friends for years. I was still in my slacks and blazer from work, but I'd tossed my tie on the dresser before he arrived.

"Caymus sauvignon blanc," I told him. "Has a good reputation, but I chose it because I designed the label." When I brought the bottle from behind my back he took it from me for a closer look.

"Very nice, with the olive and gold against an ecru background."

"The ultra-thin black outlining was the key," I said. "I ended up doing everything for them...napkins, signage, letterhead, order forms. L-W got Stag's Leap and Kendall-Jackson, too, after they saw Caymus at a trade show."

"Bravo. Quite a coup, and I'm guessing good for repeat business." He walked the bottle to my butcher-block kitchen counter and set it there.

"Hope so. I haven't heard from any of them in more than a year. There's a cycle for that kind of work."

"Law clients are the same way. When they need you, fine. When they don't, they don't."

"What kind of practice do you have?"

"Civil, mainly. Very little criminal. Real estate, water rights, insurance."

"All here in town?"

"The Bay Region and beyond. Not that San Francisco real estate isn't booming, but our firm's feeling the pinch from Willie Brown."

"The politician guy?"

"That's the one. On top of his state duties, he practices law. I'll take a refill, then let's try your beautiful couch."

GOMEZ

"Sure. I've also got a bowl of those shrimp-puff crackers they sell in Chinatown." Carrying our drinks and snacks, we repositioned ourselves in the living room.

"You could say the Transamerica Pyramid is my answer to your winery labels," Jordan stated, pointing through the window. "New, distinctive, and highly visible. I had nothing to do with the architecture, of course, but the permitting and the historical preservation issues were my life's work at the time."

"I believe it."

"For sheer controversy, though, the Mt. Sutro telecom tower was in a class by itself. I'm sorry it's so ugly, but my client had every right to build it."

"To me, they've both always been here. I lived in Berkeley until last fall and didn't pay much attention to the city."

"Our so-called progressives accept progress only when dragged kicking and screaming. I had a hand in the condemnation of the International Hotel as well, an eyesore if ever there was one."

"I only remember the headlines, but I have friends who'd hate you for it." I was thinking of Mad and Gomez. Around the time she started working for the Mime Troupe, they had been part of the fight to preserve the old hotel. A tattered poster announcing a 1976 protest rally at the demolition site was still stuck to a boarded-up storefront we had passed when she and Gomez walked me to my car after leaving El Gallito. There had ultimately been a police raid, she said, to clear out the tenants, most of them aged and sick, who refused to vacate.

"Yet for some reason," Jordan frowned, "those friends you're talking about would probably never hate dear Assemblyman Brown. He's had as much to do with Manhattanizing…whoever coined that term should be shot…this town as I have, but he gets by with it, fancy cars, fancy wardrobe and all. The rest of us play by the rules while he and his Revenue and Tax Committee browbeat whoever disagrees with him…or with his crony, the mayor."

This sounded nothing like the Mayor Moscone that Gomez and Mad had spoken about, but I let Jordan's remark ride. "No love lost, I take it."

"None, although Brown may have gone too far this time. You've probably heard that he's representing Sam Conti, the porn-store king, along with gambling casinos back east. The voters will wake up sooner or later. I'm no Puritan, but it pays to be discreet. You can't go flaunting sex in people's faces the way Conti does...or those outrageous Mitchell Brothers...and not have backlash."

"Changing the subject," I said as neutrally as I could, "I've read *Ecotopia* and left it on my hall table for you." I had no intention of discussing the Mitchell Brothers with him, despite his enthusiasm for the Adult Film Festival.

"What did you think?"

"Not as pie-in-the sky as you led me to believe. I could live happily in Ecotopian San Francisco."

"Ah, youth," Jordan replied, initially with gentle sarcasm, but gaining sincerity as he continued. "If only Gwen...Kes, I mean...my daughter, would consider a fellow like you. God knows, you're better than any at Shaman Farm."

"Thanks, Jordan. That's very kind."

"I mean it. You have good taste, you're creative, open-minded, even healthy." He lifted from my end table the copy of *Runner's World* magazine that had come in yesterday's mail. "I've seen you more than once jogging along the Embarcadero or headed out in your sweats of an evening."

"Sometimes it's for racquetball. I like to stay active. I'm establishing new habits to go with my new address."

"Smart. Where do you play?"

"North End Rowing Club."

"Charming place. I didn't know they had a court. If you ever see Swede Johansson there, tell him Jordan Mackay says hello."

"I will," I nodded, though my participation in Gomez's illegitimate access meant that I never would.

"Incidentally," Jordan said, "have you thought more about having Eve fix you up? Quite easy to do, really."

"To tell the truth, I'm leaning in that direction." In fact, since meeting Mad the previous week I'd been virtually in rut, dreaming about her, and trying to decide if masturbation fantasies concerning women you knew were more degrading than ones concerning women you didn't.

"Excellent. Do you a world of good. What physical type interests you most?"

"You're saying I have unlimited choice?"

He laughed. "Not unlimited, but certainly not narrow."

"Strawberry blonde, then. On the petite side. Doesn't have to be the Hollywood bombshell with the 36-D chest."

"Sounds possible," Jordan nodded. "Any cultural interests or foreign languages you prefer?"

"I have enough trouble with women in English," I joked. "But someone who reads, enjoys movies, and maybe knows a little about architecture or design would be nice."

"I'll see what I can do."

"And there's some kind of agency involved?"

"Yes. Eve will vet the candidates to the extent she can, but official contact will be through the service. That can't be avoided, and will set you back $500."

"Oh." I'd been unprepared for the amount.

Noting my reaction, Jordan smiled knowingly. "Seems a lot, but believe me, well worth it."

"You said there was a means test. I assumed the women wanted guys with high-end lifestyles."

"No, no, I'm afraid the means test is in addition to the fee. The agency is one-time, assuming you like the girl they send. The rest you work out with her, but it's always gone smoothly in my case and becomes routine once settled."

I was nearly sure I understood what I'd just heard, but I had trouble believing it. "You mean you pay Eve?"

"Absolutely, dear boy. That's the glory of the whole thing. I as much as told you two weeks ago."

"Well, it got by me."

"Paul, Paul," Jordan shook his head. "I enjoy delightful company, guaranteed sex with a beautiful young woman, no strings attached, or invasion of my life, or annoying visits to her parents. And no need to endure pre-menstrual mood swings. For a package like that, a man *should* expect to pay. The benefits of marriage, which themselves come at considerable cost, pale by comparison."

"Do your friends know about this?"

"Some do, some don't, though most of the latter probably suspect. I also have a couple of widows my age I squire to the opera and to dinner parties where Eve …or Tara, in her day…would feel uncomfortable. Very liberating, actually. No need to pursue for sex women who don't light my fire, and the widows probably prefer not having to fend me off. An ideal situation, don't you think?"

"And you don't worry about harming your chances for that judgeship?"

"Not a bit. My politics are the harm. Keeping company with Eve, or with Tara's replacement, once I get her selected, is about as far removed from street prostitution as a debutante cotillion is from a singles bar. In fact, everything has been structured to stay within the law."

"I'll be damned. What else can I say?"

"You can give me the go-ahead." Jordan was used to being obeyed, and my reluctance had put some bite into his voice.

"I don't know…and it *is* pretty expensive."

"You don't have to embark to the extent I have. Make one up-front investment, meet someone you're reasonably compatible with, go out, have a good time, get laid in the safest, lowest-pressure way there is, and move on to other kinds of relationships. Revisit the agency girl only if you want. It's not a lifetime commitment. In fact, there's no commitment."

"But seriously, don't you find it kind of empty? A good-looking guy like you, with the kind of money you have, there've got to be Eves who'd cozy up for free."

"Yes, of course. And by the way, you haven't posed a question yet I'm unused to answering. But at what price do those *free* young girlfriends come? It's a case of marry them, change my will accordingly, and submit to their whims…or pray that my pre-nup passes muster when they sue for alimony. No, thanks. I'll take the installment plan, where what leaves my wallet counts as incentive pay."

"There's still the emptiness. What I feel when I come home at night and know this place is solo, not shared."

"That's more a state of mind than anything, which you get used to. But Eve and I have been seeing each other for three years now. We don't have sex every time we're together any more, even though I know it's available if I wish. She honors my feelings, I try to honor hers. And she's quite accomplished. An excellent singing voice, very well read in terms of poetry. She nursed me when I had the flu last year and wouldn't take a cent. I was tremendously sad when Tara left, though I knew sometime she likely would. You don't turn those feelings off. It's not anonymous humping with a succession of hookers. That I admit is gross."

"Everything you've said about my benefiting from a transitional mode makes sense, but I'll have to get comfortable with what's involved first."

"Your choice. It's a branch of the world's oldest profession. The opportunities won't go away, however long it takes to make up your mind. Hell, I'll split the agency fee as a gift. I hate to see anyone be a hermit. But," Jordan laughed, "I'm not offering you Eve."

I laughed, too. "Maybe I've been a little dense, but on that point there's no confusion. She must have other…ah…clients, though."

"Yes. But I don't need to know who they are."

"I'm curious about another thing. Unrelated to Eve."

"Which is?"

"You already know my wife ditched me for someone else. What happened with yours? If you don't mind talking about it, I mean."

"No, I don't mind. It was ten years ago, and rarely comes up anymore. Candace and I knew one another from college. She was a senior at Cal when I was at Boalt. All the social niceties were in play, our families approved, and it seemed like fate. For a long time it was. I worked, the children arrived, Candace got her dream house. Why if this were France, we'd still be together…officially, that is."

"What do you mean?"

"French wives…of a certain class, anyway…are much more tolerant of their husband's extracurricular activities. They aren't seen to lose face."

"Really?"

"It wouldn't even be out of the question for me to have a place here in town. Nothing as grand as Golden Gateway, but what they call a *pied-à-terre*. It was credit card receipts for hotel rooms that sunk me.

"I had a separate card with my office as the billing address, but some paperwork escaped into my trousers pocket. The dry cleaner returned it to Mrs. Mackay when she was out running errands one morning. She demanded that I confess, and I stupidly did…to more than she could prove. Next thing I was out on my ear. So much for the sexual revolution."

"You said you lost your kids to the divorce as well as the 60s, and a blowup like that must have made it worse."

"Granted, but the die was already cast by then. I'd be just as much a symbol of the establishment if their mother and I were still married, and they don't much care for her new husband on the same grounds."

"I didn't mean to pry. With so many couples splitting apart these days, it makes me feel better to compare notes."

"I understand. And I'm not trying to paint Candace as some dreadful harridan. The fact is, no one woman could ever be enough for me...or most men, if they're honest... and marriages that don't accept that are doomed. But I don't really think about Candace these days. It's the children I miss. Having an adult relationship with them, and a connection to the next generation."

"Odds are good they'll come around, especially as they sense their own mortality."

"Yes, I hope so. And better that I lost them to the 60s than the 70s."

"I don't follow."

"I doubt Kes or James are involved in hard drugs, for one thing, and they appear to be heterosexual, thank god." He contorted his body as he spoke. "Could you imagine your kids preening around the Castro with those fags and lezzies? Disgusting!"

"They're all somebody's kids...aren't they?" I said, haltingly. His remark was another angle on a thought I'd been struggling with lately: that everyone, everyone — including Long John Holmes and Marilyn Chambers and the most grotesque people that you saw on BART or on the street — had once been dandled hopefully on a parent's knee, and very likely there were baby pictures somewhere to prove it.

"At least not mine," Jordan emphasized, with an unpleasant laugh.

My floor lamp flickered slightly in response to a power surge. Identical to one I'd let Jenny abscond with last year, its profile resembled an engine valve, but seven feet tall and flared at both ends, the steel brushed to a matte sheen, with decorative bands of brass. To my knowledge, she had never told her family in England about Barbara, nor had I told mine. I wondered if we ever would. Did everybody lead double lives — an official version, fitted to parental and societal expectations, and a real version not fully acknowledged even to ourselves? Or was it more complicated yet?

Which somehow led me to settle Jordan's earlier subject. "For now, anyway," I said firmly, "I'm taking a bye on Eve and her friends. But don't get me wrong. No aspersions intended, and I appreciate the offer." I swung my eyes to meet his.

"To each his own," he replied, with a look that said I was being a fool. "By the way, I like what you've done with this place. Italian modern, you call it? Does that include the low-pile rugs in dark gray?"

"Yes. They're knock-offs, but the style's from Milan."

"Your Miró and Klee prints go wonderfully. Miró's a favorite of mine."

"I noticed yours. It's a good one."

"Absolutely. Eve recognized it, too, when she and I were getting acquainted. From a numbered edition. Art wasn't Tara's cup of tea, and I'm not making that a criterion for her replacement. But," he turned to point, "who's this near the dining area? Very striking, with the reds and yellows and the slouching figures that blend into the streetscape."

"Freidrich Hundertwasser," I answered. "A post-war Austrian who shows at a gallery off Union Square. My major splurge when I moved in."

"I'll keep an eye out for him." Jordan stood and walked for a close-up view. The brightness of the ceiling-mounted track lights showed that his hair was thinning a bit and his facial skin was not as taut as it seemed from the front.

He slowly stepped back and pivoted to face me. "Another taste of wine, if I may, then I have to go. Hate to say it," he winked, "but I have a date…with someone new."

I picked up Jordan's glass and reached for the bottle. "Is Eve a real name? Or do you know?"

"The truth is, I don't know. And probably not, but real enough that she has ID for it. We've traveled together to Tahiti."

After he left I walked to North Beach for a garlicky dinner at the US Cafe followed by an internal tug-of-war over taking the feelings stirred by our conversation to the Playpen, a new live-sex show at Alex de Renzy's place downtown. There were plenty of cabs and I could be there in five minutes. I was about to hail one when I saw a woman who'd rung my doorbell looking for Jordan last month walking arm-in-arm with a bulky, fiftyish guy while the two of them gawked at a Broadway marquee touting nude encounter sessions. She gave a little smile to signal that she recognized me from somewhere, too, but her overall demeanor said I was to ignore that fact.

Though wordless, our exchange so reeked of sex-for-hire that I lost the urge and detoured to City Lights bookstore, where I bought volumes one and two of *The Diary of Anaïs Nin*. My browsing also confirmed that six volumes of the diary were now in print, that she had been the *LA Times* Woman of the Year for 1976, and that she was hugely controversial as a feminist figure. Her latest title, called *The Delta of Venus*, was such a hit that a notice had been taped to the shelf saying it was out of stock.

Until Mad's mention of Nin at Gomez's, I couldn't recall having heard her name since my senior year at Kansas, when I took the Comp Lit class that exposed me to Henry Miller. I almost bought his book *Black Spring*, too, while I was at City Lights, but decided instead to search the boxes in my hall closet to locate *Tropic of Capricorn*. My roommate had absconded with *Tropic of Cancer* as soon as the semester was over, but I was pretty sure I'd kept *Capricorn*, and that it would be among the paperbacks I'd salvaged from the shelves when leaving Arch Street. Mainly, though, both of Miller's *Tropics* had seemed weirdly smutty to me, and I'd never understood why they were regarded as hallmarks of modern literature.

The *Diary* was hard to get into on the ensuing nights, but with the sense of Mad looking over my shoulder, I persevered. Where Gomez dared not go, I would. But to cover all bases, I finished unpacking and found *Capricorn*, beat-up and faded, with the flyleaf reminding me that I'd once lived at 212 Wentworth Hall. And Miller was every bit as blunt as Nin was elliptical. They must have been an incredible pair, not to mention her long-suffering first husband, Hugo. My volume of Borges's stories also surfaced, which I put on the night table with my other reading.

Meanwhile, Gomez called to set our next racquetball date and say that he and Mad wanted me to go dancing Friday night at a bar near the airport. He asked if I'd drive, and being eager to show off the Audi, I agreed. Maybe I'd be able to unloose some of my newfound literary knowledge as well.

GOMEZ

CHAPTER 11

"You absolutely promise it's not disco?" I asked, changing lanes to pass a truck near Silver Avenue, southbound on the Bayshore Freeway.

"At Artichoke Joe's?" Mad pitched her voice to sound extra-incredulous. "You've got to be kidding." Gomez's forearm was draped against the leather of her seat, and she gave it a playful backhand swat to underscore her point.

"Don't worry, man," he assured me. "Not that kind of place. The bands do covers of 60s and 70s rock. You'll be fine."

It was dark, beginning to clear at 9 p.m. after a day of rain, and we were in the Audi, Mad occupying the other bucket seat and Gomez slouched forward from behind. We'd eaten folded-over meat pies called empanadas at Las Pampas, the Argentine restaurant Gomez frequented, drunk raw-tasting red wine, and were now heading for what he said would be "the *women and song* phase" of our evening. As they guided me to the on-ramp, he and Mad had pointed out the Centro and the nearby Mime Troupe headquarters. Both were vacant at that hour, and looked much more like nondescript warehouses than places my friends would work.

Earlier, when we'd finished dinner, I thought Gomez might try to supplant me as driver and to impress Mad, treat the car as his, perhaps by saying he knew the way and I didn't. I planned to refuse, and had readied a list of counter-arguments, but the issue never came up. He climbed into the back and insisted that she sit with me.

Seemingly daring the weather, he was in his standard, French-intellectual garb, while Mad, under her raincoat, wore a fetching, above-the-knee, suede miniskirt topped by a scoop-necked, lavender T. Following Gomez's advice from earlier in the day, I'd gone with jeans, a striped pullover and a raincoat of my own. We were all in high spirits, but at Candlestick Park had fallen silent until Mad's voice overrode the drone of the tires and the low whoosh of the defroster fan.

GOMEZ

"See Brisbane across the marsh? Has a great country-western bar for dancing hee-haw. We thought about taking you tonight, but decided it's not your scene." She was gesturing southwest, out the passenger side of the windshield.

Inky-black against the nighttime clouds, San Bruno Mountain rose to our right like the hump of a giant, kneeling dromedary. At its base, I saw the scatter of lights Mad was talking about. The Audi had meanwhile become one more blip in a pulsing stream of headlamps on a six-lane causeway along the bay's edge. I couldn't recall ever hearing of Brisbane — except in Australia — and could readily accept that it wasn't my scene.

"When you can, get in the slow lane," Gomez directed. Quieter, and closer to my ear, he added, "Mad and I plan to do a little coke before we go in. There's enough for you, too."

"Better not," I answered, "I'm driving." I felt a jab of alarm, but did everything I could to conceal it.

"*Some*body's misinformed," Mad announced. "Driving's no problem. You're hyper-alert. It'd be long worn off by the time we leave, anyway."

"I don't know the stuff well enough to trust it," I replied.

"Oooh," she mocked, again swatting Gomez's arm. "Wouldn't want to get Paul-baby out of his depth, would we?"

He lightly touched her shoulder with his fingertips. "All limits respected," he told me. "Do what you're comfortable with." The tires of the vehicles ahead threw up dirty rainwater from the pavement, and I briefly turned on the wipers to combat it.

"Sure," Mad agreed, dropping her sarcasm. "If you're not tooting, we'll stay in the car while you get a table. The bar and dance floor are way in back."

"In back of what?" I asked, mainly as a way to change the subject. "Artichoke makes it sound like a produce stand."

"Nooo," Mad said, verbally tweaking me again. "A casino."

"Since when are we in Vegas?" Bypassing the drug use question by going in ahead of them seemed my best option, but it also meant parting with the keys while they committed an illegal act in my car. Or was the whole place illegal? What if we got busted?

"Card room's the California term," Gomez shrugged. "There's no slots, roulette or dice, but certain kinds of low-stakes poker can be OK, city-by-city."

GOMEZ

"If they had craps tables, Gomez might forget to dance," Mad said, tweaking him for a change.

"Oh, bullshit. Craps is my game, but the concept is restraint. Didn't you get that from my Tahoe story?"

"Your Tahoe story is so weird, who knows what I get?" she replied.

"What Tahoe story?" I asked.

Before Gomez could answer, Mad did. "He says he goes for a week every spring, camps alone in the woods, meditates, lives on brown rice, and shoots craps at night."

"Weird. I'm with Mad on this one."

"Won't be able to this year because of my job," Gomez said, "but I did it a bunch while I was in Berkeley. Very cleansing, physically and mentally. A perfect preparation for summer excess."

"The Zen of dice," I responded. "Is that what you're saying?"

"Yes," Mad answered for him again. She pointed at her temple with a rotating index finger as freeway traffic rumbled by.

"Exactly," Gomez went on, ignoring her. "Oh, take this exit and hang a right. Joe's is on a side street just before El Camino. Anyway, I camp on the Nevada shore, in a spot nobody goes. One big meal a day...brown rice and green tea. Otherwise, I fast. No booze, nothing. I don't just meditate, I read, too. Whatever I want. Then, later, off to the craps tables, with a strict limit on how much I win or lose per night. The contrast," he laughed, "between my campsite and the rush of the casinos is hallucinatory, but I can focus on the dice like you wouldn't believe."

"Does it have to be craps?" I asked him.

"There's a lot of skill to poker," he replied. "Bluffing, memorizing cards, odds constantly changing. Craps is in the open. Just you and the little white cubes."

"I asked the same thing," Mad offered. "He says skill is another futile attempt at control. There's supposed to be something holy about submitting yourself to chance."

"What do you think you do when you get out of bed every morning?" Gomez argued. "My Tahoe trips are only a heightened form of it. The balance of control and chance. For one week, I try to give each its separate sphere. Not that you *can*, of course."

"I have control of my life," she said. "I make a point of it."

108

GOMEZ

"The illusion of control," he shot back. "We thrive on that here in earthquake country. But chance always wins."

"Kind of bleak, wouldn't you say?" I asked him.

"Not at all," Gomez answered. "Simply realistic. You want to be alive, those are the terms. I've also honored chance by flipping a coin to make big decisions."

"God, what next?" Mad groaned. "Name one big decision you made that way."

"Returning to Berkeley after Alabama," he replied matter-of-factly. "And another," he laughed, "that you're not going to like: whether we'd keep going out after I learned you were married."

I thought Mad might get huffy over the second example, but she laughed, too. "At least it was a *big* decision," she joked. "Was I heads or tails?"

"Tails," Gomez said, diving his hand onto the seat to pinch at her fanny, for which he was rewarded with Mad's loud, exasperated squeals.

÷ ÷ ÷

Artichoke Joe's turned out to have a large, wrap-around parking lot, with room for the Audi in a dark corner along the fence. By the time I opened my door and got out, Gomez had extracted a bill from his wallet and was rolling it into a tight, tube-like cylinder. Mad, on cue, began fishing in her purse.

"We'll be right in," Gomez said. "Close that, will you, to kill the dome light?"

"Yeah, sorry," I said. "The keys are in the ignition. Be sure to lock up."

"Word of honor," he replied.

"See you inside." I closed the door with a muffled thud and Mad threw me a kiss through the window.

She seemed wilder tonight, different from when I first met her, as though she might have done some coke or other drug in the restroom at dinner. I could only guess. Or maybe she was just in a good mood. I threaded my way among the parked cars, not looking back despite my anxiety about security guards poised to close in.

The building was a big, ugly, flat-roofed affair of tilt-up concrete, occupying half a city block, one story high and windowless except at the front, which was set close to the street under a faux-Western, bat-and-board porch. There was minimal exterior lighting, primarily a neon sign on a free-standing pole where the driveway intersected the sidewalk. The name of the place flashed on and off in red against a glowing green artichoke the size of a double-bed mattress. The surrounding area consisted of light industrial and commercial establishments, but Joe's, with a copse of bedraggled oleander at the far end of the porch, was the only one open for business.

In fact, it was bustling. And while I've never gambled and didn't know what real casinos were like, add a row of slot machines and what I now saw would probably be a close match for the non-deluxe end of the Nevada spectrum. Middle-class couples, white and fitting essentially the profile of my mom and dad, occupied most of the tables, although smatterings of Asians and younger whites, generally male, were also a factor. The carpeting and the green felt tabletops showed wear from years of use.

Double-knit leisure suits in varying shades of brown did for the men, while the women went with lacquered hair, blouses and contrasting vests. Card dealers and cocktail waitresses, wearing white shirts and black slacks or skirts, stood or strode about in a head-high haze of cigarette smoke amid the sound of hushed conversation punctuated by the clink of glassware and ice. Adjoining the main room were large alcoves of similar ilk, and behind was a restaurant with leatherette booths, a Formica counter, and a notice stating that breakfast was served at all hours.

I walked directly toward the rear on a tile strip separated from the gaming area by a spoked wooden balustrade that became a glass wall when I reached the mostly-empty restaurant. A wood-paneled bar, large, high-ceilinged, and crowded with both customers and every kind of beer sign, lay just beyond. Through the gap in a folded-open accordion wall I saw a bandstand and dance floor, also high-ceilinged, lit from above by banks of green and red theater gels.

The band must have been on break, but milling between the bar and the stage were fifty or so males and females who, in contrast to the gamblers out front, looked to be my age or younger. Mad had clearly dressed to fit in, since short skirts and Ts were ubiquitous on the females, and I, too, was somewhat in vogue in my pullover. No one there was dressed like Gomez, but one of the key things that made him Gomez was that he liked to have impact.

I found a table near one end of the folding wall and took possession. It was littered with empty bottles and glasses, and had apparently been serving as an unofficial way-station for the help. I put my raincoat over the back of a chair and sat in another. While a busboy did some noisy cleanup, I ordered beer from a cute waitress, trying to push aside visions of a police cruiser pulling in behind my car. Despite my distaste for the stuff, I chose Anchor Steam because the logo I designed for them, high, narrow indigo script against a butterscotch background, had caught my eye in the bar and I bragged about it to the waitress. "Oh, cool," she said, not very convincingly.

Nervously drinking, I continued to look around. I hadn't cared for much of anything at Joe's so far, but Mad and Gomez's reasons for bringing me made sense. If I were a dancer, there were definitely women I'd want to dance with, and there wasn't an overload of guys. Maybe, once the music started, I'd get into it. A metallic jingling in my ear was quickly followed by the clack of my keys hitting the tabletop.

"As promised," Gomez said, stepping away to hold a chair for Mad and help her out of her coat.

"Great table," she added. "We sent the right man for the job."

I don't know what I expected, but they didn't really look or seem different. The pupils of Gomez's eyes had perhaps become larger, and maybe he was blinking less, or at least staring more openly at everything, and his typical expression of amused anticipation may have been heightened. As for any loosening of inhibitions, there was so little hesitation between thought and word—or deed—in Gomez's normal state, how would I tell? Mad was mildly flushed, which on her looked good, and consciously or not, she'd adopted a half-smile almost identical to his.

"Where's the band?" she demanded, seating herself between him and me. For this outing there were no scarves or arty touches to her hair. To further ensure she would blend in, Mad had adopted a loose ponytail, which alternately rendered as medium blonde or pale red under the gel lights, and she'd cut back on her usual eye makeup. "Taking a break?"

"Haven't seen them," I replied.

GOMEZ

"Did you catch their name?" She began to bounce in her chair.

"The Plumbers," Gomez interrupted. "It's on that poster and on the bass drum."

Our cute waitress appeared and Gomez ordered a round of drinks, a double tequila with a twist for himself, and a *grande* margarita for Mad. As the waitress gathered my empty bottle, I pointed at it to convey that I'd have another, wanting a chance to show Mad something I'd designed.

Gomez nixed that by lightly placing his hand around the waitress's wrist. "No, no," he said. "He'll have a margarita, too."

"I will?"

"Right," Gomez confirmed. The waitress nodded, then flicked her eyebrows at me and tried to disengage her wrist, but Gomez didn't let go.

This jarred her for a second, and I saw her face cloud. "Hey!" she said.

In what seemed like one motion, Gomez lowered his head to brush a kiss on the back of her hand, conspicuously released her from his grip, and conjured a smile that would have charmed the Gestapo.

It also charmed her. "What a nut!" she laughed, heading off to the bar.

When I looked at Mad she was standing behind her chair, where she remained even after our drinks arrived, taking a swig of her margarita, and barely resting the heavy, oversized glass on the table before taking another. As the band, five long-haired guys in leather hats and Harley-Davidson tanktops, reassembled on the platform, she watched them intently.

"Mad wants to audition for groupie," Gomez joked.

"What I want is to shake my money maker," she replied, snapping her fingers in partial demonstration. "God, they're slow!"

At that the music started, and she grabbed Gomez out of his seat and onto the floor, joining a rush of other couples who had the same idea. "Paul," she called back over the growing din, "if you don't find somebody to dance the next one, I'll find her myself and introduce you." With a gotcha smiles and waves, she and Gomez merged into the melange of dancers whooping to the chorus of *Built This City on Rock and Roll*.

GOMEZ

I didn't attempt to keep them in view. I drained my beer and polished off two-thirds of a big margarita while The Plumbers played out their opening number and got into a cover of some Eagles country rock. That was more my speed, and I wasn't about to have Mad drag women over to meet me, so I found Peg—or Pat, I didn't quite get her name—standing with a group of friends in the bar, and out on the floor we went. I know Mad and Gomez saw me, but they kept their distance, which is what I hoped they'd do.

Peg/Pat, an insurance agent's secretary, I learned between songs, drifted back to her friends when a boogie-beat Doobie Brothers number came on. I danced that one with Michelle, a chubby brunette whose date had gone to get them drinks. It was fun, in a way, and I was glad I was there, but it didn't remake my life.

Retreating to our empty table for the band's next effort, I found an untouched margarita next to my melted, largely empty one. I tried just to listen and not feel pressured to do more. When our waitress passed, I pointed to my new margarita and displayed some *hey-what's-this?* body language. "Gomez," she leaned over to say in my ear, "your crazy friend."

Then came something called *My Old School*, which had heavy cowbell percussion and motivated my crazy friend to lead a weaving conga line across and around the floor. Mad wasn't with him as far as I could tell, my first margarita was history, and multiple sips of the second had gone down my throat. Covered with sweat and smiling like he'd just won the daily double, Gomez left the dance floor to join me as the music segued to a syrupy ballad.

"Thanks for the fresh drink," I told him.

"*De nada*," he answered, flopping into his chair. "Whew! That'll keep me in shape for racquetball."

"Where's Mad?"

"Went to the head. She and her purse, that is."

"Oh," I nodded knowingly. "When's your turn?"

"Had all I want." He mopped his forehead on the sleeve of his all-purpose black sweater, which I now realized was luxurious, perhaps of died vicuna. Maybe Mad had bought it for him; it didn't come from any thrift store. "Margarita number two," he went on, "was to catch you up with us...so to speak."

"Starting to feel like it has."

"Good. You realize I don't do this all the time?" He made sure he held my eyes.

"Kind of figured, but I haven't given much thought."

"Like anything pleasurable…you overdo, it's less special. You can't be high every day and still know what high is."

"Makes sense."

"Something else. You won't find Gomez skin-popping or pill-popping. If he can't get it through his lungs, he doesn't need it in his body."

"You're excepting beverage alcohol, of course."

"Of course. But Gomez is careful with that, too."

"I hope you're not saying Gomez would sniff glue."

That drew the biggest laugh I ever got from him. "No…no…" He was forced to stop by uncontrolled bouts of cackling, in which I took full part. Eventually, just as Mad returned, he managed to continue, "Gomez…Gomez ingests only…only substances…meant for human consumption. He is, after all, human." It wasn't explainable as funny, but nonetheless brought additional spasms from each of us.

"What's with you guys?" she inquired. I couldn't tell if she'd had another toot or not. She probably had, but for the moment she seemed more placid than before.

"Gomez says he's human," I answered, still laughing.

"That's news," Mad stated, glancing repeatedly from one of us to the other, the quasi-smile on her face waning and waxing in a rhythm unrelated to her eye movement. "Paul's been hustling chicks," she added, as though I weren't there. "Did you see him?"

Gomez's laughter had given way to a reprise of his own attenuated smile, but his response to her question was to raise his arms grandly over his head and direct a beatific gaze at the ceiling.

After announcing that another break was due, the band launched into *Proud Mary* as their closing number. Mad got Gomez up, and I persuaded Tracy from Pat/Peg's group to dance with me. She was slim, with short, light-brown hair. I'd seen her on the floor a couple of times with different guys, and there was something about her I liked. Maybe it's that she wasn't overly smooth, nor particularly attractive, yet she was clearly having a good time and projected that in my company as well.

GOMEZ

During the break Gomez and Mad went back to our table while I lingered a few minutes in the bar with Tracy before finding the restroom and wandering out to watch the gamblers. I was nearly sure she would give me her phone number if I asked, and was deciding whether to. I already knew she'd gone to Cal Poly and worked for an architect in San Mateo, but there were minuses to go with the pluses.

For one, she was taller than I am, and on close inspection, you could also tell she'd had a harelip—now perfectly repaired, but still. If I got her number, I'd have to invite her to meet Gomez and Mad, and given their effortless animality, we'd both feel inadequate. On the best day of her life, Tracy was no Mad.

I decided not to ask. A couple of bass-drum thumps told me the band had returned, so I headed that direction, detouring slightly to avoid Tracy's view. I sat with my friends and took the last swallow of my margarita, but before I said anything The Plumbers, acknowledging a shouted request, launched into a custom version of *Mustang Sally*. This time Gomez was the instigator and quickly whisked Mad away, motioning me to come along. I shook my head. If his goal was a dancing threesome, I was ready to go home.

That thought was ended by Tracy, bending down to request a dance. While my mind reviewed polite ways to say "No," my body rose, took her hand and propelled us onto the floor. I felt myself smile as we gyrated, more or less in time with the music, but not quite in time with each other. Perhaps a minute had gone by when Gomez and Mad bopped toward us, followed by Mad's tapping Tracy's shoulder and saying, in an artificially formal way, "May I cut in?"

Without waiting to be introduced, or to hear Tracy's reply, Mad snaked between us, dancing so close that I had to backstep and sidestep into the jumping, twisting crowd near the bandstand. Over Mad's shoulder I saw Gomez take up with Tracy, laughing and talking while he improvised a routine which involved his hands grasping her outstretched arms just below the elbows. He, as usual, looked graceful, and suddenly, so did she.

"Finally," Mad said, pirouetting and deliberately bumping me with her hip, "I get a turn with Paul. It took Gomez to rescue you from *that other woman*."

GOMEZ

"What am I rescued *for*?" She had already made me feel like a better dancer, though I was still me and the song was still *Mustang Sally*.

"Delights yet uncharted," she answered, with another pirouette and bump. Her short skirt slid up on her thighs in correspondence to the beat, and I realized that, if she'd had a bra on earlier in the evening, which I thought she had, she didn't now.

Mad stepped away a bit and bounced in place, clapping her hands and singing the chorus, joined by nearly every voice in the room. "All you want to do is ride around, Sally…Ride, Sally, ride!" And on the repeat, my voice was in there, too—for the first time in my life.

After the final verse and a triple chorus, the song was over. Mad had carried on like she was possessed, and I hoped that what I looked or sounded like had escaped notice. A slower, six-note bass progression began, to scattered cheers from the crowd, and I turned to see if I could locate Gomez and Tracy. He was walking back to our table and I saw her disappear into the bar. I took a step to follow, but Mad grabbed my arm. "Oh, no…this is my all-time fave. I'm not dancing alone."

How could I argue? Her so-called fave was a blues/funk number with sultry lyrics and a chorus that went, "You can keep your hat on. Yes, you can ke-ep your hat on." The lead singer played randy accents on tenor sax to complete the mood. Arms at her sides, Mad danced about two inches from me, eyes closed, mouthing but not singing the words, all of which she seemed to know. When the chorus came, she put her hands on top of her head, fingers intertwined, to form a hat.

Then, during an up-tempo crescendo of sax and guitar, Mad's eyes opened tauntingly and she pulled the waist of her lavender T-shirt up to her cheekbones. She followed with a grinding, 360-degree turn to proffer her naked breasts at whoever was watching. From the ripple of hoots, dozens of guys were, and more than a few women. Unable to sort out surprise, embarrassment and desire, I simply stared. Pert orbs of creamy skin, about the size of jelly doughnuts, sleek and well-defined, with diminutive, rosy-pink aureoles and up-tilting nipples, all bouncing ever so slightly to the thumping bass. She lowered the shirt to her navel, provoking minor groans of disappointment, waited, and without turning this time, hiked it up again for my sole benefit.

After five unforgettable seconds, Mad closed her eyes, down came the shirt, and we danced out the rest of the song as though nothing had happened. Gomez, sitting in front of a fresh tequila shooter, now wore a full smile. I started to lead her off the floor, but a young, no-neck, jock-looking guy intervened, asking if "…the lady with the perfect pair wouldn't dance even one more?"

"Hell, yes," Mad answered. "But the show's over for now."

"You're on," the guy said. "I have my memories."

The band laid out heavy guitar riffs that I identified, on my way to join Gomez, as originating from the Rolling Stones. Mad must have been in her element, shaking and strutting with him to *Honky-Tonk Woman*, but I made a point not to look.

"I take it Mad flashed you," Gomez laughed, when I got close.

"Not just me," I said, blushing at the thought of it and that he'd so quickly guessed. Still facing away from the dance floor, I dropped into my chair.

He took a satisfied nip at his tequila. "She's threatened that before. I talked her out of it once in Brisbane. Afraid she'd start a fight. Here, not so bad. Or maybe," he took another nip, "she just had the right partner."

Behind him, I had a clear view into Joe's wood-paneled barroom, and for better or worse, Tracy was nowhere to be seen.

GOMEZ

CHAPTER 12

Mad danced a second number with the no-neck jock, and might have made it three if Gomez hadn't waded out and told her we should go. She'd obviously had a fine time, and had loved the band, the atmosphere, and especially, though she avoided any mention of it, the attention she'd gotten by vamping me along with the whole place. I'd been painfully embarrassed at first, then ticked off, but Gomez was unperturbed and her continued enthusiasm seemed so guileless that my anger, with nothing to attach to, largely dissipated on our way out.

At the car, when he again crawled into the back seat and directed Mad to the front, she forced her way in with him, turning me into their chauffeur. "Paul's going to take us wherever we say," she announced winningly. "Aren't you Paulie-waulie?"

"Not necessarily," I answered. The big neon artichoke behind us blinked on and off in the side mirror as we rolled out of Joe's drive and pulled away.

"How about into the hills to catch 280?" Gomez put in. "Darker and less traffic. Open the sunroof. We'll have the moon and stars."

"280, yes," I told him. "Sunroof, no. Way too cold."

"Cold is right," Mad agreed. "Turn up the heater, would you?"

"Sure." I cut left for a while on El Camino, picked a likely cross street, and gunned the car uphill.

"God, what fun!" Mad said, humming and mouthing the ba-ba-ba-bu-ba…ba, ba-ba-ba-bu-ba…ba bass line from *Keep Your Hat On*. "That last set was all whorehouse music."

"As if you'd know," Gomez laughed.

"More than you think," she retorted.

"Is this what Henry and Anaïs would do?" I put in. "Dress the part, go slumming, get high, dance, carry on, be driven home to Boulevard Clichy or Louveciennes in a taxi? Or would her husband Hugo be at the wheel?"

"Maybe," Gomez replied. "Who cares?"

GOMEZ

"You and Mad," I challenged. If they were curious about my sudden command of those facts and names, so much the better.

"Take that up with her," he answered dismissively. "I'm nobody but Gomez."

"Why should I care either?" Mad insisted. "The 30s or the 70s…fun is fun. But Paul knows more about Anaïs than he let on at dinner the other night."

"Like I said, I studied Miller in college…and," I continued with a lie, "some of the context came back after hearing you talk." Having just been the foil in Mad's titty show, I was damned if I'd let her know she was dictating my reading habits. I was also glad I hadn't pointed out the Anchor Steam label. The mood she'd been in at Joe's, she'd only have belittled it.

We reached Skyline Drive and I could see the 280 Freeway below, along the near shoulder of a rift valley, but with no way to get there. We'd crested the first line of hills, and were on a ridge where fringes of redwood and madrone formed higher tiers among the oaks. As Gomez had promised, it was gloriously dark, with the clouds mostly dispersed and far more stars than we'd have seen in the flats. His wished-for moon, however, wasn't in evidence. Since we weren't in a hurry, I headed away from SF to enjoy the night sky while I searched for an interchange.

"You guys OK back there?" I asked. "I'd like to turn the heater down."

"Go ahead," Mad answered. "I'm completely cozy."

"Want the radio?"

"Thank you, driver, but no," Gomez joked. "Whorehouse music is a tough act to follow."

I heard what must have been Mad's raincoat sliding off her shoulders and wished I could get out of mine. I had already loosened it as best I could beneath my seatbelt. After a series of sharp downhill curves, lighted green signs directed me to the freeway, and we were soon northbound in very thin traffic.

"Geez, Mad," Gomez said in a surprised whisper, "illegal use of hands."

"What Anaïs really might do," she whispered back.

"In a parked car, maybe." Gomez's voice was so low I could barely hear, "Not with… with…somebody driving."

"Pretend he's a cabby." She swallowed the words into a breathy chuckle.

There was a rustling of cloth, a sigh, the sound of what must have been kisses, and audible breathing. "Mad…lay off," Gomez protested quietly, "use your head."

"I plan to," she purred. There was more rustling of cloth, then the slow ratcheting of a zipper.

My first impulse, telling them to stop, would not only have acknowledged what I much preferred to deny was happening, it would have branded me a prude. Yet with that action foreclosed, images from a dozen porn movies—the tumescent member, the oval lips, the hooded eyes turned to the camera, the dribble of juices down the chin—swept across my vision as though projected on a gauze screen floating between me and the highway's glimmering lane markers and grainy concrete.

Additional sounds, low sighs and breathing that I wouldn't ordinarily notice, continued to emanate from the back, as though amplified by a static charge. Still, nothing I heard was gross, like the slurping that porn directors position their mikes to pick up. Or maybe film slurping is dubbed in or feigned by the actresses. Regardless, the real-life sounds were achingly sexual. A strong involuntary tingling seized my groin and my underwear felt like it had shrunk. And since I needed to check the mirror from time to time to monitor traffic, not sneaking a look proved impossible.

Gomez, whose face was out of view behind my shoulder, had slumped back on the seat, and Mad knelt on the passenger-side floor, mainly identifiable by her strawberry blonde ponytail's swinging rhythmically above his lap. It was like the simulated sex you see in soft-core flicks, and I thought for a moment it was a joke. I'd been shockable on the dance floor, why not here? But in that case, they'd have been waiting for me to look so they could laugh, while instead, there wasn't much doubt I was being ignored.

All the anger I'd felt earlier returned, and now extended to both of them. What if the whole performance, the titty-show and the back seat carnality, had been planned—just to get under my skin, to flaunt what they were and I wasn't? I heard a muffled groan, some shifting of upholstery and another sequence of rustling cloth, but hell would freeze before I looked again. Spotting a big, shiny, cab-over eighteen-wheeler ahead, I decided that circumstance had of fered me a weapon, because we had entered the southern outskirts of SF and there was a lot more ambient light.

I sped up, overtook the truck and got the Audi in the lane to his left, with my rear window about even with his front hub. If the driver wanted to see in, there was his chance. He slowed a bit to deal with a merge, I slowed, too. He accelerated, so did I. And I really don't know what I wanted—Mad and Gomez to be dissuaded, to sit up and calmly ask me to turn on KJAZ, or to have them bitch that I'd spoiled their fun, or for the trucker to give us a serenade of growling toots on his diesel horn. Nor did it matter, because none of those things happened.

Without reacting one way or the other, the truck peeled off at Geneva Avenue and I abandoned my ploy, turning to watch him go while a corner of my eye swept between the Audi's front headrests. Mad's face, jaw lowered and eyes hooded as I had imagined them, was centered there, because she was straddling Gomez's lap with her back toward him. While her T-shirt remained in place, her skirt was wadded at her waist, her panties suspended at her calves, and her haunches pressed to his bare thighs.

Though she saw me, her eyes didn't open further. She merely adjusted her body and placed a hand on my upper arm. "Really, Paul," she said, "If you're going to watch, could you do it in the mirror so you can pay attention to the road?"

÷ ÷ ÷

The rubbery slap of my soles on the pavement became more muted as I got into a good rhythm. It was early Sunday morning, clear and breezy along the Embarcadero, where I had just cleared the end of Folsom Street and the shadow of the damnable, elevated, double-deck freeway that dominated the Ferry Building and the waterfront. Docks and slips, empty of vessels since the shipping industry moved to Oakland, lay ahead and behind, with wheeling flights of gulls and the full expanse of the bay as backdrop.

I was breaking in a new pair of Adidas Runners. They're incredibly stiff, but the best you can buy. To the south, the cranes and silos of China Basin and Mission Rock gave me something of a destination. My quarter-way marker, Red's Java House, would show in a couple of blocks. I felt the beginnings of a good sweat, and could at least count on a sense of well-being during the time I was out, and for a while afterward.

I'd run yesterday, too, a shorter more punishing course on Russian Hill, unsuccessfully trying to shake the malaise left by Mad and Gomez's exhibition the night before. They were sheepish when I dropped them at Valencia Street, but made no apologies, and I'd been cool and peremptory in saying good-bye. A little hung over from the margaritas, and spurred by everything I'd seen and heard, I had a night of shallow sleep and wild, horny dreams. These only compounded my humiliation, so that when I got up I was ready to call Jordan and put Eve to work on my behalf.

But first I ran, then hit the office to catch up on stuff I hadn't gotten to because of heavy client meetings the previous week. Around eleven-thirty, the phone rang and it was Gomez, as usual without a hello or other preliminary.

"Paul, I'm really, really sorry. So is Mad. We were way out of line. I walked over to the Centro to call. Tried your apartment already."

"I wish I didn't know what you're talking about."

"It wasn't aimed at you, man. Things got out of control."

"Sperm of the moment, shall we say?"

"Bad pun, but I wasn't the instigator. You know Mad took extra toots. Her husband gets home tonight for three weeks. It was a last fling kind of situation."

"You didn't have to include me."

"We wanted to. I even told her to shepherd you a bit, be sure you met people and danced…which she was into."

"Including a titty show?"

"No, no, that was freelancing. I knew she would sometime, but I figured it would be with me. Look, man, I owe you, and I'm sorry."

"What you owe me for, and Mad, too, is scaring off the only available woman I've met this year that I wanted to go out with."

"What? How do you mean?"

"Tracy, the girl you cut in on. She disappeared after that."

"The gangly one?"

"Yes. I've got to start somewhere."

"Hell, you can do better than her."

"Maybe I don't want to."

"Well, you should. I talked to her a little when Mad led you away. Not much there."

"What did you talk about?"

"Don't really remember. But she asked if Mad was with you or with me."

"What did you say?"

He laughed. "Told her I didn't know for sure, that we were working it out."

"Oh, shit."

"Look, I had no idea. I was just blowing smoke. You could go back to Joe's next week and probably find her."

"I'd have a better bet going to play poker."

"Suit yourself," he said. "Am I at least on probation? I'll make it up to you, man. Let's shoot pool at the Silver Dollar. I'm terrible. From what you've told me, you'll clean my clock."

"Yeah, I suppose." With Gomez, my saying *no* never seemed to be an option. "But you'd better not back me down or embarrass me with a woman again."

"Take that to the bank. I'll call soon about pool or racquetball."

Then, of course, he hung up, and the last of my intent to run the other way from both Mad and Gomez was drowned in the dial tone. No, my only running was for exercise, loops or out-and-backs, like today's, keeping myself in shape for whatever came next, but not leading in any new direction. Drenched with perspiration, I let the *slap, slap, slap* of my shoes return me to where I was—the Embarcadero and a beautiful morning. I hadn't phoned Jordan yet, and now I thought I wouldn't.

Other runners, guys or happy-looking couples in nylon shorts, went by outbound on the route I was completing, and we exchanged cramped little waves or nods, wasting as little energy as possible. There were running clubs I could join, I knew that. But running was the one way I'd ever found to be alone without feeling alone.

The white plywood facade of Red's Java House, always closed on weekends for some reason, slid by for a second time and the looming presence of the elevated freeway gave the sense that I was entering a tunnel with home, the sunlit Golden Gateway complex, at the far end. Partway along, on the corner of Mission, stood the Silver Dollar, the seedy dive where Gomez wanted to shoot pool. He had quite a nose for urban funk. I'd seen the place more times than I could count during my years of working at L-W, and never been motivated to go in.

÷ ÷ ÷

No sooner was the triangular wooden rack removed than *PLLOCKK!* Gomez slammed the cue ball into the fifteen others I'd amassed as his target. He sank one and was jubilant. Not so on his next try, when he dropped a corner-pocket leaner with a nifty bank shot, which then glanced off a stray at mid-table for a canceling scratch. Our first game I'd handled the break, and won easily when he scratched his last two turns.

"Shit," he said, as much to himself as to me. "Running true to form, and I'm up against a shark." He had bought us a pitcher of flavorless beer, which was perched on a stained and cigarette-burned window ledge, along with our glasses. He drank from his and handed me mine.

I braced the big end of my cue on the floor, leaned on the shaft, and took a swallow. "Like I told you, pool has always been something I'm good at."

"Must be your eye for engineering or drafting," he shrugged, chalking the tip of his cue. "Too bad it wasn't a varsity sport. You'd have gotten a letter and been boffing the cheerleaders."

"Doubtful."

"The main thing is, I dig this place, and a high risk of losing's how I pay some of what I owe."

"Don't go overboard. As long as there's no repeat, I'm willing to forgive and forget." I stepped around him to line up my shot.

"You were right to be pissed," he said. "Last thing you need while you're working through the crap Jenny left behind. There'll be more recompense than this."

I got a nice run of six balls going while Gomez employed every kind of groan and body-English as distraction. And on my miss, I gave him a terrible lie. He took forever on his setup, measuring and re-measuring the alternatives, so I re-scanned the Silver Dollar's interior to confirm my original impression. Yes, dive was the word — a large, dirty, smoky, smelly, bare-floored room with windows on two sides, three badly worn pool tables and an ornate, old-fashioned mahogany bar and back-bar. Above the crazed and yellowed mirror hung a faded oil of a reclining nude that might have been around since the Gold Rush.

Our fellow patrons, all male, included postal workers from Rincon Annex in the next block and a number of others who looked like they slept in the alley as many nights a month as they did anywhere else. The bartender, fat and mean-faced, sat reading the newspaper under a handmade sign proclaiming, **BEER AND WHISKEY ONLY - We Do Not Serve Wine**. An out-of-date calendar touting an auto parts distributor via association with a swimsuit-clad blonde hung nearby, adjacent to some oversized jars of grotesque pickled eggs and pigs' feet.

Gomez and I were the sole players, and judging from the condition of the spare cues in the corner, they'd been used in brawls no less often than for their real purpose. There was also a jukebox, permanently dark and lifeless, probably due to the gash of shattered plastic across its front, a gash with the exact taper, my eye reported, of the cue Gomez was holding. Finally, he leaned well over the table and let fly.

He didn't scratch, but didn't sink anything either. "You left me in the fucking Sargasso Sea," he complained.

"There might have been one opening," I said, "but you didn't see it."

I re-chalked my cue, ran five more balls, he put down three, then I ran the table, and the same dynamic applied to our next two games. "See," he said, "told you. My clock's never been cleaner. Let's toss back another of those pitchers."

"How do I know you didn't roll over for me? Seemed easier than it should have."

"Just not my game. You may have been present at his creation, but Gomez doesn't roll over for anybody."

"I was browsing through *Capricorn* last night, and Henry Miller's characters would delight in paying debts that way."

"Where do you get this stuff? Why would I care about him?" His expression said I was being obtuse.

"Come on. The parallels with you and Mad and her husband and these kind of places," I gestured at the room, "are a little hard to miss."

GOMEZ

He bought more beer and we took a table near the jukebox, away from any neighbors so we could spread out. "Coincidence," Gomez said. "I mean the Miller/Nin thing. Honest to god, pure coincidence."

"I could sell you a beautiful bridge four blocks from here. Cheap, too, and goes all the way across."

"So don't believe me. Look, I admit I had a case on Miller when I was in college. Did papers on him, read all I could."

"Why didn't you go to Paris instead of Buenos Aires?"

"You know why. Besides, what's in Paris? Miller's world was forty, fifty years ago. The groupies sniffing around the Place de Clichy, ordering Pernod and not taking baths, are pathetic. Argentina was original. So's the Silver Dollar. I found them myself." He grimaced to display his gums and irregular bite. "I can't stand it where everybody has straight teeth."

"What's Miller's famous quote about happiness?" Gomez had triggered a memory from my own college days, something our Comp Lit prof read to us at the beginning and the end of the semester.

"From page one of *Cancer*," he said. "'I have no money, no resources, no hopes. I am the happiest man alive.' There's hyperbole to it, but an important truth…about de-emphasizing material possessions. The idea's to live, not jump through hoops. But you're way off to think my Yale reading list has anything to do with Mad."

Who was he kidding, me or himself? I could no more buy this latest dodge than I'd bought either Mad's or his the other night. "Let's see, Miller had an ex-wife who lived in New York. So do you. I forget her name, but Miller's was Mona, and yours I remember as pretty similar." He knew I was baiting him and he didn't like it.

"Get a grip," he said with scorn. "Mona is fiction. Her real name was June. June Mansfield, which itself was changed from something eastern-European. My ex is Donna. How do you make… make June out of that?"

"OK, but for a while, Miller taught English-as-a-second-language at some kind of institute. Or maybe you didn't know?"

"I knew. So what? Next you'll tell me that Miller was a lot straighter than he portrays himself in his writing. I know that, too. Nobody undisciplined could produce such a body of work. Haven't

GOMEZ

you figured out that everybody's an imposter to some degree... Paul Stiles included? The trick is not to overreach."

"And to not get caught."

"Amounts to the same thing."

"How much does Mad know?"

"No more than she needs to...from where she came in, that is." He glared at me, but there was a cagey smile behind his glare.

He wasn't giving an inch, and I was done probing. I'd learn more by observation than from Q&A, and that would be true with Mad as well—if I ever saw her again—which wouldn't happen unless Gomez made it happen. He was right, though. I had been on the verge of pointing out that Miller was much less bohemian than the myth he'd created, and that he might not have lived very differently from my friend Andrés Gomez. My friend who was clearly my age or older, but who, in another sense, had existed for barely six months. As for his remark about imposters, could he have been reading my innermost thoughts this past month?

"Your engineering background might be good for more than shooting pool," he observed, after we'd both paused to drink. "Could also help with this great brain-teaser I've got."

"Oh yeah, what's that?" I smiled, admiring how artfully he'd changed the subject.

"A math teacher at the Centro laid it on me. We bet five bucks. Blew his mind when I came up with the solution, wham-bam."

"So it'll cost me five if I don't?"

"No, won't cost you a cent. But if you do, you get another free dinner at the Hayes Street Grill."

"Nothing wrong with those odds."

"Here it is: if you had a thousand $1 bills and ten envelopes, could you place all the bills into envelopes, write on each one the amount it contains, then seal the envelopes, and still be able to pay out any whole-dollar amount between $1 and $1,000 without re-opening any of them? If your answer is yes," he concluded with his full-charm grin, "then you have to tell me how."

"Wow. Complicated. Run through it again."

"Don't have to. I typed it up." He drew a folded paper from his jeans pocket and handed it to me.

GOMEZ

I studied the paper briefly. "Well, the answer has to be yes, or the question would never be asked. But it sure looks impossible from here."

"No comment," Gomez replied. "And there are rules. Take as long as you want, but no outside coaching…except Mad. I sent her a copy at the Mime Troupe. You guys can work on it together. Same prize, so it might be a dinner for three."

"Doesn't sound much like her cup of tea." In fact, I thought, a pursuit about as far removed from the right-brained Anaïs Nin as one could imagine.

"It isn't, really," he acknowledged. "You'll have to be the inspiration, but she has some apologizing to do, too. I passed along both your phone numbers. Hope you don't mind."

"No, I'm glad." And I was, against all my better judgement. "She's out of commission with her husband in town, though, isn't she?"

"Yeah. But she can still call from work, or you call her. The number's in the book. If she's not there, leave a message." He gave me what I guessed was a knowing smile, and we relaxed with the rest of our beer. If Gomez wanted you to like him, you were going to like him. It was useless to resist.

GOMEZ

CHAPTER 13

All the Nin/Miller lore, denials notwithstanding, could have been read as clues to what was coming, and there were more, but I wasn't looking for clues. Instead I topped up our beers and chattily asked Gomez if he would miss Mad during her *unavailability*—which was how I put it, to avoid mentioning the husband. But he just scoffed, telling me the situation was inherently ambivalent, and displaying bravado about his "other ways" to keep busy.

We ended the evening by trading laughs and tossing around oddments from the news, like Larry Flynt of *Hustler* fame's being shot by some whacko in Georgia, and the latest on an outfit called Peoples Temple, which had recently relocated from SF to the South American jungle to escape negative publicity and a fraud investigation. In trying to involve their members in programs at the Centro last fall, Gomez said he'd met the leader, Reverend Jim Jones, and thought the guy was a sleaze.

"Yeah, but wasn't part of the flap that he was on the Housing Authority, appointed by the mayor, your favorite politician?"

"Locally," Gomez answered, with a nonchalant toss of his head, "Jones got his start by picketing to put suicide barriers on the Golden Gate Bridge...which we still need, by the way. It's not Moscone's fault he went bad from there."

"Probably the last we'll hear of it," I said. "How about catching a movie one of these nights? If you...well...aren't too busy *other ways*."

"There's good European stuff around. "*That Obscure Object of Desire*, Bunuel's latest, plus revivals of *Swept Away* and *Jules and Jim*. We have to keep loosening you up."

"Never heard of any of them."

What we settled on, the following week, was *Swept Away*, which Gomez raved about having seen twice in Berkeley a few years back. It was very sexy, a man and a woman from opposite ends of the economic scale thrown together on a deserted Mediterranean island, and in my current state, very troubling. If a film—

by a female director, no less—could so believably portray the heroine's sexuality as being that animalistic and that responsive to male assertiveness, and yet be so quickly dropped from the equation when they were rescued, how would I ever figure it out?

"Well," came the inevitable question, as we navigated the theater's lobby on our way to his truck, "what did you think?"

"Strong stuff," I answered, groping for words. "If I even got the point."

"Simple. Shows what complex beasts we really are. Maybe *Jules and Jim* would have been better. Same message, different facts."

÷ ÷ ÷

Next up was another evening at Jordan's. By unspoken consent we passed on discussing Eve's would-be contribution to my sex life, although Jordan was hopeful he'd found a new regular, Marnie, to complete his lineup. He'd seen her twice, and the only hitch was that her schedule wasn't as predictable as he liked. She was French, cool and blonde, new to California, and highly satisfactory. I would be invited to meet her sometime if things continued to develop. He'd already paraded Marnie at Henry Africa's, he said, which was part of his standard MO.

"Better yet," Jordan continued, "she loves foreign films. We saw the new Bunuel last weekend."

"Um...*Object of Desire*...that one?"

"Yes. Kinky and strange, didn't you think?"

"I haven't gone, but a friend mentioned it. We saw *Swept Away* instead."

"Oh, rather a classic. And kinky, too, if you ask me. Women's kink."

"Right," I hurried to agree. "The same friend also mentioned a revival of *Jules and Jim*. Does that ring a bell?

"Definitely," Jordan said. "Another classic. French, but a bit before your time. A wonderful *ménage au trois*...and actually sweet, though it sounds kinky."

Conversation then turned to our usual banter—local politics, our jobs, his lack of communication with his son and daughter. But his movie commentary stuck in my mind and was subsumed into my conflicting feelings for Mad. Moment to moment I hoped that she would or wouldn't call about the math puzzle or to apologize, and that I would or wouldn't stop remembering how our evening at Artichoke Joe's had ended, and yet I had no ability to talk about it. There were several reasons for maintaining silence with Jordan, primarily his salaciousness, and more obvious ones with Gomez, including envy. But at least I hadn't been abject enough to invent some absurd pretext and call her.

With the weather warmer and daylight growing with the season, we had the balcony door open, making Jordan's view more commanding than ever. Following him to the kitchenette, where he discarded the rind from a baby Gouda he'd served, I saw a monogrammed potholder hanging from the cook-top and a stack of matching coasters on the counter between us.

I picked one up. A now familiar name in blue caps was printed above an open book in blue and white, beneath which was the Latin motto *Lux Et Veritas*. "I take it you're a Yalie?"

"What?" He turned to face me. "Oh, yes, the alma mater. How about you?"

"Nothing of the sort. I'm a Kansas Jayhawk."

"Stayed close to home, did you?"

"Yes, maybe too close."

"I was resentful at being shipped east, but it grew on me. Initially I thought my friends at Cal and Stanford had much the best of things."

"After growing up at Pebble Beach, why Yale?" I kept a tone of casual interest, but was preoccupied with the vast contrast between Jordan and Gomez. They were years apart in age, representing different eras, but that alone wasn't the explanation. Their taste in film seemed the only common denominator.

"Family tradition," he replied. "My father, an uncle, two of my cousins...Stevenson Academy, then New Haven. There are more Yale grads in the Bay Area than you might think, and most of us stay in touch. My son would have none of it, of course, but neither did I insist, which I doubt he appreciates."

"Kansas doesn't have an alumni group here that I know of."

"Too bad. Might boost your career. Ours is good with mutual support and all that. At various times I've been treasurer, vice-president, secretary, and happy to do it. We sponsor scholarships, steer the right kind of kids to the hallowed halls, and have bi-monthly luncheons."

Jordan led me back to the living room, where we sat on the couch. "I worry the place is going to the dogs, though," he went on. "Admitting women, for one thing. What a ripple that must make in dining commons. It'll make one here, too, if they start showing up for our lunches. And long-time ties with the prep schools are being sacrificed. As if there's a better way to assess merit." He had made himself comfortable and was refilling our glasses.

Clearly I wasn't going to inquire if Jordan knew Gomez. Not only would Gomez support the changes Jordan bemoaned, he had attended college as a different person, a person he didn't want anyone to remember. But the idea that Jordan might know Andy Steentofter, or at least recognize the name, never quite went away.

"Incidentally," I asked, "do you know Matts Freytag, the Anchor Steam beer guy? I did all the graphics work for them."

"Certainly I know Matts. A Yale man through and through. He's been a mainstay of our club. I didn't know him on campus, he's too young, half-way between you and me, I'd guess. But he ought to be happy with your design. A nice piece of work."

"He said he was. I'm happy with it myself." That gave one shred of validation to Andy's persona last fall, but what I was mainly thinking was that a Kansas alumni club might be a place to meet women. We, after all, had been accepting them from day one.

÷ ÷ ÷

At the office that week I made a few calls and struck out on local Kansas connections. There were a number of us, but no organization. And while I could have found a flurry of KU sweatshirts in the sports bars on Union Street, because the Jayhawks were in the NCAA tournament again this year, I'd never been interested in basketball.

Mid-afternoon on Thursday, Ivy, the department secretary, came in to relay a message. Round-faced and frumpy, but newly affiliated with what seemed to be a serious boyfriend, she had some knowledge of my celibate status and looked down on me for it. Bypassing the intercom gave her a chance to add facial expressions and body language to her patronizing tone of voice. I was bent over my drafting table doing mockups, but she delayed her performance until I turned in my chair.

"*Madeline* is on the line for *Paul*," Ivy announced. "Disco music in the background, and no last names required."

My mouth went dry, but for Ivy's sake I was impassive. "Good," I said. "Just a friend. Don't over-dramatize." I grabbed a packet from my outbox. "Could you get this down to mailroom ASAP?"

"Yes, boss," she replied, with heavy irony, and I waited to be sure her footsteps kept going past her desk and the doorways of the other design staff in our suite.

I picked up the phone as calmly as I could, as though Mad could see through the lines. "Hi, what's up? Gomez said he gave you my number."

"Am I forgiven?" she answered meltingly. Ivy hadn't been kidding. There was disco music in the background.

"I guess. But it was hard to take at the time."

"I'd like to make amends."

"Consider them made." I felt my palm sweating against the plastic of the phone's handset.

"No, in person, today."

"Not necessary," I told her. "Really." I recognized the music from listening to my car radio. The chorus was in French or some Caribbean patois I couldn't understand. "Where are you, anyway?"

"At home." *Voulez-vous coucher avec moi, ce soir,* came the chorus, *voulez-vous coucher avec moi*. Mad must have had her tape deck or radio near the phone. "I'll pick you up on the Embarcadero, outside your office at 4:30."

"I don't get out of here till five. Do you know where it is?"

"Yes. But today you're leaving early." ...*voulez-vous coucher avec moi*...the music pulsed. "Gomez says you put in tons of extra hours."

"OK. What'll we do? Have a drink and work on his math puzzle?"

"Oohh, one of those things, at least," Mad replied. ...*avec moi, ce soir*...crooned her accompaniment. "Watch for me along the curb." She hung up.

GOMEZ

Ivy gave me such a pair of raised eyebrows when I said I was leaving at 4:25 that she deserved to be permanently deformed. "What language did you take in college?" she asked coyly.

"None," I said. "High school Spanish was it. Why?"

"No reason. Just making conversation."

I strode quietly along the corridor, across the deck and down the gangway, sure that Murphy's Law would send one of the higher-ups looking for me with a hot deadline before I escaped. But my luck held. Even so, it was clear why I had ruled out trying to date anyone at L-W. There would be rumors, notes would be compared, and things I wanted private would no longer be private. Ivy was probably upstairs right now, finagling a late smoke-break so she could watch from the deck while I got into Mad's car.

In fact, what vehicle was I looking for? Mad hadn't said and I'd never seen her behind the wheel. The Embarcadero was always a big jam-up at rush hour. What if we missed each other? I reached the street, noted again what a lovely spring day it had been, and realized that a half-hour off work would be an extra half-hour of soft breeze and golden sun: no fog, no foghorns, and just a few wispy clouds.

There were never many pedestrians on this section of the waterfront, but strangled lanes of auto traffic pressing north to the Golden Gate and Marin had already formed. I looked around and checked my watch for the third time since leaving my desk.

"Paul," I heard Mad laugh from twenty feet away. "Eyes wide right."

On the outer edge of the sidewalk, with only a low concrete barrier and the bay behind it, was a burnt-orange, early 60s Karmann-Ghia, whose paint and chrome showed some wear from all those years, but had been well cared for. The low, curvilinear hood was pointed away from me, the driver's door was open, and Mad stood against it smiling, with one palm raised in a diffident wave.

"Oh, hi." I started toward her, my first step easy and confident, but each thereafter more tentative. My left foot wanted Ivy to be spying from above, my right foot didn't.

Mad wore the same Capezio flats, pleated batik skirt, and black leotard top I'd admired when I first met her at Gomez's. This time, though, she had not only braided a pastel scarf into her hair, she'd wound a long, wide swatch of chiffon in pale, melony greens and pinks twice around her neck so that it hung nearly to her ankles and made lazy winglets as the air around her moved.

Drawing even with the car's bumper and stubby tail, I slowed further, realized I'd been staring, and dropped my eyes. "Hop in the other side," she instructed.

The passenger door was locked, so I reached through the open window, grasped the inside handle and did as she said. I'd never been in a Ghia before. I'd seen lots of them and liked their look, but it was amazing how low they were and how little knee-room I had. Mad folded herself beside me, slammed her door and started the engine. A chugging roar came from the back, about the level of our shoulder blades.

Through the windshield a runner, a guy my age in electric blue shorts and a loose-fitting tank top, no doubt also out of work early, loped straight at us along the sidewalk, frowning at Mad's parking technique. She cut left in front of him after spotting a slight break in traffic and scraped the muffler as we jounced off the curb. The runner went by close on my side, visible now from thighs to navel only.

"If you hadn't called, I'd be running tonight just like him," I said.

She gunned the motor and speed-shifted to produce a semblance of acceleration, merging us onto Bay Street. "Well, then," she replied with a quick glance my way, "we'll make sure you get some exercise."

"Good." The idea of a stroll with her at Fort Mason or the Marina Green after our drink formed in my mind. "Do you always park like that?"

"As a last resort," she laughed. "I figured I could charm myself out of a ticket if you showed up about the same time as the cops." One length of her long, gauzy scarf was billowing out the driver's-side window, forcing her to retrieve it and after several tries, wedge it under her leg.

"I'd be worried," I joked, "if your hero was Isadora Duncan."

"You think I'd take it that far?" Her reply ended in a giggle.

I was pleased she could laugh with me, not just at me. "By the way, what was that music on the phone when you called? It's popular now, I ought to learn the name."

Mad ran her eyes appraisingly across my face, as though I might have made another joke and she wanted to be sure, then an swered, "I...ah...forget. Whatever tape was going. I didn't realize you'd hear."

With no signal or hesitation, she followed this with a sudden, tire-screeching turn through oncoming traffic onto Polk, ran the four-way stop at Francisco and barely halted for the next one. To keep from grabbing the dashboard, I grabbed at another topic. "I wasn't expecting to see you while your husband's home."

"At the moment he's not. He left for LA this morning and I'm meeting him later at the airport."

"I meant home from Asia. What's in LA?"

"More of his oil project. They're discussing a shipping terminal for liquefied natural gas, whatever that is."

"I know the basic science."

"Fine. I don't want to. But if you ever meet Clark, you'll have something to talk about."

We approached the corner of Broadway, the locus of Henry Africa's, and I wondered if we'd have our drink there. I had peeked through the windows once or twice, finding the place loaded with wooden masks and carvings, refectory furniture, painted animal hides and hanging tropical plants, but I'd shied away from going in. It was the city's most renowned *meet* market—or make that *meat*—for singles, exactly the kind of pressure I didn't need. To arrive with Mad, however, and perhaps run into Jordan, would have been the biggest score I could then imagine.

"Where are we going, Henry's?"

"No, Gomez's." The stoplight dropped in our favor and she shot across the intersection.

"Oh." I'd wanted her to myself for once, but so it went. "I didn't figure he'd be off work yet."

"He's not. He has class now and some kind of community meeting after that."

"Well, the drinks will be free. Serves him right, since it's his puzzle." I was getting my wish after all.

"Oh, yes, the famous puzzle."

"Do you have any theories? I've been working on a few."

She laughed warmly. "You really are sweet, aren't you?"

"I don't know." I sneaked a look at her, but she was too busy to notice.

GOMEZ

"Well, you are. And no, I have zero theories on putting dollar bills into envelopes."

"I think it has to do with prime numbers or square roots...you know, some mathematical law, but I haven't started mapping them out."

By now Mad had swung west to Gough and was on a route to Gomez's I often used myself. "What made you ask about Henry Africa's?" she inquired.

"We went right by it."

"We've gone by lots of places."

"This guy I know...my neighbor, actually...likes to go there."

"Looking for action, I assume?"

"No, that's what's funny. He takes his dates, you know, late, after they've...they've made love...and they sit in a corner, just taking in the scene, handicapping the contestants and betting matchsticks. They're the only two neutrons in a world of electrons and protons."

"Your analogy's beyond me," she said, "but that is funny. Have you told Gomez?"

"No, I just found out, and it doesn't seem like his kind of thing."

"Maybe not...more mine, really."

As she rode the clutch down the long hill and across Market Street in the slanting sunlight, Mad entertained me with Mime Troupe gossip. Their key benefactor, somebody-or-other Goldstine, was also being courted by the Pushrods, a so-called guerrilla tap-dance collective, and by an unofficial Troupe spin-off, the Pickle Family Circus. It was turning into the fund-raising Olympics, Mad said, and she was scrambling to meet the competition.

"Once you get that wrapped up, could you move into the performance end?"

"I already am. In life. Like everyone, whether they admit it or not."

On Valencia, Mad dared fate by boasting about her parking karma, but a spot virtually in front of Gomez's building opened the instant we pulled up. "See!" she crowed.

I got out, unlatched the alleyway gate, and Mad went ahead to extract a key from the interstices of the arbor near the foot of the steps. It was the first time I'd been there by day, and an arc of what

GOMEZ

my aunt used to call **tea roses**, little pink ones with spare, small, spiny leaves, clung to **the rickety** wood above me and were just starting to bloom, their **scent** competing with the garbage cans. The former upstairs tenant, the deceased mother of the hapless, drugged-out guy who'd preceded Gomez, must have been a gardener.

Mad unlocked the door and in we went. At certain times of day dust is more visible, and there was a patina of it on the dully shining floor around the rug. Unquestionably, Gomez wasn't home, and except for a few books and an empty wineglass on the table, and some odd dishware in the sink, the place was as tidy as mine. In fact, the bed was even made.

He had led me to believe that his *other ways* of keeping busy included women, but if so, any consorting with them was apparently being done elsewhere. It took only seconds to reach that conclusion, although Mad seemed to be making a similar survey at her own pace, and perhaps with a similar objective. Was that why we'd come, so she could document a strange, misplaced jealousy?

"Find us something to drink, would you?" she said from the table, where she was corralling Gomez's books, re-shelving them, and selecting others.

I looked into the door-less lower cupboard that comprised the pantry. "There might be beer in the fridge, but what I see here is an open jug of Burgundy and some tequila."

"Make it tequila, and check if he has limes."

"He does, in the fruit bowl."

"Bring one over, along with the bottle and a knife. Oh, and two glasses."

When I arrived with the bar supplies, Mad had replaced what I assumed were volumes from Gomez's Miller collection with Nin and Durrell titles, arranged around the empty wineglass in nearly identical fashion.

"Do you know where he keeps scratch paper and something to write with?" I asked. "Otherwise we won't get anywhere on the puzzle."

"The dork!" she exclaimed. "He knew I'd find this." She pulled a last book, hardbound, from the shelf she was raiding and shook it at me. "It's never been here before."

GOMEZ

"Find what?" We were both standing, and for some reason we stayed that way.

"*Two Sisters*, a novel from the 40s by Gore Vidal. It has a character based on Anaïs that she absolutely hated." Mad put the book under her macramé purse on a corner of the table.

"Looks like you're going to burn it," I said.

"I might. But pour us a little of that Suizo."

While I did, Mad sliced wedges of lime and squeezed them over our glasses before dropping them in. "How did Gomez come up with something that obscure?" I asked, trying to be cool. "It has to be out of print."

"The man has limitless angles. You can bet he cadged or bartered for it somewhere." She held up her glass, implying that I should do likewise. "One taste and you'll never be angry at me again," she said, coming closer than necessary and touching the rim of her glass precisely to the rim of mine. "To the dream," she nodded.

"Will I be ensorceled?"

"Yes."

We drank, just a sip each, and I dared to look directly at her. "Well, I *was* a little angry…before you called, that is…but I wasn't as soon as I heard your voice." She didn't look away.

"And now?" Her nostrils fluttered slightly, suggesting that she might be nervous.

"Definitely not now."

I stood holding my drink against my chest, realizing that I was still wearing my blazer and hadn't loosened my tie. She turned, took a second sip of tequila, walked to the bed, and kneeled across its corduroy cover to place her glass on the night table at the far side, beneath the windows. "Next," she said, working the louvers to open the shutters a bit, "the perfect amount of light." Because she had stepped out of her shoes, I saw the pink, bare soles of her feet, isolated against the bedspread and the fabric of her skirt.

When I'd last been there Gomez hadn't had shutters. Or if he had, my powers of observation were off. But I remembered the night table, and also that on the near side of the bed was a straight-backed wooden chair. Mad eased herself into it, sitting so that she was back-lit, more in profile to me than straight on.

GOMEZ

Pushing her hips forward on the seat, she raised her knees so her feet were well off the floor and her skirt's hem hung at the tops of her calves. She reached beneath it and hunched gently from side to side, sliding her panties down her legs and into her hands. Without looking at me, she folded them and leaned to put them under Gomez's pillow. I was transfixed.

"Do you like this skirt?" she asked softly. "I remember your eyes on it the night we met."

I took another swallow of tequila, which until now, I'd always thought tasted awful. "Yes, I do. It must be Indonesian."

"I bought it there at Christmas, but Graciela helped me add the pleats. She sews marvelously." Mad had readjusted her position and placed her feet back on the floor, sitting now with her whole face toward me. I saw an abbreviated, expectant smile, but couldn't make myself meet her gaze.

"Would you like to know what the pleats look like from the inside?" she asked, just above a whisper.

"How would I do that?"

"Take off your jacket and come over here."

Remembering what happened seems as unbelievable as experiencing it. I let my blazer fall off my shoulders and down my arms, until I could drape it over a chair. Then I began to remove my tie.

"No," she said, "leave that on. I like the idea."

Not knowing I was moving, I walked to her. She took my hands, pulled so that I bent at the waist, then tilted her mouth up in a kiss. Suddenly I was the wire short-circuiting the terminals of a generator. In an explosion of sensation, Mad's tongue darted lustfully against mine, I tasted and breathed the tequila we'd been drinking, and a sharp jolt shot up my spine from my crotch to my brain and back to my knees. When the kiss ended and she again pulled on my hands, my legs buckled and I knelt in a spasm of anticipation.

Through the cloth of her skirt I saw her legs spreading. After that I saw very little because she lifted the hem, sat forward in the chair again, and drew me into a dim tent filled with her cinnamon perfume and a narcotic undertone of seaweed. The flesh of her thighs was smoother against my face than buttered suede, and the steady pressure of her hands on my neck guided my mouth to where she wanted it.

GOMEZ

Though I'd often seen this act on film, I had never actually performed it, and I'd have had stage fright if I'd known it was something Mad expected. But everything evolved so spontaneously that a primal Paul, an unrepressed oral maniac, took charge and knew just how to proceed. Giving pleasure became my sole purpose, which was itself pleasure. In concert with her breathing, Mad groaned and moved on the chair, making subtle changes in my access that kept matters fresh and exciting. I had no thought of time or place, or of ever doing anything else.

The first thought I did have, when thought returned, was of wanting to see Mad's face, and to know whether my ministrations were producing the kind of wanton expression I'd seen in the mirror of the Audi two weeks ago. But my mouth couldn't be in the tent while my eyes were outside it, and outside I might have to talk, or operate on some level beyond the physical.

Mad sensed my distraction and eased away. "My god," she said. "I knew you'd be horny…but…my god…"

At this point I became aware of my cock, jammed in my shorts, bigger and harder than I ever remembered, and already dribbling semen. Mad swung one leg over my head and stood up, expelling me from the tent as she turned to lift part of Gomez's bedspread off of the blanket. I struggled to my feet and sat in the chair. Unwinding her long scarf, Mad stepped out of the skirt, stripped off her top, and shrugged loose from the filmy half-bra she'd had under it. My fantasies of her unblemished skin and how the rest of her must be shaped had turned into a living hologram. I might have sat there, wordless and watching, if she hadn't perched opposite me and begun undoing my tie.

"Come on," she breathed into my ear, "I'll never be more ready."

Seconds later my clothes were on the floor, Mad was beneath me on top of the blanket, and my cock found its yearned destination with no further prompting. Before shock at what I was doing could slow me down, she tilted her hips and made my thrusts uncontrollable by moaning repeatedly, "Let it go…ahh, that's good…ahh, that's right…let it go."

This completed, at least temporarily, the conjuring of a new Paul, one who forgot about his undersized member, who came once almost right away, and who barely softened as he continued

GOMEZ

thrusting to come a second time minutes later—wildly, blindingly, violently —without regard to consequences, without regard to who this woman was or why she was receiving him, or why there, on the still-made bed of his only real friend, Gomez.

CHAPTER 14

The base of Mad's spine fascinated me. It was slightly concave and lined with minuscule, down-soft hair, which, though invisible to the eye, yielded deliciously to my fingertips. Just there, where the divine, rising curve of her hip began, two pliable sinews seemed to intersect, then upwell to outline the curve.

While she stroked my scalp, as it lay against her shoulder, I slowly traced my hand, again and again, from behind her knee, along the back of her thigh, and up over the softness of her buttock to lingeringly rest, before I reversed course, at that special place. Any other woman I'd known, and certainly Jenny, would have long since been up and taking a shower, but Mad showed no more interest in untwining our bodies than I did. Instead she made murmuring purrs to say she liked what I was doing.

As long as my eyes were closed and our luxurious skin-to-skin contact continued, I could forget where I was and not really worry about the truckload of remorse I knew was careening toward me. **Gomez Drayage Co.** the truck's signage would say, and with a curious lack of feeling, my brain even supplied an appropriate logo featuring pampas grass and a carefree gaucho.

"Paul," I heard Mad whisper, "what are you thinking?"

I opened one eye to find a plane of creamy skin angling down to the symmetry of her right breast. No, I wouldn't mention his name now, not if I could avoid it. "Oh..." I reverted to a previous thought, "how it would feel to go through life and be as fantastically good-looking as you are."

She kissed my forehead. "And you deny it when I say you're sweet."

"I'm only reporting the facts."

She gave a breathy laugh. "I'm a late bloomer, that's for sure, but perhaps I've finally bloomed."

"Meaning what?"

"In high school I was the ugly duckling, and in Beverly Hills, that's a big burden. College wasn't a whole lot better."

"Not believable."

"Try me with braces and thick glasses. Thank god for contacts, and it took all the technology in Hollywood to straighten my teeth. When my little brother was riding around yelling 'Look, Ma, no hands,' I was in eleventh grade saying 'Look, Ma, no tits,' and I still had rubber bands in my mouth. Then…there was my nose."

"Huh?"

"My nose job. It's no secret. Stop pretending."

I sat partly up so I could see her in the dimness. "I'd never have guessed."

"Yeah, right. But I'm glad I waited, because surgical methods really improved. By age eighteen the teeth were taken care of, and while I was at Mills I got contacts and the tits shaped up on their own. The nose, such as it is, completed the package. I went home a few years after graduation and had it done down there."

"By a doctor to the stars, no doubt."

"Sort of. I still took a long time coming around to it, to feeling that this me would be no more false than any other me."

Falseness—mine, hers or anyone else's—was the last thing I wanted to discuss right then, so I made sure the topic lapsed. "What was your major? At Mills, I mean."

"Oh…drama. I thought you knew."

"Maybe I forgot." She'd learned a lot about me the night we met, but I'd been so careful to be obliging, and so much under her sway physically, that some of what she'd said and what Gomez had told me beforehand might have failed to stick.

"Well, it teaches you to present yourself, and to overcome being shy…both of which I badly needed."

"Then the you I'm hearing about and the one I see…and smell…and touch…" I veered my hand to run a light touch up her abdomen, between her breasts and to her chin, "…have less in common than distant cousins."

"If you're determined to bathe me in approval," she smiled, "I accept. But it's also true that looks like mine have come into vogue these days, so I'm going to enjoy it while I can. I think you're in the same boat…for guys."

"Me?"

"Sure. Shorter hair, nicer clothes, careers instead of communes. The shaggy 60s and blow-dried 70s are over. On Sundays the Hyatt

GOMEZ

Regency has started having dressy tea dances and people our age and younger are flocking there."

"Being in vogue. That'll take some getting used to."

"I doubt I'm wrong. If Gomez gets a new suit...or lets me get him one...we're going to the Hyatt next month. Of course *he* spotted my nose job right away, or says he did. Something else he's supposedly up on."

At this mention of his name, the remorse truck arrived to dump its load. She felt my body tense and shift on the bed—Gomez's bed. "Shhh...relax," she said. "This was more or less his idea. Since he and I don't have an exclusive relationship...and we obviously don't ...providing what's most important for you right now has to be right. He doesn't want details from either of us, and why should he? What is, is. Let yourself live."

I wasn't entirely reassured, and had yet another reason to be shocked, although the now obvious clues I'd missed quickly lined up in my mind. But in some ways, having his permission made things worse. An affair on the sly would give me more stature. "And if he walks in?"

"He won't."

"How do you know?"

"I know." She reached for her tequila on the night table, took a sip, and handed the last of it to me. My own glass was empty and on the floor somewhere.

"But he could." The possibilities were grimly insistent. For Gomez to come banging through the door outraged would have been bad enough, but for him to show up with happy congratulations would be a hell of its own kind. I heard a wall clock ticking in the kitchen, yet had no sense of time. The "ideal amount of light" that Mad had arranged earlier, and it had been ideal for the removal of her panties and events thereafter, had by now dwindled to nearly nothing, all of which was the spill from adjacent buildings or street lamps at the end of the alley.

I also realized that Mad's oversized chiffon scarf had been folded into a makeshift coverlet, and that we were lying on it rather than directly on Gomez's blanket. Not only hadn't we gotten into the bed, she had improvised the bedding, both of which suggested precautions to prevent discovery, yet her follow-up was to matter-of-factly counsel that I treat our tryst as a form of group marriage with today simply being my turn. I drank the tequila and this time it did taste awful.

"Alright," she agreed, breaking the silence, "he could. But he's not going to. He'd never miss this meeting he has or cut out early. It's after seven, though, so we do have a problem."

"What?" A renewed surge of anxiety made me sit up farther.

"No, no." She took the glass from me and kissed my cheek. "A minor one…I assume. It's too late for me to drive you home and still get to the airport to meet Clark. Could I drop you at BART? Would that be OK?"

Suddenly I felt cold, needed to get dressed, and wanted to be able to see what I was doing, but wasn't sure I wanted Mad to see me or even me to see her. The dark was a better keeper of illusions.

"Well, would it?" she repeated mildly. She had rolled away and I knew she was locating her clothes.

"Yes, BART's fine. In fact, I can walk over to Mission to get on." I scrambled from the bed, and lit the light in one of Gomez's closets, partly closing the door so the room would stay shadowed

"I'd be glad to take you, really," she said, slipping her tight-fitting black top over her head. Just visible in the background was Gomez's Diego Rivera print—a flower vendor whose stolid figure bent forward under his load in counterpoint to Mad's contortions, trying to align her flopping sleeves from within.

"Use the extra time to be sure we're fully reassembled," I told her. "I'll put back the tequila and stuff, you do the bed, then go find the bathroom. I don't have anyone to be presentable for tonight. I'll wash the drink glasses, too."

"OK, good. But only wash one. Put that away and leave the other on the counter. He'll know I was here from the books."

It took me less than five minutes to get into my clothes and police up the residue from our drinks, with one dirty glass left conspicuously out. When I finished Mad was in the bathroom primping and humming what sounded like the disco song I'd heard during her phone call. I folded my tie and slid it into an inside pocket, adjusting my blazer and smoothing my hair by using the glass surface of Gomez's framed Martin Luther King photo as a mirror. I supposed that it dated from his Alabama days, but really didn't give the substance of his past any thought.

GOMEZ

"Do you think I could borrow this Gore Vidal?" I called to Mad. In the additional light from the open bathroom door I saw that her long scarf, tightly folded, was now on the table edge with the book, where her purse had been.

"It's permanently out of circulation," she replied. "Too defamatory."

"Are you Anaïs's alter-ego or her protector?"

"Don't get carried away with the alter-ego business. That's just a private joke with Gomez."

"Sorry."

"But protector...of her memory...I'll admit to. And I'm not alone. Plenty of women feel that way now. She's a rare example of feminine freedom."

Somehow the splash of water in the sink and the sound of a cabinet being closed triggered me to walk to Gomez's bed. Mad had remade it perfectly, which I'd expected, but I ran my hand under one of the pillows and was shocked to find her panties still there.

"Mad," I called more loudly, "you forgot your...your... underwear. Do you want them, or do they belong with your scarf?"

"No, leave them where they are." Her voice sounded no closer to me than before.

Was this another private joke? I started to comply, but couldn't. Instead, the panties, crumpled to prevent their showing, went into my coat pocket as I adroitly restored the pillow's position. Retreating to the table, I felt nervous and giddy, aware that I had acted not merely to cover our tracks, but for a more seamy reason. Another dimension of the charge this produced was assuming that she planned to meet her husband in a very public place wearing nothing under her skirt, and then to go home with him.

Mad stuck her head out of the bathroom. "Thirty more seconds," she said. "And in case you're wondering, a smart woman always keeps extra undies in her purse. I'm wearing a tampon, too, so Clark won't get overly interested."

"OK...I'm ready." Thank god she couldn't see me blushing, not only from what she'd said, but from what I'd done, and how easily I could have been caught.

This wasn't just a triangle, non-traditional as it might be, it was a quadrangle. To ensure that harmony prevailed, she had sex with me, jokes with Gomez and well-practiced excuses for her husband.

And that was just today. Other days her pattern would likely adapt and be different. While I was sorting this out, Mad turned off the light and strode from the bathroom.

"We'd better say goodbye here," she stated, putting her purse on the table and coming to snuggle against my chest with her arms around me, "but don't muss my face."

I was overcome and began kissing the top of her head through her hair. She'd refreshed her cinnamon perfume, which surrounded me as it had when my head was between her legs, however long ago that was. I went from pitying Clark to a grudging admiration for him. No one seemed to possess or control this remarkable creature, but he had a far more enduring claim than did I—or Gomez, for that matter.

"You were wonderful," she said into my neck. "So loving. You're not through with me, I hope. I don't want to be through with you."

This was beyond what I could have asked for, and almost more than I had dreamed. Gomez and Mad's giving me a onetime gift was hard enough to comprehend, much less that it would continue. "I never want to be through with you."

"Never? That we can't guarantee…either of us. But I'll call again as soon as I can."

She slid away from me to gather her things while I extinguished the closet light. "I've been reading Anaïs's diaries the last few weeks," I said in the darkness.

"Have you really?" came Mad's delighted reply. She had drawn the outside door open and was standing in its frame. "How far have you gotten? What do you think?"

"Now that I'm into them, I'm hooked," I said, squeezing by. The door locked behind us. "Sometimes she's as real to me as I am to myself." I felt the cool night air on my face and smelled the incongruous roses on their incongruous arbor in a skuzzy Mission District alley. "I'm just starting Volume III. She and Hugo have arrived in New York and are getting settled."

"That would be 1941," Mad nodded.

"Right," I confirmed. We descended the stairs with her leading and the rose fragrance growing stronger. "But earlier, with Henry …and with Gonzalo and Otto Rank, it feels like a lot was left out."

GOMEZ

Mad gave a quiet laugh. "A lot was," she added. "About her father, too. Remember that Hugo's still living, and read between the lines. How much *should* she have said?"

I reached to touch her arm and she placed her hand on mine for an instant. "OK, then, Paul…goodnight. I've got to run." After re-hiding Gomez's key, she quickened her pace in the walkway and before she reached the gate, was lost in the shadows.

Rather than try to keep up, I advanced in slow, easy steps. The cyclone fence and its razor wire were behind me, as was the barely visible yard of wrecked autos, but there were no lurking gang members or anything to suggest them. It was a benign spring evening.

The fear I'd felt in February had been replaced by amazement. How could what had just happened possibly have happened? It couldn't, but there was no mistaking the sound of Mad's car pulling away. Emerging, I walked a quiet, unlit block of 22nd and two teeming blocks of Mission, where I was the only Anglo face, and took the steep, deep escalator down to BART.

For the rest of the night, on the train, in the streets, or at home reading Nin's diary on my couch with a sandwich balanced in my lap, I felt none of my usual alienation. It had been such a constant in my life, and had so worsened since Jenny left, that its absence was like being reborn. I was composed and fully engaged in everything I did. The miraculous events of the afternoon seemed no longer miraculous, but predestined. I had so wanted Mad that, by the force of my desire, she had been delivered to me.

Of course those feelings didn't last. By the time I got to work the next morning, and for days afterwards, I swung unpredictably and in no order from: knowing I was a fool to be involved with either Mad or Gomez, to knowing that I had at least allowed them to play me for a fool; to feeling happier than I'd perhaps ever felt; or to agonizing when the phone rang over which of them it might be, which I wanted it to be, or which I dreaded it was. Gradually, though, the fact that Mad didn't call outweighed all else. I had her panties to savor and admire, but the whole episode became ephemeral, like remembering a dream.

Running was about the only thing that helped, although a big design project for a new electronics firm near San Jose kept me hopping, too. It was top secret and rush-rush and I'm still not supposed to talk about the specifics. Before long I also began worrying about the long silence from Gomez.

The *ménage* he'd thought he wanted, now that he had to live with it, might not be what he really wanted. Maybe Mad had reported back and he was pissed. Or had the panties been a prearranged signal that things were OK, and I screwed it up? I called him at the Centro and didn't get through, but I was so anxious when the receptionist came on I demurred at leaving a message.

To pass the time, I again entertained Jordan at my place, which we extended by going out to dinner in North Beach. We got along well and it was fun. I told him I'd had a date recently which had been very — fulfilling, is what I think I said — and he immediately sensed my meaning.

"Hats off," he said, with a sly smile and a raise of his glass. "About time."

"Thanks."

"Will I meet her?" There was something beyond friendly curiosity in his manner, something proprietary.

"I don't know. I'm pretty sure I'm not the only guy in her life."

"Even better. You're out of your shell now, so enjoy the field."

Jordan also told me, in very broad terms, about legal cases he'd worked on over the years, everything from proving industrial espionage to crafting the operating agreement that allowed the *Chronicle* and *Examiner* to share a single printing facility and produce a combined Sunday edition. I was more in a mood to listen than to talk, which gave him the role he preferred.

Finally, about ten days after I'd been with Mad, Gomez did call. I was at work, so maybe he attributed my stiffness to lack of privacy or to the deadline pressure I quickly mentioned. Regardless, he appeared not to notice and was his usual rapid-fire self. We set a racquetball date and he filled me in on Mad as though I'd want to know and had no other means of finding out. If he was that determined to play a game of mutual ignorance, what choice did I have?

Her husband was due to return to Asia the following week, and to spend time together, the two of them had gone to Palm Springs before he left. "That's the crappy part of being with someone who's married," Gomez went on. "*Their* schedule controls everything."

"Guess that's right." And it was right, I was learning myself.

GOMEZ

"Pisses me off that I miss her. You probably do, too. Being...ah ...*The Three Musketeers* has been fun. She said she apologized for Artichoke Joe's."

"Yeah, she did. We had a drink after work one night. Mad and I are fine now, and I do miss seeing her."

"You guys work on my math puzzle at all? She's been so much on the fly I forgot to ask."

"A little," I said. "Very preliminary."

"Like what?"

"Well, we think it illustrates a mathematical law...some established pattern."

"So far so good. You want a hint?"

"OK."

Gomez laughed. "Not a major hint, just this: conceptually, what you said about its illustrating a law isn't wrong. But don't expect a chestnut as venerable as the square root of 12 quadrillion, 345 trillion, 678 blah-blah-blah, where the series reverses at 9."

Trying to picture the digits he'd skipped, I joked, "Every little bit helps." To myself, however, I gulped. Math going into the quadrillions was a chestnut, and his envelopes were harder? Yet the bluffing we'd just laid on each other about Mad called for a continued show of confidence. "I can already taste my free dinner at Hayes Street."

"Listen, I'm sorry I've been so out of touch. The Centro's had me meeting myself coming and going. I took on an extra class for a guy who quit, and we've had political meetings out the gazoo every night.

"Can't be helped, either," he went on. "The city's got this squirrely new Board of Supervisors...you know, elected from the neighborhoods instead of at large...and the Centro gets city funding. Pain in the ass, even though I'm glad for the change. There's bound to be hassles...moving from plutocracy to democracy."

I had followed the issue to some extent in the news, and had heard Jordan grumble about it, but I wouldn't have guessed it would impact Gomez. "You're the man for all seasons, by the sound of things."

"I'm no stranger to politics, you know that. See you for racquetball."

GOMEZ

CHAPTER 15

Maybe Gomez was such a master at being normal — normal for him, that is — because he only had one speed. All bases between us were now touched, all fictions nicely preserved, and I supposedly had a one-third interest in a girlfriend, or some proportion, anyway, which was an improvement over where I'd been.

The bonhomie also carried over to our sweat-drenched contests in the rowing club basement. On my part, I felt a greater sense of rivalry, that on some level we were jousting for Mad, not just that he was a benefactor I resented needing. As for Gomez, he was always so competitive there was little room for ramping up.

He probably noticed my intensity when I won a couple of close games I normally wouldn't have, but he didn't alter his approach or his attitude. "You can kick my ass at pool, but I'm not sitting still for this," was all he said, adding later, after out-hustling me the rest of the night, "My football coach told us a hundred times, the most dangerous thing in sports is to let a guy think he can beat you."

But playing hard seemed to clear the air as far as I was concerned, so I was receptive when he called again to say he'd finessed a couple of Giants tickets. They were off to a great start and had won ten of their first twelve, according to the sports page. Vida Blue, a former Oakland guy who had switched teams, would be on the mound. And Gomez, of course, had us right behind third base, not in box seats, but the next best thing.

It was a night game, offering a taste of Candlestick's infamous swirling winds along with the discourse on baseball philosophy he'd wanted to lay on me last fall when we were painting and he was Andy. He began with the design of the field, which I had to concede was extremely pleasing, its neatly laid out and raked base paths set off against the mower patterns of the immaculate green turf. Our heroes were facing Houston in a match-up Gomez claimed would be almost as hot as one with the Dodgers.

My frame of mind was good, for the moment a phase of relishing my encounter with Mad and feeling that Gomez and I had a stronger bond as a result. Since it was the swinging 70s, why not get with the times? He'd driven us to the game, snaking into the parking lot via a back route off Third Street, and with the Ranchero's windows open and the radio on, I actually enjoyed the damn thing. The fact that its mufflers were so loud used to bother me, but Gomez made us both smile by winding the rpms on his up-shifts to accentuate the roar, and popping the clutch whenever he decelerated. To sustain that mood, I fetched big cups of beer as soon as we arrived.

He couldn't believe I'd never been in a major league ballpark, but it was true. In fact, I'd never attended a game with paid admission in any sport since high school. And in a way, the admission charged here was only theoretical, since our seats hadn't cost him a dime, but he waved off my queries as to how he'd done it.

"Jesus," he said, biting into a jumbo dog loaded with mustard. "You at least know the basics, right?" With his other hand he gestured toward the field, where the players were completing their warm-ups.

"Balls and strikes, innings and runs? Yeah, that stuff I have down."

"Well, I'll try to give you the nuances. Of which there's a lot."

"As *all* baseball buffs insist," I gibed.

"If you're smart enough to grasp them, wise ass: the delicate balance between offense and defense, relatively little action, each one discrete, and all having to be precisely executed."

"In other words, slow."

"Not slow, deliberate. Maybe I dig it so much because I'd never be good at it."

"I'll take racquetball," I said. "No matter how bad you screw up, you can get it back on the next shot. Here you might not have a chance in the next hour."

"Think of it as Zen. The one American game to really catch on in Japan. Which reminds me, I'm reading *Shogun* now and it's knocking my socks off."

"I'll give baseball my best shot. Could we save Zen for another time?"

"Sure, but shut your yap and watch. The lead-off man's up."

A wiry guy who was the Astros' second baseman made Blue throw pitch after pitch and Gomez hung on every move. But finally, after a bunch of foul balls, the umpire called the guy out on a foul down the third base line not even half way to the bag. "All right!" yelled Gomez, adding to the swell of approval around us.

"I thought you couldn't strike out on a foul."

"You can if it's a bunt. Didn't you see him double-up on the bat?"

"Why should that matter?"

"Fundamental rule: preserves the balance of offense and defense."

Things moved deliberately along, helped by further visits from the beer man, while I got an earful of the infield fly rule, the squeeze play, the strike zone relative to the batter's size and stance, who has the right of way on the base paths, and the sanctity of not having a designated hitter take the pitcher's ups. To Gomez, the road to hell was paved with designated hitters, and the American League had already gone there. Two gritty plays at third, one a successful tag and the other a tag-beating slide, required no explanation, although Gomez and a skinny, sixtyish guy next to him analyzed at length the fine points of how the fielder's throws had affected things.

By the seventh-inning stretch the Giants were ahead 4-2 and Blue sat in favor of a reliever. In fact, that was the final score, but during the change-over the evening became an emotional struggle it was everything I could do to handle, because Gomez delivered a Mad update that was doubly devastating for how matter-of-fact he seemed. She was back from Palm Springs, her husband had taken off to Indonesia for a month, and Gomez had seen her twice since then as far as I could tell.

"Honest to god," he said, lowering his voice, "we did the damnedest thing the other night. We'd been hanging out at my place kind of letting nature take its course, when she jumps up and says we're going to Henry Africa's."

To mask how destroyed I was by this, I intentionally choked on my beer.

"You alright?" he asked.

"Yeah, sure. Sorry," I gasped, buying time. "But what do you two need with a pickup bar?" Needless question, since I knew where the idea came from.

"Exactly what I said. And why drive half way across town for a drink we could have at El Gallito?"

GOMEZ

"So?"

"She wanted to feel the hustle, but float above it. Sit in a corner watching hormones on parade. I dug it more than I like to admit, and Henry's was sure the right place."

There was a sharp crack from the field and the crowd let out a collective groan that turned to a cheer when a long drive streaked past us, hit the left field foul marker and bounced out of bounds. While my attention had been wandering the Astros had put two runners on with one out in the eighth, and only luck saved the Giants from giving up a three-run homer along with the lead. Gomez now refocused on the action, jabbering excitedly to the skinny guy, who was leaning over his shoulder.

Both the Giants and I regrouped and finished the night in face-saving manner, although they recorded a win while my lot was to paper over a loss. If Gomez noticed, I guess he chalked it up to an OD of baseball, which he dealt with by switching subjects to talk about *Shogun* on the way home. Not great literature he took pains to say, but nonetheless a great book — a distinction he seemed to think meant something.

÷ ÷ ÷

With Jordan away on business, Gomez preoccupied by Centro politics, and Mad's favor extending to Clark and him but not me, I regressed badly on the sex front. How I could feel so betrayed made no sense, when constancy had never been the remotest possibility, but betrayed was how I felt. Running should have helped, and believe me, I tried, yet even that let me down.

Three times I went late to Henry Africa's to spy in the windows for Mad, dreading to see her at a corner table with Gomez — or perhaps some guy I wouldn't recognize — looking languid and jaded in a flowing, silky outfit. Other nights I went to The Playpen and the O'Farrell, steeping myself in porn punctuated by fleeting contact with anonymous female flesh. No matter that the movies, as well as the dancers' shaved and stylized nudity, became boring, the compulsion to return overwhelmed me. And on those nights, as a testament to how craven I'd become, I took Mad's panties with me, hidden in my pocket.

GOMEZ

Finally, having neither seen her at Henry's nor found a way to assuage my hurt, I wore them to The Playpen under my trousers in what must have been a bid for maximum self-disgust. They were too small and cut into my scrotum, but I didn't care. I touched myself, felt my hardness press against the smooth black fabric, waited until a dancer who looked as much like Mad as possible began to circulate among the rows of seated men, and commissioned lap dances from her, three, one after another.

Of course she wasn't Mad, however dim the light. She was too thick at the hips and used the wrong perfume, but with each dance she became more accommodating, reaching a hand down to touch me where I'd been told the house rules forbid. By then she'd also mussed my hair and had been softly blowing in my ear.

"What if," she asked in a voice that was clearly private, "I earned myself a tip nobody needs to know about?"

This had never happened before, but maybe it was a benefit of my picking a seat well away from other patrons. And in the thrill of it, beguiled by her emerald thong-bikini and youthful skin, I forgot that there was a new feature to my wardrobe.

"Yeah, what if…" I replied, scrooching slightly forward so her hand could stay in front of her and there'd be no sign that anything extracurricular was going on.

I quickly got very hard and was ready to burst when she teased my fly open an inch and put one finger inside to run it along my nylon-encased cock. Your instinct is to prolong that kind of pleasure, to arch toward the touch, but just as I began doing so, my super-ego rang the alarm. Though her finger had missed the lacy frill at the waistband and the lower hems on her first pass, it would be only a matter of seconds before my secret was out. Peremptorily, I grabbed at her shoulders, pushing her away while I straightened in the seat, then instantly pulled down again so her fanny was centered on my lap.

We were now in a classic posture for the practice of her trade, and she lost no time in rocking her roundness expertly against my shaft to cause a gusher that appalled me and that I tried desperately to conceal. But the dancers all have a sixth sense for it, and the protocol is that they slow and then stop, regardless of whether the music has stopped or not, and ask if you want another dance.

GOMEZ

The guy is supposed to say no, whereupon she collects for services rendered and moves on before dampness can seep to the outside of your trousers. A good system, basically, which Candy — that was the name she gave — and I duly followed. I sheepishly threw in a ten-dollar tip, received a nodding smile, and saw my ten go into the sole of her slipper, separate from the bills clutched in her hand. For that maneuver she temporarily occupied the seat next to me, before standing to bend forward and place the tiniest of goodbye kisses on my temple.

"You should've let me earn my tip," she said, assuming her full height and walking away. "I like it when guys wear that sexy Playboy underwear."

The music for this fiasco had been the new hit *Lay Down, Sally*, which was still blaring while an angular blonde with a Dutch-boy haircut writhed naked on stage. Using her show as cover, I rose before Candy reached the side aisle, drew my raincoat around me and fled in the opposite direction through the lobby and into the street.

I'd taken a cab down, but decided to walk home. At least in foggy SF you can wear a raincoat at night year-round without looking out of place. And on these shameful outings I always did, because submitting yourself to public inspection with a spreading wet spot on the front of your pants was a bad alternative. It's better not to lose control, but you have to be prepared.

÷ ÷ ÷

My close call with humiliation had additional consequences. For one, negative conditioning must have set in, because I haven't been to The Playpen since, and I've almost stopped straying into similar venues. I say almost, since I really am trying to be honest here, and claiming greater purity would be a lie. What is true, though, is that I've had no further periods of — well, addiction, for lack of a better word — when I go back night after night, hating what I'm doing yet powerless to stay away.

For another, I was forced to launder Mad's panties — by hand in my own bathroom, of course — to rid them of my stink, which pretty much denatured them for all purposes. The barest hint of her cinnamon perfume survived, but the essential leavening of seaweed was gone and my final connection to that surreal evening at Gomez's seemed to go with it. I possessed by devious means a pair of women's underwear, I kept them hidden inside an old pair of hiking socks in the far reaches of my dresser, and that was that. Also, running started to work again as a diversion, which allowed me to feel OK about myself for the first time in weeks.

But then, almost as soon as I'd come to terms with her offhand dismemberment of my life, Mad did call. The real Anaïs Nin would have a metaphysical explanation for such uncanny timing, but Mad offered nothing beyond a recent trip to see her mother in LA, which had lasted longer than planned. That this coincided with troubling events on my end through most of April was apparently happenstance, however much it had felt otherwise. Nor would those events ever be revealed to her. In fact, I was chided for not having left even one message at the Mime Troupe she could have received and returned while away. I had been on the verge of trying more than once, but what seemed like the certainty of being rebuffed had paralyzed me.

Her call came on a Sunday afternoon at home when it could as well have been my parents, which is what I anticipated when I heard the ring.

"Hi, it's Mad."

"Oh, yes, hi." If the sub-floor hadn't been reinforced concrete, I might have melted through it.

"Are you alone?"

"Sure, why?"

"You sound guarded, like we might have to speak in code. Anyway, I've been thinking about you a lot."

"It hasn't seemed that way."

"I know, I'm sorry I didn't call sooner. I was away with Clark and again because of my mother's breast cancer."

"Sounds bad. I hope she's OK."

It was supposedly in remission, Mad told me, although disfiguring surgery had been required the previous year, and her mother was still weak from the follow-up chemo. "But I'm home now," she added, "and Clark is out of the country. You didn't call me either, you know."

I promised to do better, once again kicking myself for being so passive, and finally came around to the inevitable name. "Gomez told me about Palm Springs, but he didn't mention LA."

GOMEZ

"I don't think he knew. It came up fairly suddenly. I do have a confession, though."

"About what?"

"I took him to Henry Africa's...you know, the way you described your friend as doing. It was fun, too, but I should have taken you first. I wish we'd had time the night I dashed off to meet Clark."

"It doesn't really matter." I was lying, of course, yet why relive a source of pain when the voice I most wanted to hear was saturating my consciousness?

"There's something else I've wanted to do. Can you come over here Tuesday night? Gomez refuses because of Clark, so I don't ask him anymore, but I could make it quite special."

"Honestly, Gomez's place was pretty weird, in the midst of all his things. Even if I don't know Clark, your place might have the same aura."

"No, no, I have my own space...my studio. I wouldn't be comfortable in Clark's and my bed either."

"OK...what time?" I would have caved regardless, but the studio made it easier.

"Nine o'clock at 385 Blair Road. If you have something to write on, here's the directions."

÷ ÷ ÷

Piedmont may be contiguous with Oakland, but it's another world. In fact, Arch Street, where I'd lived in Berkeley, and that I remembered as being classy, might not meet Piedmont's zoning codes. The streets are overhung with mature trees, mostly sycamores, and lined with those graceful old street lamps that look like fluted asparagus stalks with phosphorescent tips. And at night, hardly a car goes by or is visible, because parking at the curb is tightly restricted.

As for dwellings, 3,000 square feet would be on the small side, with at least 4,000 the norm, and the overgrown ranch-style houses typical of the Bay Area's other toney suburbs a rarity. Instead, two and three-story affairs of stone, brick or stucco predominate, set on large lots with expanses of lawn and foliage. To drive slowly along checking the directions Mad had provided, even in a new Audi, made me wonder about attracting the police on suspicion that I was a jewel thief.

Dense shrubs, oleander and ficus, shrouded Mad's driveway, where the address, nowhere else visible, was painted on the curb. I drove past and circled back, rehearsing what my exit route would be if I needed one, and making sure that I'd arrive exactly at nine. Toward the house, once I pulled in, the drive widened into a parking apron with a detached, three-car garage on the right and the house to the left. It was stucco, a two-story neo-Mediterranean villa with broad, rectangular windows and a flagstone walk curving up to the door.

Nice, no question, you'd have to say very nice, but approximately mid-range for the neighborhood in terms of size and design. A shallow, arched portico projected from the front wall to shelter the door, which was lit by a single bulb in a torchiere of black metal. The door itself was of heavy planks with hand-smithed black studs and metal strapping, all held in place by three large hinges of the same material. I was in a state of advanced excitement, sexual and every other way, when my finger found the button in the doorjamb and produced a gong sound within.

I'd been expecting Mad, and wondering what exotic headgear—a turban, perhaps—she would effect this time, or whether she'd be naked under a kimono or sarong, but the person confronting me was short, with straight, ear-length, black hair, tobacco-brown skin and flat, compressed features. Her eyes, though, gave signs of a smile, and so did her voice.

"*Buenas noches, Señor* Paul. My name is Graciela, please come in."

"Oh, hello, glad to meet you." I stepped inside.

Graciela was forty, if I had to guess, and wore a maid's dress of black cotton with white cuffs and a white apron. She backed away from me across the terra-cotta tiles of the entryway and onto the polished wooden floor of the hall and living room. Mad and Clark had opted for a Spanish Colonial look, but the pieces were well selected and not overtly massive. I've had so much reason to think back on that night I wish I'd spent an extra minute to fix more of the household details in my mind. The only one to stick was a full-size Gustav Klimt reproduction of very high quality, in a gilded frame hung in the stairway landing, a semi-nude woman, in profile, posed against a gold-embossed background of peacock feathers.

"*Señora* Madeline waits for you in the cottage," Graciela said. She turned and looked over her shoulder. "Come this way. It is behind the garage."

I followed Graciela down the hall, out the rear of the house and across a stone patio, where she stopped. "There," she said, pointing to the right.

A path of crushed granite led across a low garden of rosemary, sage, agapanthus and geranium. White flecks of lemon blossom showed on a dwarf tree at the far end and their sweet smell broadcast in the air. Flanked by stands of bamboo, a modest shingled structure in the manner of Julia Morgan stood beyond the garden, along the lot line, emitting a glow of golden light from its partly open door.

"When I first come," Graciela observed, "I think I hab' to live out there, but *Señora* Madeline so generous she give me big room in main house."

"Thank you, Graciela," I said. "*Buenas noches.*"

"*De nada, Señor* Paul. Hab' a nice bisit."

Φ Φ Φ

PART IV

The hider must have a seeker. That is the game. A seeker who is not too cruel. Not too observant.

> John Fowles
> *The Magus*
> Revised Edition, 1977

GOMEZ

CHAPTER 16

It's amazing what your mind can compress into forty or fifty seconds, in this case eight months of my life in the time it took to exit the Embarcadero Freeway on my way home from Mad's and find the ramp for Golden Gateway's underground parking. Maybe second-hand smoke from her Thai weed or the mood left by the *luminaria* in her cottage had amplified the effect, but what would a novelist need to cover that much background? A hundred pages at least, which would take hours to read.

And by morning, fundamental things about my life did seem to have changed. I was at an all-time peak in expressing my sexuality, with the understanding that more would follow, and though Gomez was still my sponsor in being a full-fledged male, I wasn't beholden to him in the same way. He was centrally involved, but no longer just in the sense of winking and handing out puzzles in which Mad had little interest. Now he himself was the puzzle and she was completely signed on.

I lost no time the next night in calling Jordan to pursue the Yale angle, but I got a recording on one of those new machines that let you leave a message. I wondered how much installation was involved and what he'd paid for it. The idea that I could have a truly private home answering service had great appeal. No worry about snooping intermediaries like Ivy at the office, and if Mad called day or night, I'd absolutely know.

Meanwhile, maintaining normalcy with Gomez in other respects became imperative, so I decided to work seriously on the envelope problem. I didn't take a wad of ones out of the bank or get ten envelopes and number them, but I dug up an old spiral binder, wrote GOMEZ on the front with a marking pen, and labeled the first ten pages as Envelope 1, Envelope 2, Envelope 3, etc. Then I tore out a couple of back pages for scratch paper and jotted a list of math concepts, drawing on vague memories from my engineering classes and buzz I'd overheard from Jenny and her lab colleagues.

GOMEZ

GOAL: Array one-dollar bills in ten sealed envelopes such that a person asking for any amount between $1 and $1000 can be given exactly that amount without opening any of the envelopes.

Possible Solutions:

Factorials

prime numbers

irrational numbers

roots/powers: square, cube, quadratic

logarithms

geometric progressions

golden sections

The last is a design parameter dating back to ancient Greece, something I learned after my switch from slide-rule land. I doubted it would apply. I threw it in mainly as a morale booster, so I'd understand at least one of the items without the need for further research. They were also related to a famous numerical sequence with a name I couldn't quite remember, but that would go on the list, too, when I did. Reopening the binder, I wrote $1 on the Envelope-One page and $500 on the Envelope-Ten page. Not much, yet as far as I'd gotten in thinking about a solution, since Mad had offered no suggestions.

The only way to give someone $1, if that's what they asked for, would be an envelope containing a single bill. Also, if you had a single, your other nine envelopes could be even numbers, since you could always add $1 to get any possible odd number. The envelope with $500 seemed equally obvious. If you could cover all amounts from one to five hundred with the first nine envelopes, adding $500 would let you cover any amount from $501 to a thousand.

By then I was spread out on my glass-topped dining table, with the leavings of my TV dinner pushed aside and a refill of chardonnay. I'd run the length of Embarcadero after work, showered, and was enough into Gomez's puzzle to have hit on prime numbers as a likely solution. I wasn't familiar with all their properties, but I knew what primes were and that 2 was the lowest. Since $1 was a given, logic favored a series starting at 2. On another scratch sheet I sandwiched the beginning eight primes between the first and last values I'd arbitrarily deduced: [$1] 2, 3, 5, 7, 11, 13, 17, 19 [$500].

Less promising than hoped. So many primes were of low value that you'd have to discard some and move up the series or you would run out of envelopes. But where did the discarding start and where did it stop? Without certain low values in, you couldn't fill all the later gaps. It also looked as though primes could only be summed into an exhaustive sequence of 1,000 ordinal integers if you treated some of them as negative numbers when needed. Since there's no such thing as an envelope containing minus dollars, Gomez would have died laughing if I brought him that.

Irrational numbers, like the square root of six, or $\sqrt{6}$, proved useless as well. The integer series comprised of their squares began helpfully at 2, but quickly showed the same drawbacks as primes. At a loss, but just in case it had some relevance after all, I then placed at the bottom of my list the 12-quadrillion numerical palindrome I remembered from his hint. Maybe seeing it on the page would spark new ideas, although I had no intention of getting myself sidetracked into trying the calculation. For all I knew, the X in $X=\sqrt{12{,}345{,}678{,}987{,}654{,}321}$ would turn out to be irrational anyway. My dictionary, not an *OED* but a good one, had already proven useful for mathematical definitions, and further consultations were clearly in the offing.

Yet with those thoughts came a jarring pang of loss over Jenny. She had all this stuff nailed. Not that I'd cheat and ask her the solution, but she would know off the top of her head the properties of factorials, primes, irrationals and on down the list, which would have prevented many false starts like those I'd just made. In fact, she would love to be asked, and I could seemingly hear her voice and her clipped accent tossing ideas around over coffee on our sunny back patio in Berkeley. However much I'd buried the feelings, our marriage hadn't been about nothing.

And now, other than to call her at work, which I stopped doing soon after she left me, I didn't even know for sure where she lived. I had the phone number for Barbara's place, where Jenny had moved initially, but she would surely have used her share of the Arch Street proceeds to find them a better address. There was a strong chance Jenny would have a listed phone either way, so it would be no trick to call information, and I considered picking up the phone.

GOMEZ

What prevented it was remembering that Jenny hadn't called me at home or at work since escrow on our house had closed. Not once.

Gomez had a theory that women were never really done with their ex-spouses or lovers. If a guy has been significant in their lives, they invariably wanted to be friends and gain validation by tapping the lingering regard they assumed you held for them. It might take a while, he said, for their feelings to coalesce and for them to make contact, but they always did. I asked if that had been true for Donna, his ex.

"Of course," he said. "Mad will, too, when the time comes. And so will Jenny. That's why I brought it up. Think ahead to how you want to react when she does."

"Jenny'll be the exception," I told him, keeping the possibility at arm's length.

Sitting there months later, looking at my GOMEZ notebook and scratch paper, I realized that subconsciously I had wanted him to be right. I wanted Jenny to call and to try to initiate something, a coffee date, dinner, something. And if she did, it was no longer automatic that I'd refuse. Instead, with my confidence newly armored by Mad, I might say yes and enjoy being unattainable.

The phone rang so loudly I started and sent my pencil skittering onto the floor. No, it couldn't be Jenny. I felt dumb entertaining the idea. But perhaps Mad, which gave me a flutter of a different sort, though a far better chance that it was Gomez, and I'd better loosen up and act natural. If I inadvertently gave away Mad's and my latest gambit, he would quash any chance I had at a real relationship with her before it began.

I waited two more rings and answered with a bored, "Hello."

"Paul, Jordan here. What's this question you have?"

"Turns out to be two questions. For openers, where'd you get that slick phone machine?"

"A Panasonic. The latest thing. You like it?"

"Enough to know I want one. As long as they don't take my whole wallet."

"Less than a hundred bucks at Good Guys on Chestnut Street. I'd invite you over to see it and meet Marnie, but we just got in from dinner and she's freshening up for…activities of a more private nature."

"Understood. My main question was if you could help me find a Yale alum who I think lives in the Bay Area."

"Highly possible. What's his name and when did he graduate?"

"Andrew Steentofter, spelled S-T-E-E-N. I'm not sure of the graduation date."

"I don't recall hearing of him. How old is he?"

"Thirty-eight or so."

"Oh, a youngster. Let's see...that would mean class of '61, probably. I'll check 1959 through '63. All the records are by year. You never mentioned having a Yale friend."

"He's not," I said. "I'm trying to help out a woman I know."

"Would she be the alluring creature you've hinted about?"

"Yes, pretty much."

"Well, bravo. Glad to do it. She'll think you're a man of great influence. I'll get back to you tomorrow."

"OK, thanks. The years you're targeting sound right."

A week ago, the thought that Jordan was consorting with Marnie not fifty feet from where I sat would have been quite unsettling. As it was, I straightened my apartment, thought about my morning wardrobe, read a little more Anaïs Nin, and got an early start on a good night's sleep. And the following night, awaiting Jordan's call, it didn't bother me to know that Mad and Gomez were out dancing to Brazilian music. That was their scene, not mine.

"I half wondered if I'd get a recording," Jordan joked, when I answered on the first ring. "Last time we spoke, you sounded ready to buy."

"This coming weekend for sure. Any luck with my missing Yalie?"

"No sign of him."

The excitement I felt didn't wholly override my disappointment. As much as I liked conspiring with Mad, I wanted Gomez left intact. "Is that conclusive?"

"Far from it. I only checked the old rosters from when I served as secretary, then called the fellow who's in office now. In other words, for the class years where we'd expect to see this Steentofter, he doesn't show as subscribing to the Yale magazine and hasn't been in touch with our local association to supply an address."

"That's quite a bit. All I could reasonably ask."

"Actually, there's one more thing. I could call Yale itself. No reason not to. They'll confirm his degree, but they won't give an address unless he's current with his alumni dues and has indicated he wants to be contacted."

"As long as you don't mind. He played football there, too, he says."

"I thought you didn't know him."

"Oh...I don't. Just what I've heard."

"Still useful. Sports give us second line of inquiry. Do you happen to know what college he was in?"

"I thought Yale was a college."

"Residence college. That's how Yale is organized."

"No, I don't." Nor did I remember Gomez's having said a thing about residence colleges.

"Too bad. Might have helped. I'll pursue the football connection, but would it shock you if Steentofter turns out to be a fraud?"

The answer was still yes, despite the blind leads so far. "What makes you ask?"

"Well, I ran into your L-W client Matts Freytag at lunch yesterday. I told him you and I are neighbors and he sends a hello."

"Oh, good."

"Matts was class of 1960, so I asked if he knew an Andrew Steentofter. He didn't, which might not mean much. Yale is a good-sized institution. But Matts played football there himself. Not a star, necessarily, but on the team. See what I mean?"

"Yeah, sounds like Matts would have to know him." Especially, I thought, since Gomez had once claimed to know Matts.

"Perhaps Steentofter is out to impress your lady friend with his athletic prowess. Or perhaps he went to Podunk U. and thinks Yale is a better pedigree. I'll dig a bit more, but so far things don't smell right. May take a few days, though."

"I appreciate this a lot, Jordan. Thanks. A few days is great. Let's have dinner again some night."

"Fine. And I still want you to meet Marnie. Could we include your new gal and make it the four us?"

"Not just yet."

"I can be patient where the chance to meet beautiful women is concerned."

"On that score," I said, "you wouldn't be disappointed."

GOMEZ

I wondered, though, if he might eventually propose other kinds of foursomes, an option I never wanted Mad presented with. For all I knew, she'd be receptive, and it was bad enough worrying that a threesome involving Gomez and me was already on her mind — or perhaps his. If so, the investigation she and I had launched should blunt that off by serving as a wedge between us and him. Even in porn films group groping didn't much appeal to me, and I had no intention of adding it to my life.

÷ ÷ ÷

Saturday I did acquire an answering machine, which I spent a good part of the afternoon wrestling out of the box and learning to operate. Then I went for a run, ate at MacArthur Park across the square from my building, and saw a really dumb movie, *Animal House*, at the Gateway Cinema downstairs. A couple I recognized from the restaurant were in the ticket line, so we sat together and were seemingly the only disappointed patrons in the house. Their names were Bob and Carol Houser. They lived on a shoulder of Telegraph Hill, and asked for my number, saying they'd invite me over.

Sunday and Monday I worked my fanny off on behalf of L-W's secret technology client, but continued to think about Jenny. It would be an extra reward to have the first message be from her, and hoped she'd think a recording device meant that I was much in demand socially. But even if she wasn't first, I'd bought spare tapes, and when she did call, I planned to remove the one with her voice so it wouldn't get erased.

Imagining that Jenny would call just because I'd focused my thoughts on her smacks of parapsychology, which I don't believe in, but stranger things had already happened. Look how my situation with Mad worked out. I also had a fantasy that I'd get Jenny and Mad on the same tape, that they'd both be asking to meet me somewhere, and that I'd play their voices back afterward any time I wanted.

Instead, the first message was from Gomez, giving me grief over how decadent my new toy was. And it's true, I had set the machine to pick up quickly so that I'd have to interrupt it to talk, letting me first hear who was there and how they were reacting to a

GOMEZ

Paul who was a little less available. The directions said I could then record a whole conversation without the caller's knowledge by just letting the tape run. In Gomez's case, though, I hadn't been home, and no one else had called yet to play into my scheme.

His message was, "Christ, I hate these things! If you aren't going to pick up your phone, have it disconnected. Be honest, like me. I don't pretend to want calls at home. Anyway, time for more racquetball, and you've got to catch this new flick, *Annie Hall*. I saw it last night at Serramonte and was knocked out. So call me, dork-face, when you want to sweat."

The next message wasn't Jenny either, and again I hadn't been there. It was Jordan, saying, "Well done, fellow technophile. Imitation is the sincerest form of flattery. The Yale alumni office can't verify your man Steentofter, and they don't find him in football team photos in the relevant yearbooks. I don't know that I'd go to court on this evidence, but the guy seems phony. Or maybe he attended and dropped out. Keep in touch."

First thing next morning I called the Mime Troupe from work. "What's wrong with you, man?" came a strangled male voice on the other end. "She's never here this early. Nobody is. I wouldn't be myself if I wasn't sleeping on the floor."

"How about taking a message for her?"

"If I have to. Is it about money?"

"Could be."

"OK, shoot. We've all got to eat."

"Tell her to call Paul Stiles at L-W Design right away."

"She have the number?"

"Yes," I replied, and he hung up.

The following afternoon, Mad called back and Ivy put her through without further comment. "Hi," Mad began, "I'm guessing you have news, or did you just want to hear my sweet voice?"

"Why not both?" I longed to dive through the phone wires and be where I could see, smell and touch her.

"That would be better than news alone," she replied warmly.

"Can we meet for a drink? Today? A little bird from Yale's been whispering in my ear."

"Today would be hard. Why can't you tell me now?"

"Too complicated. And we need to decide what's next...you know, on our project. How about Pier 23, near my office, on the little deck out back?"

"Alright," she sighed. "At five. Clark can think I was delayed in traffic. It's so easy to hop on the bridge from there, maybe I'll be OK. The problem is, he and I are going to a symphony concert tonight in Berkeley."

"Well, I really want to see you."

"I want to see you, too."

It's a short walk from L-W to Pier 23 so I got there almost on the dot. After making sure nobody I knew was in the bar, and that Mad hadn't arrived, I ordered two glasses of the house cabernet and carried them past the saucy, bare-assed cowgirl mural in the hall and out to the deck. As I'd hoped, it was deserted, with more breeze and gathering fog than the trendy after-work crowd wanted to deal with. In flat, dull light, I sat at the farthest of three weathered picnic tables and sipped from my glass, listening to gulls screech, and to bay wavelets slap the pilings.

Mad, dazzling but unorthodox as ever, joined me a minute later. "Wine," she smiled approvingly. "Just what I need to beat this weather."

Her feet were in wedge-soled black mules, while the tight leggings of her usual black leotard served as both stockings and slacks. Over her shoulders, extending to mid-thigh, was a heavy cable-knit sweater of natural, undyed wool. She wore no makeup except her kohl eye-liner, and had her hair entirely tucked into a loden-green cloche hat. Before sitting, she leaned across the table to place a mesmerizingly demure kiss on my cheek. "Hi," I breathed into her ear.

"Sorry I'm such a mess. We were doing inventory today."

"Nothing I see resembles mess." All my feelings for Mad at this point were dangerously ill-advised, but I let myself revel in them. "I just hope you're not parked on the sidewalk."

"No," she laughed. "Legal this time, but still free...a broken meter on Greenwich. Regardless, I can't stay long." She tipped her glass toward me, then drank.

I returned the gesture. "Quite a wonderful hat," I said.

"Thanks. It's borrowed from one of the costume hampers we were going through."

GOMEZ

"A nice fringe benefit."

"Definitely." She settled further into her seat. "But please...tell me about Gomez. Was he not at Yale?"

"That's how it looks. Or he went briefly and dropped out. There's no alumni record for Steentofter my friend can find."

"As I suspected. Kind of sad, don't you think."

"Very sad," I agreed. "Where do we go from here?"

"What do you mean?" Perhaps due to the breeze, Mad's head was down slightly, but even filtered through her lashes, her glance was direct.

"You questioned other things...and since then, so have I. If Yale is false, it doesn't mean all the rest are. He still could have played college football. Something wrecked his leg and knee."

"I know. It's hard to imagine how he dances the way he does, and chases you around the racquetball court."

"That's why we need a master list...of what should be checked out, which items to work on next, and who'll do it, you or me." I'd brought my briefcase, and had begun carrying the GOMEZ notebook around in hope that math puzzle ideas would pop into my head at random moments. I reached under the table to feel in the center pouch for the spiral binding.

"Yes," Mad nodded, "we do need a list. I've forgotten some of the things already, and I don't know how many I can take on. But what on earth is that?" She pointed to the notebook. "You even have his name on the cover."

"It's for the envelope puzzle," I explained. "We can use a blank page at the back for our list."

"A whole notebook for that silly puzzle?" Mad rolled her eyes impatiently.

"Yes, it's tricky and I'm still cranking on it. Why?"

"I bet he acts so super-smart all the time because he *didn't* go to Yale. I'll try to help with the background check, but don't count on me for math."

"I don't mind. I'll figure the thing out. It's fun."

"For you, maybe. But here's what. When you solve it, we'll have an excuse to make him take both of us to Hayes Street. We're bound to have unraveled more of his life by then, and we can lay it on him face to face. We won't be mean, but we'll call his bluff. The Gomez persona is such a work of art he should keep it as long as we're in on the joke. We can help him shine. You know… Andrés Gomez, written up in Herb Caen and getting invited to ritzy parties. Wouldn't that be a riot?"

"It would if he goes along, but don't be too sure he will."

Her eyes were simultaneously mocking and serious. "Madeline Klein," she stated, "can be *very* persuasive."

I laughed. "A verifiable claim. One I've seen in action."

"Then, come on, Paul. Really. I have to hurry."

I flipped open the binder and we huddled over it, flattening the pages against the table to evade the wind, and prompting each other while I wrote furiously. Our brainstorming captured the three items she'd cited in her Piedmont cottage last week, along with a number of others neither of us had voiced.

"Spinoza!" Mad burst out. "And Teflon! Those are too rich! He's never brought them up, or his Communist parents, either."

"What about the Mitchell Brothers porn audition?"

"He showed me the photo. I thought it was hysterical, but I believed it. Just the kind of thing he'd do." She laughed with delight, as though this was the most fun she'd ever had. "Oh, and one more. We already have EST, but put down that he supposedly knows Anaïs's brother. He must have invented that to impress me, too."

By the time we were done Mad was shivering and had pulled her hands inside the sleeves of her sweater. I felt cold, too, and put my jacket collar up. Walking toward the door into the bar so she could leave, Mad stayed close to me and wrapped both her arms around one of mine. "Another warm San Francisco night," she joked, "like the old rock song."

"Yeah, that guy'd never been here," I responded.

She stretched to kiss me glancingly on the lips. "I've got to run," she said. "Too bad we don't have time to get personal." She brushed a hand across the front of my trousers and I felt a surging erection.

"Yes, too bad," I replied, stopping to press my groin against the side of her sweater where it bloused below her hip. The contour of the hat made her eyes seem larger and her mouth all the more bewitching.

"Lack of time is just part of it," she said. "I'm not in full form. I've got my period."

GOMEZ

I gave her a doubting look, as humor, but also because her remark evoked a memory of past subterfuge. "No, I mean it," she protested. "For real. But I have a fabulous plan for our next…*encounter*. You'll have to be patient."

"That might be easier if you'd kept your hand to yourself a few seconds ago."

"I know, but I wanted to see how naughty you can be. What if you masturbate at nine o'clock tonight? I'll imagine you're coming inside me while I'm at the concert with Clark."

CHAPTER 17

What I did after getting home from Pier 23 may be obvious, but at least I waited until the appointed hour.

Before that bout of telepathic eroticism, as if to show that my sexual compulsions were under control, I clearheadedly fixed dinner, reworked the Gomez questions Mad and had I drafted at Pier 23, and made further progress on the envelope puzzle. Anal-retentive or not, my neat list of math concepts had been worth the effort, and I applied the same technique to Gomez, putting his various phantasmagoria in chronological order. Mad and I had also parceled out the labor on certain items and agreed that the others would remain up in the air. I listed that, too, by adding either our initials or a double question mark in parentheses after each entry.

I was pretty pleased with the result, so I planned to Xerox one for Mad at L-W the next day and mail it to her office. None of the items were earthshaking, of course, which is what made them fun. The original I kept, stapled into the GOMEZ notebook.

<u>Items in Question re: Gomez (a.k.a. Andrew Steentofter)</u>
Spinoza is a blood relative (??)
Father/mother were Communists, 1930s (??)
Family resided in Bennington, Vermont, 1940s/50s (??)
Father invented Teflon, approx. 1950s (PS)
College football scholarship, late 1950s (PS)
Yale graduate, approx. 1961 (PS and MK)
Resided in Greenwich Village, early 1960s (??)
Lived/worked in Buenos Aires, Argentina, mid 1960s (MK)
UC grad student - Ph.D. Ren. Lit., late 1960s/early 70s (MK)
Faculty, Stillman Coll., Alabama, late 1960s/early 70s (MK ??)
Black Panther Party congressional candidate, approx. 1970 (??)
Friend of Joaquín Nin (brother of Anaïs), 1970s (MK)

GOMEZ

Attended EST session in SF, early 1977 (MK)
Auditioned for Mitchell Brothers porn film, late 1977 (PS)

The reason I offered to pursue Teflon was that Jordan had said his firm did patents, so he could point the way. Yale I was done with unless Jordan provided a new lead, but I could easily inquire at the O'Farrell Theater to find out if the Mitchells held porn auditions and if they took photos of the sort Gomez had shown me. That I was already familiar with the theater and its environs wasn't something Mad needed to know.

She planned to ask at Las Pampas Restaurant about the Argentina story. She'd become friendly with the owner and thought he would help on the q.t. We both knew from the *Dairies* that Anaïs had a brother who was a performing musician in Europe, though how Gomez could possibly be in his social circle defied imagining. The specifics had been kept vague because Gomez was supposedly going to surprise Mad with an invitation to meet the brother. The best she could do was nose around among her Nin fan club contacts to learn if the brother was still alive and where. She also had a potential way to unearth things at UCB, and if that panned out, Gomez's file would have to show where he'd done his undergrad work and might include material related to his teaching at Stillman. Lastly, she would use a connection from her EST days to see if he was known there.

Through Jenny I had my own *in* at the University, but I'd persuaded Mad that Jenny would be risky because she knew the Steentofter name from when Gomez painted our house. My real concern, though, was an absolute unwillingness to ask Jenny for a favor. I was determined that she'd call me, and if I had to wait forever, I would. The remaining items on the list were too obscure or too geographically remote to do much with.

As for the other puzzle, the math one, I ruled out four more possibilities and decided what to home in on. Jenny liked to say that the most important thing you can know in science is that what you're working on *has* a solution. Next is to learn the incorrect answers, because eventually you'll learn the correct one. Both precepts were applicable; I knew there was a solution, and I was recognizing blind leads more and more quickly. By the time I put it aside, the page of concepts looked like this:

GOAL: Array one-dollar bills in ten sealed envelopes such that a person asking for any amount between $1 and $1000 can be given exactly that amount without opening any of the envelopes.

Possible Solutions:

~~Factorials~~

~~prime numbers~~

~~irrational numbers~~

roots/powers: square, cube, quadratic

~~logarithms~~

geometric progressions

~~golden sections~~

(Clue?? X=$\sqrt{12{,}345{,}678{,}987{,}654{,}321}$)

~~Fibonacci numbers~~

Irrationals and primes I had already axed, and factorials were another waste. Not only were many of the gaps between calculated values too large to fill with combinations of the other values, you'd drastically exceed the $500 you were trying to work with by the time only six of the first nine envelopes had been used—assuming, that is, you always started with $1 and Envelope Ten always held $500. What I mean is, alone $6! = $720, and the progression of $1!, $2!, $3!, $4!, $5! and $6! sums to $873, with envelopes seven, eight and nine left over. Then, when you added $500 from Envelope Ten, the total became a very unhelpful $1,373. Still, doodling with factorials gave me two insights.

The first nine envelopes didn't have to add to exactly $500, nor did the tenth have to contain exactly $500 either. As long as every preceding integer in the total of the first nine envelopes could be produced from some combination among those nine, their total could exceed—but not be less than—$500. Whatever dollars remained from the $1,000 grand total would go into the tenth envelope. Moreover, you didn't have to use all of the envelopes. Some could actually be empty without affecting the answer.

Like factorials, logarithms were also worthless. They're not integers, but I remembered from my first engineering class the orderly progression of their mantissa segments in the tables we used. The contents of Envelope Two might correspond to the rounded off mid-point, for example, of the Log 2 table, and Envelope Three to that same point in Log 3, etc. Upon checking, though, nothing enabled me to extract a discrete subset from the continuum of values, nor would the potential dollar amounts in those ranges represent a solution.

Next to go were golden sections, redundant because they have the same 1:1.618 internal ratio as Fibonacci numbers, whose name I'd finally dug from memory so I could look them up. And for a while, Fibonaccis seemed promising. The beginning series is: 1, 1, 2, 3, 5, 8, 13, 21, 34, 55, 89, and so on. What grabbed me was that you could combine various of the envelopes to fill all the gaps. But there was a fatal defect; even modifying the sequence to exclude the first of the duplicate $1 envelopes, the next nine Fibonaccis totaled to a paltry $142, far short of the $500 I needed.

Regardless, valuable knowledge had been gained. The correct series would start slowly and get large fairly fast, though not too fast. Since both the surviving concepts, roots/powers and geometric progressions, could satisfy those conditions, I'd put in a solid night's work. The 12 quadrillion numerical hint he'd been so casual about might even come in handy, if only to disprove something else.

Then the moment arrived for my virtual date with Mad, so after putting the scratch sheets and the GOMEZ notebook back in my briefcase, I retrieved her panties from their hiding place and fed my lewdness with the last traces of her cinnamon perfume.

And for once, I didn't feel pathetic or degraded. I had permission, so it wasn't in the usual sense a solitary act. During our Berkeley years Jenny had explained pheromones to me, and I wondered if Mad's could have survived the washing. All mammals secrete them, Jenny said, to trigger mating behavior. Since they are technically odorless, it was an unanswerable question, but the panties did seem to heighten things.

Not that heightening was required. I had experienced Mad's touch to a critical part of my anatomy only hours before, and by now knew her body and appetites more than well enough to summon inflammatory images. Reality, in fact, mixed with fantasy in ways that were difficult to distinguish.

Later, in the dark with the covers pulled up, I tried to comprehend how it was that I'd lived eight years as a married man with a drawer full of women's panties in my bedroom and had never been motivated to investigate much less abscond with a pair. I also wondered what Gomez did with the specimens Mad apparently left under his pillow from time to time, and I wondered about her sex life with Clark.

Jealousy would be stupid—and futile—but I *was* curious. Asking Mad directly was one approach, if the moment seemed right and it wouldn't put a pall over our time together. Or maybe Gomez knew, and with some minor prompting would supply answers without too much digression into the Zen of underwear fetishes. Still, we'd all done so well relying on unspoken acknowledgment there was no reason to press matters.

And in the same mode, I had gradually accepted Mad's vision that a soon-to-be defrocked Gomez would remain sufficiently intact to continue as the nucleus of the Three Musketeers. Together, perhaps we *would* conquer new worlds, with an increased truthfulness among ourselves, and a subtly outrageous facade to present to everyone else. The notion that Paul Stiles from Topeka, Kansas could be comfortable in such a life didn't even seem that much of a stretch.

Next morning, in preparation for mailing Mad's copy of the Gomez list, I composed the following note to accompany it:

> Thursday
> May 18, 1978
> Hi— Here's our homework assignments. Due dates are flexible, but let's compare as we go. I hope you were thinking about me last night during the concert, because I was certainly thinking of you. Did they play Ravel's *Bolero*?
> The Third Musketeer

÷ ÷ ÷

GOMEZ

The rest of the month Mad was with Clark and out of circulation as far as Gomez and I were concerned. We continued our racquetball contests, and he had a new favorite song, *Two Out of Three Ain't Bad*, by a raspy-voiced rocker named Meatloaf. Driving in the Ranchero or in my Audi, Gomez would search the radio dial and sing along. Beyond that, he was so keen on *Annie Hall* he wanted to go again—with me. He was right, too. Very clever and funny, and even though it involved the end of a relationship, it didn't leave me feeling down. Thanks to him and Mad, I really was getting over Jenny.

I had also become so used to the tap-dance of pretending our three-way *ménage* wasn't happening when we all knew it was that concealing Mad's and my burrowing into Gomez's past felt like more of the same. Rather than his being offended, it could be that he expected it, that he'd intentionally baited us with the grandiosity of his claims. But with this second—real or false—secret to keep, I became less cautious with the first.

The hats and style Diane Keaton had affected as Annie in the film gave me such a strong sense of Mad on the deck at Pier 23, which was the last time I'd seen her, I took the conversation in a normally proscribed direction when Gomez and I hit the Washington Square Bar and Grill afterward. We were at a front table along the wood-paneled interior wall, he seemed preoccupied, and the place was boisterously crowded.

"From what I hear," my foray began, "what's-his-name... Clark...is in town, and Mad has been a scarce commodity for the rest of the world."

"You got it," he affirmed, taking a pull on his beer. He face was aimed past me, toward the back of the room. "Geez, there's every kind of local politicos in here tonight."

"I'm glad somebody would know," I replied. "Not me."

"Well, take my word. I'm talking Mel Wax, one of the mayor's top honchos, Willie Brown visiting from Sacramento, and Corey Busch, Moscone's press guy, who helped keep the Giants from moving to Toronto. And damned if everybody's maverick, Quentin Kopp, isn't in another booth."

"Yeah, but my question was about Mad." I craned around for a quick look and recognized Willie Brown in a back corner, as though posed for a media shot.

GOMEZ

"Right," Gomez answered. "We went dancing at the Hyatt just before what's-his-name got home, and I've seen her once for lunch since. How about you?"

"She left a message at my place a few days ago to say hi." Which was true, but it was more than hi. She'd expressed satisfaction with how nasty I was, regretted that *Bolero* hadn't been on the concert program, and said she'd started some of her homework. And yes, I had removed the tape and saved it.

"That damned machine," Gomez groaned. "I'm going to boycott the thing or just give you the raspberry."

"Great, I'll know exactly who called. But I'm curious. What do you suppose goes on between Mad and what's-his-name that she acts so…so unmarried?"

"I never ask," Gomez replied. "Her problem. I don't know, I don't want to know. Ask her yourself if you're that curious."

"Whatever, it's hard to figure. You think he's impotent? They don't have kids. Or is it one of these open marriages you read about in the Sunday supplements?" This was as bold as I could imagine myself being.

"Told you, I don't know. Maybe he's a swinger, maybe he doesn't give a shit. I dig being with her, she has limits, and I roll with them. I'm too busy now to have a demanding relationship anyway. Oh, are you guys still working on the math puzzle? Has Mad been much help?"

"She has…as indirect inspiration, I guess you'd say." I thought he might laugh. "But I'm getting real close, and when I solve it, Mad wants the Musketeers to all have dinner at Hayes Street."

He remained distracted. "So she says. Tell you what, when you're ready, write down your answer and have me make the reservation. Bring the answer with you. If it's right, I'm buying. If it's not, you are. I'm surprised you don't have it by now, anyway."

"Well, you're not the only one who's busy. I'm part of a team at L-W that's going hell-for-leather with a new technology outfit in San Jose. Top secret."

"Sounds like Apple Computer to me," Gomez smirked.

"No comment," I rushed to say, but he already knew from the twitch of my mouth that he was probably correct.

"You think the Centro doesn't have eyes on the South Bay?" he asked sagely. "There's going to be tons of electronics jobs, the way things are shaping up."

A dark-haired guy, a little paunchy, with glasses and a five o'clock shadow, was squeezing by us carrying a suit coat, his suspenders showing over his starched white shirt. Making a fist with his trailing hand, he brought it down in a light gavel-stroke on Gomez's black vicuna shoulder. "Hey!" he said.

"Yo!" Gomez replied, startled. "How's it going?"

"Give you one guess," the guy smiled, backing out the door.

"That's Mel Wax right there," Gomez nodded. "A bona-fide big cheese."

"You should be a regular here," I joked. "The mayor himself might be next."

"I've met Moscone a couple of times. In fact I saw him at Henry Africa's the night I went with Mad. He saw me, too, but I didn't try talking to him."

"Not like you to shrink back."

"A matter of common sense. He was with a very interesting-looking black chick, and I got the impression they were there for the same reason as Mad and I."

÷ ÷ ÷

"Teflon," said Jordan on my office phone, "is a trademarked name for polytetrafluoroethylene. Both the trademark and the patent are held by DuPont Chemical Corporation, and DuPont is shown as the inventor. Patented 1953, renewed, 1970."

"Ah, yes, 'Better Living Through Chemistry.'"

"Right. They own that, too. Why did you want to know? Your man Steentofter again?"

"No, no," I lied. "It's so I won't appear dumb with a new client. All I asked was how to find out. You weren't supposed to do the legwork."

"Don't worry," he chuckled. "We have secretaries for that. Your message described the job, I turned it over to one. See how efficient using phone machines can be?"

"Well, thanks, I really appreciate it. If I need to learn more, how could I?"

"The Kearny Street branch library has the business collection. Except for brand new awards, they track all US patents, current or expired. Sally went in person, but the staff will check if you call."

"Wow, easy as that." Me, the son of a librarian, and it took a lawyer to explain.

"Even in the modern world," he quipped, "citizens get something for their tax dollars. Don't forget that we need to make a dinner date."

"I won't, and I'll buy. You've earned it."

"I'm not so sure, but you're stuck now."

As soon as Jordan hung up I dialed and had the woman who answered revisit the records Jordan's secretary must have scanned. While I was on hold, I pulled out the GOMEZ notebook and started a page for Teflon. Since I had time, I started pages for Yale and the Mitchell Brothers, too. Upon returning, she confirmed what I'd learned from Jordan, which I jotted down.

"Do you have the book in front of you?" I asked, wondering what she looked like. Her voice sounded too sexy for a mom — mine or anybody else's.

"Yes," she answered.

"Are any names shown for the people involved?" My pen was ready.

"Let's see...a few. The technical summary was written by Dr. Steven Keltner, Vice President for Research, and Dr. Hollis Banks, Research Chemist, both of DuPont Laboratories, Wilmington, Delaware. Philip Addison is shown as corporate President and CEO. That's it. There are also stipulations that research findings be shared, because they were partly government funded. Perhaps the Journal of the American Chemical Society would have more."

"Do you have access to it?"

"Here, no. And I'm not sure the main library goes back that far. You might try Berkeley or Stanford."

"OK, thanks." I tried UCB, made my request, and was told they would call me later. After lunch they did, but Keltner and Banks were again the only names, and Wilmington, Delaware, a long way from Vermont, was the only location. Or was Vermont false as well?

That night I put on my raincoat and walked down to the Tenderloin and the O'Farrell Theater. With a mission to accomplish, I vowed that I wouldn't go beyond the inner doors, but felt the pull of titillation despite myself.

There's no outside ticket booth, it's in the lobby, a large, sterile, well-lit expanse of crimson carpet that belies the adjoining complex of dim, closed spaces where the lap dancing, movies and peep-shows are. Nobody lingers going in and out, it's too bright and too open, a perfect buffer between any puritanical passers-by and the sordid pursuits within. A bouncer, deliberately looking the part, is always stationed toward the rear, with a ticket guy and a chrome cash register at the free-standing glass counter in the middle.

Tonight's ticket guy resembled an over-age, gone-to-seed James Dean, with dead eyes and a weak chin, whom I'd seen occasionally on prior visits. I waited until a couple of departing patrons cleared the exit, then approached. "Can you talk a minute?"

"About what?"

I drew as close as I dared. "Well, do the owners ever audition talent for the…you know, films they make?"

"Why, you got a chick you're trying to push?"

"No, no, I'm curious, that's all."

"Auditions aren't my department. Get lost, or buy a ticket and go in."

"Is there somebody I can talk to?"

"Hey, Larry," he called to the bouncer, "this guy's got an item under his raincoat he thinks the world should see. You worked auditions lately at the other location?"

The bouncer raised his head and looked at me with what passed for a smile in his line of work. "Nah, it's been quiet."

"Did they have any last December?" I asked while I had the bouncer's attention.

"Beats me," was his answer.

"You law enforcement?" the ticket guy demanded. "Or a PI?"

"Neither. I swear. I'm trying to play a joke on a friend. A guy."

There was a burst of loud rock-and-roll as two Asian men, talking rapidly in what I had to take on faith was a language, came out of the dance area and made their way to the street. The ticket guy regarded me coolly while they passed, finally saying, "I'll do you a favor and call the boss. But if he wants you gone, Larry is happy to help."

GOMEZ

I saw him put a phone to his ear and dial three digits. "Artie, hi, it's Roy. I got a guy downstairs wants to know about auditions for a joke on a buddy of his. You have time, or should we run him off?" After a pause the guy said, "No, I already asked," paused again, said "OK, here," and handed me the phone.

"Who am I speaking to?" a baritone voice inquired.

"This is...Phil...ah...Phil Stark," I lied. "Thanks for taking the call."

"Alright, Mr. Stark, how can we help you? Please make it quick."

"I have a friend who brags that he auditioned for a film with Green Door Productions last December. Another friend and I think he's bullshitting and want to prove it."

"Green Door is one of our companies. What's your friend's name?"

"Could be either of two names. Andrés Gomez *or* Andrew Steentofter. That's S-T-E-E-N."

"Hold a minute. I'll verify if we *don't* have a record of him. Otherwise, my answer will be no comment. Do you understand?"

"Yes."

In sixty seconds or so, time enough for more out-bound males to traverse the lobby, one of them with an unfortunate blot on his slacks, the voice returned. "No record of either person in December or April, and those are the only sessions we've run recently. Or could be a name you don't know. Most people we deal with use aliases."

"Oh," I said. "But there was something else. He showed me a photo, a Polaroid of him and another guy, with Green Door and the date handwritten on the back. Does that sound legitimate?"

The guy on the phone gave a little, keening laugh, low in his throat. "No. Unless our good camera was broken, the date would print automatically, we usually shoot one subject at a time, and we don't provide them copies. I'd say your friend's having you on."

"Thank you Mr., ah...I didn't get your name."

"Let's keep it that way. But by all means, have fun with your new info. I'm watching on the security cameras, and I'll ask Roy to escort you out. Put him on, would you?"

"Security cameras?"

GOMEZ

"We run a tight ship, Mr. Stark. The staff need to know they're accountable for their actions. Some nights it would help if the customers knew, too."

I didn't wait to be escorted, I waved and left on my own, keeping my eyes averted as I sidestepped some new arrivals. I was now zero for three on substantiating Gomez and wanted to share this news with Mad as soon as I could. Not that I was happy with everything I'd learned, especially regarding the security cameras, but the off mood I was left with might have done more than my resolve in sparing me another passage through the flesh-pots. That, at least, counted as a win.

GOMEZ

CHAPTER 18

The Sunday after Memorial Day Mad arranged a tryst for us in Sausalito at the Alta Mira Hotel. I had left messages with her office alluding to an update on my investigations, and her response, after a half-week's gap, was to set a date, time and place. She would rent a room, we'd meet there at 2:30, and before dark have dinner on the terrace.

Like many Bay Area people, I'd already experienced the Alta Mira's famous brunch. The food, including complimentary champagne, was good, the weather sunny when nowhere else was, and the views of Belvedere Island, Angel Island and the bay were without peer. It just hadn't occurred to me that the rambling, pink stucco edifice was a hotel in anything but name. I found, however, after winding my way up the wooded hillside and yielding the Audi to an eager parking attendant, that if I bypassed the entrances to the restaurant and the terrace, proceeded through an arch buttressed by two huge vases of gladiolas, and crossed the Persian carpet in a stately foyer, a small registration desk of hand-waxed redwood was set into the far wall.

"Hello," I said to the man behind it. "I'm Mr. Klein. My wife has already checked in."

In a wrinkled poplin suit, with his graying hair combed over a thin spot at the crown of his head, he looked exactly as I would picture the headmaster of a prep school. "Nice to see you, sir," he replied. "Mrs. Klein is in 402. Here's the key. I'm to tell you, also, that she made a 6:15 dinner reservation."

He pointed me to the elevator, and in a state of lightheaded anticipation only slightly less than I'd felt visiting Piedmont, I began my ascent. The hotel portion of the facility was small, no more than a dozen rooms per floor, with ours toward the top front. From the hall layout it seemed that I'd be entering a rectangle of no great size, with little available light, so when I gave a warning knock and pushed open the door after turning the key, the effect was of a flashbulb going off, though my eyes adjusted instantly.

GOMEZ

"Hi," Mad greeted me. "Isn't this place glam?" She was sitting up in bed, wearing only a silky, peach slip, with her legs under the sheet and the rest of the bedding folded back. Her hands held a copy of *Vogue*, and she had thrown open all the curtains and panes of a large bank of casement windows to maximize the sun, air, and most importantly, the 180-degree land-and-marine-scape, with the masts of scores of berthed sailboats splitting the low foreground like pencils jutting from a jar.

"Yes," I agreed, closing the door. "Terrific. Reminds me of a place Jenny and I stayed in Nice. Just don't tell me who else you've been here with."

"Alright, I won't," she laughed. "But I have an itch I want you to scratch for me."

My memories of that afternoon are more the overall mood than the intimate details. It was an ecstasy of skin, with hunger on both our parts, just enough familiarity to ease nervousness, and plenty of novelty to breed passion. But one detail was that Mad made me come in her mouth. When you hear guys bragging or telling jokes, the term is always *let* rather than *made*, but in this case I tried to disengage out of ordinary courtesy and she pulled me to her and upped the tempo to where I had no choice.

She didn't stop for a minute or more afterward, either, which sent crippling waves of pleasure through my cerebellum. I mean, in porn movies the men pull out and the women make a big fuss, so I always figured that was how things were done. And since no evidence remained, it was obvious where my sperm went, but Mad seemed wholly unconcerned.

I'm sure the fact that she got me to smoke dope with her when I first arrived played a part. I only took a few puffs, but Gomez was on the right track when he said weed was for making love. And if he said coke was for dancing, maybe I should have tried it at Artichoke Joe's, or should elsewhere, given the chance. Mad and I carried on like the proverbial rabbits—or is it minks—then napped, wrapped around each other, until after five when the air turned cool and the sun dropped over the hill behind us.

"OK if I shower first?" she asked as we awoke. "I'd love to get you in there with me, but the stall is tiny."

"Go ahead," I answered, "For erotic purposes, I'd need more recovery time anyway." I held her another five seconds, kissed her shoulder, and reluctantly let go. She sat up cross-wise on the bed and I noticed how spare and lacy her rose-gold crotch hair was, the texture of my pubescent sister's when I used to spy on her as a kid. Embarrassed by that memory, I forced myself not to look when Mad walked to the bathroom door.

"Would you close up?" she called. "It's getting chilly."

Since only low-flying aircraft could have seen in, I went naked to the windows and cranked the casements shut except for a small crack. Tagging along, between my thighs, was Roger, Mad's new name for my penis, shrunken to smaller than usual by his recent exertions, and smaller than I wished he was, but not posing any handicap in my suddenly flourishing sex life. Maybe Clark was small himself, and that's what Mad was used to. Later, while I showered, Mad dressed, and while I dressed we talked.

"I won't have time to linger at dinner," she said, sitting cross-legged on the surface of the writing desk in a pale-green, A-line shift, "so let me say what I found."

"About Gomez/Steentofter?" I pulled a polo shirt over my head as I spoke.

"Yes. EST doesn't have a record of him, at least not in the regular files, Argentina is negative or inconclusive, Cal is positive but inconclusive and Anaïs's brother is nowhere to be found. It's like you with Yale. You'd think something...some one thing...would check out."

"My other two didn't check out either."

"I forget what they were."

"The Mitchell Brothers audition and Teflon," I reminded.

"Oh, right, what happened?"

I told her and read some specifics from the GOMEZ notebook, which I'd brought along. To sum up, I said, "The same words you used...negative but inconclusive."

She then explained further about Cal and Argentina while I took notes. Gomez had been a graduate student at UCB, but his records were sealed for non-payment of fees. One of Mad's drama professors had since become a dean, and Mad got her to inquire under the guise of considering Andrew Steentofter for the Mills faculty. Cal would confirm neither the years he was enrolled nor anything else, although if Mr. Steentofter would pay what he owed, any other irregularities could perhaps be resolved.

GOMEZ

The Las Pampas Restaurant was more ambivalent yet. Ignacio, the owner, thought there was Argentina in Gomez's Spanish, but he heard other strains as well. He was nearly sure Gomez had visited the country, or read up on it, but there was little more he could say. Gomez was *un buen hombre* and a good customer, and that's what mattered. But at that point Rosa, one of the cooks, had poked her head out of the kitchen and told Mad that Gomez could be New York Puerto Rican, like her. He knew some of the old slang, she said, and some of the neighborhood lore. He just hadn't lived around Puerto Ricans in a long time.

As for Joaquín Nin, he was thought to be in the US, but was no longer performing and had become a composer. The source for this was the Nin fan club president in LA, who recommended that Mad also quiz the information operators in all the cities where Gomez and Joaquín might have crossed paths.

"It's an unusual name, too," she concluded. "Most places there weren't any Nins, and none with the right initial."

"Probably unlisted," I said. "Think how notorious Anaïs was. He must have gotten really tired of it."

As we rode the elevator down to dinner, Mad described two other things she'd done, strictly on whim. I was carrying the notebook, but didn't stop to write. Two days before, she'd called Black Panther headquarters in Oakland and asked about past political campaigns.

"Who wants to know?" a hard-edged female voice had replied.

"I do. I'm trying to track down an old friend," Mad said.

"Old friend who? Old friend where?"

"Well, this was in Alabama, around 1970."

"Hey, dumb ofay bitch, don't be callin' here? Why'd we know about that shit?"

Mad and I laughed while crossing the foyer, but every turn our quest had taken made it more like swimming in Jell-O. Her final angle had been oddest of all.

"Remember the commune you mentioned, where he was living when you first met? Well, I drove that part of Alcatraz Avenue and recognized it from your description."

"Great! There's got to be people around who know more than we do. A guy named Howard, for sure."

GOMEZ

"Yeah, but nobody was around. The place is boarded up and the yard filled with trash. I tried a couple of the neighbors, but none would talk to me, except one old lady, who said 'those people are trouble' and I 'should never get mixed up with them,' like it had been a safe house for dope dealers, or something."

"Hard to believe. It sure didn't have that feel the time I saw it. But I never got Howard's last name, which doesn't help much."

"If it's even a real name. But I'd be furious to think Gomez was just some hustler from Spanish Harlem, and he's conned both of us."

"From my standpoint, quite a ride."

"That's not the point," she shook her head. "I think we should confront him."

"No, no...way too soon. We haven't really proven anything. We only know what we don't know. For example, I'm pretty sure he told me Oakland and Huey Newton weren't the only Black Panther Party back then. And I'm still working on his math puzzle. That's our cover for getting him to Hayes Street."

"So what?" she shrugged. "Tell him you've solved it."

We were shown to a table, and unlike brunch, when the place was always mobbed, dinner was a quiet affair with fewer than fifteen parties seated. And by reserving early, Mad had gotten us on the terrace railing, under an umbrella that we didn't need at this hour, and with a view, except for some intervening treetops, almost as grand as our room's. The East Bay was in full sun, but fingers of fog were probing into the channels between the gumdrop profiles of the islands, and the western hills threw shadows on the water. We ordered her a crab Louie, poached salmon for me, and at my instigation, a bottle of Caymus Chardonnay.

While our waiter was fetching it, I could finally tell Mad about my design work for the top new wineries, which I showed off as soon as he came back to pour. She admired everything about the label, and the wine as well, saying she would try to get some for future fund raising events. I then mentioned Anchor Steam beer, whose label she knew and thought was equally sharp.

With my professional accomplishments praised, my sexual appetites sated, and the last of the dope working its magic, launching a more delicate topic seemed easy. "Clark is out of the country again, I gather?"

GOMEZ

"Not till later in the month. He's playing golf with some business cronies at Pebble Beach. He'll be home by ten. That's why I can't stay."

"Obviously he wouldn't be pleased at how you spent the afternoon."

She raised her eyes from her bread plate. "He wouldn't want to know. And he'd rather not suspect. I'm willing to honor that. But it did complicate trying to see you."

"I knew there was something."

"There was something else, too. I had to break a date with Gomez and his new suit. Another tea dance at the Hyatt. It's the only place we go that plays tangos."

"Oh, that is touchy." And astonishingly gratifying, at least to me.

"Don't worry about him. He started this. He sees me during the week in the Mission sometimes. And when Clark's gone, he sees me a lot."

We were getting away from Clark's potential inadequacies and into Gomez zones better left alone, so I changed the subject again. "How's your mother, by the way?"

"About the same. Depressed and frightened, and I don't blame her. With cancer, you can never trust that it's gone." Mad had placed a pearl-buttoned, white sweater across her shoulders, which she adjusted every so often to prevent it from sliding askew.

"Is breast cancer what Anaïs died of?"

"Hers was worse...still reproductive organs, but worse. And all those cancers follow family lines. Your risk is higher if your mother has it, and also if you don't have children."

"Do you want children?"

"Clark does, I don't. It's all moot, though, because I can't. It's just such a shock to think your tits can kill you, or your cervix. I've learned to be orgasmic and to really like sex. I don't want that taken away from me."

I reached to touch her hand and she responded with a firm, welcoming pressure. "Sorry," I said, "not the best choice of topics."

"It's alright." Her voice was low and constrained. "What is, is."

We sipped at wine until the waiter brought our plates. After she'd sampled a few bites, Mad put her fork down and made sure

GOMEZ

she had my attention. "Well," she said, "what are we going to do about Gomez?"

"I don't know. Maybe nothing."

"If you won't confront him without facts, we need more facts."

"Or let things continue as they are. It's pretty clear our suspicions were justified. Why not accept that and live the dream, as you say?"

"I can't bear the uncertainty. I could probably accept anything, as long as I knew... and as long as he copped to it. I even still like the idea that we'd conspire to keep his persona flying." She began eating again.

"I guess there's a couple of new approaches. Like a record of him at Bennington High in Vermont, or maybe DuPont has a plant near there, where his dad worked."

"Those sound like long shots."

"Unfortunately," I nodded. A busboy cruised by and lit a glass-chimnied candle on our table.

"If it's just us," Mad continued, "the best resources left are Clark and your ex...but I guess they're off limits. Jenny might be able to cut through the impasse at Cal, and Clark has State Department contacts who could probably check for a Steentofter passport. You can't get to Argentina without one, and the dates would be shown. The trouble is, what reason do I give for asking?"

If she was fishing for me to call Jenny despite my misgivings, I didn't bite. I wasn't into it to anywhere near that degree, nor did I want help from Clark. In fact, I was into it primarily because Mad was, and so far our little quest had brought us together exactly as I'd hoped. "Yeah, I agree, both are off limits. But what if you and I paid those fees at Cal? Then your Mills contact could access his file."

"It was over $2,000," Mad said flatly. "With late penalties to be added on top."

"Ooh. Way bigger than I thought."

"We also might not learn much. He could have faked a Yale degree applying to UC, and hasn't paid because he got caught and was thrown out. Why spend all that on learning more of what's not true? I want to know what *is* true. Remember when *Newsweek* ran the expose on Bob Dylan? About how he was a nice Jewish boy from Minnesota named Zimmerman, and not a freewheeling hobo?"

"No."

"Well, that's what I want, and there's only one way to get it. I come up with the money and you find a reliable detective."

"You're kidding. How would I do that?"

"Through your lawyer friend, the one who helped with Yale and Teflon. All the major firms use private investigators. We joked about it before, but this time I'm not."

"That's an awfully big step."

"Come on, Paul," Mad urged. "You have to say yes." Her voice was dulcimer sweet.

And, of course, I did say yes, although she had to badger me for another five minutes and explain that the money would come from her trust fund and be invisible to her husband. Moreover, to be sure she had no traceable connection, I would be our sole contact with the detective. Both were signs that this might always have been her real plan, but I took it as a spontaneous reaction to the lack of success we'd reported so far.

÷ ÷ ÷

After a dessert of sorbet and coffee we walked to the parking lot to say goodnight while the young attendant recovered our cars. Mad leaned into me and kissed my neck. "I had a lovely time…and Roger got to conduct a whole new rendition of the *Bolero*." A teasing smile formed on her lips.

"It made the first one seem like a chamber ensemble."

"I have a special treat planned for us at the end of the month, after Clark leaves."

"What's that?"

"A surprise," she said. "Something al fresco. You'll have to take a day off work, though, and promise to follow instructions. Agreed?"

"Should be OK."

"I'll give you as much advance notice as I can, but try to be flexible."

"Sounds mysterious."

Her teasing smile returned. "Not mysterious, sensuous."

The Audi eased up next to us and the attendant, older than the one I'd seen that afternoon, got out proffering my ignition key. As soon as I took it, he used the same hand to push his lank hair back from his eyes, after which he rotated the palm to receive and stash my tip in the outside pocket of his tunic. Only then did I realize that his other arm was missing and that the sleeve that should have housed it was also missing, the aperture at the shoulder sewn closed.

"Vietnam," he mouthed bitterly, noting my glance before I looked away, but I'd been reminded of Gomez's damaged knee. Could the war have had something to do with that, and with why there were such gaps in his past? I remembered his serenading me with a lewd verse from an army song. Where had he learned it?

Once I got in the car Mad reached through the driver's window and curled her fingers into mine. "I'm tremendously excited," she said, "at the decision we made. Call right away when you get a line on someone."

And in a matter of days, I not only had a line on someone, I'd solved the math puzzle. It hit me driving home across the Golden Gate, and who knows, maybe the dope I'd smoked helped. I wasn't absolutely sure until I sat in my living room, ran the numbers on my pocket calculator and wrote them down. Envelopes two through nine were a classic powers of 2 progression, and Gomez's hint, intentionally or not, may have done more harm than good. All my wheel-spinning on factorials and Fibonaccis could have been avoided if I'd focused instead on an exhaustive way to get from \$2 to \$16 using the fewest envelopes, and generalized from there.

Finishing my calculations, I transcribed them onto a single sheet, which I folded and wedged into the GOMEZ notebook. Done, finally—although with Gomez himself, it was one more thing I'd have to play dumb about until Mad's and my latest tactic bore fruit. Then I could claim I'd just come up with the solution, and we'd all be off to Hayes Street for a very, very interesting evening.

Two nights later Jordan and I went to Fior d'Italia near Washington Square for deep-dish lasagna rich enough to clog all the major arteries. The remedy for that, he insisted, was a Chianti which came in a tall, Bordeaux-type bottle, no woven straw in sight, and was the equal of any red I'd ever had. I was paying, but Jordan knew the place, so I let him do the ordering.

He had begun by guiding us to a corner table in the back room, under one of the many gilt-framed oil portraits of what I took to be the owner's ancestors. But even if they'd been bought at auction someplace, they looked terrific against the grayish-maroon paint on the walls, a higher gloss version of the wine in our glasses. Also, since it was Tuesday, things were quiet and our waiter maintained a slow pace.

After Jordan caught me up on his women and his other doings, I posed the question I'd been saving. "Am I right in guessing that you or your firm know a private detective who could help with more of the Steentofter business?"

His face displayed the most interesting expression I could imagine seeing on it, a mix of amusement, guile, approval and disbelief. "Well, well," he said, drawing out the words. "This has turned serious. Who is the fellow really, a rival?"

"Not so much that. An ex of hers...of my lady friend's. She's the one who wants to know, but wants me to do the work."

"I see. I'm going to say I believe you, even if I don't. And yes, I know plenty of investigators. They're a dubious lot, for the most part, and Rufe's the only one I'd recommend."

"I thought roof was something that kept the rain out."

"Ha," Jordan parried sarcastically. "I mean Rufus Bonhof. He's the best. I used him during my divorce, to try digging dirt on my ex to get out of the corner she had me in. No luck, but he did a hell of a job. He's picky about the clients he takes, so I'll call and say you'll be in touch. His number's in the book. They'll give you the location."

"Thanks. Sounds like I'll owe you another dinner."

"No, but I'd settle for some *tiramisù* as tonight's dessert."

"Fine, whatever it is."

"A sort of chocolate rum cake. Tell me, though, am I right to think your lady friend is married?"

"Let's say you are."

"And Steentofter is her husband?"

"You're a little off base there."

"Wait, I've got it. He's the father of a love child."

"Now you're way off base."

"Well, it's better you didn't spend your nest egg on one of Eve's friends. You'll need it to pay Rufe. He's good, he's just not cheap."

"It's her money anyway."

GOMEZ

"This gets more decadent by the minute," Jordan chuckled. "But I forgot one thing. Rufe is black. I hope that doesn't put you off."

"Of course not. Why would it?"

"You never know. And do keep me posted, especially if there's some kind of Yale connection after all."

CHAPTER 19

Since I hadn't thought to ask how the name was spelled, that morning found me running my finger down all the Bahnhoffs and Bohnhofs in the white pages before getting it right. I then waited until late in the day so Jordan would have time to clear my path. After a few rings, a youthful female voice answered, "Bonhof and Associates. May I help you?"

"This is Paul Stiles on referral from Jordan Mackay. I'd like an appointment with Mr. Bonhof as soon as possible."

"Yes, we've been expecting your call. Let's try for tomorrow afternoon."

"Great. When?"

"Perhaps 2:30? From 3:30 on looks difficult."

"Mmm...alright. I'll move some meetings and free up an hour."

"I have you booked. We're in Suite 1-C at 1736 Stockton Street. Thank you."

I'd been extremely nervous, but it turned out to be like calling my dentist, except it was easier to get in. I also began anticipating the things Bonhof might ask, and decided to try Liz, the sexy-voiced librarian, with another DuPont question.

"Yes," she said. "As long as it doesn't have to be current to this year, Standard & Poors has that information. I won't take long, if you can hold."

"OK. I'm mainly interested in the 1940s and 50s, so don't worry about current."

When Liz returned, she had this to say: "It was more of a job than I thought, because the company is so large. I checked the oldest S&P volumes we have, for 1972 and earlier, and there are no DuPont facilities of any kind in Vermont. The closest is Springfield, Mass., which is a paint-manufacturing plant. As far as I can tell, there are no research facilities north of Philadelphia, and most are clustered around Wilmington."

"Thanks a lot. That's very helpful."

"You're welcome Mr. Stiles. It's what we're here for."

Another round of inconclusively negative findings. Next I concocted a story for Ivy and put her to work. And by the following day, a few hours before my Bonhof appointment, she had made the calls I'd asked her to.

"Am I wrong about this?" she mused, sidestepping through my narrow office door. "You don't have authorization for an assistant, and you wouldn't be in charge of recruiting if you did."

Damn, I thought. What a pain she was, and apparently no one had told her that round-faced, round-cheeked women shouldn't wear short bangs, nor should bodies like hers be clothed in miniskirts. "I know that, Ivy. It's hypothetical. I met the guy at a party, he was looking for a job, and claimed to have taken a lot of design and drafting classes in high school. If he's for real, I want to alert personnel, that's all."

"Well, he's not for real." She dropped her plump behind into one of my Van der Rohe chairs and, legs tightly together, lifted her feet off the floor. "New shoes," she said. "They hurt." She was wearing what looked to be cheap pumps from Woolworth's, devoid of all arch support.

"What about him doesn't check out?" I replied, making sure to sound casual.

"No drafting classes, no nothing. Didn't even go to Bennington High. They scanned from 1950 to 1960. No Steentofter, period."

"Could there be more than one school? Like separate voc. ed. or technical? I don't know how big the town is."

I asked that question. One, and it draws from the whole area."

"Either a fake or a flake," I said resignedly. "Thanks for trying. His phone number goes in the wastebasket."

"What's he been doing since then? Why go all the way back to high school?"

I had to think fast. "Being an artist, he says, a painter. In New York and South America."

"Arrgh, everybody's an artist these days." She swung herself forward in the chair and stood. "You didn't meet him on Castro Street, did you?"

"No, Ivy, Castro Street is not where I hang out."

"I swear half the guys in this town do. Thank god for my sweetie, Brad." She started toward the door. "There's a Bennington College, you know."

"Really?" Maybe that was the answer. Gomez had gone there, not Yale.

"Yeah, but it's all female. That's why I was kidding about Castro Street. You're sure he's a guy, right?"

"Oh, oh, I get it. Yeah, I'm sure."

She stopped in the doorway. "How come Madeline hasn't called lately? She looked like quite a catch that day she picked you up."

"I didn't know your desk had a view."

"I was on deck for a smoke break. Can I help if I have eyes?"

As soon as Ivy left I jotted her Bennington news into the GOMEZ notebook. And yes, Mad *was* quite a catch, not to mention that her detective idea was more and more winning me over. Except for grad school at Cal, not one thing had even begun to check out. Our choices were give up, or hire a pro. It was that simple.

÷ ÷ ÷

Not only did Bonhof have Jordan's recommendation, it was an address I could walk to in fifteen minutes. In fact, I must have been by it countless times, never guessing that a real-life detective would be located in a standard North Beach neighborhood. But I'd never seen the building per se, because it turned out to be set well back from the street, through a wisteria trellis and up a brick walkway between the garages of two neighboring structures.

If I had seen it, though, I wouldn't have forgotten. Suite 1-C was shoulder-to-shoulder with four similar spaces facing onto the deck of an L-shaped shingle structure with broad, overhanging eaves and a colonnade of carved wooden posts along the perimeter. In the courtyard bounded by the L, a koi pond, specked with lily pads and rimmed with mossy rocks, burbled quietly. The style brought to mind Mad's cottage, but it was more formal, and more intricate.

At a reception desk inside sat a middle-aged man in shirt sleeves, whose tie was loose and who was writing so urgently in the margins of a typescript he barely looked up. He had a fringe of short, dark hair but was otherwise bald, and his complexion was ecru, say, in the range of light beige. To the extent I thought about it, he was southern European, or possibly Lebanese.

"Someone will be right with you," he mouthed absently from beneath a pair of half-frame, tortoise reading glasses.

I rechecked the doorplate, wondering if I was in 1-B or 1-D by mistake, but definitely saw the name Bonhof. There was no source for the female voice I'd spoken to on the phone, nor was anyone black to be seen, here or in the cluttered inner office, which was partly exposed to view. No doubt this guy was one of the associates, and Bonhof himself would keep me waiting—unless I was being fobbed off on the associate.

"Sorry," he said, still distracted. "Pam leaves at noon and Gloria doesn't get in till 3." He pushed the typescript aside and began hunting across the desktop until he found an appointment book. Flipping it open, he rustled the pages.

"Do you know if this building was done by Bernard Maybeck?" I asked him.

"It was, yes," he nodded. "Good eye. Most people guess Julia Morgan."

"I didn't realize there were Maybecks in this part of town."

"All his others are in Presidio Heights." He glared at the book. "I wish to hell Pam would leave this thing open to the right day. Oh...here...are you Mr. Stiles?"

"Yes. Paul Stiles."

"God, of course...Jordan's neighbor. Come on in." He got up and went to the other office. I could tell from the way he moved his six-foot frame that he had once been wiry, and though he no longer was, he carried the extra pounds well.

I followed. "Do you know where Mr. Bonhof is?"

He snatched off his glasses, waved them in his hand and gave a burst of sonorous laughter. "Damn that Jordan. I should've known. I'm Rufe Bonhof. He told you I was black, didn't he?"

"Well, no, but he...ahh...described..."

"Of course he did. Always does. Besides, it's true, even if he makes a joke of it." Bonhof reversed course and shook my hand. "Almost forgot to press the flesh. Sit down. We'll send for coffee when Gloria shows up."

I reviewed his face, validating my first impression; there were no Negroid characteristics. He sensed my uneasiness and laughed again to defuse it. "I'm Creole...from Louisiana. Came to the Bay Area as a kid in the 40s when my daddy got work building ships.

GOMEZ

You've heard of the One-Drop Rule? A Southern thing about blood? Well, I've got my one drop, or maybe two, so I'm black. Whatever the hell that means. I always tell clients up front. Saves surprises, saves discomfort. Unless I'm working undercover, I don't want to pass. I want to be me. Jordan likes stealing my thunder is all."

"The guy I want you to find is supposedly Hispanic, and he's blacker than you."

Bonhof laughed at that, too. "Everybody's blacker than me. My daddy, my sister, my kids...and their mama is white. Everybody but my cousin, the New York book critic. I'm blacker than him."

New York book critic? When it came to embellishing, this guy and Gomez might make a pair. They also both assumed that you'd laugh at whatever they thought was funny, whether or not you laughed first.

"Shall we get started?" he asked.

"OK, sure."

"This is a missing-person case, you said? Jordan didn't fill me in."

"No. Like that, but basically creating a dossier of his life."

"I see. Tell me more while I take notes. There's a case outline form I like to use." Bonhof put his glasses back on and picked up a clipboard.

"Fine. What do you want to know?"

"Start with his name, age, marital status, places of residence, and so on."

Partly free-form, and partly steered by him, I recounted what I knew, or thought I knew, explaining that nothing had yet been successfully verified. "And the point is not just to prove this stuff false, but to learn what the truth is."

"Understood. I'll reconstruct everything, which will tell us what's false. Where is Steentofter now? Do you know?"

"Living in the Bay Area under an alias."

"You're sure?"

"Yes, I even know the alias. But it's critical that you not alert him or speak to him directly. His current situation isn't part of this."

"Is he a criminal or associated with criminals?"

"No, not that I'm aware of. Why?"

"To gauge the hazards. Also, there are gaps in what you've told me that could represent prison time. You know...Greenwich Village, then suddenly off to Argentina; Berkeley, then suddenly off to Alabama. Call it my suspicious nature."

"Prison seems out of the question, but…but…" I faltered, thinking of what Mad had said about the former commune house and the warning she'd received.

"But what?" he followed.

"Well…that past address I had for him on Alcatraz Avenue ended up being trashed and abandoned within a matter of months, and the neighbors seemed kind of spooked…intimidated."

"Then prison isn't out of the question, though more likely it's something else. Any sign of plastic surgery?"

Before I could reply, I heard a door close behind me, then footsteps along with the bumping of objects being laid on a wooden surface. And Gomez *had* shown knowledge of surgical techniques, more than once as I remembered, but never pertaining to himself.

"Gloria, honey," Bonhof called, "come meet Mr. Stiles."

In Maybeck buildings everything is of bare wood—walnut, teak, cedar—stained or polished to bring out the grain, and assembled into strong verticals and horizontals. The effect is soothing and warm, heightened in this instance by narrow mullioned windows that ran almost continuously around the exterior walls, set above eye-level, where they brought in light while assuring privacy. All the hinges, door-handles and other fixtures were of brass, deliberately tarnished to accent the wood by subtly echoing it.

Against this background, as I turned in my chair, a female face reminiscent of Bonhof's appeared. But the new face was a tone darker than his, pecan would be a good description, surmounted by a short Afro and featuring a shy, full-lipped smile.

"Don't get up…please. I'm Gloria," she said, pointing at Bonhof, "his daughter." She was angular and pretty, in sandals, black velour bell-bottomed slacks and a print blouse—Senegalese, perhaps—of browns, blacks and grays. "I'm going to the corner for coffee. Want some?"

"Nice to meet you," I said. "Thanks, coffee would be great."

"You're reading our minds," Bonhof put in. "I'll have a cup too."

"Cream or sugar?" Gloria asked me.

"No, I don't need it."

As she began to depart, Bonhof's eyes lit. "Wait," he said. "You didn't ask me about cream and sugar."

"I'm trained by now, Daddy," she replied with mock weariness. "I bring you coffee nearly every day." She swung her eyes to me. "A black man drinks black coffee. I'm sure he's told you all about it."

"Yes, but he skipped that part."

"Good," she laughed on her way out, "maybe he'll start skipping it with me."

"I didn't invent this race-obsessed society," Bonhof protested gleefully. "I'm just trying to live in it."

"Daddy, please…" she called over her shoulder.

"That's a real sweetheart, that gal," Bonhof nodded. "Hell of a painter, too. Goes to the Art Institute over on Russian Hill and works here after class. My married daughter, Pam, comes in mornings while her little one's in pre-school. Pretty slick for the old man, don't you think?"

"Absolutely," I agreed, gesturing to my right. "Did she do these, by the way?" Four deft line drawings of fish and animals, interspersed with idealized human figures, were arranged on the wall—sketches, it seemed, for a larger piece.

"Those are by the black artist Sargent Johnson," Bonhof replied. "Fine work. Gloria framed 'em for me, though. And that collage in the front room is a Hayward King… Now let's see," he continued in a more professional tone, "what's behind your interest in Steentofter? Is he a personal enemy, a business rival, a romantic rival?"

"Actually, he's my best friend." I'd never phrased it that way before.

"Say what?"

"And no matter how things develop, I hope he'll still be. But he's put out so much baloney, I need to call him on it. In a way, I think he wants me to."

"Well, what you've got has been laid on thick. There's Yale and Cal for intellectual zing, football for valor, Argentina for cosmopolitanism, then his supposed family ties to Spinoza, Communists and Teflon, plus addresses in every cultural-political hotspot for the last twenty years." Bonhof paused to laugh. "Greenwich Village, Berkeley and Alabama…a portrait of the zeitgeist! Not that unusual in some circles, I guess, but stacked up with everything else, he's either a multi-layered phony or a real phenom."

"You're leaving out San Francisco in the late 70s."

"Right. EST and the Mitchell Brothers thing...plus his name-dropping about Anaïs Nin. Doesn't change my assessment."

"What did you mean when Gloria first came in...you know, about plastic surgery and the 'something else' besides prison?"

"That he's a fugitive, of course. Surely you've heard of the Weather Underground, Mr. Stiles...to pick one example."

My jaw fell open and my tongue must have been hanging out. "Those wackos who blew up things to protest the Vietnam War?"

"Yes, like government offices at the Ferry Building here, and in a more celebrated instance around that time, blew themselves up... some of them, anyway...in Greenwich Village. What's your answer regarding surgery? On his face, that is."

I simply couldn't believe it. Yet certain facts did fit—the maimed knee, the chronological gaps, the aliases and location changes, his familiarity with mechanics, math and guns. "No facial marks or scars I've ever noticed. You really think, " I asked, "Steentofter is...well...a terrorist?" The word amplified how alarming the concept was, my esophagus seeming to burn as I spoke it.

"I don't think anything at this point. He could just be a draft-dodger who didn't go to Canada or Sweden. In my business, you never prejudge. But being open to all possibilities isn't prejudging. I'm not the type to blunder into traps if I can help it, and I hope Jordan told you I don't work cheap."

"He did. I still need a sense for what that means." With the realization that even these last questions had, for him, been routine, the worst of my tension began slowly to drain away.

"It means I'll turn this around for you within forty-five days, and I have a flat rate of $4,250 for dossiers."

"That *is* pretty steep." I knew Mad had money, but she and I hadn't talked about how much.

"Argentina's a long way from here, depending on what turn things take. It may be more famous for the tango, but it was also the natal home of Che Guevara...and of the *Montanero* revolutionary movement...models for many of their recent US counterparts.

"That's not a prediction, and is probably nothing. Old houses in North Oakland get boarded up all the time, and any number of people from hippies to movie stars change their names for no sinister reason."

GOMEZ

Gloria returned with a steaming paper cup for each of us. "Italian roast," she said, circumspectly, "from Malvina's. Daddy likes it strong." Almost before I knew she was there, she was gone again.

"It'll take more than this stuff to put hair on my fat chest," Bonhof observed, as we both took sips. Then he was back to business. "And sorry to say, my prices aren't negotiable. I take fifty percent up front and the other fifty on completion."

"I guess that would be OK. I'll have to check."

"Wait a minute, now. Are you working with somebody else on this?"

"Maybe...sort of."

"Mr. Stiles! I level with you, you level with me. That's the deal."

"Then, yes. For whatever difference it makes." I drank more coffee.

"Male or female?"

"I'd rather not say. All your contact will be with me, regardless."

"*If* I decide to take the job." He gave me a severe look over his glasses frames. "Does this person have any legal or family relationship to Steentofter?"

"No."

"Any criminal involvement?"

"No."

"Is this person in love with him?"

"No, she's...well..." I caught myself too late, "she's not."

"A woman, then?"

"Yes. A friend, same as me."

"That's all?"

"Yes."

"Can I trust you, Mr. Stiles?"

"Yes."

"Why is your woman friend remaining anonymous?"

"She's married, and wants to keep her husband out of it. In fact, he could be someone you or Jordan know." All of which was supposition. Mad hadn't stated her motive.

"Jordan has no part in this. Anything you tell me is between *us*."

"Good. That's important."

"Do either of you have photos of Steentofter? Current ones, of course, but older ones would be the most helpful."

"We might. I'll have to check on that, too. So...you'll take the job?"

"I should say no...but yes, I will. Odds are it won't be that difficult...or dangerous...and in terms of professional pride," he looked at me as though he were going to wink, "it's a lure that your own efforts came up empty."

"I can let you know tomorrow about the money."

"And the photos?" Bonhof reminded.

"Yes, those, too."

"Any other questions?"

"You said before that you work undercover. Will you on this case?"

"Not likely. Here's what solves cases like this." Bonhof patted his hand on a large, double-row Rolodex sitting on the low filing cabinet near his desk. "It's what I have that other folks don't. Anything else?"

"Will you be handling most of this, or will one of your associates?"

"Associates!" he laughed. "Now that is funny. There are no associates, it's just a name. Or you could say I have hundreds of associates," he patted the Rolodex again.

"I wanted to be sure."

Bonhof looked at his watch. "We need to wrap things up, but I have a final concern. I understand you work for L-W Design."

"Yes."

"Do Milt Landau or Roy Walters know you're dealing with me?"

"No."

"Best keep it that way."

"Sure, but why?"

"Jordan used to be their attorney. Did he tell you?"

"Yes, but I'd forgotten."

"Well, I had a lot to do with why he isn't any more."

"That was about the time I started there, and I never knew the details. What happened?"

"Confidential. However, if Steentofter is a co-worker of yours or tied in with L-W, I'll have to refuse the case after all."

"No, he isn't. But I'm dying to know what went on with L-W and Jordan."

"If he clears me to tell you, I will. That's up to him." Bonhof stood and shook my hand again, as firmly as when I'd arrived. "Please excuse me, Mr. Stiles. I have an important call coming in. Let me hear from you yes or no tomorrow. The forty-five-day count begins as soon as I receive your first payment."

On my way out I surreptitiously got a better look at Gloria, who waved but was busy on the phone. What would it be like, I thought, if I were five or six years younger and could date art students?

CHAPTER 20

Mad gulped at the cost, too, but gave the OK when I emphasized how favorably Bonhof had impressed me. And by then, if she'd needed additional persuading, I'd become so engaged myself that I might have kicked in the first thousand dollars. I also felt no need to burden her with Bonhof's more dire speculations, since he'd quickly downplayed them by stating benign alternatives of greater plausibility. But it was fortunate I called as soon as I returned to my office, because she was leaving the next afternoon for a long weekend in LA and wanted to get to the bank beforehand.

To ensure full confidentiality on her end, she would mail me two counter drafts payable to cash, which I would dole out as needed. Another piece of luck was that Mad had snapshots in her desk that a Mime Troupe photographer had taken when Gomez visited there earlier in the spring. Photos of him would arrive with the checks. I relayed this news to Bonhof via Gloria, assuring her that the job was on.

Jordan was away somewhere with Eve, so I left a thank you message saying things had gone well and lobbied him to have Rufe tell me what had happened regarding L-W. I admitted I was prying, but promised to keep all revelations strictly under my hat. Saturday I ran in Golden Gate Park and Sunday I had a nice brunch with my new—I guess you'd say friends—Bob and Carol Houser at their place on Telegraph Hill. I hadn't really expected them to follow up on the vague invitation they'd offered at the Gateway Cinema, but they did.

Finally, to guarantee that all the Bonhof preliminaries got taken care of, I walked the first check and the photos over to his Stockton Street office late on Tuesday, which was also a way of seeing Gloria. He hadn't been in, but everything went safely into his case file. Gloria was in a sunny mood and told me that her favorite artist was Joan Brown, an Art Institute star from the previous decade, of whom I'd never heard.

GOMEZ

From this it emerged that she would give me a tour of the Institute some Saturday to see the Joan Browns in the permanent collection, as well as an apparently famous Diego Rivera mural in the auditorium. I asked about Gloria's own work, and she agreed to show some of that, too. She was booked the coming weekend, but would definitely find time. I suppose it didn't hurt that I knew a bit about Maybeck and worked at L-W, where she would *"just love"* to visit if she ever could. I wondered what she thought she was doing. I had wanted to find out if I would dare to flirt with her, and for my trouble I got flirted with instead.

Gomez continued his heavy involvement with Centro meetings, although we got in one round of racquetball and had our usual fun and conversation. It seemed strange not to tell him about Gloria, since I wanted an outside opinion on whether to try dating her, and he'd be the ideal source. Yet how could I describe who she was or where we'd met?

Not only could that compromise the investigation, it was easy to envision his insisting on meeting her himself, then charming her socks off and relegating me to third wheel by tagging along on our tour of the Institute or of L-W. And on what basis could I object? He'd willingly been my sponsor with Mad, and without her, I would never have had the confidence to approach Gloria in the first place.

But those concerns faded, and the month of June settled into an amiable groove. Gloria had told me no news was good news in the early stages, so I didn't worry about not hearing from her father. Mad phoned to talk and to verify that the checks and photos had arrived, and my big project for Apple Computer continued to go well. The only off note was something called Proposition 13, which passed by a huge margin on the state ballot, putting many government services in danger of elimination. If it weren't for Gomez's climbing all over me prior to the election I'd have voted yes, but I ended up being glad I hadn't.

The election aftermath was yet another thing keeping Gomez busy, although Jordan was overjoyed that his property taxes would be cut, and he agreed to think about what, if anything, of the L-W saga Bonhof could tell me. Jokingly, he suggested that I trade tidbits about my mysterious married woman for his giving Rufe the go-ahead. In refusing, I reminded him that he could always tell me about L-W himself, without anyone else the wiser. No, he said, he'd been sworn to secrecy, so it would have to be Bonhof. All of this, however, pointed in the same direction: the world was a far more devious place than I'd believed till now, and for better or worse, I was part of it.

÷ ÷ ÷

Toward the end of the month I got twitchy and called to check Bonhof's progress. Naturally I waited until after 3 o'clock so Gloria would answer, but the voice I got was his. "Mr. Stiles...of course I remember you."

"I was wondering how the Steentofter dossier is going."

"I prefer not to give interim results. Too many things are subject to change. Please understand, there's almost a month left of my forty-five days."

"Very true, but can you tell me anything?"

"I'll go this far. Your man exists under the name you gave, and he's left a trail. It's a bit of a palimpsest, but the breakthroughs are starting to come."

"Sounds promising."

"Yes. I don't anticipate insoluble problems."

"Is Gloria there, by the way? She said something about giving me an Art Institute tour."

"I was going to bring that up," he replied. "The school year is over, and she went back east with her mother for a few weeks. I'm making do with a temp. But when Gloria mentioned the idea, I reminded her that you were a client and she'd have to shelve it."

"You mean there are rules?"

"Indeed," he went on. "*My* rules. Given the nature of the work, it's a bad idea to socialize with clients. She should know. I've said it many times."

"I guess I see your point. The tour thing came up by accident."

The phone vibrated with one of his laughs. "Now I don't object to your going out with my daughter. Your parents might, hers don't. The age difference is more of a worry, but that's for her to decide. She's always had her head screwed on straight."

"I wasn't looking on it as a date, exactly."

"Well, Gloria was. And she's really not such a youngster herself. She was a junior at Santa Clara when the art bug bit, and she'll have her MA from the Institute next spring."

"So I wouldn't be a complete cradle-robber?"

"No, you just better be divorced like you said. I'm a bad man to have down on you."

"Everything's in order there…except I'm still your client."

"As I told *her*, you won't be forever. Give it a month after the job is done to let the dust settle, then you can do your tour to start the new semester."

"Alright, I'll keep that in mind."

"Say," Bonhof continued, "did you talk to Jordan about L-W?"

"Yeah, I did. Why?"

"Well, he hasn't gotten back to me on it. I'll have you into the office to pick up the dossier once I'm done. I always do that face-to-face. If I've heard from Jordan, we'll cover the other, too."

As soon as I lowered the phone and began jotting a reminder to look up the word palimpsest, Ivy was hovering at my elbow to tell me with exaggerated seriousness that *Madeline* was on the other line. I nodded and waved Ivy out the door.

"Did you know tomorrow was your day off?" Mad said.

"Oooh, not good. Couldn't it be Thursday?"

"If I *have* to wait, I will. Anticipation is an aphrodisiac."

"You've been helping me understand that."

"You'll understand better by Thursday afternoon," she teased.

"How so?"

"It's a surprise, remember?"

"That's what you said, but it has to start somehow."

"Do you know Mountain Home Inn on Mt. Tam above Mill Valley?"

"Yeah, I've seen it."

"Meet me there at 10 on Thursday morning. You and Roger are going hiking, so wear comfy clothes and shoes."

"Oh, right," I said. "You told me al fresco."

"At least you were listening. Another thing…have you heard from Bonhof? If you tell me now we can skip the Gomez talk while we're together."

From my standpoint, a welcome idea. Although he was our unifying force field, having to swap theories about him every time I saw her only highlighted my junior status. Even the news that she'd broken a date with him to meet me at the Alta Mira, while a victory of sorts, hadn't resolved that feeling. "You picked a perfect time to ask," I said. "Bonhof and I just got off the phone."

"Well?"

I filled her in, to which she replied, "Damn, that means another whole month. But while we're on the subject, I checked something else last week."

"About you-know-who?"

"Yes. He's officially on the Centro payroll as Andrés Gomez. They don't show Steentofter at all. I figured out how to ask discreetly, so I did."

"Interesting," I said, trying to sort out what this news might mean. "I hope you really were discreet. With Bonhof poking around too, we don't want anyone to catch on."

"Don't worry. I made like I worked for a credit bureau and was looking for several other names, too."

"Aha…pretty clever. And with all the Bonhof stuff, I forgot to tell you, but I solved the math puzzle. It was so simple I should have had it the first day."

"Aren't you the smarty!" Mad enthused. "All we have to do now is wait. Mr. G. has a big jolt coming when he takes us to dinner."

"Shall I explain the answer?"

"If you want, but not now, and not on Thursday. We won't have time."

"I can while we hike."

"Don't be too sure," she laughed. "I'll see you at Mountain Home, OK?"

÷ ÷ ÷

It took less effort than I expected to get Thursday off. Also, since I let twenty-four hours elapse before submitting the request, Ivy didn't remark on my absence's being related to Mad's call. That was no guarantee Ivy had failed to notice, or that she hadn't blabbed to her office buddies, but the lack of snide innuendo was a relief.

GOMEZ

As for anticipation and its aphrodisiac properties, I was overwhelmingly horny by the time I left the city, although waiting produced a more pleasurable benefit as well. We'd had a spell of fog earlier in the week, which looked to be over, so the weather in Marin would be gorgeous. The Golden Gate itself was clear, but the air was milky with vapor, agreeably muting the sun's energy as I crossed, while the bay's surface reflected and boosted its power farther inland. To the west, fog still hung along the headlands and the ocean was obscured.

Having never been to Mt. Tam except on weekends, I found a major difference in traffic. Past Mill Valley nobody was on the road, so I raced the Audi through tight turns in a hillside eucalyptus grove purely for the joy of feeling it respond. The sunroof was open and *Handyman*, a new James Taylor song, trilled from the radio.

Mountain Home's parking lot was un-peopled as well, with Mad's Ghia one of two vehicles there when I arrived. The other was a rental belonging to a family of German tourists who preceded me through the door. Steep-roofed, and constructed of heavy, dark timbers, the place had a Bavarian theme, which perhaps had attracted them. Mad sat at a window table with a cup of coffee and a partially eaten piece of strudel. A barely articulate surfer-girl in lederhosen and an embroidered blouse intercepted me to take my order before I sat down.

"Hi," Mad said, smiling, though she showed the same indistinct nervousness I remembered from the afternoon she had seduced me in Gomez's apartment.

"Hi. Roger extends his greetings, too."

She smiled again. "I'm always glad when he extends himself, and the weather's super."

My coffee and pastry came, so we both ate, helping to offset the fact that her nervousness had begun infecting me. Mad was in square-cut khaki hiking shorts and a long-sleeved T. Her hair was loose, but the beguiling hat I'd admired on the deck at Pier 23 rested on the table near her plate. And she was apparently up to other wardrobe tricks, too, because her breasts were unencumbered by any additional fabric beneath her shirt.

Pointing at her feet, I said, "Hey, running shoes. I didn't know you owned any." Since I'd consented to have today's surprise unfold at its own pace, I stopped myself from asking if she'd traded her bra for them.

"Inspired by you," she answered. "They're fabulously comfortable even if they are geeky. And boots are overkill on most of these trails."

"Good. Geeky or not, they're all I brought." I held my own feet up. "But I wish I'd worn shorts instead of jeans."

"I almost didn't because of poison oak." Mad unbuttoned a pocket at her hip, extracted her keys, removed one from the ring, and placed it on my side of the table.

"Now give me yours," she said.

"My what?"

"Ignition key. We're trading cars."

"We are?"

"You promised to follow instructions. Besides, Roger wants you to."

With misgivings, I did as she asked. Gomez was the only person to have driven the Audi but me, and I'd been with him. Mad would be solo, and her driving habits weren't comforting. She finished her coffee, slid my key into her hand, stood, bunched her hair, and put on the hat. Hidden under it had been a sealed envelope, oddly lumpy, with my name written on the front. She slid it toward me, her nervousness seemingly gone.

"After I leave," she said, with insistent eye contact and her hand touching my arm, "go out to the Ghia, open the envelope and read what comes next. You won't be sorry."

Giving an impish look over her shoulder, she walked to the door, and against a subdued babble of German from our fellow customers, I saw her get in the Audi, adjust the seat, and pull onto the road heading west. I paid for our food and contorted myself into Mad's car. Within the envelope, which I kept below the level of the dashboard and windows to defeat the possibility of prying eyes, were a tightly rolled marijuana cigarette, a book of matches, a Xeroxed map segment, and the following note:

> Paul--
> Today is about anticipation and fulfillment.
> We will not speak while we're together no

matter what happens. Remember, we will not speak.

Drive to Stinson Beach and leave my car at the Matt Davis trailhead. The map shows where. If you need to eat, have something in Stinson before you park. Lock the car and wedge the key under the inside of the left rear tire. At exactly 12:30 begin hiking up the trail. When you get into the woods a bit, go behind a tree and smoke the joint. Enough to get stoned, like you did in Sausalito.

Then keep walking. It's steep at first, but eventually you'll reach the grassy upper slopes and the trail will flatten and trace southward above the sea. I'll do exactly the same, starting from the upper end at Pantoll. Your car will be there, with the key hidden as described.

At some point along the hillside we'll meet. When we do, grab me and kiss me. I'll break away and run to a secluded place. Follow, and catch me where I stop.

When we part, continue uphill to your car and go home. I'll find mine at Stinson. We may be together for a half-hour or an hour-and-a-half, I don't know. But you <u>must not</u> say anything, nor will I. If you do, what's developing between us could all be ruined.

Mad

PS. On the off chance that other people are there when we meet, ignore me, pass, and keep going. Give them time to move on, then turn around. I'll do likewise. We'll meet a second time and follow the plan. Don't worry if we have to evade people, it will just build anticipation.

Clearly the above had an effect on Roger there's no need to describe. Nor will you be surprised to learn that I saved the note and still have it hidden with the tape of Mad's voice, her panties, and a few other odds and ends related to that time in my life. When I take them out, as I occasionally do, Roger is cued to remind me of his presence, but the strength of his reaction is nothing like it was upon the note's first reading in Mad's car. And while that initial tumescence was short-lived, it returned off-and-on and of its own accord during my drive to Stinson and my hike up the trail.

Regardless, her plan wasn't complicated, and she seemed to have things timed out perfectly. The Ghia was under-powered and almost comically noisy traversing the mountain's shoulder, but it handled well and I got used to it after a few miles. Passing Pantoll Camp, where the road forks to ascend the summit or drop to the coast, I tried to spot Mad waiting in the Audi, but she wasn't to be seen. And when I thought about it, I realized that she knew I'd look and had made a point of waiting somewhere else.

The signs along that stretch say Panoramic Highway, an apt name. I couldn't pinpoint the last time I'd driven it, but I remembered that I was with Jenny and we'd been wowed coming over for an early dinner and a walk on the beach. This trip, however, all my pores were tingling as Mad's car wound in and out of the trees, up and down the side canyons, and eventually down through the fog to the headlands leading into town, and I felt half stoned without so much as a whiff yet of her dope. It wasn't just that a semi-familiar place had become new and exotic, I myself was new and exotic.

Looking constantly at my watch, I bought a sandwich in the local store and ate it at the dead end of a cross-street near the water. By 12:30 I had located the trail and left the Ghia as Mad instructed. By 12:35 I was a hundred yards up, among dense redwoods that were dripping moisture the receding fog had precipitated on their branches. And by 12:37 I was off the trail behind the tipped-up rootball of a giant fallen trunk, inexpertly sheltering a succession of matches in order to take three—no, four—solid, throat-burning hits on the joint. Mad hadn't told me what to do with the stub, so I buried it among the redwood roots because I didn't want to have it on me in case anything weird happened. That was my last practical thought of the day.

Roger and I began to climb. On a series of plank bridges I crossed and re-crossed a creek that was always within hearing as it poured down a channel of chest-high ferns, but was frequently blocked from sight. Then I switchbacked out of the canyon to break through the redwoods into mixed oaks and madrones on a ridge so steep that long flights of steps had been cut into the trail to permit ascent. I was a mile or more from the car in gray, filtered light. Despite the coolness and my fit aerobic condition, I began to sweat and my heart pounded in my ears.

Finally, as though levitated by external powers, I rose above the forest canopy and the fog at the same moment. I heard Steller's jays, I heard the breeze rustling the madrone leaves below me, I felt sun on my skin, I saw a red-tailed hawk wheeling in the updraft, and I saw the tumbled and furrowed top of the fog stretching away like a vast, unmade bed with the Santa Cruz Mountains as headboard far to the south. But of human life, I heard or saw nothing.

Continuing to climb, I reached a knoll with my first view of where I was headed. The trail now became a brownish ribbon laid to follow the grassy folds and curves of the sun-struck, sun-bleached hillside, trending gently up through isolated copses of live oak and around a sculpted outcrop of serpentine rock two miles ahead. With a renewed rush of anticipation on both Roger's part and mine, I squinted, scanning for Mad. I still saw no one.

I became increasingly aware of the sun. I was thirsty, and I'd left my dark glasses, water bottle and hat in the Audi, not imagining I wouldn't have access to them. The trail veered into a rocky defile and paralleled a dry, winter-only stream carved into the slope and overhung with pungent bay laurel. At the defile's shaded apex the trail crossed the streambed, making a hairpin turn to wind back into the sunlight on the other side. After a short interval I rounded a shallow ridge and entered another defile, this one even more pronounced. Suddenly my skin prickled and I drew a sharp intake of breath.

Against a rock in the deepest shade sat a longhaired aboriginal man in a deerskin loincloth, bare-chested and wearing a shell necklace. His eyes were closed and he appeared to be meditating, with his hips resting on his heels in a modified lotus position. At his throat, where a tracheotomy vent would be placed, shone a ruby jewel. Dizzy, I involuntarily raised my forearms as though to protect myself, and in that instant he disappeared. My pulse rate soared.

Taking time to collect myself, I slowly advanced. Jays squawked, I heard the breeze, and a ground squirrel scampered away scolding me *tisk-tisk-tisk* for disturbing his acorn hunt. There was no other sound. It hadn't been Mad in disguise, and it certainly hadn't been a native shaman or anyone else. It could only have been something my mind and eyes had constructed from the pattern of shadows, rocks and the roots of a large tree. Yet studying them from all available angles, I couldn't reconstruct what I knew I'd seen.

I felt cold, though I was sweating, and I speeded my pace to pass that spot, to put distance between it and me, and to regain the sunlight. Beyond the laurel grove and the dry stream the trail began to run flatter through open savanna, but the irregular contour of the hillside limited my view to no more than fifty or seventy-five yards ahead. The red-tailed hawk I'd seen earlier had been joined by another, both now sailing and circling in the pure blue sky.

Below me the golden grass dropped to a fringe of woods, then to a longer, steeper face of rock and brush a thousand feet through the fog, all the way to the invisible sea. Which was I more stoned on—Mad or marijuana? An impossible question, but never had I experienced my moment-to-moment surroundings as intensely as in the last hour.

A slight leftward curve brought me to a broad, grassy bowl, and there on its opposite flank was Mad. I saw her hat first, then the scissoring motion of her bare legs. She gave no indication that she saw me, and I quickly lowered my head to avoid sending an inadvertent signal. We were about 125 yards apart and apparently had the bowl to ourselves, with Roger so hard he began to impede my progress toward what he wanted.

In erotic dreams, or in mine, anyway, this is when a Boy Scout troop would march by or my mother would drop in for a visit. But on Mt. Tam, Mad and I suffered no such setbacks. Time seemed to slow, making each of my steps take ten full seconds and every footfall land with a prolonged, echoing thud, as the tufted grass along the trail rasped against my jeans. Head still down, and over the noise of my breath, I heard Mad's shoes scuffing the earth, growing closer and closer.

Her shadow reached me first. I stood aside as though letting her pass, but she leaned to brush an arm against my chest. The sensation was like a visible flare of pleasure. I roughly seized her shoulders, twisting her body against mine and forcing our mouths together. She replied with a groan, equally of protest and desire, yielding her lips briefly, then turning away as she shoved me hard in the chest.

I released her, surprised at the force she'd used, and she darted down the slope, running rapidly through the grass. She had a twenty-foot lead before I took any action, the initial one being to make sure we were unobserved. Since we were, I joined the chase. My longer stride let me close the gap to fifteen feet by the time Mad reached the margin of the grass, where she zigged and zagged into the trees. I realized she'd been avoiding poison oak, and carefully did the same. She dodged around a rock-pile and jumped down into a small clearing in a stand of Monterey Pine at the edge of the cliff. Patches of fog still hung below us, with the sun just beginning to glint off the water where the fog had burned away.

About half way across the clearing Mad looked back, saw me, stumbled to her knees, then sprawled forward on the tawny carpet of pine needles. It was a bit of a pratfall, the only part of her act that hadn't been flawless. But seconds later, when I caught up to her, she was on her knees trying to crawl in the direction she'd been running. I threw myself down, wrapping my arms over her back like a beginning position for judo class.

She struggled, but I horsed her over and immobilized her legs by tangling mine around them. I saw her face and eyes clearly for the only time since we'd met for coffee, and what I saw there seemed very close to fear. I never intend to be in that kind of situation for real, and I pray that I would find a terrorized woman to be profoundly non-sexual, but to my shock, Mad's expression was the strongest aphrodisiac yet in an aphrodisiac-filled day. My hands groped under her shirt to cup her naked breasts, and I ran my mouth against her sweat-salty neck, tracking upward to capture her lips.

As before, she briefly responded, then pulled back, struggled, responded again for a longer period, then pulled back. This was to be the mode, but I was undeterred. Her nipples were erect and her panties, when I pried open the buttons of her shorts, were so wet at the crotch that they clung to the creases of her flesh. Roger, meanwhile, was doing all he could to unfasten my jeans with no outside assistance.

After repeated cycles of response, pulling back and struggle, my shirt was off, Mad's was wadded at her neck, her hat was gone, her shorts and panties were around one of her calves and my jeans and briefs were down to my shoe tops. She would dig a heel in the pine needles, push up, roll away, then roll forward to catch Roger between her legs and bathe him with her slipperiness, but always manage to deny him entry. I began to thrust at her, masturbating, almost, against her inner thigh or her pubic hair.

Suddenly she altered the sequence, flopping onto her stomach and starting to crawl away again. I lunged onto her back, pressing her down, using a hand to open space between the pine needle-rimed globes of her rear, driving my hips to again graze Roger across her flesh and finally into the overripe fig of her vagina. She perhaps could have pulled away, perhaps not, but she no longer tried. Instead she gave a short, shrieking cry, rocking back to meet me in an accelerating rhythm until I released spurt after spurt into her and she gave the cry again, longer, and broken by gasps. Emanating from somewhere, I heard my own voice make guttural accompaniment.

But we weren't done. My spasms continued until there was no more to ejaculate, yet Roger remained hard, and Mad abandoned all pretense of escape. She rolled onto her side, faced me, placed a leg over my hip and brought me back inside her, while I licked forest detritus from her breasts. Her prohibition against speaking had seemed bizarre at first, but I now forgot the impulse and fully gave myself to the physical. Mad attacked my mouth with her lips and tongue, as though she were starved for it, and we established a steady, plunging rhythm that focused my entire consciousness in the tip of my cock. With her breathy groans in my ear, I came a second time, a single insistent shot that verged on pain.

÷ ÷ ÷

When truly satisfied sexually, Paul Stiles either sleeps or assumes a sleep-like state. By June of 1978 I was still discovering that, having not understood the concepts of sexual and satisfaction as being related until my tutelage by Mad. And I say sleep-like, because I would swear I didn't sleep on Mt. Tam. I was at some level aware that she was easing out of our mutual embrace, and that the sinking sun had penetrated our little grove to shine uncomfortably on the back of my neck.

GOMEZ

Yet move as I might, I couldn't escape its rays. The *M* of Mad's name, with a question gradually forming to follow the *a* and the *d*, was on its way out of my throat when I caught myself, silenced it per our agreement, opened my eyes, and realized she wasn't there. My shirt had been draped over me from my waist to my knees, I was blotched with pine needles, and I was alone. It was 3:30 p.m.

I was still stoned, too, in a mellow, residual way. A thousand feet below, miles of ocean were now clear, with newly revealed fishing boats and freighters moving slowly past as though they were pieces in a board game. I got dressed, forged a meandering route up to the trail and continued toward my car.

I felt completely at home in that primitive environment and in what I had done. No matter how clever or complex, or how elaborately dressed or coifed, I was an animal. I experienced animal pleasure, animal passion, animal lust. I could remember it, deny it, analyze it, marvel at it, or feel guilt about it, but I was an animal, descended from the rutting moose, the great apes, and Australopithecus. And like me, they all must sometimes have seen the spirits of their ancient ancestors along the trail.

PART V

The man who is reborn is always the same man,
more and more himself with each rebirth. He is only
shedding his skin…and with his skin, his sins.

> Henry Miller
> *Tropic of Capricorn*
> Grove Press Edition, 1961

CHAPTER 21

If I hadn't stayed on the coast trying to catch further sight of Mad, I might have been home in time to answer the phone when she called. As it was, the machine picked up, so I wasn't altogether in limbo.

On the way to find the Audi at Pantoll Camp, which was half-an-hour more of hiking, mostly through wooded uplands, I had plucked sprigs of bay leaves, crushed them and smeared the essence on my face and neck. It was sensual and exhilarating, and probably long known to California Indians, because it turned out to repel insects. But the heavy herbal aroma still didn't override the dope smell in my car. Recklessly, Mad's toking had begun before she left the parking area, or worse, while she had been driving, which I normally wouldn't tolerate. In this case, I was so taken by how extraordinary she was, like no woman I'd ever imagined, that any thought of making it an issue quickly faded.

With no conscious plan, I drove beeline back to Stinson and the lower trailhead, keeping all my windows open for a maximum airing out. Mad's Ghia was gone, of course, and though I later stationed myself behind some brush in a pullout near the junction of State Route 1 and Panoramic Highway, she didn't come by. I gave it twenty minutes, then returned to SF. And what I'd wanted wasn't to talk to her after our episode of silence. I wanted to see her, preferably from a distance, while knowing that she'd come there because of me, and to prolong that sense by following her a few miles, if I could be sure I was unobserved.

"Oh, you beast," her recorded message began. "That was fantasy brought to life, something I've dreamt of for years.

"I didn't want to spoil it by meeting you on the road afterward, so I went north through Fairfax to the Richmond Bridge. Now for the bad news. Since I'm busy with family through mid-July, I'm not sure when we'll be together, but I'm sending a gift to tide you over. It will arrive in a few days.

GOMEZ

"I'll just have to make do with my memories, and let Clark wonder why Ravel's *Bolero* is always on the turntable when he visits the cottage. Good-bye, Paul-the-beast."

Beast, I thought, wow, and I'd been one, but the fact that I wouldn't see her for an undefined period wrenched at me. Gift or no gift, what Gomez said months ago had been right: when somebody was married, you operated on their schedule or not at all.

Saturday I worked to make up for my Thursday off, and Sunday I went for a long run on the Embarcadero, which got me mixed up in the Gay Freedom Parade, because I tried a shortcut on the way back. You couldn't live in the city and not know the damned thing was going on, but at the wrong corner I forgot. The next morning's paper said that over 300,000 people had attended, and that Market Street was completely closed. Not all 300,000 were gay, of course, but an amazing proportion were. The rest were the usual street personalities, plus other locals for whom any excuse to have a parade and party is good enough.

The speeches and awards were at the Civic Center, so at least I got to miss those. Mayor Moscone, Congressman Burton, Willie Brown and the new gay Supervisor Harvey Milk were among the speakers, with Milk apparently upstaging everyone. "This is America, too," he reportedly said. "Love it or leave it."

On the heels of Proposition 13, the anti-gay Proposition 6 was coming in November, seeking to deny their ability to hold teaching jobs. It had lots of people fired up, pro and con, including the singer Anita Bryant's national movement advocating the pro side. As for the con side, I got surrounded at one point by a wacky entourage in clown suits and had to wear a *No on 6* button before they'd let me pass. "Oh, nice legs," the tallest clown joked, eyeing my nylon shorts.

I didn't think of myself as anti-gay, I was just tired of their making a big deal of it. Being hetero was no automatic bed of roses. Jenny had come to the 1977 parade with Barbara, I remembered, right after they'd announced their partnership. I also remembered that she'd thought about coming in previous years, but I hadn't understood the significance, because she was always more political and more into causes than I was.

And this year, to top it off, a beautiful day, putting the lie to standard complaints about SF summers. The paper also said Milk had received death-threats because of his key role in the Anti-6 campaign and the hard-hitting speeches he was giving against it. You'd have never guessed, though, to see him go by in a big white convertible, waving and smiling. Behind him in another convertible were two guys dressed as President Carter carrying a banner of Carter's recent pronouncement that "Human Rights Are Absolute." There were brass bands, jugglers, and all kinds of everybody else, and a Mime Troupe float, too, though Mad wasn't part of it.

Gay doctors and plumbers marched in pink lab coats or coveralls, along with drag queens and a wild contingent of so-called Dykes on Bikes in heavy leathers gunning their Harleys to a roar with their clutches disengaged as they coasted by. But it was a low blow to hear them chant, "Two, four, six, eight, are you sure your wife is straight?" Jenny was undoubtedly there, accompanied by Barbara, and I desperately hoped I wouldn't run into them. They'd never join the dykey bikers, that wouldn't be Jenny's style, but there was plenty of room in the crowd, if not elsewhere in the parade.

It was colorful and I was trapped, so I tried to enjoy it. A common theme for the marchers was to carry signs saying where they were from, I guess to emphasize how diverse SF's gay community was, and I was impressed. Maybe, using an atlas, you could find a state or country not represented, but at the time I couldn't have named one. I even ended up glad I'd come.

How could I have felt so blindsided by my marital collapse when all these people, from every walk of life, of every imaginable age, and from every corner of the world, were in some part what Jenny was? And why would she have wanted to acknowledge it any sooner than she had if the Anita Bryant types were so bent on discrimination that they ran ballot initiatives to legitimize prejudice?

In a weird way, and I do mean weird, I felt left out. Gays seemed to have a bond I'd never known with any group. But having already considered the idea, I knew that being gay wasn't a choice for me. And not for anybody, I was gradually beginning to concede, given the increasingly likely genetic component. Besides, with Mad in my life, I'd absolutely choose to be straight.

While I was near Carlotta's Fountain at the foot of Kearny Street, a blocky guy, sort of baby-faced and wearing a cheap suit, steered his way along the curb. He had a sour expression and was neither spectator nor participant. He was in his thirties, and with him were a college-age guy and girl who had the ultra-clean look of Mormon missionaries. They were trying to pass out handfuls of *Yes on 6* ribbons, but in that crowd, no takers. The assembly of clowns I'd seen earlier kept pace a few feet behind them, hissing.

Right in front of me the blocky guy turned around and glared. "This is a public street!" he declared. His face reddened, he spoke aggressively, but he didn't yell. "These two have as much right to be here as you do! And I have the same right!" He squared his shoulders and resumed his original course.

The clowns hissed louder, but they stopped following him. "Who was that," I asked the tall one who'd admired my legs.

Through garishly made-up lips, he — I think it was a he — answered, "Supervisor Dan White. An ex-cop. Of the whole Board, the only one to vote against our parade permit. We hope he gets run over by a motorcycle."

I was going to ask him more, because I'd heard Gomez mention White recently, when I got distracted by Gomez himself. He was disguised and standing on a flatbed truck, but I was sure it was him. Sharing the truck were a dozen teenagers of uncertain gender or gender orientation who lounged guardedly on pieces of used living room furniture. **Tenderloin Youth Shelter** said a crude, magic-marker sign on the cab. **Friendly, Safe, and Better Than Home** said another.

The Bob Marley song *One Love* belted from the truck's portable PA and Gomez was lip-synching into a broom handle with a spent tennis ball speared on it for a mike. He wore a dreadlock wig, sunglasses and frizzy goatee, and was dressed in an old tuxedo with a big *No on 6* button on the lapel. What he was doing there I couldn't fathom, but every time I decided it wasn't him, he moved or scanned the crowd in a way that convinced me it was. And clearly, he didn't want to be recognized; nor did I, so I dodged behind a lamppost.

In a minute he was safely past, but an implosion in my chest signaled a new problem. Two feet away was the back of Jenny's head. The shapeless, blunt-cut blonde hair was unmistakable, though I didn't recognize the blouse she was wearing or the woman, a tough-looking brunette, around whom she had her arm. They began to turn my way, tracking the next vehicle in line, a vintage Packard marked **KQED Broadcasting**.

GOMEZ

I ducked behind the lamppost again, but for naught. It wasn't Jenny. Right height, right coloring, right build, but wrong face, a New York accent and not, thank god, her.

÷ ÷ ÷

Fourth of July and the following weekend I spent partly with the Housers, who apparently enjoyed my company, and partly with Jordan. At the St. Francis Yacht Club he played host for fireworks offshore of the Marina Green. Eve was sick, he explained, and Marnie was out of town. The atmosphere was stiff, but the view was great and I had a good time. Jordan pointed out people whom I knew only from reading Herb Caen, who was even present himself, as one more target for Jordan's catty remarks.

It turned out that Jordan had also given Rufe the OK to talk about L-W. Drunk on Scotch, he flashed a grim smile when I asked what had spawned the decision. "It's my revenge," he said, "on you for asking, on Rufe for his part, and on L-W for the whole damned thing." Beyond that, he wouldn't elaborate.

The Housers and I went to a new show, *Beach Blanket Babylon Goes to the Stars*, which was their idea and was a real kick. There'd been lots of hype, so I worried it would be a letdown, but not at all. It was as nutty as the Gay Freedom Parade, yet with no pretense of serious purpose.

The next Monday Mad's gift arrived, in an appropriately plain brown package, which contained a book, in a plain brown jacket of its own. At least the back was plain. The front featured a sepia-toned photo of a young, 1920s-style woman posed in an empire chair such that her thighs were tantalizingly revealed between the lace border of her slip and her stocking tops. *Delta of Venus* the cover read, with a secondary line saying Erotica by Anaïs Nin. I felt an immediate shiver of desire.

This was the title that had been sold out at City Lights the night I'd bought my editions of Nin's *Diary*. I sat and flipped it open, not waiting to clear away the wrapping, remove my tie, or pour my usual after-work wine. It had been published posthumously, just that spring, but consisted of fifteen pieces Nin had written in New York during the early 40s for $1 a page, as a way to earn money after her forced relocation from Paris. A shadowy dealer or collector of pornography had hired her, Miller and other struggling writers to supply him. But Nin, also according to the preface, hadn't been her patron's favorite, her approach being too cerebral and not sufficiently physical.

Among the contents were the stories *Mathilde*, *The Ring*, and *Lilith*. Those I devoured on the spot, imagining Mad as the female sensibility and her voice reading aloud. Roger soon demanded exercise and got it. I had planned to go running, then have a quick supper from the freezer, but running fell by the wayside and I went to eat in Chinatown so I wouldn't be tempted to read more at the table. I forced myself to use chopsticks, too, as a form of impulse control.

Mad's mantra was anticipation, she had demonstrated its power, and I undertook to practice it. I would limit myself to one of Nin's twelve remaining tales per week, defined as Monday through Sunday, skipping those weeks in which I saw Mad herself. On the designated night, whatever I decided it to be, I could read that week's tale as often as I wanted, but I couldn't reread any other until I'd read all.

Despite the opinion of the collector who commissioned them, the first three had seemed abundantly physical to me, yet they were antithetical to the leering *Hustler* grossness that had gotten Larry Flynt hauled into court and later wounded by an assassin. It takes all kinds to make a world, they say, but I felt I was finally getting closer to knowing what kind I was. Or if not, at least knowing the kinds I wasn't. Maybe I liked sex a lot more than I'd realized, but that didn't make me a creep.

Meanwhile, carrying out my high-minded plan posed complications. First I had to rearrange my sock drawer to make room for a book. If I balled up my dress hose and piled the athletic and casual socks flat, I could wall off a secret area and then put a layer of athletic socks over it. Inside were Mad's panties, now in saran wrap, her note from Mt. Tam, two tape cassettes of her voice, a postcard of the Klimt nude I'd seen at her house, a cassette of Ravel's *Bolero* I sometimes played in my car, *Delta of Venus* again folded in the paper it had arrived in, and another note that I'd found tucked into the paper when I reused it to hide the book.

GOMEZ

For Paul-the-Beast,

Something to keep you and Roger company while my trapeze swings into my other life for now. I know you'll like it, because it's an all-time favorite of mine, and my men always do.

Speaking of Roger, I've decided there's a very sexy place he should explore. The idea has seemed too intimidating until lately, but he and bestial you are the perfect team. You'll find what I'm talking about in *The Boarding School*.

I also have suspicions that you took the panties I left at Gomez's the night we made love there. I needed an extra pair after lunch last week, looked where he usually puts them, and other likely spots, but they were gone. If you're guilty you have to admit it.

Mad

The practical difficulties of erotic rationing were thus minor compared to the psychological ones, and clearly I would read *The Boarding School* next — as in next week, if I could wait — though I knew what she meant without reading it. I also knew why Roger would make the idea less intimidating, and it was the first time she'd in any way referred to his size. She hadn't done it accusatorily, but I felt accused nonetheless, and my hopes that Clark's equipment was smaller than mine were now out the window. Yet her idea was exciting, too, very much so.

Then there was the news that she'd been looking for panties after a recent lunch at Gomez's, and that *all* her men, presumably including Clark, liked the Nin book. It didn't take much to read between those lines. I had a place in her life — or in one of her lives — and if I could keep generating the requisite denial of the larger picture, this was the most rewarding relationship I'd ever experienced. If not, a long fall with sharp rocks at the bottom was where it led. One thing sure, I'd deny any knowledge of the missing panties and phone her at the Mime Troupe tomorrow to make my point.

÷ ÷ ÷

GOMEZ

Since she wasn't around when I called, my message had to be cryptic, but this much should have been plain: I was falsely accused. The guy I talked to, the same insouciant voice that had once claimed to be sleeping on the floor, got no inkling from me of what wardrobe item might be in question or whether it was Troupe property. I said only that Mad had asked for an accounting, I was baffled, she needed to try somewhere else, and I was relying on him to convey those facts. I gave a good performance.

A few hours later Gomez checked in, and by now Ivy was used to putting his calls through without screening. "Long time no see," he began.

"Yeah, too long." This was a ploy on my part, a sign of the change in our friendship. I owed him a call, but I'd procrastinated since the parade. It was hard enough to gliss along against the double dissonance of Mad and Bonhof, and now came something else. Why had he been there? Was he merely supporting a worthy new cause, or did he have a third life, separate from Gomez and Steentofter? "What've you been up to?" I added.

Surprisingly, he neither dodged the question nor turned it around in accusation of my own lapse. "Been out of town," he replied. "I had a chance to head to Tahoe for my annual brown-rice/craps-shooting scene." His voice seemed more subdued than usual.

"Right, I remember. Submitting yourself to chance."

"As we've discussed...and I even won a few bucks. A good omen for the year ahead. I'm looking at heavy-duty changes. And there's weird shit going down, too."

"Really? Fill me in." I nervously shifted my grip on the receiver. Was he onto Mad's and my nosing around? Or onto Bonhof?

"That's why I called. But not over the phone. Can we meet for a drink at six?"

"Tonight? Where? Silver Dollar? Washington Square B&G?"

"Someplace new I'm hanging out, called Hieronymus Boxx...at Precita and Folsom. You'll dig it."

"OK, I'll be there. But come on, don't I at least get a preview?"

"I can't risk being overheard. I'm not calling from where you think."

"Oh." I assumed at that point he would hang up, per the Gomez norm, but he didn't.

GOMEZ

"What've you been up to yourself?" he asked.

"Not much. Work...plus hanging around with one of my neighbors and a couple I know who live on Telegraph Hill." I could have left it at that, but I was tired of letting myself be bulldozed by him. "And believe it or not, I went to the Gay Freedom Parade."

"You? Why?" There was a distinct pause, then he jabbed, "Must have been looking for your ex," trying to put me on the defensive.

I didn't fold. "That'd be reason *not* to go," I responded calmly. "What happened was I blundered onto it while I was out for a run. No planning involved. It was really colorful. You ever watch one?"

"Nah, not my thing. Live and let live is the best I can do in that department. Seen Mad lately, by the way?"

"No," I lied. There was nothing about Mt. Tam I could safely mention. His question had sounded neutral, but he'd deliberately cut me short on the parade, and I was as sure as ever that he'd been there. "I've got news for you, too."

"What?" He seemed edgy.

"You make me wait, I make you wait."

"Touché," he replied with an approving laugh. "See you at six."

According to my map, Precita and Folsom intersected two blocks south of Army Street at a small park adjacent to what was shown as Bernal Heights, which bounded the Outer Mission to the east. It was completely new territory for me, half a mile farther than Gomez's apartment, and I couldn't think why he would have picked it. The weather was wildly windy and gray-black when I set out, a sudden reversal from a mostly sunny day, the kind of sky that in Kansas would have people cowering in their cellars.

Here it only meant that the fog was in, obeying a logic that defied all prediction. Although I had to detour at several points, because of traffic and because the Heights' transverse bulk blocked streets that would otherwise have gone through, I still got myself parked near the fantastical confines of Gomez's new hangout by just past the hour.

CHAPTER 22

From outside, the building was a tall, ornate Victorian in the Carpenter-Gothic style, painted in contrasting shades of green, with rose, purple and yellow decorative accents giving the effect of a psychedelic T-shirt. It had no doubt been a hotel or rooming house at one time, and the floors above the ground-level Hieronymus Boxx Cafe looked to be a warren of small apartments, some facing the narrow swath of trodden Bermuda grass and windswept shrubs that passed for a park. At the park's center a gaggle of children who might have been from the same Mexican village as Graciela played on a bent and rusty jungle gym.

Inside was an artists' paradise, its walls adorned by continuous, inter-linked murals of quirky street scenes à la Bosch, Breughel or Hogarth, all of whose work I'd studied but could never keep straight. Since Hieronymus Bosch seemingly figured in the establishment's name, I assumed he was a major influence. Also, that Bosch was Dutch—or I thought he was—might explain Gomez's attraction to the place.

The bar ran along the wall paralleling the entryway, while a dining room spread leftward, evolving toward the front, along a row of low windows, into a less formal setting with newspapers piled about and no tablecloths. Old-fashioned globe lights hung on chains from the ceiling, but no Gomez in sight. A bearded guy of indeterminate age, in coveralls, sat reading the *New York Times* and nursing a glass of red wine. He, I and a workshirt-clad couple sharing a pizza in the far corner were the only customers.

Planning to install myself at a window, I skirted the grand piano separating the sectors of the room. From behind me came footsteps and a male voice. "How about something to drink?"

When I turned back, a lanky six-footer with flowing chestnut hair and a matching mustache was advancing in my direction, while a service door adjoining the bar swung closed in its frame to show where he'd come from. He stopped a few feet away. His woven belt, pantaloons, pleated shirt and paisley doublet announced that, for him, the annual Renaissance Pleasure Faire I'd read about in that week's *Chron* was an everyday event. Add a rapier at his waist and he would be a movie extra.

"Sure," I replied, taking him in. "A carafe of the house red will be fine."

"Big or little?" He had the overused vocal chords of a former rock singer.

"Make it big, with two glasses. I'm waiting for someone."

"Don't sit up front if you're gonna' eat. Food's only served back here."

"Just drinks as far as I know. Unless my friend wants dinner. You'll probably recognize him. It's Gomez."

"Who?"

"Gomez. Andrés Gomez. He's been hanging out here lately."

"Oh, yeah…sure…Andrés. The piano guy from Argentina. He's too much…and he just scarfs on my old lady's quiche."

"Piano guy?"

"Hell, yes. Terrific. Does Tampa Red boogie-woogie, Beethoven, other classical. Everybody in the place shuts up when he plays. He says he studied it back east."

"I guess I don't know him that well." I spoke matter-of-factly, but what I'd said made me feel hollow.

"You somebody from his new job? You have the look."

"No." I masked my surprise. "I think job is what I'm here to learn about."

"I won't spoil the story, but it's a hot-shit deal." My host returned to the bar while I got a table with a full view of the street and sidewalk.

He brought my wine. "I'm Wally, by the way," he stated, pointing to his chest. "Keep coming in, man. We opened a few months ago, and we'll treat you right."

"Are these murals your work?"

"Yeah, some. My old lady's, too. But we let anybody add on if they submit an idea and can handle a brush. It's a neighborhood thing."

"Very impressive."

"Hispanic murals, like you see all over the Mission, are only one kind. I dig them, but other traditions need to stay alive. Andrés has his eye on the wall above the piano. I guess he used to paint. Says he plans to work up something. They're fun as hell to do."

Wally left to wait on a somber, thirtyish female in a granny dress and combat boots who had come in to sit at the bar. Drinking my first glass, I ran my eyes back and forth between the street, looking for Gomez, and the closest mural. It was hysterically complex, with pigs being slaughtered and smoked into hams and bacon by Russian peasants and Greek helots on the steps of the Transamerica Tower. The color tones and shading were from a fifteenth-century canvas, but the crowd included all manner of odd figures and details—a cubist Picasso nude, a warmly impressionist Renoir family, an ICBM staged for launch, Richard Nixon, Pancho Villa, John Lennon, the Lone Ranger, Eleanor Roosevelt, Barbra Streisand, Fidel Castro, Mata Hari, Willie Brown, Long John Silver, King Kong and endless others.

I was antsy at having to wait, but found myself smiling. The fog outside reached as low as the rooftops, like my childhood model-train town in the basement if I'd hooked up the vaporizer and left it on for a week. Scraps of newspaper scudded down the sidewalk and across the park. Into a spot at the curb, empty except for a mound of fresh dog-do, pulled a dark blue BMW sedan, a nicely kept older one, with a stubby, angular trunk and ovoid chrome grill. Wherever the Ranchero ended up parking, it wouldn't be there.

A guy with two or three inches of combed dark hair and a neat bristle of mustache got out and hurried into Hieronymus Boxx without looking up. He wore a stylishly cut business suit, white shirt, no glasses and no tie. He was, I realized with a delayed jolt, Gomez.

"Hey, Andrés!" I heard Wally call. "Your buddy's up front with some wine unless he's drunk it all."

"Wally, my man," Gomez replied. I couldn't quite see around the corner, but it sounded as though backs were being slapped and high-fives given. "Marsha," Gomez continued, presumably to the granny-dress woman, "how's it going?"

"The usual," she grumbled, giving way to a louder female voice that must have been Wally's old lady, saying, "If you play *Moonlight Sonata* I promise to cry."

GOMEZ

Hop-stepping around the piano, Gomez swung into view. "Shit, Paul, sorry," he said. "I wanted to get here first to provide the welcome." He scraped back a chair and dropped into it.

"Wally was an OK sub," I replied. "But what's going on? This Andrés stuff?"

"Kind of a new me." Gomez looked up while pouring his wine, causing him to spill dribbles of it on the table. "Not new, new...you know, but a new variation." Sliding his glass clear of the spill, he took a long drink.

I steeled myself for one of his charm attacks. "Let's see," I said, "contact lenses, new haircut, new mustache, new car, new job according to Wally...and that's a hell of a sharp suit." There was essentially nothing of Gomez left, or of Andy, either.

"Pierre Cardin," he announced, regarding his coat sleeves with satisfaction. "On sale, of course, two for one, but the only threads like this I've ever had."

"And the job?" I asked, while registering that he, not Mad, had been the buyer.

"That's my real news. I was going to string you along, soak up your stuff first, but since Wally let the cat out, here it is: I'm working in the Mayor's Office."

"The mayor? Doing what?"

Gomez was loving every second. "Special Assistant for Community Affairs," he answered. "Good bucks and good clout. Too fucking much, huh?"

"Amazing. We should've ordered champagne." I raised my glass.

"Thanks," he returned the gesture. "I told you, heavy-duty changes. Basically, I do whatever George wants, but my main assignment is keeping peace between Dan White's Irish Catholics in the Crocker-Amazon and the Hispanic Catholics in the Mission...*and* not letting Harvey Milk's gays splinter the Moscone/progressive coalition. We can piss off downtown and survive, and we can piss off the cops, a lot of whom don't vote in SF anyway, but we can't piss off the neighborhoods. I'm not alone on it, but I'm the eyes, ears and legs."

"Wow!" I said, but also gibed, "And things move fast. Not just Mayor Moscone... but *George*. You must be in solid."

"Well, I haven't god-damned sold out," Gomez shot back. "Since Alabama, and especially since Watergate, I've never thought of doing politics again. This is different. And yeah, George, that's how he wants it. From what I'm seeing, I'd follow him off a cliff."

"Selling out's your worry, not mine. But big cities don't run on good deeds and twinkle dust. There's been a lot of stuff in the paper about campaign contributions from Howard Hughes and from that People's Temple guy, and about hidden give-aways to settle the city employees' strike. Leave cliff-jumping to somebody else."

"It's a turn of phrase. Look, George is a practical politician. He cuts the deals he has to cut. Here's what gets me excited. As a person, he's completely for real. He lives on his salary, and after all those years in the State Senate his savings account isn't much bigger than mine. And who do you think decriminalized marijuana and assured abortion rights in California? Or got free school lunches for poor kids?"

"I was never that much into politics, but what about the chick you saw him with at Henry Africa's? He's married to someone else, right."

"Right. As for the rest," he said with finality, "I don't really know, and I don't ever plan to know. But this is more than a job. It's the one thing I've believed in for a long, long time. And yeah, other changes are part of the package. I hoped you'd be on for the ride, same as before."

"Meaning what?"

"Usually when I've made turns in my life, like Alabama, or coming back to Berkeley, or from over there to here, people get goosey and don't stick. Or I dump them. But now it's the same town and I'm still Gomez...which I have to be whether I want to or not."

"Wouldn't Steentofter be just as easy?"

"Easier in some respects, harder in others. But it's not an option."

"It's your name, for Christ's sake!"

"Not exactly...and not any more. I did a legal change a couple of months ago, to match the Social Security number I gave the Centro. Beside, I'm fenced in by affirmative action. The mayor needs me as Gomez. I don't come right out and say I'm Argentinean ...second generation, or whatever...but I let people believe it."

"I thought you were Hispanic either way."

GOMEZ

"I am, but I have to look like and sound like. George can't be leaning on the police to integrate the force and not do the same himself."

"And that's not fraud?"

"I hope nobody finds out, but no. You can change your name to anything as long as there isn't criminal intent. At the time I did it, the mayor and affirmative action weren't on the horizon. But I'll be buffing up the rest of my Hispanic credentials just in case."

"While consoling yourself with a new car, new clothes and a new look. How do you keep the identities straight?"

"No problem, I'm used to it. But how did *you* get to be such a cynic? What I saw last fall was a sweet little lost boy."

We both laughed and took another drink. I didn't accept cynic, but there was an answer to his question I didn't give. The transition from lost boy to whatever I'd become had everything to do with him, and I wasn't going back. He read my silence and my facial expression as criticism and made quick efforts to cover.

"The clothes and the look go with having an uptown job. I've got to be straight, not too ethnic...or too bohemian. It's a matter of credibility. I have to be *of* and *about* neighborhood politics, but not parochial. The car, too. My mechanic always had the hots for your Ranchero, and he was working on this classy old Beamer as a hobby, so we traded. You and Mad don't get to drive your German cars and leave Andrés behind."

"Does she know about this?"

"The suit, yes. The rest broke all of a sudden, and I'm only on the new job four days. Officially, that is. The Centro cut me slack before because of the advantage to them if I worked for George. Anyway, I wanted to tell you first. Also, September 1, I'm moving to a nicer pad," Gomez raised a thumb over his shoulder to the Heights, "up there."

"Is the price of admission that I have to call you Andrés from now on?"

"Could be important," he nodded, with one of his half-smiles. "I still answer to Gomez, but I try to downplay it. Andrés has more cachet for how I'm operating."

"But you are telling Mad, right?"

"I guess, but remember what else I said when I called...oh, my new place will have a phone, and I'll give you the current office number as soon as my cards are printed. Anyway, I said there was weird shit going down, and truth is, I'm not sure where Mad stands. I want your advice."

My heartbeat thumped in my ears. "What kind of weird shit?"

"She's getting possessive...or something. Ignacio at Las Pampas said she hit him up on my background, and there was a call to the Centro asking about me, which I'm pretty sure was her. When Hilda, in the business office, who's a natural mimic, passed along the word, the voice she imitated sounded exactly like Mad."

"So?" I dodged. "Take it as flattery. Anaïs pursuing Henry."

He grimaced. "That schtick's getting old. Seems like she's prowling my apartment, too, and is always trying to buy me stuff. I don't feel the same ease between us."

"But she's married, for god's sake. Why would she be possessive?" There was just enough truth to my argument that I could sound convincing.

"What *you* don't know about women would fill a semi-trailer. Her husband gave her a gun last winter. Who's to say she didn't buy a replacement after it got stolen?"

My heart thumped louder. "I hadn't thought of that." Which I hadn't, though I now remembered their banter about the gun the night I first met her. But were Mad's motives for hiring Bonhof less innocent than I'd believed? No, impossible.

"Aahh..." Gomez went on, moderating his tone, "good chance I'm overstating. Things have even seemed distant between you and me lately, and that's my fault. I've been eaten up with angling for this job and having to keep it hush-hush."

"I haven't noticed anything," I said, though I had, even without the changes on my end.

"Good. You've already helped. I'll crank up the sweet talk and try to bring Mad around. Just don't let her know I'm moving. I'll explain the new job and the new look, but longer term, I want to set boundaries if I need them, and not give her a key."

"My lips are sealed," I answered, conflicted, but relieved that this aspect of the conversation hadn't gone worse. "Besides, I don't actually know where you're moving."

"Right, but the point is, you will. Mad, maybe yes, maybe no."

I refilled our glasses, emptying the carafe. The less of Mad's time Gomez took, the more there would be for me. That thought enabled what I said next. "Jumping back to your new job, has it by any chance gotten you involved with something called the Tenderloin Youth Shelter?"

Gomez choked on his wine, no more ingenuously than I had on my beer at the ballpark three months ago, but spared his new suit by managing to swallow what was in his mouth. "God!" he rasped. "Sorry. What did you say?"

I repeated my question, adding, "Seems like a good cause, something Moscone might support."

"He supports all kinds of stuff. Why ask about that one?" Gomez's voice and manner fell short of belligerent, but not by much.

"Don't bite my head off. I was at the Gay Freedom Parade, remember? The shelter had a float, and I thought I saw you hanging around it at one point."

He sat forward in his chair. "Yeah, well, I told you I was at Tahoe. You want to watch fruits bounce through the streets, you're on your own. I can't stand what goes on in the Castro bath houses or the S&M bars south of Market. I was still kicked back on the beach that day, growing my mustache and visualizing the dice cup."

"I figured it wasn't you. Just wondered. You might've been back by then." But for once, because Mad and Bonhof had sensitized me, I knew he was lying. I'd caught him off guard, and compared to the glibness of his usual spiels, this one didn't fly.

Trying to relax, Gomez flexed his shoulders, then attempted a joke. "Wish I knew who the guy was. I've been so busy lately, having another Andrés would be a boon."

I cleared my throat. "Are we ready for my own ridiculously inconsequential news?"

"Sure. I didn't mean to get so carried away with mine."

"It's time to make reservations at Hayes Street. Mad and I solved your puzzle."

"No shit? I'd given you up. People usually get it right away, or they don't."

"I…we…should have gotten it right away. But the answer's written down and sealed, the way you wanted, and you'd better be ready to pick up the check."

"Don't be too cocky. Did you use all the envelopes?"

GOMEZ

"Yes. And it's a smooth progression." By now, in fact, I could do it in my sleep. The powers of 2—squared, to the third, to the fourth, etc.

"All ten values?"

"No. There's exceptions."

"One exception, maybe. If it's plural, try Occam's Razor."

"What the hell's that?"

"Not what I shave around this with," he replied, flicking a finger across his upper lip. "It's a basic principle of logic: the simplest solution to any problem is usually best. Named for William of Occam, a 14th century Brit."

"I'll take my chances with what I've got. So when's our free dinner...Mad's and mine?" He'd thrown me, though, with his latest hint. My solution had two exceptions, 1 and 489. "She's really gotten into the puzzle thing lately," I bluffed.

She had also argued that we didn't need the answer, we only needed to say we had it. She'd happily let Gomez crow about our math failures as set-up for the real unveiling. And it wouldn't bankrupt me to pick up his tab, but I wanted to beat him on all counts, especially since his deliberate lie of minutes before.

Gomez took a slim leather folder out of his suit pocket and consulted it. "Looks like way the end of July. It'll have to be after what's-his-face...the husband...leaves again."

"Good. I'm more available than she is. Work it out with Mad and I'll be there." Bonhof's deadline was July 20, so any time after that suited her and my purpose. By then I'd also solve the damn math puzzle, and I'd run it on one of the new Apple computers we were getting at L-W if that's what it took.

"Speaking of dinner," Gomez said, casting his eyes to the back of the room, "I've got a meeting at 7:30, but the food here is good if you want to stay."

"Maybe I will. And isn't this the street where Patty Hearst was arrested? She's all over the paper now because of finally going to prison."

"No. That was the Harrises, her kidnappers and later on, conspirators. They had a hidey-hole across the park. Patty was busted out by the Cow Palace, near where my meeting is. Strange, but in Berkeley, Camilla Hall, another of the kidnappers, who always seemed completely sane, lived in our commune for a while. I used to bullshit with her in the kitchen until one night she just disappeared. Then the FBI showed up to deconstruct the place looking for clues. They questioned me, too."

"Better you than Paul Stiles," I said. "What ever happened to her?"

"She had the thickest glasses and thickest toenails of anybody I've ever known, and got killed in that big LA shoot out. Which is when Patty went underground."

Geez, I thought, the guy never gave up. Now he'd been questioned by the FBI, had the inside scoop on Patty Hearst, and a ready-made explanation for why his former neighbors in Oakland would be spooked. I was tempted to add all of it to Bonhof's list. "Too bad you have a meeting," I said. "I understand Andrés plays fine piano." I pointed at the keyboard.

"The little I play, I play well."

"Boogie-woogie and Beethoven are what I'm told."

"Two of his sonatas and three Chopin nocturnes. All thanks to my *maman*."

"How so? You never mentioned it."

"Never came up," he shrugged. "She was a concert pianist in northern New England. Whacked me with a ruler if I didn't practice. But by junior high, she could see it wasn't going to take."

There were witnesses to his playing, so he couldn't be faking that. His mother as a concert pianist sounded far-fetched, and there was no trace of him or his family in New England anywhere I'd looked. "Some of it took," I replied. "I'd like to hear you one of these nights."

"Boogie I picked up down south. The classical pieces I've known since I was a kid. I concentrate on those, do them the way my mom liked. It blows people's minds when the first notes come out," he laughed, "and I don't play unless it's a good instrument."

"Ever play for Mad?"

"No. Great idea. I'll use it to soften her up. Bring her in here and lay on the Chopin. Find out what's in her bonnet." He bounced to his feet. "Hey, I've got to run. I'm supposed to be inconspicuous, a fly on the wall, but I better be on time."

CHAPTER 23

The food probably would have been better at Hieronymus Boxx than the greasy burger I ended up with later at Pier 23. But I was so annoyed at the fuss people made over Gomez on his way out, and by the fact that the room seemed both darker and smaller all of a sudden, that I left. Darker, of course, made sense. We were well on toward twilight, and there was fog besides. Smaller related to his four-star physical presence. Weary as I'd become of it, whether as Andy, Gomez — or even Andrés — rooms expanded when he was in them and shrank when he wasn't.

Since that alone would be enough for most people, why did he always have to be such a bullshitter, so wired-in, he claimed, to every damn thing, spinning one pretense after another? For all that I was drawn to him, and I still was, I was repulsed as well. And seeing him at the parade, followed by his determination to deny it, raised possibilities that were truly bizarre. How did he know what went on in the Castro bathhouses and S&M bars? Was he gay? Bi? Transsexual? Was that the reason for his sanguine attitude toward Jenny when I'd told him my situation last year? And where did Mad fit?

It now seemed that she was kinky enough to be involved in an affair with a non-male male just for sport, and a second with me to scratch her remaining itches. Naturally Gomez wouldn't mind. In that scenario I was his surrogate, not his rival. The Miller-Nin angle had been a diversion, a way to lend glamour for my sake. If the credit on that supposed Mitchell brothers photo had been falsified, why not the image itself? Is that what Mad thought was so funny? Or did Gomez's interest in plastic surgery mean he'd undergone one to provide a male appendage, and the flesh had been taken from the back of his leg? An uncircumcised version would probably be easier to construct.

Helplessly rolling this through my mind while I ate, I was struck that the Three Musketeers consisted of two psychopaths and me. The upcoming dinner at Hayes Street might not be just to confront Gomez, it could represent my initiation ceremony after a period of hazing they'd both engineered. Yes, I would be first to see whatever Bonhof came up with, but after I had the basic facts I might be no closer to figuring out what was really going on. All I knew was that it gave me heartburn, and whatever restaurant I chose that night wouldn't have much mattered.

The next morning I largely recovered my balance. Everything was contingent on Bonhof's findings, and they were due soon. If, for instance, Gomez had changed gender, or been a fugitive, or fudged his entire résumé, Bonhof would assuredly discover how, when, and where, and I would have the means to lever Mad into telling me what she did or didn't know. My only real option was to play the game to the end, which was easy with her, since she was currently unavailable to me anyway, but harder with Gomez. I'd have to avoid him, but I missed the old Gomez, my friend, before the doubts, before my own the lies and deception—and before Andrés. If being lured into libertine behavior was my fate, maybe Jordan's was the voice I should have listened to.

It still seemed right, though, to alert Mad to Gomez's suspicions before she saw him again, and this time when I called the Mime Troupe she was there. She was also rushed to leave for a meeting, which kept her from pumping me for more than I wanted to say.

"What bothers him most," I pointed out, after relating the incidents he had cited, "is he thinks you're being possessive."

"How silly," Mad disparaged. "But I should have known someone at Las Pampas would leak. I implied it was a romantic matter, so they'd keep quiet."

"That could sound like possessiveness."

"I suppose. And the Centro woman's imitating my voice was just bad luck."

"Did you look around his apartment for more than panties?"

"Yes and no. He'd already left, so I opened a few drawers and eye-balled his mail and desk papers while I was at it."

In the odd dynamic between us, I was relieved that it was Gomez himself and not someone else she'd been entertaining there. And he might not even be capable of the kind of entertainment I'd always assumed. I found myself hoping he wasn't, despite my shame at wishing him or anybody that much grief. "I was afraid Gomez might be onto Bonhof, too," I said, "but he gave no sign."

GOMEZ

"Good. I was stupid. I should have butted out."

"Anyway, you'll be hearing from him soon about Hayes Street. He knows we've solved the puzzle, and he's shooting for the end of July."

"That's ideal," she said. "Clark will be overseas and we'll have Bonhof's dossier. Oh, oh…they're asking for me in the director's office. I've got to go."

"Give me one more minute. Gomez is also looking to meet you this week at a new hangout of his. He has some big news. A lot of news, actually. You're in a hurry, so I'll let him tell it."

"I don't know. I may put him off and get an update from you. It's hard to pretend when nothing he says ever holds water."

I went on to voice Gomez's worries about a changed mood among the three of us and emphasized that she should smooth things over with him in person. I said I'd tried to do the same when I had seen him. She closed by asking if I liked her gift. I affirmed that I did, and mentioned the disciplined pace of my reading, which earned me points, judging from her laugh. We didn't have the time or the privacy to discuss specifics.

"I'll want a full accounting…sometime," Mad concluded wryly, "and too bad about my missing wardrobe item. I was just sure you had it."

÷ ÷ ÷

Having gone public, so to speak, with my rationing system seemed to make abiding by it easier. I held off until the following week before reading *The Boarding School*, which certainly did convey Mad's message of forbidden delights, but not in quite the boy-girl terms I'd expected. And looking back, I guess that's how things always were with her—not quite as expected. Meanwhile, I spent more time on the puzzle solution and couldn't find an error. Maybe Gomez's warning that the correct mathematical series included only one exception had been meant to throw me off.

I also began thinking about Gloria Bonhof again, and about taking her to Hieronymus Boxx for dinner and to see the murals. Knowing such a unique place in such an unlikely part of town, and having Wally recognize me, was bound to make a good impression. For openers we'd go when I was sure Gomez wasn't there to hog the stage, but a later return to demonstrate that I not only knew the proprietor but was close friends with the engaging pianist could permanently establish my cool. I wouldn't have to mention that everything about him was smoke and mirrors, except—apparently—his keyboard touch.

She was another big reason to anticipate completion of the dossier. Once that was behind us, things with her could develop. It also seemed that I would be privy at last to Jordan's buried history with L-W. But most important, Mad would have to come clean on any scams she was pulling, and Gomez and I could cut through the crap and operate openly with one another for what would be the first time. If it all worked out, I was even willing to call him Andrés. Otherwise, damn it, he'd stay Gomez. I didn't need him anymore to finesse things with Mad, so if I had to go my separate way, I would.

Jordan left for his annual do at Bohemian Grove, but the Housers filled in by inviting me to another dinner at their place. I knew I should reciprocate, have them for cocktails since I didn't like to cook, but so far they were treating me as an interesting stray without the rigid taking turns you fell into with some people. The following weekend they were off to LA for a mini-vacation, to take in some museums and see a new play, *Zoot Suit*, that had gotten rave reviews. They were excited that the production was an offshoot of the famous, to them, Teatro Campesino from Ceasar Chavez's farmworker union. They were devotees of his, and when younger had marched, boycotted grapes and all that.

And finally, finally, Bonhof called to set up a meeting on what would be the forty-fourth of his promised forty-five days. I told him I wanted it as late as possible, to guarantee that I wouldn't have to go back to L-W, but I was angling for Gloria to be on duty as much as anything. I didn't give Mad notice of the date, nor did I return the friendly message Gomez left on my phone machine. Not seeing or talking to either of them until I knew as much—or more—than they did might give me the upper hand for once.

Breezy, partly sunny and partly foggy, July 20th was one of the longest days of my life. I looked at my watch so often that Ivy commented on my way out, "You must have something great planned with Madeline. You're jumpy as a cat."

"Today is business," I replied icily. "Exclusively *my* business, may I add."

"You mean I won't see her car pick you up if I happen to be on deck?"

"No, because no one is picking me up."

"Whatever, you've been a whole lot easier to work for these last couple of months."

I walked via the most direct route, but it still seemed to take twice as long as my prior trips and the brick passage skirting the koi pond felt like one of those endless concourses in an airport terminal. But as on my first visit, Bonhof was at the front desk, wearing his reading glasses, and alone.

"Sorry I'm not Gloria," he winked. "She definitely told me to say hello. Pure coincidence, but I had to send her to the courthouse to file some papers in a pending case. It was a rush deal, honest."

"Honesty," I joked, "now there's a concept, and since you brought it up, I *am* disappointed not to see her. Please be sure she knows that, and say hello for me, too."

"Will do," he said, standing to shake my hand.

"When does the embargo you've imposed expire?"

"Let's say September 1. She's not involved with anyone right now, so you don't have to worry. Come inside where we can stretch out. There's lots to cover."

"September?" I asked, following him to his office. "I was hoping you'd ease up." The afternoon light slanted beautifully through the windows and diffused across the paneled walls and the low-reflection glass of his framed art.

"If anything blows because of the Steentofter dossier, we'll give it time to blow." He sat behind the desk, took off his glasses and motioned me to a chair at one side.

"It's that sensitive?"

"No, not that I see. But if it comes out that you or your silent partner know things our subject would rather you didn't, and he learns why, who's to say? Better safe than sorry."

"OK, September, then. But I'm dying of suspense. What've you got?"

"First I'll brief you on L-W, and there's a parallel with Steentofter in things not being what they seem." Sunlight now shone on Bonhof's bald scalp as well. "It's not our main purpose here, and I won't necessarily name names. Nor am I swearing you to secrecy, as such, but you can never mention...or drop the slightest hint... that Jordan or I were your source."

"Agreed. Jordan said it was his revenge."

Bonhof gave a short, involuntary laugh, his voice cracking like an adolescent's. "Might be tougher on you than on L-W. Ready?"

"Yes. Today I'm submitting myself to chance." I liked the sound of that remark and so, I gathered, did Bonhof.

"OK, here it is. A certain well-connected lawyer was going through an ugly divorce. In hopes of mitigating the damage, he hired a private investigator to tail his wife and dig for dirt. Investigators don't much like that kind of work, but it pays the bills.

"The wife had begun spending time with the unmarried Mr. L, co-owner of a large design firm. The investigator was too good at his job. In combing through Mr. L's finances and phone logs for evidence of gifts or weekend getaways, it was inadvertently discovered that Mr. L had paid illegal kickbacks to officials of the Convention and Tourism Bureau of the city in which his firm is located.

"In return for said payments, Mr. L's firm received a string of lucrative contracts, tourism being the city's largest single industry. Also emerging was that these kickbacks were facilitated...for a fee, of course...by a prominent local and state political figure, an attorney who is the same race as the investigator."

Bonhof looked at me. "How we doing, Mr. Stiles?" he asked. "Always amazes me how *white* white-folks can get in situations like this."

"I don't like what I'm hearing, but I don't want to stop."

"Design," Bonhof nodded, "can be as rough a business as any. You don't get to be top dog by staying on the porch. Anyway, some slight evidence...very slight...of possible hanky-panky between Mr. L and the lawyer's wife did turn up. Against the investigator's advice, the lawyer used this to confront his wife, thinking he could bluff her into reducing various claims against him. Instead she laughed in his face. Mr. L, it turns out, is exclusively gay, though so deeply closeted that the investigator had failed to..."

"Unbelievable!" I erupted. "He's a hard-body, a tennis buff, and is all over the society pages escorting Cassie Mondrian to the opera or some starlet to the Academy Awards."

"As it happens, Mr. Stiles, a little further probing revealed that Ms. Mondrian is gay herself, but finds Mr. L to be a quite convenient escort. Moreover, she's much more presentable than the succession of Filipino houseboys with whom Mr. L consorts in private."

"Unbelievable!" I said again.

"Not at all, I assure you. In any event, the lawyer's wife said that she would publicly out his biggest client in order to clear herself, if it came to that, so the lawyer, to preserve his golden goose, backed off."

"But that doesn't get…" I was going to say Jordan fired, but Bonhof interrupted.

"Then," he continued forcefully, "in one of those twists that so amuse the gods, a losing bidder in that year's contract renewal brought suit against both Convention and Tourism and Mr. L's firm."

"You know, I do remember. L-W had just settled that case when I started working there, and…"

"The lawyer," Bonhof interrupted again, "in an ethical dilemma, decided to inform Mr. L that the lawyer's firm could not mount a defense, because he had knowledge of facts contrary to Mr. L's assertions of innocence. When the lawyer's wife revealed to Mr. L how this knowledge had come into the lawyer's possession…that is, by the lawyer's having had someone spy on his own client…the lawyer's firm was unceremoniously fired. Mr. W, Mr. L's business partner, was aware of this decision and supported it.

"In other words, regarding professional matters, though not in those of the heart, the lawyer was entirely scrupulous and got canned for his trouble. The prominent political figure continues to represent Convention and Tourism, earning additional fees."

"Wow," I put in, "I can sure see why Jor…why the lawyer is pissed." With a sigh, I also wondered how much of my last paycheck had been tainted money.

"And his revenge, you see, is to have you report for work daily at the floating palace of design with a better sense of how the toast there came to be buttered."

If I'd been pale white before, in Bonhof's description, I felt prickly and flushed now. The duplicity just cited didn't portend well for Gomez. I had told myself five times a day for the past week that I'd written him off, but at some level I had been rooting for him, the way he did the Giants. No matter how bitterly he grumbled that they were folding again after a good start, he always followed the scores.

"Now it's Steentofter's turn," Bonhof stated. He picked up a heavy envelope, from which he extracted two, inch-thick documents in brown, faux-leather bindings. When he put the envelope back down, it wasn't empty. "Oh," he added, "you have another check for me, I believe."

"Yes, right, I do." Opening my wallet, I passed it to him.

"Thanks," he said. "Here, we'll trade." He handed me a dossier with the typed name Andrew Baruch Steentofter visible in the cut-out window on the cover.

"Where do we begin?" I asked. I felt a strong emotional surge, and sweat oozed into my undershirt from beneath my arms.

"Why don't I summarize, then you ask questions? The dossier is in strict chronological order. We won't get to the point for quite a while by starting at page one."

"OK."

"This was a very interesting exercise, by the way. To a greater extent than any case I've had, everything Mr. Steentofter alleges about himself is true."

I was dumbstruck. Bonhof tried, I think, not to laugh, but ultimately couldn't hold back. "Sorry," he said. "If you saw yourself, you'd laugh, too."

"How can that be?" Now that I had my wish, I couldn't believe it. "How can that possibly be?"

"There was one detail, an innocent lie in most circles, that threw your earlier queries off. Andrew B. Steentofter is 42 years of age, and soon to turn 43. When you and Jordan checked at Yale, thinking he was 38, you were four years too late."

"I'll be damned."

"Remember my saying the man was a phony or a phenom? Well, it's the latter. His short bio is this: born, New York City, 1935, almost the minute his parents stepped off the boat from Rotterdam. Grew up in Vermont, went to high school at Deerfield Academy in Massachusetts, was a scholastic stand-out and star halfback, earning himself a scholarship to Yale.

"During the last pre-season practice for freshman football, he suffered a disastrous knee injury. He had several reconstructive surgeries as a result, but never played organized football again. Since the Ivy League doesn't have athletic scholarships per se, on he went, but with no recognition in the sport."

Speechless, I made eye contact with Bonhof and nodded that he continue.

"At Yale Steentofter majored in English, worked part-time in the dining commons, worked summers as a house painter, and graduated summa cum laude. He was peripherally involved in alumni affairs until he taught at Stillman College in Alabama. He then got into a dispute with Yale over what he called their elitist admissions policy, and their refusal to share endowment funds by adopting Stillman as a sister institution. According to Yale, he's been a non-person ever since. You'll find correspondence in the dossier to back that up."

"Yeeow," I said quietly, more to myself than to Bonhof.

"Essentially *my* reaction when the Yale info came in. After his BA, Steentofter lived on 4th Street in Greenwich Village during one of its more fertile periods, worked as a handyman for a property management company in Spanish Harlem, and later spent two-plus years in Argentina...I have his passport records. Officially, he was there to teach. I didn't pursue what he actually did, because I didn't think it was germane in light of everything else."

"You're right."

"Next he returned to the Village, married a Donna Louise Smith, and enrolled at Berkeley in Renaissance Literature, over a period of years and with the Alabama interruption, completing his coursework and later his dissertation. No worries about military service, either, what with the bad knee and the marriage, although he did volunteer as an anti-draft counselor for a time in Oakland. Should I go on?"

"Not really. But what isn't true? Did he run for Congress as a Black Panther down South?"

"Yes," Bonhof put on his glasses and opened the dossier, "and he received better than 13,000 votes. They were a Democrat splinter group, though, nothing to do with Bobby Seale and Huey Newton."

"What about EST?"

"Steentofter took the training, or most of it, but he was such a gadfly they refunded his money on the condition that he never talk to journalists or anyone. That was perhaps the most challenging fact to come up with. Werner Ehrhard guards his realm like King Solomon's mines."

In a sense, Bonhof's had opened a sinkhole under my chair, but I was too elated to sink. "What about the Mitchell Brothers?"

"There are limits to my magic, Mr. Stiles. A person named Benny Steen, who might or might not be our subject, auditioned there last winter, but it was a night on which the photo equipment malfunctioned."

"Is there any record of his being questioned by the FBI?"

"Yes, in 1974. He apparently lived in the same building as a suspect in the Patty Hearst case." Bonhof was now jumping from page to page in his copy of the dossier.

"Why does he owe UC Berkeley a bunch of money?"

"As we've seen, Mr. Steentofter resists authority. When he returned to UC from Alabama, he obtained a subsidized apartment in married student housing. He entered a lottery, in fact, to qualify. He then lived there most of a semester without evidence of a family, someone reported him, and the University demanded that he get out and retroactively pay full market value for the unit. A standoff began which to this day has prevented the award of his degree."

"I'll be damned." As Andy, he'd told me he was single by then, but his hustling a low-rent apartment sounded typical.

"That's twice you've damned yourself now." Bonhof smiled, not just at his own remark, but as though this job was as close to a career high as he'd had in a while.

I smiled back. It had become fun for me, too. Wonderful fun. "What about his parents? I've got to know that part."

"Were they Communists?" Bonhof responded, paging the dossier again. "Good chance. All the signs are there, but proof positive would be hard to come by. In the Netherlands, the family name was Steen. They added the suffix *tofter* upon emigration, because they had papers to match."

"Anything else?"

"His mother's family name in southern France was Fontana. She was a pianist of some renown, and his father actually did invent Teflon." Here Bonhof laughed loudly. "Or helped invent it. The father taught chemistry for modest wages at Bennington College, but worked summers for DuPont in Delaware. He was part of a research team specializing in plastics and coatings. DuPont owns the patent, but by corporate policy, they share royalties after five years. Dr. Vincent B. Steentofter is among the recipients."

"What's left from my original list? I can't think."

"The list? Let's see, I put it in an appendix. Oh, yes, Spinoza. Again, tough to verify, but it seems likely. I need to find the page. Ah, here. Baruch, or Benedict, Spinoza, the fifteenth-century philosopher, died childless but had one sibling. His sister married into a family of converted Jews named Steen. Now Steen, in Holland, is as common as Jones in the US...or Gomez in Spain...so this gets rather vague. All I can say from our present remove is that every generation I can trace of the relevant Steen family going back to the 1790s has a male child whose given name includes either Baruch or Benedict. From that I'd surmise they either are related to Spinoza, or believe they are.

"And finally, Dr. Joaquín Nin Culmell, brother of the celebrated Anaïs, and a noted pianist and composer in his own right. He resides in Berkeley, teaches on the UC music faculty under his mother's maiden name Culmell, and had his house painted in 1976 by someone you know. Currently, however, he's on sabbatical, working on an opera titled *La Celestina*, based in part on an unpublished dissertation by Andrew Steentofter."

"I'm completely in awe. How do you do this?"

"I never answer that question. My livelihood depends on clients believing they couldn't do it themselves."

"Well, we can't have Gloria going hungry."

"That one," Bonhof chuckled, "will earn twice the money I ever do. Any more questions?"

One thing still didn't sound right. Private school would explain the void Ivy had found at Bennington High, but Gomez said he'd grown up poor. "How does a family in that economic bracket afford out-of-state prep school for their child?"

"Very perceptive. I wondered myself. The DuPont royalties weren't yet coming in, but many private schools and colleges have mutual tuition waivers for faculty children. Dr. Steentofter took advantage of that for both his sons. The younger brother, by the way, later attended West Point and has served much of his life overseas in the military."

Even the existence of the brother I'd heard mentioned had checked out. A wash of nervousness accompanied my next question. "OK, this one's off-the-wall. Has he ever been homosexual or changed his gender, surgically or otherwise?"

"Why would you think that?" Bonhof had the thoroughly perplexed expression he must have seen on me a few minutes ago. "It wasn't on your list."

"Like I said, off-the-wall."

"Nothing showed up, and it would, as closely as I looked."

"You're right. Stupid. I can't believe I asked. And I guess we're done. What's left for me is to tell my partner."

"Well then, Mr. Stiles, it's been a pleasure. I'll keep a copy of the dossier, you take the other two. Usually I don't make that many, but in this instance I have a second client, whom I strongly suspect works at the Mime Troupe." With raised eyebrows, he checked me for a reaction, then slid my dossier in with the extra, placed the envelope in my hand, and stood in preparation for seeing me out.

"So," I asked, to divert him from further speculation about Mad, "shaving four years off his age was Steentofter's only secret?"

"No, no, not what I said."

"That's what I heard you say."

"I said that the things you wanted verified were all true."

"Oh."

"But I imagine you know, for example, that his legal name has been Andrés Baruch Benedict Gomez since early May, and that he's recently begun working for the mayor?"

"Yes, all but the two middle initials. And Centro Social de Los Obreros before that."

"Do you know why he changed his name?"

"Not really. Do you?"

"No, although he's clearly prone to reinventing himself. As for why, I found nothing salient, except that among Sephardic Jews of the Iberian Peninsula a so-called *marrano* tradition arose, due to fear of persecution, and it carried over to Holland as well. *Marranos* periodically took new names and often passed for Christians. Spinoza himself adopted the name Benedict after an attempt on his life by a mysterious assailant."

Bonhof came around his desk and I stepped into his path. "I don't think you've answered my real question."

"Like anyone," he shrugged, "your Mr. Gomez has a few secrets. Nothing related to what you've asked about, but we can go into them if you like. And of course, they're in here." Bonhof pointed to his dossier copy on the desktop.

"No, forget it. I know more of L-W's secrets than I ever wanted, and I don't need anybody else's. I also see the parallel you're drawing. The reverse of my expectations was true in both cases, but it's possible to have too much truth."

Bonhof seemed pleased. "Exactly the lesson I hoped you'd draw," he said. "This man is your friend and he's worth hanging on to. When he tells you the rest some day, which I predict he will, you'll have come by it fairly and have no grounds for doubt."

Bonhof and I started toward the door. "A final detail," he said. "As of late June Mr. Andrés Gomez joined the North End Rowing Club, a bunch of maniacs who swim year-round in the bay. Does he know how bloody cold the water is?"

"He only plays racquetball there, he doesn't swim." But I smiled to myself that as Andrés he was a member and no longer an interloper.

Bonhof and I reached the door, then vigorously shook hands. "Thanks," I said. "This is the happiest ending imaginable."

"You're very welcome. Gloria looks forward to hearing from you in September."

÷ ÷ ÷

By the time I walked home, I knew what to do next. It came down to trusting Gomez. Proceeding directly to the garage, I drove to Mime Troupe headquarters. The six o'clock news was over when I got there and parking had opened up. I was thankful, however, for the extra summer daylight, because the neighborhood looked just as chancy as Mad had always described it. I didn't see her car anywhere, and I not only assumed she wouldn't be around, I preferred that she wouldn't.

The heavy, metal-sheathed door dating from the building's warehouse days took two hands to push aside, but it wasn't locked. Beyond the threshold a long, high, windowless hall ran both left and right, lit at each end by a single bare bulb in a mesh cage. No one was in view, but I heard commotion and indistinct voices coming from a doorway ten yards to my left. I followed the sound into an auditorium-sized space with a level concrete floor and all sorts of scrap lumber and stage sets pushed against the walls.

Along the front were several low platforms, rehearsal stages apparently, one of which was lighted and busy. Actors and actresses, some in costume, some in street clothes, were positioning themselves and delivering lines in response to instructions from two would-be directors pacing about at floor level. Prop and costume people stood at the ready, while other watchers with no identifiable roles sat in a scatter of folding metal chairs. In the offstage gloom I smelled pizza, coffee, cigarettes and French fries.

As I got within ten feet of the back-most chair, a twentyish guy stood up from it and came toward me, eyeing Bonhof's envelope clutched beneath my arm.

"Can I…ah…help you with something?" he said warily, and I recognized his voice from past phone conversations. He had a corolla of longish hair, a rat-face, and smudged circles under his eyes.

"Yes. I have an important delivery for Madeline Klein." If he recognized my voice he gave no indication.

"She's not here. The office is closed till nine or ten tomorrow."

"No problem. I just need to leave this on her desk."

"Guess we could try. My name's Speedball. I'm the caretaker."

"Good to meet you. I'm Paul." He didn't acknowledge the hand I held out.

Speedball led me back past the entryway to the opposite end of the hall. On squeaking hinges he opened the second-to-last door and leaned in to switch on a light. "That's her," he said, pointing.

Thankful that his worn sweatshirt and jeans were fairly clean, as was his hair, I squeezed by him and into Mad's office. Or the office she shared, since there were two desks, one a heap of barely sorted binders and paper, and the other, clearly hers, neatly laid out for the following day.

I scanned the walls and desktop for a photo of Mad, Clark and Mad, or other personal mementos, but the only distinguishing feature was an unframed reproduction of a Klimt peacock that hung above her phone. Otherwise, the vertical-lath sides of what was little more than a closet displayed a welter of posters and postcards from past Troupe productions with names like *Frijoles*, *TartTough*, *She Conks to Stupor*, and *Hotel Universe*.

GOMEZ

Speedball stayed watchfully in the doorway. "OK if I use a pen and some paper?" I asked.

"Sure. Just don't mess nothin' up. Mad's real particular. Makes me shake out her rug, empty the wastebasket and all that shit. If she didn't look like such a royal piece of ass, I wouldn't do it."

"OK, thanks," I said, feeling an unexpected kinship with him, "I'll be quick."

Mad's chair, when I sat, held a teasing residue of her perfume. I opened a drawer and quickly found writing supplies, but nothing with them was a candidate for addition to the cache relating to her that I kept at home. After a few false starts with a cranky ballpoint pen, I folded and rubber-banded the following note to Bonhof's envelope, leaving it in plain view under a paperweight.

> 7/20/78 (6:30pm)
>
> Mad,
> Here's both our copies of Bonhof's report. You're going to drop your teeth. Gomez is 100% for real, except he's older than he admits. We need to deep-six this whole thing and all celebrate together at Hayes Street, whether my puzzle solution is right or not. Call me at home as soon as possible from someplace you'll be free to talk. I miss you,
>
> Paul

"You one of her moneybags types?" Speedball wanted to know.

"Not really. These are just reports. Pretty boring stuff."

"Yeah, like you'd be leaving wads of cash," he giggled. "I could always hope."

"What's going on out there tonight?"

"Extra rehearsals for *Electrobucks*, our latest gig. We opened it July 1 at Marin Civic Plaza, but there's lots of rewrites to work in."

"I thought mime was silent."

"No, man, that's pantomime…with white-painted faces. This is commedia dell'arte. Sometimes I do bit parts or hand puppets."

"Oh, ah…wish I had time to hang out and watch. What's it about, anyway?"

GOMEZ

"Sex, money, feminism. All the hot topics. This is the happening place, man. We're where it's at, especially since *Zoot Suit* has hit so big down south."

I re-balanced the paperweight, swiveled Mad's chair in Speedball's direction and got up. He backed into the hall as I approached. "Catch the light switch for me, would ya?" he asked.

"Sure." I also pulled the door closed. "What's the connection with *Zoot Suit*? I only just heard of it from some friends."

"A big smash, and that guy who did it, Luis Valdez, was here for years until the farmworker thing. Writer, director, whole ball of wax. Before my time, but they still talk about him. He's really put us on the map. Mad can't stop smiling since the news broke."

Speedball led me to the exit and as a goodbye gave a little palm-up wave at his belt-line. I felt good, and knew I'd done exactly what I should have. Since Mad had paid for the dossiers, they were hers, but I hoped she would do what she should and burn them in her cottage's fireplace.

Walking back to my car I swerved into the street to avoid a couple of drunks, but they didn't really look that dangerous. It must not have been Gomez I'd seen at the Gay Freedom Parade, I decided. I was wrong and had just been having damning thoughts because Mad and I had fed ourselves so much misinformation. I'd mistaken that New York blonde for Jenny from a lot closer range.

But another fun thing to do with Gloria, I realized during my drive home, would be to see the Troupe perform the *Electrobucks* piece Speedball had told me about. I didn't think it would be smart to introduce Gloria to Mad, but Mad wasn't in the audience except on special occasions. Just mentioning Mad's name to let Gloria know that I had an in with the Troupe would be enough. I could benefit from their new reputation even if I'd been too un-hip to attend before now.

Maybe the Housers would want to double-date. I was about to be a guy with a married lover, an interracial girlfriend, connections in the art world, and on close terms with both a top-rank lawyer and somebody on the mayor's staff. This had been one hell of a year, but I'd come a long, long way.

GOMEZ

CHAPTER 24

For whole new reasons I was eager to hear from Mad, and Speedball had made it sound as though she'd be at work the next day, but by late afternoon, still no luck. Of course it was Friday, and she was a volunteer, so she might not show up whatever Speedball thought. But even when I put her out of mind, my new knowledge about Milt Landau made everything at L-W seem off. The boat's exterior hull was more stained with soot and rust than I'd remembered, there were encrusted seagull droppings on the decks and railings, and inside, the brass fixtures looked duller and the mahogany trim could have used refinishing.

As he and Bonhof had surmised, Jordan's revenge actually was harder on me than on the company. One way to address that was to act on what I knew, but how? Those kickbacks were ancient history, settled out of court, and probably with all further claims barred. Nonetheless, they pissed me off. When the next bid cycle came around, I wanted us to get the Conventions and Tourism contract fair and square. And we could, with our talent level, unless some other hustlers ponied up the kickbacks instead.

A different mayor had been in office then, but it was Moscone now and Gomez worked for him. Moreover, Gomez was already calling the guy George, so blowing the whistle might not cost me any skin. I had no idea what the mayor's relationship to Conventions and Tourism was in a formal sense, but formal or not, if Moscone played things as straight as Gomez claimed, nobody on the City Hall end would get away with rigging bids. Let's say that took care of the future, what about the past?

I was tempted to leak the whole story to Ivy, Filipino houseboys and all, because she was so tuned into the L-W grapevine the rest of our co-workers would know in a flash. But she was also so indiscreet that it was bound to come back on me. Then what? Anybody at L-W who made half a try could link me to Jordan, whom I'd promised to protect. He had already paid plenty of dues on this. Besides, who gave a damn about Milt Landau's closet sex life? I had stuff I wanted kept private, and so did Gomez and everybody else on the planet.

Kickbacks were the issue. Were they still going on, and were there other tainted contracts? Ivy could find out, but I wasn't sure she or the other staff would get very stirred up. Maybe that was just how business was done in SF, or anywhere, and as long as the Christmas bonuses kept coming, I'd be the only one who cared. Yet how much did I care? Revisiting history could end up jeopardizing my job, not just my bonus.

Who I really wanted to bounce all this off was Gomez, a further reason to be thankful that the trust issues between us were resolved. Given the exceptional person he was, his gifting me Mad seemed that much more plausible. And teaming with her to inquire into his background had not only validated it convincingly, there were no known ill consequences. To me, in fact, the consequences had been entirely positive.

I had Gomez back, I had met Gloria and I'd definitely become better at dealing with women I was attracted to. I'd also amassed enough new sexual experience to be able to wall off the harm done by Jenny, I was making friends like Jordan and the Housers, and I'd come to terms with having Mad in my life on a nonexclusive basis. And from reading Nin's *Diaries*, I no longer wondered about Mad's motives.

If Anaïs was the prototype, an expansion of Mad's circle beyond Clark and Gomez was to be expected when an eligible candidate came along. Luckily I had been found eligible. I also needed to recognize that the circle would continue to expand, although Nin typically didn't end old relationships when she began new ones. She gradually reallocated her time, trying to maintain a reciprocal energy between her and the men who could accept her freedom.

Gomez had figured that out immediately, asking from Mad the same in return. I could do it too. I would make myself. Moreover, the knowledge that she liked me and had sought me out had been empowering in ways she and Gomez couldn't have anticipated. With a woman like her in my corner, a woman guys at the Mime Troupe or at Artichoke Joe's went ga-ga over, and who sent me sexy notes and gifts, anything seemed possible.

So yes, I would have preferred Mad on my office phone at 4:55 that day, but Gomez was the next best thing.

"Paul, it's Andrés."

I smiled, as though I'd newly learned how. "Oh sure, Andrés. Who else?"

"Don't give me a load of shit." I saw his own smile in my mind.

"No problem. From here on, Andrés it is."

"Good. Thanks. And we're set for Hayes Street. How's Wednesday, August 2nd, at seven?"

"Nothing in the way here. Does it work for Mad?"

"Yeah, she and I had a lunchtime reunion at my place early in the week. Things are seeming mellow again. And man, is she jazzed about a Three Musketeers dinner."

"Well, I am, too. Especially because I get to leave my wallet home." Since Artichoke Joe's and my involvement with Mad, I hadn't wanted all three of us to be together, but the way things were currently aligned, I was ready.

"Don't bank on your math skills yet," he chided. "Anyway, Mad swears it wasn't her asking about me at the Centro, and says she only got into it at Las Pampas because one of the kitchen help claimed I was Puerto Rican. She thought Ignacio should stick up for me as a *porteño*."

"A what?"

"*Porteño*. It's how Buenos Aireans refer to each other. Not that I am one, really."

"Hey, listen, you were right about Hieronymus Boxx. I didn't eat there that night, but I'd like to. It seems terrifically cool."

"How about Thursday next week? A little wine, and they have dynamite quiche. I'll even show off and tickle the ivories."

"Sure, that'd be fun. What time?"

"Could we make it six-thirty? Six turns out to be hard for me nowadays. And Dutch treat, no pun intended."

"Fine," I laughed. "But I do want to hear more about your job, and I've got a city government thing I want to talk about."

"Then that's the agenda. We have to start making time for racquetball, too."

"Absolutely."

"I'll turn into uncle piggy if I keep eating at these political receptions and don't exercise. Oh, get this. I actually joined the Rowing Club. No more sneaking in, and I even have a locker. We can shower there and do show and tell."

GOMEZ

I knew what he meant, and for once, didn't mind. "This Andrés guy has really gone uptown. Since I don't have much to show, I'd better have a lot to tell."

"If not," he laughed, "make something up."

Gomez's gibe was funnier than he knew. Twenty-four hours ago, if he'd talked about making things up, I'd have thought he'd lowered his guard and spoken candidly for a change. Instead, it was a joke we could share.

Naturally this reminded me of Bonhof, and one beat later, Gloria. "Have you heard of a local artist named Joan Brown?"

"Funny you should ask. She swims at the club, and that water will freeze your po-po. But yeah, I just met her. She's good buds with a new friend I need to tell you about."

OK, there was no escape. Gomez or Andrés, he had fingers in all pots, and on top of that he was hanging out with Gloria's hero. "Sounds like po-po has been reinstated in the vocabulary," I ventured.

"True," he replied. "I wondered if you'd notice. But toothpicks aren't back and neither is automotive repair, so don't take anything for granted."

"Whatever helps me get a line on Brown's art. I hear she's quite the ticket."

"That's what I hear, too. Supposedly has gallery shows in New York and LA... besides SF."

"Do you know which gallery? Here, I mean."

"No, but you could call a few of the big ones, like Vorpal, and ask. It's pretty much a network."

"Or you could ask your new friend." Not that I doubted him, exactly, but he spun out so much of this stuff that it was tiring even when it was true.

"Sure. I'll check and tell you next week at the Boxx."

÷ ÷ ÷

Late Saturday morning I got home from a long run along the wharves, west past the Rowing Club, through Fort Mason, across Marina Green and all the way out Crissy Field to Fort Point under the Golden Gate Bridge. The machine was blinking that I had a message, and it was Mad, quiet and businesslike, saying she'd try again

GOMEZ

in an hour. To be sure we didn't miss, I stayed in my sweats and read the paper on the balcony with the sliding door open and the phone pulled as close as I could get it on the living room floor. When it rang, though, it startled me.

"Yay, you're there," she said.

"Yay, it's you," I answered.

"These haven't been the easiest calls to make."

"Where are you, anyway?"

"The Claremont Hotel. In the lobby. I had a beauty appointment at the spa. Clark flies out Monday for three weeks and he's feeling needy, so I couldn't call from home."

"I don't blame him for missing you," I said.

"We need to talk about Gomez. I saw the dossiers. What was the point of your note...you know, about deep-sixing everything?"

"Just what I said. Burn the whole lot. I never want to see them again. Any fun we'd have with a phony Gomez will be twice as good with him real. Besides, you heard about his new job. He doesn't need a social boost. He'll be in Herb Caen on his own."

"Oh, yes, I heard. He was sweet as pie the last time I saw him. Wants me to come to that Boxx place for a piano serenade. And it's Andrés now, no less."

"You don't think that's cool?"

"How much of the dossier did you and Bonhof cover?"

"Enough. Everything important."

"Then whose side are you on, mine or his?"

"No one's. There are no sides."

"Paul, you fool. Andrés Gomez is a living lie."

"Baloney. Except his birthday everything he said checks out."

"It does not!"

"Mad, we're all entitled to a few secrets. Look at you."

"That's different. I don't hold myself up as a paragon."

"Forget it. Let's have our dinner, share some laughs, and figure out where the Three Musketeers ride next. Andrés can get us invited to some pretty interesting places, I bet, and I'd also like to see what the Mime Troupe crowd is like."

"Oh, you would, would you? And he's already got you trained to say Andrés. I'll bring the dossiers to Hayes Street, we'll go with the original plan, and if he can take it half as well as he dishes it out, the Three Musketeers might survive."

GOMEZ

"No, really, Mad, burn the dossiers."

"I won't."

"Well, I'm sorry, I can't go through with it. If you bring the dossiers, it's dinner for two."

"If that's how things have to be, that's how they'll be. No more free pass for Andrew Baruch Steentofter."

"OK, he lied about his name. Or to you, he did. Did you notice his own parents lied to him? He should have been Andrew Baruch Steen."

"No wonder he likes you. You're gullible."

"Bonhof says I wasn't gulled."

"For the last time, Paul, face up to what you're refusing to know, meet us at Hayes Street, and make him admit what he knows."

"Mad, if you insist on that, I not only won't be there, I'm going to warn Andrés when I see him next Thursday at the Boxx."

"Now we do know whose side you're on, don't we?"

"I'm on the side of stopping this before it ruins the two best human relationships I've ever had."

"Oh, god. You and your illusions."

"Look, I'm sorry. Everything has just gone sideways from what I expected. Think about it, and I'm pretty sure you'll decide I'm right."

"Think about it! How condescending! Do you suppose I paid that much money without thinking? Bonhof didn't address Gomez's lies about Graciela, either. She's still not Guatemalan and there were no death squads where she came from."

That part had slipped my mind, and wasn't on our list because we already knew the truth. "Mad, I'm sorry. There's arguments on both sides. But you …we…don't have to haul out printed reports to talk about Graciela. I agree, he has to cop to misleading you, and I'll back you up if you want."

"No picking and choosing. Come to Hayes Street and back me up on all of it."

"I just can't."

"So Gomez's little lap-dog is wimping out. Fine, I'll go it alone. But don't you dare warn him."

"Maybe you and I can get together after Clark leaves and talk things through some more. I really want to see you."

GOMEZ

"I wanted to see you, too. But if you're going to act like this, I don't."

"Please, Mad. We'll find a way to compromise. Or flip a coin, submit ourselves to chance."

"That's the dumbest thing I ever heard."

She didn't slam the phone down, she just hung up, but it had the same effect. How had this happened? Every pernicious possibility was now reopened, but I couldn't believe Bonhof had blown it, or had steered me away from anything important. She'd never met him. I had.

Still, my picture of what was to come had abruptly gone surreal. Mad was refusing to see me, she'd hung up rather than continue to talk, and I was due to meet Gomez—I mean Andrés—for some kind of heart-to-heart in less than a week. If I played lap-dog for either of them, I'd be a wimp to the other. Unless I walked completely away and became a wimp to both.

÷ ÷ ÷

As you can imagine, the next few days weren't pleasant or easy, and the rest of the weekend, with no planned distractions, was particularly hellish. I eventually went for a walk Saturday night, ended up at the nearly empty Silver Dollar, and got so drunk that I shot an improvised form of pool with myself and engaged the endlessly sullen bartender in conversation. He might not remember it that way, but I do. Horribly hungover, I barely got out of bed on Sunday, and when I did, got drunk again at a lower Broadway bar I've never been able to find since. But at least I'd walked, not driven, on that dismal round or I might have done myself far greater injury than a second hangover, and wrecked the Audi besides.

Starting Monday I was a bear with Ivy, who undoubtedly divined that trouble with Mad was the reason, but was too intimidated to make any comments. As for the hidden scandal at L-W, it hardly mattered by comparison. My abused head and I decided to tea-total the rest of the week and pretend that everything was fine — at work and at home — but the latter fiction was difficult to sustain. By Tuesday evening no more word from Mad, I couldn't bring myself to call her, and what I'd thought of as the new Paul Stiles had come largely undone. Yet my position on the dossiers hadn't chan-

GOMEZ

ged. I wanted them destroyed, and if she did that, and never mentioned their existence, I would have offered just to play dumb at the dinner without warning him first.

I considered other alternatives as well, including either staying with the original plan or ducking the whole thing, but none of them felt right. By the same token, losing Mad seemed unbearable. How could things be over between us? I'd experienced *over* with Jenny, and this hadn't gone near enough acts yet. Then again, Mad and I weren't bound by any of the normal ties. My next brush with freak-out came Wednesday night, one week before the Musketeers scheduled reunion at Hayes Street, though I somehow avoided further recourse to booze. But finally, when Mad still hadn't called, and hadn't returned the calls I'd left at the Mime Troupe, my attitude hardened.

Nobody who told as much truth as Gomez—or Andy, or Andrés —had, deserved to be blindsided by two of his friends with a detective's report in a public place. Or even by one of his friends. If Mad didn't back completely off, I would neither be party to it nor stand idly by. I'd carry out my threat to warn him face to face, hopefully in a way that wouldn't cause both me and my chair to be blasted out through the Boxx's roof. That met the ethical minimum, yet how the hell could I phrase it to be sufficiently diplomatic? I didn't know and I might not know as of the time I walked in the door, but my right brain had better start producing. Plenty of good design ideas had flowered for me when I'd been under pressure, but here the stakes were higher. I must have been nuts to suggest that Mad and I flip a coin.

Once I warned him, and she knew I'd done it, which I would make sure she did, she'd have to change her approach. She might back out of the August 2 soiree at Hayes Street, but conceivably we could get past that and reschedule, since there were things the three of us still needed to talk through. I didn't plan to portray her as the villain. In fact, she—and even Gomez—could end up respecting me more if I made this a success.

÷ ÷ ÷

What was it about Hieronymus Boxx and fog? I waited as late at L-W as I could on Thursday, hoping Mad would call, then ran home to my garage in breezy sunlight and drove aggressively the length of Folsom Street to get to Precita Park by six-thirty. Yet in that few miles and thirty minutes, a clammy miasma was already down to the rooftops and whipping through the notch between Bernal Heights and Potrero Hill like a winter mistral.

And there'd been a reason I thought Mad would call. Earlier in the day, after saying that a reply was needed as soon as possible and providing my L-W phone number, I had left with Speedball the most provocative message I could think of, "What would Anaïs do?" It should have been as clear to Mad as it was me that Nin didn't burn bridges, despite her life's many turns.

"That's a weird one, man," Speedball had said. "Help me with spelling," which I did, until he added, "Oh, yeah, the French writer chick. Never knew how it was pronounced."

When I reemphasized how urgent this was, Speedball went on to say, "Yeah, yeah, I remember you from the other night. What was your name again?"

"First is Paul, last is Stiles. Be sure you put it down that way." My hope was to get her attention by sounding neither threatening nor weak. Now, pulling the Boxx's door closed against the wind outside, I had to accept that it hadn't worked.

Anticipation may be a great tonic when the event in question is pleasant. Tonight's appointment with Andrés felt more like a court date for sentencing. My guilt was well established, if not confessed, and waiting only made it worse. But, except for frantic emotions on my part, the scene at the Boxx was a freeze-frame of my previous visit, though the room was a bit more crowded.

I took the same window table, ordered a big carafe of red wine, and informed the hovering Wally that Andrés would be arriving any time with the intention of playing the piano and eating. Flamboyant as ever in a black velour vest and paisley trousers, he treated me like a regular, which I noticed he did with everyone. He was also enthused at the idea of free entertainment. The problem was, Andrés didn't show.

By seven I'd drunk more than half the wine, was getting buzzed despite my pledge to the contrary, and had grown weary of examining the row houses across the park to guess which one had harbored Patty Hearst's accomplices. And through all this, the second hand on my wristwatch swept steadily along while the minute hand seemed never to budge.

"Don't sweat it," Wally consoled as he cruised by for a second or third time. "Drés always gets sucked into meetings or gets lobbied when people see him on the street. The poor dude's never gonna be on time for the rest of his life."

Which was a contrast with the old Gomez, who made few appointments, didn't have a phone, but was invariably prompt. I just had to adapt. But what I did was worry my guts out. One angle I'd thought of, assuming he did show, which seemed less and less likely, was to build on his recent joke about making things up. I wouldn't say that a private investigator had been involved, but I could tell him Mad and I were talking one time and had gotten curious because his bio seemed so amazing, and we'd figured he was daring us, so we asked around and made a few calls, learned his real age, had other questions, and... Shit, it sounded brainless even to me.

Maybe I'd build on his new job instead. Ask if he realized how unusual his résumé was, tell him I'd thought he might be exaggerating, didn't care that much, and Mad had wondered, too, but now his job added another whole layer. Had they checked him out before he got hired, or taken him on faith? Ideally he would pick up on that and I could steer into saying that Mad and I were aware of certain discrepancies and wanted a chance to clear the air. He'd be angry, and probably cancel Hayes Street even if Mad didn't, but at least he wouldn't be open to ambush by her and her accusations.

Finally, Andrés—already known as Drés here at the Boxx—was an hour late, the wine was empty and I signaled Wally to bring my bill. I knew I shouldn't be driving, but damn it, I was too upset to eat and was going home. Could be there was something on my phone machine that would offer a way out. If not, any action was better than just sitting. At that point, came a staccato knock-knock-knock on the outside window, and I turned, with my pulse making an answering staccato, sure it was him.

But it wasn't. A short, well-put-together woman, good-looking, with a mane of wavy, hennaed hair hanging to her shoulders, focused her gaze above my head and waved. She wore a paint-marked smock or apron of some kind under an old Navy pea coat, and had gorgeous brown eyes. I'd estimate her age at thirty-five, and could read the word "Wally" on her lips, though her voice didn't carry through the glass.

"*Susana! Caio bella!*" he called, returning her wave as he approached to collect my money. The woman smiled, then walked out of view.

"Who's that?" I inquired, fighting my tongue not to slur the words.

"Susan DeFeo," he answered. "You wouldn't have to ask if Drés was with you. She has the hots for that boy, and she'd be sitting in this extra chair. If he does come in, you want me to tell him you waited?"

"Yeah, please. Have him call me at home."

"Will do. God, that Susan's a babe. Half the guys in the Heights are in love with her, and the other half haven't met her yet."

"Andrés has always been lucky that way," I said, though assembling and speaking even that simple statement took special concentration.

"Some guys are. And him you don't mind. He's supposed to be getting a new place up on Elsie Street, but I'll bet you five bucks he moves in with Susan by Thanksgiving."

"How'd they meet?" I was determined to show Wally I was OK.

"Right here," he said. "She was doing touch-up on a mural when he first came in. A hell of an artist. She's tight with the Zen Center and that crowd…and with Joan Brown, too. Only a matter of time before one of the downtown galleries picks her up."

It scared me how drunk I was. I drove ultra carefully, windows open and glad for the cold fog. At 23rd and Folsom I got an idea, flipped the turn indicator during the next block, and made a left on 22nd. Behind a creeping low-rider in a turquoise Impala that was shiny as a brand new surfboard, I crossed Mission, reached Valencia, and saw Andrés's BMW parked along the curb to my right. Great, he was there. Maybe he was changing clothes, or had lost track of time, or forgotten what day it was.

I turned onto Valencia, and three cars ahead of Andrés's was Mad's Ghia.

CHAPTER 25

I slowed, sped up, slowed again, saw there was nowhere to park, and on impulse, pulled onto the sidewalk in a driveway down the block. I'd probably get a ticket, or even towed, but I was drunk enough not to care.

Then, with no sense of having traveled the sidewalk or unlatched the gate, I was in the passage outside Gomez's apartment and heard Mad's voice through a partly open window. "How do I know about June?" she challenged shrilly, "I'll tell you…when you tell me what happened to my gun."

"What is this, the Spanish Inquisition?" Gomez yelled.

"I wish," Mad said contemptuously.

"You know what happened. Somebody stole it."

I stationed myself under the rose arbor. At this stage of the season it was covered with thorny foliage, but no blossoms. The lighted window shone above me, ahead by two or three feet. My resolve to intervene and to buffer him somehow, as I'd intended at the Boxx, was gone. I was afraid to disclose my presence, much less announce it.

"Right," she scoffed, "and the somebody was you."

"What if it was?" Gomez's concession had the tone of a demand.

"Talk about nerve! I don't want more trouble with Clark than I already have. He's been asking. Give the damn thing back!"

"As soon as I got home to SF that night, I threw it in the bay at Mission Rock."

"Bullshit!" she shrieked.

"Go on, search the place, who cares."

"I have," Mad announced.

"Don't think I didn't notice. But there was nothing here showing June's name, and you didn't find your fucking gun, did you?"

"There's other places you could hide it. Where do you get off stealing my property and throwing it in the bay, if that's what you even did?"

GOMEZ

"Guns breed trouble. You didn't know how to use it, and I wasn't going to run around with a married woman, armed by her husband, while I wondered what *he* was packing."

"Don't be an ass! How dare you bring that up!"

"Don't be a bitch. One less gun in the mix had to be a plus."

"I don't believe you."

"I don't care."

"The same as you didn't care about Graciela."

"Says who? I helped save that woman. You did, too."

"Not the way she tells it, Gomez, or whoever you are. I think I'll call you Baruch. That's the only name you keep."

"My name, you consummate, pluperfect bitch, is Andrés Gomez. If that was good enough last December, it's good now. And what the hell do you mean about Graciela?"

"You tell me, you damn fraud."

"Screw you! I'm done answering questions. How do you know about June?"

"I read it…in here." A dossier plopped loudly on Gomez's kitchen counter or table. I recognized the sound from Bonhof's office, but to be audible from where I was Mad must have hurled it down.

"What the fuck is that?"

"It's your life, Baruch. Take a look. Keep it, in fact, in case you can't remember how old you are."

"Who's Bonhof Associates?" I heard, or imagined I heard, pages being flipped. "Christ," Gomez added, "there's every kind of shit in here."

Mad's response was cold. "It struck me as the antidote to shit. June is on page 63, among others. The whole sordid story, right up to date."

Distress overrode Gomez's anger. "Where did you get this?"

"Paul hired a private investigator."

"Pa-ul?" he said. Anguish and disbelief made my name come out in two syllables. I felt scorching anguish, too, and though I wasn't entitled, even some disbelief.

"I paid," Mad went on, "but Paul found him."

"What the hell does this have to do with Paul."

"Thanks to you," Mad replied with mock sweetness, "he and I have been lovers since April."

GOMEZ

"You what?" Gomez roared.

"You heard me."

"There's no words for the bitch you are. I knew better…god damn it, I knew better than to get so cunt-struck from the day we met. All I said was flirt with him, loosen him up so he'd relax around women…and you start sucking his dick."

"Since when do you tell me what to do? I'm not your harem girl to pass around. I'll come on to Paul or anybody I want, and set my own limits."

"And that little Judas asks all the time how I feel about Clark. He deserves you, that guy, and you him."

"Paul cost you nothing. I've been way more available to you lately than you were to me."

"Why not just boff your way through the Mime Troupe? Why does it have to be my so-called friend…the one I'm late meeting for dinner right now, the turd?"

"Maybe if I was less suspicious of your lies, it wouldn't have been Paul. Or if you hadn't tried dangling me in his face. We both want the same thing from him, anyway. He's who you're most jealous about, that he won't keep fawning at your feet."

"I should have known you were off the deep end after Artichoke Joe's."

"Baruch," Mad stated flatly, "doesn't get to be the star of every show he's in."

"Of course, it's too much to expect from Mr. Mini-Dick with the lezzie wife that he'd turn you down."

"Why didn't *you* turn me down last winter if I was such trouble?"

"Get out of here, bitch!" Gomez shouted. "Get out! Go home to your precious diary and write French. And FYI, I read that almost better than I do Spanish."

"So the dossier implies. To no avail, though, or you wouldn't be so shocked. I'm just sorry we aren't having a public conversation at Hayes Street, but Paul has wimped out."

"That's what wimps do. Now hand over my key."

"Not a chance. You want security, change the lock."

"Kiss my po-po. Give me the key…before I…"

"Before you what?" she cut him off. "Assault me? The mayor would love that on the police blotter."

GOMEZ

I heard footsteps and realized Mad was gathering herself to go. Without thinking, I hurriedly tiptoed to the back of the building and ducked under the porch stairs with the garbage cans. Just me and the other rats, it seemed. I felt nauseous, my breath sour in my throat. The door above was yanked open and a split-second later its handle thudded against the wall. Someone came out, who, from their lightness of step, had to be Mad.

"Wait," Gomez said, apparently from the doorway. "Where is she? Did your fucking snoop at least uncover that?"

"Who...your darling June?" Mad answered.

"Yes, for Christ sake!"

"No phone or address that I saw. We didn't request any, but read for yourself."

"As soon as I change my lock," he said sarcastically.

"I might decide to throw your key in the bay," she replied, starting down the steps, "in case my gun needs company. Or...maybe I won't."

The heels of Mad's trademark Capezio flats clopped on the wooden treads, carrying with them her slim ankles and the calves and thighs I had kissed in the sunlight of our Sausalito hotel room. Gomez's door slammed shut, and I ached to catch up with her, the Alta Mira version of her, and to whisper her name, but that version was no more. Then, through the gate, I heard the Ghia make a screeching U-turn and roar away in the wrong direction for Mad to spot my car.

With Gomez storming and muttering around his apartment, I began to extract myself from beneath the porch. My suit, if I hadn't already destroyed the knees, was definitely headed for the cleaners. Crouching, undecided, I heard groans at the weedy base of the cyclone fence little more than a yard away. A hand clawed at the wire and a form with arms extending from a dark-colored pouch of cloth pulled itself into a sitting position.

Although I was protected by the fence, the foggy twilight had become night and I was terrified. I shrunk back, gasping, but the form, staring blankly with unkempt black hair and a dirt-smeared face, was aware of my presence. It pointed a finger toward me, made a gurgling sound and an additional low groan. At that point Gomez came out with another violent slam of the door.

GOMEZ

"The bastard!" he said, drawing a deep breath. "The prick! I see him, and he'll be sorry." He pounded down the stairs. "I should've read that damn diary when I had the chance."

The form outside the fence lurched to its feet and crabbed sideways along the mesh to confront him. I could now tell that the form was male and wore a set of filthy, disheveled army dress greens under a torn sleeping bag swathed across his shoulders. "The chick needs a gun?" he whined. "I'll get her a gun. Cheap, no questions asked."

Gomez stopped at the bottom of the stairs. "Fuck off, Armando! I've got enough goddamn snoops to worry about!"

"I live here, *mano*."

"You haven't lived here in a year, asshole. Hang around and the *Chingados* will kill you." Gomez strode away, finishing the sentence over his shoulder, his neck and jaw framed in the space between two stair steps.

Armando scuttled along the fence. "I was the first *Chingado*," he said, whining and bragging at the same time. "*Lo primero*. Fucker Boy number one."

"I hate gangs, and I hate guns!" Gomez yelled. "Leave me alone!"

"You got other company back here, too," Armando said weakly.

I froze in place. Not only could Gomez have discovered the whole perfidious mess these past months by deciphering Mad's diary, he could easily notice the Audi parked down the street. And if he did, whether he'd heard Armando's last words or not, he'd be searching the passageway in another minute ready to fight. That's what guys were supposed to do in this kind of situation, and it was Gomez I'd be fighting, not Andrés. Gomez was who I'd betrayed, and for me there would be no Andrés. I'd never be a partner to that identity, not now.

But if I stayed where I was, he'd have to talk me into the open before there'd be room to fight. And maybe if we talked, and my true contrition came across, we could forgo the manly cliché. If he caught me in the concrete passage things would unfold too quickly to end without blood and bruises. I deserved to get beaten up, wanted to, in a way, and I wouldn't have fought back except to guard my face, yet I wasn't ready to make myself seek it.

GOMEZ

So I waited, as small and invisible as possible behind a stinking, dented garbage can. I even suppressed my breathing, but could hear Armando's rattling in his chest from where he clung to the fence fifteen feet away. It got darker, and with each elapsing second, the odds of Gomez's immediate return decreased.

"Hey, Ernesto," came a voice from the auto salvage lot. "*Mire! La puta del barrio.*"

"No!" Armando cried. He threw the sleeping bag aside and tried to climb the fence.

"*Con ojos tan malos,*" came a different voice. "*Es el joto del barrio.*"

Running footsteps approached. "No!" Armando cried again, futilely thrusting his body upward.

Two bronze men in their early twenties, both wearing headscarves and jeans jackets, grabbed Armando by the legs and pulled him down, their weight tearing his fingers from the wire mesh, which he re-grasped wherever he could. All three were breathing heavily.

"We should off you right here," said one of the men, the one I thought was Ernesto.

"No," Armando pleaded. "It wasn't my fault."

"It's about *confianza*, you scum."

"Loyalty?" Armando said, his fear fully evident. "I've always been a *Chingado*."

"Not any more, scum. You forgot about the *nos*...you only remembered the *yo*."

Armando stumbled out of their grip, desperate to reach 22nd Street, but before he'd gone two paces Ernesto caught up, linked his arms together like a club, and swung them fiercely at Armando's side. Although he tried to duck, the force of the blow drove him into the fence, the tension of which bounced him back to receive an elbow and forearm to the chest from Ernesto's companion. Armando grunted from the impact, groaned in pain, then bounced again into the wire.

Without fists, but with their arms and shoulders, the men began to play a savage game using Armando as the ball and the fence as their playing surface. Ernesto would bash Armando into the steel mesh toward the other man, who bashed him back on the same trajectory for return shot by Ernesto. I heard their grunts, the hollow slam of flesh on softer flesh, and the metallic springing of the fence, which drowned out most of Armando's groans. It went on appallingly and hideously, past their victim's becoming an unconscious, inanimate object, until they let him fall into the alley of his own weight.

Ernesto spit on him, but reached to hold the other man away. "Got off easy this time, the shithead," Ernesto said, winded from his effort.

"Who are the Fucker Boys now?" jeered the nameless one. "*Digame, joto. Quienes son los Chingados ahora?*"

Laughing, they retreated up the alley toward 21st, leaving me in utter silence, but with a new problem. The longer I waited to be sure of avoiding them, the greater the chance of meeting Gomez returned from the Boxx after not finding me. Unless he'd gone to my place and staked out the garage. I counted my breaths for five endless minutes before emerging, slunk as close to Armando as I could, determined that he was alive, realized my drunkenness had disappeared, and scurried out of the passage, across Valencia and to my car.

Perhaps thanks to a **For Rent** sign on the building that I hadn't noticed when I'd parked in its drive, no one had called the cops, so I got in and drove home. At Golden Gateway, I circled the block twice looking for a dark blue BMW or any lurking figure, but saw neither. Even so, the thought of an avenging Gomez in headscarf and denim was almost believable. Once the garage's gate closed behind me, however, I relaxed a bit, only to have anxiety give way to despair.

Leaving the lights off, I locked and dead-bolted the door of my unit. The sound bestowed a wonderful illusion of security, notwithstanding that the enemy responsible for all this woe had accompanied me up step for step clothed in my crumpled suit and was already inside. I turned, and from the opposite wall a flashing red pinpoint in the dark said I had a phone message.

Actually there would be two messages. One from Mad, gloating at how she had reached Gomez first and thwarted my attempt to warn him. The other would be from him, containing imprecations just short of death threats. I decided they could both wait until I called the emergency room at SF General to report an injured and unconscious man in a Mission District alley.

GOMEZ

With that job done and the lights still out so I wouldn't have to look at the garbage stains on my pants, I changed into my bathrobe, washed my face and hands, and plodded over to the machine to face my accusers. Surprisingly, there was only one message, and to my even greater surprise, it was from Jenny.

Given the events of the last three hours, the smugness I'd anticipated feeling if she ever did call was dissolved by the easy familiarity of her voice. The remnants of London in her accent had lapsed further into the standard Bay Area vernacular, but still held an unintended charm.

"Paul," she said haltingly. "Rather hope you don't mind, but I got your number from information. I miss you and want to talk. I'm sorry for what I put you through…for what I put us through…and hope you'll be willing to meet sometime. My number here is 848-2279. Barbara has moved, so I'm alone. I know you hated to call and have her pick up. Please ring back when you've a chance."

So Gomez was right again. Women didn't let go, and Jenny had in fact called. Nor did I doubt that Mad would, too, though I saw little value in what I expected her to say. But Gomez had also been wrong. Despite his denials after we'd shot pool at the Silver Dollar, there *was* a June in his past, an important one by the sound of it, and while he obviously wanted to reconnect, his prediction hadn't held true in her case.

GOMEZ

CHAPTER 26

Word from Mad came the following day. Twice she tried me at work, but I refused the calls. When I got home, the message light was lit and she had this to say:

"Well, Paul, you've been hiding, so you must already know, but I nailed Gomez between the eyes. I told him everything…and I *mean* everything. He was angry and abusive, which he wouldn't have dared at Hayes Street, but I couldn't wait and have you spoil it after all our work. And don't let him guilt-trip you about us. He gave that his blessing no matter what he says. I imagine he and I are through, but there's no reason you and I should be. Please call me, even at home. Clark is away till mid-August."

I'd saved Jenny's message; Mad's I erased. Over the weekend I lived on peanut butter sandwiches and vodka, and thought of my apartment as a bunker. I kept my machine on to screen calls so I could avoid ugly surprises, but the phone didn't ring. The Housers were away on their LA museum and theater trip, Jordan was still at Bohemian Grove, Mad must have been waiting before she tried again, and Gomez remained unaccounted for.

My next selection from *Delta of Venus* was due, and I'd been thinking of a long one called *Artists and Models*, but if I removed the book from its hiding place under those circumstances, it would have been to throw it off the balcony. The whole time I'd rankled at being manipulated by Gomez, Mad had been pulling the strings. I could make sense of it only as a revenge plot, revenge for his asserting power over her, with the goal that he be humiliated but unable to give her up. I was to be her cheering section and her solace if it misfired.

It also registered that I had no stereo or TV to fall back on. My clock radio and car tape deck represented my lone sources of broadcast news and entertainment. Jenny and I had owned nice equipment in Berkeley, but I'd stupidly let her claim it all, and was still punishing myself by doing without. I resolved to remedy that, but the thought of shopping made me exhausted, and I wasn't going to buy just anything.

Instead, while I waited to hear from Gomez, I read *Shogun*, which I'd bought on his recommendation. I could be a hermit a long time before I got through its 1,200 pages. Yet the longer his silence persisted, the more convinced I was that *Shogun* would be the last thing we'd have in common. If he was going to call or thrust himself on me, it would be out of anger. Once that cooled, he'd decide I wasn't worth the bother.

Starting the next week, I pursued him. At first I had Ivy do it, just as I had her fend off Mad. The latter worked better than the former. When she continually found him unreachable, I took over. I also considered tracking him down personally, but I was afraid that appearing at Valencia Street would be overly confrontive given how angry he'd been, and I didn't want to risk being Armando with Gomez as the attacker. That scene, in fact, was still invading my dreams. And at his office he might do something wild enough that it would get him in trouble with the mayor, or I might mess things up for him with Susan DeFeo if I wandered into the Boxx and caused an uproar.

Another concern was that Mad would come to L-W, add drama by parking on the sidewalk, and force me to deal with her. If I had to, I supposed I could, but how, I didn't know. To steel myself, I began erasing her messages at home the instant I recognized who they were from. She and I really hadn't spent much time together, but I missed her, or the idea of her, so intensely that blank tape was my surest defense. The other tokens of the obsession she'd nourished I also managed to leave untouched and hidden.

Then there was Jenny. At least she hadn't called back. I was dubious about seeing her, but I wanted her to stew while I figured it out. And oddly, what tipped the balance was Jordan's return from Sonoma County with photos of his daughter Kes and the new grandson he'd intuited was on the way. Jordan hadn't been informed of the birth, and the baby's father had already migrated to another commune further north, but Jordan was so enthralled that there had been rapprochement all around.

"Bastard or not, the little tike looks just like me," he announced, thrusting a deck of snapshots into my hand. "See…how about those eyes?"

GOMEZ

Jordan wanted to provide money, which Kes, nice-looking and a perfect match for Wally if he were single, was now willing to accept—all for the benefit of six-month-old Raven, of course. And the kid *was* cute. A future SF visit was in the planning stages, and they'd all take a tour boat to Angel Island, and go ashore to look for angels, as they had in the past. I was invited, too, if I liked the idea, and I said I might. Although I'd congratulated him on it only obliquely, my opinion of Jordan had been on the ups since hearing Bonhof's account of the L-W intrigue, and notwithstanding Jordan's strictly pay-to-play view of male-female relationships, this latest news gave him a further boost.

If he could bridge a familial gap of that magnitude and that duration, why could I not make peace with Jenny? I wasn't thinking she and I would get back together, though I might gain some smarmy satisfaction if she were to propose it, but the diminution of bitterness I saw in Jordan had another kind of appeal. My life had become a string of messes all the way back to Jenny. Most of them I couldn't undo, so why not turn one of those negatives into something neutral, even if positive was out of reach? Then, possibly less damaged, I'd go on not to glory, but to Gloria.

A week later I returned Jenny's call, my grip on the phone so tentative and labored it felt like I was wearing one of those restraint jackets the cops use. By the third ring I thought I'd been reprieved, but no sooner did that seem possible than she picked up.

"Sorry to take so long getting back to you," I lied. "I was out of town."

She gave a nervous sigh. "Nice, I hope. Business or pleasure?"

"A little of each."

"Oh. And you didn't mind my calling?"

"No, it was alright. How've you been?"

"Healthy. Work is fine. But a little at sixes and sevens since things went frosty with Barbara. How are you?"

"I'm healthy too, and work is booming. I missed our Berkeley house a lot at first, but I've made friends over here and am starting to really like city life."

"I'm glad. It's so good to hear your voice. I thought it would be."

"Yours certainly surprised me on the machine."

"I do miss you, Paul. Perhaps not much can be done about it, but could we at least be friends?"

"I don't know. I've been very bitter. I don't want us to be enemies, though."

"That would be something. You know that I'm sorry. I said so in my message."

"Yes, I heard." The shorter my answers, the less emotion I'd reveal.

"I should have apologized sooner. It was such a drastic change for me, such a realization, that I couldn't admit to regrets or entertain doubts at the time."

"I've come to understand all of that much, much better in the past year."

"Then you accept my apology? You haven't said."

"I want to. I could mouth the words. Let me experience the feeling and tell you another time."

"Yes," her voice softened, "alright…which means there will be another time."

"I guess it does." That was the implication of what I'd said, though it hadn't been the conscious intent.

"Could it be in person? I'll buy us dinner?"

"I'm not sure."

"Oh…I don't want to cause trouble. Is there someone else?"

How I wanted to say yes, to reinforce that idea in her mind. Yet if I did, I wanted it to be true. "In a way there is," I answered, thinking of Gloria and Mad, "but not someone with whom trouble would be caused."

"Come on then, Paul, what could it hurt?"

"A dinner," I said, "would have to be Dutch."

"If it must. But I'll come to the city. You surely know of wonderful restaurants, and I'd love to pop in and see your place."

"I'm not quite ready for that. We can meet at Hayes Street Grill, two blocks behind the Opera House."

"Sounds perfect." Jenny was always transparently happy when she got her way, and that hadn't changed.

"Understated, but very nice," I said.

"When?" she asked.

This had already gone too fast. I wasn't ready to set a date. "I'll need to check my office calendar and call you back."

GOMEZ

"And you promise you will?"
"Yes, Jen, really, I will."

÷ ÷ ÷

My work calendar, if I'd stuck to the truth, would have made a poor excuse. It was August, many people were on vacation, both clients and at L-W, and I was getting significant pressure to fly home to Kansas for my sister's birthday. The thought was that we would celebrate mine then, too, since it was coming in September.

According to Bonhof, Gomez was also having a birthday soon, and I'd begun wishing I'd looked through the dossier more carefully. I was deeply curious about June and whatever else had set Mad off, but I rejected using her as my informant. Sending Gomez a birthday card might break the ice. Or would that make things worse by highlighting knowledge I'd gained by unfair means?

Something in all this made me postpone calling Jenny and continue to hedge with my parents. If just one of the moving pieces, Gomez, Mad or Gloria, would stabilize, so I knew with certainty where things stood, perhaps I'd be able to make other decisions. Gomez and Gloria I absolutely wanted in my life. Mad I wanted a safe distance away. I also didn't recall being forbidden to call Gloria, the embargo had involved just our not seeing each other.

I decided to try Bonhof's office late in the day, make pleasantries with her, talk over future plans, and have her check the file copy of the dossier for Gomez's birthday. It would be better to know, even if I did nothing with the knowledge. When he'd almost slipped away before, I'd reeled him back in with the Ranchero. This was different, but I wasn't inclined to give up.

Around 3:00 Ivy pushed through my partly closed door, a code I use to say that I'm to be disturbed only if it's something vital. And as I'd noted to myself earlier, she had a new haircut and new skirt, but they were more of the same, not a new look. She was staying with short bangs and advertising her shapeless knees no matter what.

"Two things," she said. "First, Mr. Landau wants to see you day after tomorrow at 10:00."

"What's going on?"

"A very important client, he says."

"Must be, if he's handling it himself."

"You're his hero after all that Apple Computer stuff. Don't forget the ever-loyal Ivy on your rise to the top."

"Oh," I said, moderating my irony as best I could, "no worries about that."

"I mean it," she replied. "The other thing is, I think I understand why you've been having me give Madeline the cold shoulder."

Shit, I thought, she's here. Now what? A screaming, yelling denouement, on deck in front of everybody? "Really?" I croaked.

"Yes, you romantic devil, there's a *Miss* Gloria Bonhof on line two. She says you know her."

Yo-yoing from alarm to rapture, I can only guess what color I turned, but Ivy was certainly witness. "I thought so," she stated, adding, "OK, ta-ta," as she withdrew and closed the door till it latched.

"Mr. Stiles?" came Gloria's voice, though not as tenderly as I'd hoped.

"Gloria, hi. Please call me Paul."

"That wouldn't be a good idea."

"Why not?"

"I'm calling for my father."

"Official business, then. What's on his mind?"

"He thinks…and I agree…that if you hear this from me, you'll know it's final."

"Hear what?"

"Your friend, Mr. Gomez, is being extremely difficult. Someone was thoughtless enough to give him a dossier, which, of course, had our firm's name on it."

"He doesn't have the address, does he?"

"Not so far. As you know, we don't give it out casually. But anyone who's at all determined can find us. This is exactly the situation we try to avoid. My father says he told you."

"He did, yes."

"You'll appreciate, then, that he can't take the chance…and I can't either…of having anything more to do with you. I'm sure that you're a fine man. We seemed to have a lot in common, but my father, my safety, and my family's business come first."

"What has Gomez…I mean Mr. Gomez…done."

GOMEZ

"So far only threats. That he'll sue for invasion of privacy. That he'll break into the office to get any other files if we don't turn them over to him. He wants more information about someone in the dossier, and refuses to believe that we don't have it."

"I'm really, really sorry. Please, tell your dad I'm not the one who breached security."

"I don't think it matters who. The fact is, we've got an angry, threatening man calling us two and three times a day. My father also says Mr. Gomez works for the mayor, which could spell additional trouble."

"If I can reach him…Mr. Gomez, that is…I'll try to back him off. But he's very upset, and hasn't returned my calls for over a week."

"Whatever you can do will be helpful. Just don't think it will change anything for you and me."

"What if we wait another month…you know, all the way to October?"

"Please, no, the decision is final. We took you strictly as a favor to Mr. Mackay, and what's happened shows why we're so careful. Nearly all our clients are law firms and insurance companies, who shield us from this kind of thing."

"I'm terribly sorry."

"I'm sorry, too, Mr. Stiles. In multiple ways. At least you seem to understand."

"I'm trying."

"I was supposed to tell you something else. Mr. Gomez ought to be aware that our office is guarded after dark, that the files are in a locked vault, and that there are surveillance cameras and an alarm system night and day."

"There are?"

"Yes, of course. That's one of the reasons we're located off the street. You mean my father didn't tell you that you were on TV?"

"Not that I remember."

"It's another of his standard jokes…the ones he drives Pam and me crazy with."

÷ ÷ ÷

When Mad called again the next morning I was so weakened by a sleepless night that I almost had Ivy put her through, but what I did instead was call Jenny. We picked a Wednesday evening toward the end of the month to meet at Hayes Street, though I regretted it as soon as we hung up. With no Mad and no Gloria, I guess I wanted a woman of some kind in my life. Jenny had made herself available, but she also seemed to be reading more into my response than I thought she should.

I explained the delay in our getting together by saying I was headed to Kansas in the interim, a decision I made only as the words came out of my mouth. My next call was to a travel agent about booking flights, something I'd normally have Ivy do, but I didn't want to hear her clucking that I hadn't put in for vacation. I was meeting with Milt Landau tomorrow, and I'd clear it with him.

While Gomez remained as unreachable as ever, I'd made headway with his City Hall secretary. She knew I was persona non grata, but my persistence and my lack of histrionics must have made a good impression, because she eventually agreed to deliver a personal message rather than merely log my call.

"Many days Andrés isn't here at all," she warned, "so it may take a while. He checks in constantly by phone, but I know that hasn't gotten results for you."

"Thanks very, very much. Whenever you can get it to him is OK. I'll be brief. Ready?"

"Wait a second…alright…now."

"Paul Stiles accepts full blame for what has happened. Please call him ASAP. If possible, he will help with the additional information you need. Mr. B does not have it, and any further attempts to find it there could have seriously negative consequences."

"Is that everything?" she asked.

"For now."

"And he has your number?"

"I'm quite sure he does."

"Here's what I'll do then, Mr. Stiles. This sounds rather sticky, so if I'm not able to give it to him by Friday, I'll read it onto his answering machine at home."

I was dumbstruck. "He has a mach…ah…I mean, a phone? He never did before."

"He's always had both since starting work here. It's unlisted, though, so please don't ask."

GOMEZ

÷ ÷ ÷

Another nearly sleepless night and I was ready for my meeting with the big boss. Or the big boss on the business side, since Roy—I mean Mr.—Walters, our other founding partner, and various of his higher-ups oversaw most of the creative work. Milt—I mean Mr. — Landau and his branch of the officer corps stroked the biggest clients and made sure our paychecks didn't bounce. I'd always gotten along well with both in my infrequent contacts with them, and judging by the firm's success, it was the proper division of labor. Their spacious offices adjoined one another at the offshore end of our floating quarters, with knockout views of the islands, bridges and bay.

This was my first visit to the executive suite since my enlightenment session with Bonhof, and things at L-W continued to look and feel different. As usual, the physical environment was spiffier than at the onshore end, but the aura among support staff in the open area outside the conference room seemed colder and harder-edged compared to my memory of the meeting last spring to kick-off our Apple Computer project. Even the fact that the coffee there smelled better than at the break station in my department now smacked of decadence rather than any devotion to quality.

Landau himself was welcoming enough, and he projected an efficient confidence, with his tan, his muscular frame, his earnest handshake, his Italian silk suit, his neatly coifed, thinning hair, and his two-pound Rolex watch. If he was gay, anybody could be—Steve McQueen, Rock Hudson, Paul Newman—anybody. Also on hand was his secretary Roz, to take minutes, while several of the top creative people, Sam Prentice, Diva Hampton, and Gus Spode, one of whom usually ran the project groups I was on, rounded out the home-team side of the table.

Across from them, positioned to be thrilled by the seeming nearness of the Golden Gate and Alcatraz through the panoramic windows, were three guys I didn't recognize, wearing cheaper suits that didn't fit as well as ours. Two of them were jowly, and the third, older but more fit, locked eyes with me the minute I came in. I guess he was trying to see who'd blink first, which I was quick to do. To me, those games were ridiculous.

GOMEZ

Once Roz finished hustling coffee for everyone, making sure we had a chance to appreciate how compelling a forty-five-year-old woman's body could be in the right tomato-red outfit, Landau was off to the races.

"Except for Mr. Stiles," he began, pointing at me, "we all know each other from prior iterations. Paul, here, is not only one of our sharpest young talents, he's recently been seasoned on a number of high-profile projects in the wine and computer industries that have his clients begging for more.

"Diva and I will share the overall lead, as in the past, but to bring new energy and ideas, and to promote our mutual interests in the best possible manner, Paul will be your principal contact. He's surprised at the moment, which I wanted him to be, and he has a raise coming he doesn't know about, either."

I blushed, my circulatory system did what felt like a disco routine, and the L-W people accompanied their smiles with a patter of applause. The three outsiders contributed halfhearted smiles of their own, as though I were the runner and they were the gauntlet. "Thanks," I said. "I really am surprised, but I'll give it everything I've got as soon as you let me in on the secret."

"Not a secret, a plum," Landau went on. "As a reward for your fine work at L-W, let me introduce Don Figgis, Stan Calhoun and Rod Bolton of the San Francisco Bureau of Conventions and Tourism."

They stood to shake my hand across the table, and it was Bolton who had given me the laser eye, which he did again from closer range while we all returned to our seats.

CHAPTER 27

What was there but to leave town and try to get my head screwed on straight? I couldn't think of anything, so, feeling by then like a stick figure or a zombie under alien control, that's what I did. The C&T job was a competition that came around every five to seven years, not a true low-bid process, and Landau was happy to give me time off along with my raise so I'd be rested and ready when things really started hopping. Proposals were due November 1, with a decision on whether we'd retain or lose the contract to be made by mid-December.

The question was whether a week with my parents would screw my head on or further screw it up. It would be great to get away from anything reminding me of Mad, Gomez or Gloria, or of the fact that this was the first time the C&T job had been in play since the confidential settlement of the kickback scandal. Had everybody learned their lesson, or would my work merely be the cover sheet in an envelope filled with cash? In Kansas there was exactly nobody with whom such things could be discussed, nor would I mention having agreed to an upcoming dinner date with Jenny.

Nonetheless, my impromptu vacation was beneficial. I finished reading *Shogun* and otherwise moped around letting my mother and sister take care of me. The fact that I didn't seem happy, which I acknowledged, was commented on but attributed to heartbreak over the divorce from that woman they had all told me not to marry. Last Christmas the topic had still been taboo, but now they'd reached consensus: it was time I snapped out of my funk. I tolerated a few days of this, then found ways to change the subject.

A couple of times I drank beer with my dad while watching Royals games on TV. Maybe if we'd been listening to the radio in the garage I'd have tried to raise the issue of dick size with him— what a grotesque crock of crap it was, and how wrong he'd been to burden me with his fears. On the plane from SF I'd promised myself I would, but sitting in the living room I chickened out. He was impressed, however, that I'd been to a Giants game that spring, and impressed that anything as normal as baseball could flourish in the Bay Area. His view was that, starting at Denver and proceeding west, the US got progressively kookier until it reached the Pacific. Once I accepted that and began recounting all the substantiating anecdotes from Herb Caen I could remember, we got on fine.

My sister's birthday, which included her husband and kids, was like something from the Midwest edition of *Good Housekeeping*, but she seemed pleased and I was relieved to get mine over with early so I wouldn't have to feel deficient celebrating it alone next month. A guy, their logic went, can always use a few more shirts and pairs of socks from J.C. Penny, and I agreed, even though the guy I had in mind worked behind the receiving counter at Goodwill. I also had to take into account that my sock drawer was very short of room.

When I got home, there was one last message from Mad to delete, nothing from Gomez, and nothing, for better or worse, from Jenny. Nor were leavings from any of them among the pink noteslips that Ivy put on my desk at L-W. I did have one message from Gomez's secretary, bless her diligent soul, confirming that she'd relayed my exact words to him both via his phone machine and in person. Her name turned out to be Elaine, and her number was also on the slip, so I saved it on the chance I'd try again.

I had now done everything I could think of to heal the wound, and failed. The irrefusable bait should have been my offer to help in locating the mysterious June, but the only way to make good on it would have been with further help from Jordan. On the other hand, no more calls had come in from Bonhof Associates, so perhaps my indirect contact with Gomez had caused him to stop harassing them. As starved for good news as I was at that point, I let myself believe it.

÷ ÷ ÷

The dependable and perfectly punctual Jenny was waiting at the doorway of the Hayes Street Grill when I arrived, and I couldn't have been more than sixty seconds late myself.

"That must be your new car…your Audi…I saw you getting out of," she called cheerfully. "Very spiffy indeed."

GOMEZ

Spiffy—I remembered now that I'd picked that word up from her. "Thanks. I think so, too."

She was in a nicely draped cobalt-blue dress, a color she knew looked good on her, with an off-blue accent scarf and some jangly silver bracelets. Her familiar blunt-cut hair even seemed to have had its blondeness highlighted for the occasion. Since I couldn't remember the last time I'd seen her in makeup, the overall effect was of a different person—perhaps a different gender—than the Jenny who'd been Barbara's companion.

Another difference was that she was noticeably nervous. I was, too, but I hoped not so noticeably. It would have been absurd to shake hands, and I didn't want to give or receive a peck on the cheek, so I stopped about a foot away and let her see that my eyes were taking her in. "I'm glad we did this," I said. "You look great."

"As do you," she smiled, reaching to feel my cuff. "Quite the sharp worsted jacket. What is it, Italian to be this soft?"

"Right," I acknowledged. Stepping aside, I held the door for her. "Here, in we go."

The room was busier and noisier than it had been during my January dinner with Gomez. I also took a moment to scan the room to make sure he wasn't there, a possibility that had added to my nervousness. He wasn't, but at a larger table toward the back were a woman and two men, laughing and toasting one-another in a recreation of what Gomez, Mad and I might have looked like if everything hadn't gone tilt.

A remark from Jenny returned me to the present. "This place is marvelously handsome, Paul, with all these mirrors and fresh flowers."

We were put at a table not far from where I'd sat before, and Roberto, the waiter Gomez knew from the Centro signaled that he would be with us soon. "You said you'd gotten to like city living," Jenny went on. "I can see why, but the blustery cool outside is a bit of a shock."

"The East Bay hills," I said, "are tropical by comparison. Of course Berkeley has urban pleasures of its own, which is why you and I didn't come this direction much."

"I think I got us so swept up in the University orbit from the day we first moved there that it became too much the center of things."

GOMEZ

We went on to study our menus and exchange the predictable small talk about Kansas, with Jenny inquiring about my parents, my sister and her family, and my asking to be caught up on Jenny's co-workers and relatives. When Roberto arrived I steered Jenny to the composed salad, just as Gomez had steered me, and I prevailed on Roberto for a bottle of the same Rhone wine.

"I know it's not shown," I said, pointing at the list, "but I had it once before with Mr. Gomez."

"For a friend of Mr. Gomez, we will find some," Roberto answered.

"Have you seen him recently?" I asked with deliberate unconcern.

"No. He was due in a few weeks ago but had to cancel. He is very busy now with the mayor."

"Yes, I know."

"He sees Mrs. Yost, our owner, sometimes during the day. She lets him park in the alley when he must go to the City Hall for meetings."

Having noted that Gomez's favorite, the grilled monkfish crusted with herbs, was the evening's special, I ordered it, and made a point of assuring Roberto that I was sticking with red wine so Jenny could register a quizzical expression.

"Another wild man from the pampas," Roberto laughed.

"Who's this Gomez fellow?" Jenny asked while Roberto was away.

"An Argentinean guy I play racquetball with. This has been a hangout of his, and he introduced me to it. I'm steadier with my running than with racquetball, though."

"Well." Jenny was impressed. "I'm off racquet sports these days, and here you are, being athletic, ordering special wines and going about with intimates of the mayor."

"It sounds like a bigger deal than it is," I said modestly. She probably thought the wine was doubly expensive because it was unlisted, but Gomez had said otherwise.

"How do you know him?"

"I'm doing some design work for the city."

"Why ever did I worry? You've done fine over here without me."

"It's taken extra effort," I said.

The wine, perhaps because I'd made it sound exotic, was a hit when it came, and so were the bread and the composed salad. "The presentation is fabulous," she announced. "And ideal for me. You know how I like to keep my food separate on my plate."

"*That* I *do* remember." My reply was joking, because I wanted to see if I could still make her laugh.

It worked. Though Jenny's teeth were small for her jaw, she'd always had a ready smile, and the restaurant's light was kind, smoothing, in concert with her makeup, the facial pores she was often self-conscious about. "Just don't be making mirth about my other habits," she joked back.

"I'll try to show restraint." Jenny is also the type who washes and peels all fruit and who meticulously de-strings her bananas before consuming them.

"I think some of that drove Barbara batty," Jenny said.

"You can tell me what happened if you like."

And to my surprise, while we ate, she did—the story being that she and Barbara had fairly quickly lost interest in each other and drifted apart. No big blowup, no high drama. "Perhaps," Jenny concluded with some poignancy, "sharing so much with your mate... things like perfume, PMS and the tampon supply...undermines intimacy instead of building it. Living with a man, even an undemanding and compatible one, lends the necessary mystery." She gave a fond look in my direction.

"Maybe it was just Barbara," I offered, "and not an inevitable result."

"Very sweet of you to say. In any case, I'm left with the little house I bought up on Keith Street and an assistant I wish worked in some other lab. I'd be happier if one's sexual proclivities weren't the accepted basis for relationships, if our species had arisen through mitosis, not meiosis."

"I'm afraid my science vocabulary has eroded in your absence."

"Oh, sorry. Mitosis is sexless...pure cell-division. Meiosis mixes X and Y chromosomes through some form of fertilization. I'm loving this lamb dish you recommended, by the way."

"Good."

"And what of you?" Jenny asked. "I recall rather a cryptic answer when I asked if our meeting for dinner might cause problems with someone else."

GOMEZ

"I had an obsessive affair with a married woman...exciting by any standards, but it's over. I was foolish, just not foolish enough to be in love with her."

"How extraordinary!" Jenny said. "Who would have predicted that answer? You've also put your finger on the worst of it for me. I did fall in love with Barbara, and thought it would sustain. At first it felt much like us back at Kansas...we sustained."

"Yes, we did, for a time. And as long as we're suddenly able to be so honest with each other, I ought to tell you that I fell in love this past year too, and that I still am in love, though it hasn't gone well."

"Now you've really astonished me, Paul, as if the married woman already hadn't. Who's this other one? Do you mind?"

"I'll give you an outline. The details are too convoluted."

"Alright."

"Do you remember Handy Andy, from Berkeley, the guy who painted our house."

"Oh, yes, quite the vivid personality. He was a legend among people he worked for. I tried to hire him again to make repairs on my new place, but he'd disappeared."

"Well, it was him."

"He helped you meet her, the one you fell in love with? Is that what you're saying?"

"No, it's him that I'm in love with."

By this time Jenny and I were waiting for the lemon tarts and coffee we'd ordered, so she didn't have a mouthful of food to choke on, which from the strength of her reaction, was fortunate. "Oh, my god, Paul!" she said, but at least kept her voice down. "You poor thing. I know how that hurts. You think you've redefined yourself... or they've redefined you...then bang, they're gone."

I was at a crossroads. I'd planned a disclosure along these lines while on the plane from Kansas. I hadn't told my family Jenny and I would be seeing each other when I got back, nor had I extended her greetings to them as she'd asked.

On the heels of being trumped by Mad, dumped by Gomez, dumped again by Gloria, then dropped into the polluted mire of the C&T job, I had wanted Jenny to feel not only that I was completely out of reach, but always had been. The way she'd made me feel when she left. To punish her with the devastatingly subversive fact that she, too, had been deluded as to who her spouse really was, had been living an additional lie all those years. Nothing could slam the door more decisively on the reconciliation she was apparently hoping for. I had wanted her to want it and to be denied.

I was tired of bouncing from being Jenny's sap to being Mad's sap and then back to Jenny, never the initiator, always the sap. To hell with that. And if Jenny hadn't been so disarming in person, so open, and so sympathetic when I'd started springing my trap, I might have gone ahead.

But there was another problem; it wouldn't be true and wouldn't be fair to Gomez. When I'd seen his face framed between the stair steps outside his apartment, the shape of his jaw convinced me all over again that he *had* been on the truck at the Gay Freedom Parade. Yet I knew beyond doubt that he wasn't gay, or even bi.

That the Milt Landau news had seemed unbelievable was because I knew only the public Milt Landau. Gomez I knew in depth, and Bonhof would have disabused me if I'd been wrong. No, Gomez wasn't perfect, but who was? If he were here, he'd play this straight, no matter how far-fetched it might sound—and who better to model on?

"I don't mean it the way you're thinking," I told Jenny. "We were never lovers. It was a friendship, a powerful one, and I did...I do...love the guy. I'm even willing to admit that there was a physical dimension to it. I liked being around him physically, but that wasn't what it was about."

Jenny looked at me, still agog, while Roberto brought our desserts. "I'm afraid I did misunderstand there," she said. "Is that all you want to say?"

"Pretty much. He and I got along terrifically well at the Arch Street house, and he moved over to the city when he left Berkeley. The best and most amazing friend I've ever had."

"Why past tense?" she asked.

"I wasn't worthy."

"I find that hard to believe. He had a long German-sounding name, didn't he?"

"Yes, Steentofter. It's Dutch."

"Looking at him, I always figured it was an alias," Jenny smiled. "He probably started as Emiliano somebody before he was Handy Andy."

GOMEZ

"No, it was his real name," I said.

"And was he really a Berkeley Ph.D.? I also remember hearing that he was an opera buff and could quote passages from *Don Quixote* verbatim."

"All that stuff is true...and lots more."

"It still doesn't make you unworthy. Or did the married woman figure in?"

"We don't need to get into that. What's done is done."

"We've both had incredible roller coaster rides these last twelve months, haven't we?"

"We have indeed. How would you feel about a little cognac to close our evening?"

"I'd like it very much. And don't forget, we're splitting the tab."

I told Roberto what we wanted, then turned back to Jenny. "I was going to propose another idea on who pays."

"What's that?"

"I have a wonderful math puzzle. Just your cup of tea. If you can solve it before we leave, I'll buy. If not, you buy."

"Can I hear the problem before I accept?"

"Sure." I proceeded to spell out Gomez's $1,000 envelope problem, but with no extra hints.

Our cognacs arrived and Jenny smilingly held out her snifter for a toast. "I don't accept," she said.

"Why, too tough?"

"No, because you're trying to trick me into letting you pay."

"You really think I would do such a thing?"

"Yes, because I've already solved it."

"In that case, please don't accept. It's too embarrassing." My god, how long had she taken, fifteen seconds?

"A very clever formulation, I admit, but we're still talking about mitosis."

"Non-sexual reproduction?"

"Yes, of course. One becomes two, two become four, four become eight, and so on. The tenth envelope would contain $489 and the other nine would add to $511."

"My solution took hours...hours spread over several weeks. In fact, when I first heard it I thought it was impossible."

"That's what's so clever. But even the most plodding cell biologist knows that any progression of doubling has the property that all possible integers preceding any given value in the series can be made up by combining some or all of the prior values."

"I'll be damned. I treated the first and last envelopes as exceptions and was thinking powers of two for the rest."

"That gives the same result, but less elegantly," Jenny said. "The tenth envelope is the only special case needed, which is Occam's Razor to a T. If we were still together, and you had asked, I could have saved you lots of time."

"If we were still together, I'd never have known about the puzzle. I got it from Handy Andy. He solved it fast, too." And in arguing for the simplest answer, that selfsame razor of logic would have applied almost as well to the questions I'd asked Bonhof.

"Nothing to quarrel over then," Jenny proclaimed. "We split the tab."

"Fine. I'm put in my place once again."

"You probably know what I'm about to bring up, don't you?"

"Possibly."

"Well, I told myself I wouldn't jump the gun like this, but we've been able to talk so openly tonight...I...ah...I'm not able to help get your polymath friend back, but you can have *me* back if you wish."

"I'm truly touched, Jen. It's not what I'm looking for, I don't think, but tonight has made me want us to be friends."

"That's something. That's a start, isn't it?"

"It's definitely something, but it may not lead toward anything more."

"To go on record, I'd like us to try again, and for that we'd certainly have to be friends. I'm just not promising to be a different person, to be someone I'm not."

"I wouldn't want you to be."

"Yes, but you seem a different person, Paul, a better person. I mean it."

"Different, I can see. Better, I doubt."

"I wouldn't expect you to move, either. I put you through that a year ago. I could easily rent my Berkeley place and do the commuting from here. I know I behaved badly."

"We're really better suited to be friends, and as friends we don't have to worry about trying to live together."

GOMEZ

"You've learned some new approaches to meiosis with your married woman and found you like them, is that it?" Meant to be witty, her remark carried an undertone of regret as well.

I chose my words with care. "Truthfully, that would be a factor."

"At least say you'll consider the idea. Meanwhile, find us another fabulous restaurant for our next date."

"How about the Alta Mira in Sausalito?"

"A Sunday brunch?" she asked.

"No a dinner, fairly soon, so the weather will still be nice."

"I'd be delighted. When."

"Let me call you within the week. One step at a time, alright?"

CHAPTER 28

Her name was Kara. She was half Norwegian, or said she was, blonde, a little bigger-boned than Mad, and nearly as pretty. Like Jenny, she was two years my senior, though Jenny looked it and Kara didn't. Physically, in fact, you could say she was the dream version of Jenny, and bolstering my defenses against Jenny's reconciliation idea was why I'd given Jordan the green light on setting me up with someone.

In his view I was finally thinking rationally. He knew I'd disentangled myself from the married woman he'd never been able to get me to talk about, and knew I was back in touch with my ex, so he was more certain than ever that baggage-free female companionship and reliable sex were the ideal prescription. Kara he'd heard of through Marnie, not Eve, and I had to pony up the hefty agency fee, plus the results of a VD test, but once those were taken care of, the rest all blossomed per Jordan's assurances.

And keeping my hormones in balance worked, in the sense that I transcended my occasional wavering of will with regard to Mad and worried less about Jenny's track record of persuading me to do whatever it was she wanted. She and I were seeing each other every two weeks or so, which had restored a degree of continuity to my life given our shared history. I was even feeling safe enough to consider having her at Golden Gateway for a pre-dinner drink, and had OK'd in concept that she would host a meal for us at her place sometime. I'd always thought people who insisted they were good friends with their ex-spouses were phony, but I was now beginning to see it as possible and appreciating its value.

Yes, Kara was expensive, but I'm skipping monetary specifics. A date lasted twelve to eighteen hours, extending, for example, from dinner on one night through breakfast the following day, although Kara didn't seem to be a clock-watcher. Our first official outing, after we'd met once for coffee, consisted of a meal at Fior d'Italia with Jordan and Marnie, whom we joined afterward for a revival showing of *Godfather II*, then went our separate ways.

GOMEZ

Though she was genial and bright, Kara let me do all the initiating in terms of social activities and of sex. It was actually quite unbelievable. If I wanted to do things I'd seen at porn theaters or that I'd learned from Mad, I didn't have to justify or explain, we just did them. And she wasn't wooden about it, either, she was involved. Of course my taste doesn't run to S&M or other stuff she might have wanted to veto. Jordan was also right in predicting that she'd like that I was younger than her typical client. For our second date I made a risky move by taking her to the ballet with the Housers, and we all got along great. I'd have been mortified if they ever found out, but how would they if I kept my mouth shut?

Jenny's new attitude, deciding that she was bi but could control whether or not to express her lesbian side, she attributed to having a shrink. And while the shrink was a lesbian feminist herself, professionally she was a pragmatic neo-Freudian—her own words, I was told—and didn't have a problem with Jenny's plan to be nominally heterosexual as the best way to function in a homophobic world. That was the limit of what I wanted to know, but it was said in a spirit of full disclosure during our dinner at the Alta Mira, and made sense as an underpinning for Jenny's renewed interest in me.

As far as my own objectives went, having her as an asexual confidant would be best, but if she got into another relationship, I'd rather it be with a guy than a woman. Call it prejudice or insecurity, I was tired of explaining the Barbara thing to myself, still wished Gomez and Mad hadn't known about it, and had no desire to revisit that experience. On the other hand, I'd always held the same skeptical attitude toward shrinks and the claims people made for them as I did toward being friends with your ex, so Jenny had given me something else new to think about.

Meanwhile, at the office, it was hammer down on the Conventions and Tourism job. And like all big design projects, there were innumerable trial balloons. I enjoyed my new role, even though I was spending my raise on Kara faster than it was coming in, and especially enjoyed assigning the grunt work to other staff. Day-to-day I saw very little of Milt Landau and found Diva Hampton to be a good head. She was available when I needed her, and while her age, her voice and her pear shape suggested the classic Jewish mother, she didn't obsess or constantly look over my shoulder.

GOMEZ

What we ultimately came up with could be used against almost any background color, and could display in an area left blank the names of specific events or attractions the city might want to feature. The blank was the circular center of a shiny, flat, round-shouldered cable car bell drawn to look three-dimensional, with a pull-cord ringer mechanism at the lower left and the cord hanging vertically below, as if the bell were flush-mounted on the page the same as it would be on a car's wooden interior wall. From there we departed realism to fan out miniature, half-tone silhouettes of SF landmarks—Coit Tower, the Transamerica Building, a Golden Gate Bridge pylon, the Ferry Building, Mission Dolores, Twin Peaks and Seal Rock—like sun rays emanating from the top of the bell.

For reasons of space we had to overlap the building and tower icons on the wider Seal Rock and Twin Peaks icons, and distort the scale to make their heights fairly equal, but it was a wow when we were done. In one easily apprehended image we captured the local destinations most familiar to tourists, implied that they were all within a cable car ride of each other, which they aren't, and that SF was usually sunny, which it's not.

Then Diva hit on the perfect slogan by tweaking the efforts of a couple of our junior team members. And before, when I said she was a Jewish mother, I meant one from the kibbutz, with thrusting coils of kinky hair, a complexion seemingly darkened by generations of desert life, and a wardrobe that never strayed from earth tones and loosely cut fabric. When she laid the words **A Place Like No Other** along the lower edge of the bell in bold sans serif type, however, her tough-eyed smile confirmed that she, too, thought we had a winner.

Even at the time I was aware that my occasional diversions with Kara and Jenny were an attempt to recover from Gomez and Mad, as was some of my absorption in the C&T job. But that wasn't the whole story. Since my name would be on L-W's entry whether we won or not, and whether we engaged in bribery or didn't, it was damn well going to be good. That way, if we lost and sued because somebody else paid bribes, we'd have a leg to stand on, and if we won it wouldn't look like a put-up deal even if we had paid bribes. I hated having all that in the back of my mind, but so it went.

And proving that my creative juices could still flow despite so many clouded emotions was pretty satisfying. The complexity of the

GOMEZ

C&T design couldn't have differed more from the simple, wordless logo of an apple comprised of bright, pastel stripes and missing a bite at one shoulder that I'd developed for our computer industry client. There I'd pared away ninety percent of what everybody else on the team had submitted. Here the result had evolved through accretion. But different as they were, each image was totally scaleable. Without losing their identities, they could be portrayed as not much bigger than a silver dollar for use on a letterhead, or as big as a putting green for billboards or the sides of busses.

OK, enough patting myself on the back. The key point is that we made the November 1 deadline and I rejoined the human race shortly thereafter. Anyone who's been wrapped up in that kind of project, especially one as all-consuming as the C&T job was during late October, will understand that the day immediately following is like waking from a coma. I was disoriented, had piles of unread mail, magazines and newspapers, and discovered that the rest of the world had been marching along without me.

Baseball season was over, the Giants had missed the playoffs, and in football the 49ers were getting pounded. There was also a new Pope—from Poland, no less—the Grateful Dead had triumphantly returned to SF after performing three live concerts at the Egyptian pyramids, and the even-tackier-than-we-all-feared Pier 39 had just held its grand opening, filling the streets with dopey people in T-shirts saying **I ♥ San Francisco**. Having to look at things like that are the curse of being a designer, but I half feared that some inane parallel to the shirt and its slogan had been entered in the C&T competition and would win via financial grease.

On top of all this, a statewide election was coming up in a week, as part of which Proposition 6, the hotly contested anti-gay initiative, would be decided, and Jerry Brown might be replaced as Governor by a Republican who would appoint Jordan to a judgeship. Jordan didn't really expect such an outcome, but hope, he said, springs eternal. Although I had concealed at first that I was working on something for C&T, I told him toward the end and said that no signs of hanky-panky had surfaced that I knew of.

He was curious, I could see, but he did nothing to prolong the topic or to acknowledge that he knew where the clearance he'd given Bonhof must have led. When Jordan was keeping his mouth shut, he really kept it shut, and his only reply was a laconic, "In that flock, it's hard to tell the vultures from the carrion."

We were talking in the hallway—I sweaty and in my running shorts—outside his door after we'd accidentally ridden up in the elevator together. "By the way," he went on, "where are you on this initiative…the anti-gay one…that's on the ballot?"

"I'll be canceling your vote, I suppose, since I'm against it."

"No, no, I'm against it, too. Kes has me convinced. Besides, who am I to outlaw people's sexual preferences in their own homes?"

"Good point," I laughed.

"Reminds me, though, I heard a hell of a funny joke the other day, but you probably won't want to share it with Kara."

"OK, I'll bite."

"How can you tell if your roommate is gay?"

"Don't know," I said. After all, I hadn't guessed my wife was.

"Because," Jordan began to strangle on his own laughter, "his dick tastes like shit."

Something I did share with Kara that weekend was the oddest agency date she said she'd ever had. My plan for the late afternoon and evening was for her to accompany me to Pacific Stereo where I bought a TV, a tape deck and other equipment I'd had my eye on. The TV was a 19" Sony Trinitron, pretty much the best set going, and I rounded out the JVC 400 tape deck with a pair of Bose speakers, a McIntosh 1080 tuner/amp and a Dual A-19 direct-drive turntable. It took us two trips in the Audi to get it all home.

On the second trip we stopped for takeout Chinese, which we ate by passing the containers back and forth in my living room while I set up the stereo. The TV went in the bedroom. When we were done and I'd temporarily stashed the packing boxes on the balcony, I shut off the lights and we drank wine and listened to KJAZ for a while until I had Kara give me—well, a blow job—on the couch lasting the whole length of the Ravel's *Bolero* tape from my sock drawer. After that I got her off in bed with a dildo she'd brought and we settled down to watch *Saturday Night Live*. I didn't even consider telling her that she was the only woman to visit my apartment since I'd moved in, but eight years late, the 70s had not only arrived for Paul Stiles, he was learning to enjoy them.

GOMEZ

In the morning, following more aerobics under the sheets, I handed her an envelope that she calmly stowed in her purse. As she was leaving, I asked why she kept calling what we'd done odd.

"Not odd, like weird," she answered. "Just odd for...you know, us. It's the kind of thing I'd do with my boyfriend if he was back from the Navy a couple of weeks. Next time you think about having a quiet evening at home, let me know in advance and I'll bring some of my own tapes and a couple of joints."

I told her great, good idea, but otherwise let the remark pass because I didn't want to hear more about the Navy boyfriend. If I wasn't careful, it could end up like Mad's annoying references to Clark. But the thing was, I'd had a great time, my place was now complete in some indefinable way, and letting Jenny visit seemed a logical step. But in the interim, as though a theater curtain had gone up, I became so taken with the ready availability of good music and having my pick of televised entertainment that I couldn't comprehend why I'd willfully done without.

Building from just the Ravel, and with little conscious planning, my tape and record collection grew by the day to include the whole Gomez canon: Steely Dan's *Greatest Hits*, *Workingman's Dead*, Bob Marley, Miles Davis, a pulsing salsa album by Cuco Valloy from the Dominican Republic, Jacques Brel, Argentine tangos, Beethoven piano sonatas, Chopin nocturnes, Bach cantatas and a boxed set of Wagnerian opera. My other adaptation to plugged-in life, which took a little time to master, was remembering not to throw out the weekly TV supplement from the Sunday *Chronicle*. And definitely, whether or not it took Kara's help, I'd be getting myself a supply of the sacred weed too.

÷ ÷ ÷

Even with no program guide, TV was great for keeping track of the election. Jerry Brown won a second term, the anti-gay initiative went down to an astonishing million-vote defeat, and Harvey Milk, the gay SF politician who'd led the state-wide campaign against it, looked more and more like a rising star. Then, at the end of the week, came a second political surprise. The Board of Supervisors guy, Dan White, that I'd heard Gomez complain about and had seen at the Gay Freedom Parade, quit in a huff. Since he was a reactionary numskull who'd cast a lot of tie-breaking votes, and appointing his successor fell to the mayor, George Moscone would have a working majority on the Board for the first time since he'd been in office. Gomez must have been ecstatic, and I could imagine his buying rounds of drinks at the Boxx to celebrate.

Three months had gone by, and it still felt like everything I saw or did related to him, but maybe that's just how it is when you've been in love and squandered your opportunity. Yet in a matter of days the TV news reminded me of him again, because Leo Ryan, a local Congressman, flew off with an entourage of journalists to investigate the exiled People's Temple cult somewhere in South America. Gomez had said their leader was dangerous and had bilked a lot of the members, and Ryan sounded like he took the same view.

But that was all Gomez by association. Gomez himself was on TV the following night, standing along the edge of the stage when a wild melee broke out at a dump Dan White rally in an Outer Mission neighborhood. White had announced that morning that he was retracting his resignation. The rally was to show support for alternate candidates on the ground that the resignation had been formally accepted at a Board meeting the previous day, so the seat remained vacant no matter what White now did. White had responded by crashing the rally.

Lunging at people and yelling into the mike, White, whom the newscaster said had been carrying a gun for which he held a concealed weapons permit, insisted that he'd been elected by majority vote and that as long as he wanted the seat, which he did, it was his until the term expired. At several points Gomez looked like he might jump onto the stage to confront White, but I knew Gomez was supposed to keep a low profile, so he bided his time and eventually a very articulate woman named Goldie something-or-other got White calmed down. Legal opinion was, however, that he would be out of luck unless Moscone chose to reappoint him.

The next morning I requested a private meeting with Diva. Since she acted puzzled when I closed the door, and more so when I stipulated that I was trusting her to keep everything I said in confidence, I got right to it.

"Look," I began, "I don't know the score exactly, but I've worked here for seven years and heard rumors."

Her eyes narrowed as she placed her elbows on her desk and leaned toward me. "What rumors?" she said evenly.

"There was a lawsuit the last time the C&T job was up. We were accused of making kickbacks, and the rumors say the accusations were true."

"We got the job, and the suit was settled out of court."

"I know all that. But what about the rumors? True or false?"

She cleared her throat. "I didn't have anything to do with C&T back then."

"This is important to me, Diva. I won't do anything wacky, but I need to know."

She remained quiet, and so did I. Through the window behind her I could see truck traffic, like a fast-moving parade of sow bugs, on the upper and lower decks of the Bay Bridge. Cars, which would have been the ants in that insectary, were too low to be visible above the guard-rails from where I sat.

"Is what I say also in confidence?" she asked.

"Yes."

"Then the rumors are true. Milt and Gus handled what there was to handle. I don't know the amounts or any of the details."

"Thanks," I sighed.

"So?"

"Where do we stand this year? Are the same sorts of favors expected?"

"I don't know. I hope not, but maybe. That Rod Bolton is a slippery SOB. All of a sudden he's been asking for additional information, and Milt says it could be a sign."

"What kind of information?"

"Oh, written releases that none of the images we used are under copyright by somebody else. Penny-ante crap like that."

"I don't get the connection."

"Sometimes the indemnity limit mentioned in the release request is the ante for playing the game. Bolton says they're very impressed with our work and just want to line up the ducks. Milt's handling that, I'm not...and neither are you."

"It doesn't gall you?"

"Of course it galls me. Galls me to hell. But what are you gonna' do? God, don't tell me you're the type who thinks he can fight City Hall."

"I'm the type who's just found out how to say no to his ex-wife. But I do have a channel to the mayor that might nip foul play in the bud."

"Tempting, I admit, but don't go that route."

"Trust me. Totally discreet. No fingerprints on it, mine, yours or anybody's."

"There better not be. I still say no, but whatever happens, you're on your own. Even if I'm rooting for you, I'm not backing you and this meeting never took place."

I laughed. "Exactly how I remember it. What meeting?"

Diva laughed, too. "Anything else you want to know?"

"Now, no. But make me a promise. If we get the job, and had to buy it, tell me. Not the amount, just a rueful yes. Or if we lose the job because we didn't buy it, tell me that."

"OK, Paul, I promise. What I know, you'll know. Just don't eat your heart out, and for god's sake be careful. I'm betting you come up empty anyway. No need to take one in the chops."

I went back to my office, shut the door and composed a letter on plain paper to Gomez containing the basics on the last two C&T design competitions plus a heads-up on Rod Bolton. I closed by saying I thought the mayor himself needed to know, and that I'd be an anonymous Deep Throat for whatever additional information I could provide. But anonymous, I emphasized, was the key word, which I was trusting him to enforce. Then I sealed the envelope—also plain with no identifying marks—wrote his name on it, and called Elaine, his secretary.

"Mr. Stiles, yes, hello. Aren't you the person who wanted to reach Andrés Gomez?"

"That's me."

"Were you successful?"

"No."

"I'm very sorry. I hope you got my message saying I tried."

"Yes, and I appreciate the follow-through, but I have another favor to ask."

"Surely you realize I can't force him to call you. If it's city business, I can refer you to someone else, but he gave the impression it was personal."

"That time it was, this time it's not."

"Oh."

GOMEZ

"I want to mail you something. Inside will be a sealed envelope for Andrés. It's deeply confidential and for his eyes only. Please take my word that it's city business, deliver it to him personally, unopened, and stand by to be sure he at least begins reading."

"It's not going to explode is it?" She wasn't joking.

"No, no. I'm sorry this sounds so strange. Andrés may be down on me, but I have a very high opinion of him."

"So does everyone here. Why don't you just mail to him directly, then?"

"Because I'm afraid someone else might open it first, or that he'd throw it away unread if he saw it was from me."

"Oh, my goodness."

"Would you be willing? It's important and I don't know where else to turn."

She took an audible breath. "I'm a bit nervous, but alright...I'll take the chance."

"Thank you, more than I can say. Seriously. Now what address do I use to get this onto your desk?"

I mailed my handiwork on the way home, went for a run, dug some food out of the fridge and popped on the news to learn that Congressman Ryan and four members of his entourage had been seriously wounded by gunfire at a jungle airstrip near Jonestown, the People's Temple compound in a small, godforsaken, equatorial country called Guyana.

÷ ÷ ÷

As days went by, the news got spectacularly worse. Ultimately Ryan, an *Examiner* reporter and 913 other people were dead, the latter in the most grotesque mass poisoning/suicide anyone had ever heard of. All the victims, or nearly all, were from SF. I didn't know any of them myself, but Ivy did, Kes Mackay did, and so did Kara. Gomez, I would've bet, also did.

After a People's Temple hit-squad had attacked while Ryan and his group were preparing to leave, James Jones, the cult leader, declared Armageddon and arranged for himself and his entire cadre of followers, some at gun point, to drink lethal Kool Aid. Two hundred of the dead were children. The scene, however, was so chaotic that the body count and identities trickled out over an agonizing period.

GOMEZ

The city was in shock, comparable only to the John Kennedy assassination many reports said. Everything at L-W ground to a halt and Ivy wept off and on at her desk.

At some point Elaine called from the Mayor's Office to confirm that my letter had arrived, that she had handed it to Gomez, and that he had read it with great interest. In fact, he'd asked her to thank me. She and I agreed, though, that a lot of things that had seemed important the week before didn't seem like much now.

"I knew several Temple members from volunteering on the mayor's election in 1975," she went on. "Not that well, and not recently, but I can't believe they'd willingly line up and comply. One of the women I met had three kids there with her."

"Yeah," I said. "Put in perspective, my issue with Andrés is small potatoes, and so's all the Supervisor hoopla with Dan White."

"Ever since it started, that business has seemed more absurd than a Mime Troupe skit," Elaine replied.

"Are you a Troupe fan?"

"Oh, yes."

"Have you seen *Electrobucks*, their new one?"

"Two weeks ago, for my thirtieth birthday. Not their best, but after Christmas I'll find another friend and go again. They steadily add and embellish, so it'll be a fresh experience."

"I haven't seen it myself, but it's on the agenda."

"Well, enjoy," Elaine said. "It's been nice talking about something normal after so much horror, but I've got to say goodbye."

With all his theories about the collective insanity of the Bay Area seemingly vindicated, my dad called on Thanksgiving to see how I was doing. Fine, I said, which was objectively true. If I weren't exposed to newspapers or TV, everything in my own little world was OK for the moment. I had hope that Gomez would rein in any extortion attempts by C&T, and I had vague hope that his doing so would provide a means for reestablishing contact with him. Mad was leaving me alone, while Kara, Jenny, Jordan and the Housers gave me a social life.

Not that I said any of that to my dad. Just the word fine and some mutual babble about the weather and a cold he'd recently gotten over. But when he pressed his point, implying that there must be nascent People's Temples on every street corner across the city, I lost my temper.

"Yes, we had Patty Hearst," I interrupted, "and but you can't hang Jim Jones on San Francisco. He was weird, and folks picked up on it and ran him out of town. He was down there to escape legal action. He didn't grow up here, he wasn't liked here, and he certainly doesn't represent us. No real San Franciscan would behave like that."

And damned if he didn't back down. "You're right, son. What do I know? They don't give us any news on the TV except sensationalistic crap."

Jenny had invited me for Thanksgiving dinner, but I politely declined. At the time I didn't have other plans, I just thought it was too domestic a thing to do. I was short of cash that late in the month, which meant no Kara for a while, but I invited the Housers over for wine and to check out my place before we went across the way to MacArthur Park for a holiday meal. It was pleasant, low key and just what I needed.

Saturday morning's paper told me that Dan White had lost a bid for an injunction to prevent his seat from being treated as vacant. It also said that security in and around City Hall had been tightened in the wake of the Jonestown disaster because more Jones-inspired hit-squads were rumored to exist. Nonetheless Mayor Moscone had celebrated his forty-ninth birthday the night before at a large fund-raising dinner in the ballroom of the Fairmont Hotel. Gomez was undoubtedly there, for all I knew wearing a tux, but didn't appear in any of the photos.

Still, over the long weekend I began to think that he would call, and kept checking my machine. When he hadn't by 10 a.m. Sunday, I drove alone to Mt. Tam, parked at Pantoll and hiked a round trip of the entire Matt Davis trail, buying a stale sandwich in Stinson Beach to eat on the way back. It was a cold, sunny day with glorious views in every direction. I didn't encounter any aboriginal spirits, and I didn't detour to the clearing where Mad had staged her mock rape, but I was acutely conscious of what I'd lost since then and how little I felt I'd gained in return.

GOMEZ

CHAPTER 29

I was at my desk late Monday morning when word swept the office that Mayor Moscone and Supervisor Harvey Milk had been gunned down in City Hall and were dead. Minutes later word came that Dan White was presumed to be the shooter and was still at large. L-W's staff had already been rocked by the repercussions of Jonestown, but this amounted to a typhoon.

Ivy ran onto deck and threw up over the railing. I tried to clear my desktop because further work would be impossible, accidentally slamming my hand in the drawer while I was at it. But physical pain felt welcome by comparison, and I sat watching creases of blood collect in the skinned flesh of my knuckle.

Almost everybody wept, wandering from office to office exchanging hugs. It was more than the brain could process, and I imagined scenes like this taking place throughout the city and rippling outward across the bay and the state. Radio and TV waves would arrive first, then the real impact, the psychic one, would follow, lessening with distance like an earthquake. I wrapped a Kleenex around my sore finger and went to the break room, where I knew somebody would have a news broadcast on. It had been brutal, I learned, with many bullets pumped into both men, but they were the only known victims.

By noon, in the company of his wife, White had given himself up and was in custody, and by 12:30 L-W closed and sent us all home. The weather had so far been unremittingly foggy and didn't look to improve. I bought a to-go sandwich out of habit, but had no appetite and forgot to eat when I reached my apartment. Instead I dropped the bag on the counter and made a beeline for the TV. Flipping impatiently from channel to channel, I looked for Gomez and tried to piece together what I could.

Gradually, and in no particular order, it became known that White had evaded the new metal detectors by climbing through a basement window, assuring those who saw him that it was OK because he was a public official and in a hurry. He then dropped in on

GOMEZ

the mayor, claiming that he was following up on a demonstration his supporters had staged on the City Hall steps earlier in the day. He shot Moscone first, reloaded, dodged out a side door into the hall, went to Milk's office, said calm hellos to people he knew as he passed, murdered Milk, then dashed away in the subsequent confusion.

As the rumors, terror and shock spread, things were so jumbled inside and outside the building that the first police vehicle to arrive rear-ended another car and sat at the curb belching radiator steam. Willie Brown was reportedly the last person to see the mayor alive, having met with him on something just prior to White's arrival. Brown confirmed that Moscone had no intention of re-appointing White and had been ready to announce a new pick. And later a new appointment actually was announced, not for White's seat, but that of Board President Diane Feinstein to be Acting Mayor.

Various overwrought city staff were interviewed during the afternoon and I watched anxiously, thinking Gomez might be among them. This would completely take his knees out—the good one and the bad. Not only was Moscone his hero, Gomez might lose his job. Feinstein would almost certainly have her own cadre of advisors and community liaisons to bring with her.

Gomez didn't show up on screen, however, and no one mentioned his name. But tearfully discussed over and over was that Moscone had given his tickets to yesterday's 49ers game to one of the junior clerks and had instead gone, while I was taking my hike on Mt. Tam, to a matinee performance of *Tosca* at the Opera House.

Finally, with Dan White jailed and sequestered from the press, and the news beginning to repeat itself, I ate my sandwich, put a Band-Aid on my finger and made a bid for sanity by going for a run. The Embarcadero was vacant of auto traffic, and the expanse of slips and piers lining my route to China Basin might have been the waterfront of a ghost town. It remained foggy and gray and the few people I did see had their heads down, neither speaking to nor looking at each other. Although I ran hard and worked up a sweat, it felt silly and meaningless, as though I were a lone hamster scampering in a treadmill.

But when I got home, there was a message on my machine from Mad. "Paul," it said, "I really need to speak to you. Please, please call. No matter how angry you are, this can't wait. I'll be at home. It's OK if Clark answers, just ask for me."

Her voice sounded weak and distressed, but whose anywhere in a fifty-mile radius on that sickening and shameful day wouldn't have? Under the circumstances maybe I'd relent and do as she asked, but not right away. Still, I did want to talk to someone, so I picked up the phone and dialed Jenny.

"God, I'm glad you called," she said before I could identify myself. "Are you alright?"

"As a relative term, yes, I'm fine. No direct effect except a 3-D preview of hell."

"What about your friend who knew the mayor? The Argentine guy?"

"He's OK as far as I can tell. You sound pretty rattled yourself."

"It's a nightmare. Jonestown was horrible beyond words, but this...losing Harvey Milk...feels like it happened in my living room."

"Moscone was pretty worthwhile, too, from what I'm told."

"I know, but you probably didn't hear Milk at the Freedom Parade in June. He was magnificent."

"I didn't hear him speak, but I saw him go by on Market Street, waving from his white convertible."

"You mean you were there?" Subdued or not, Jenny's approval couldn't be missed.

"Sure, I've become a real San Franciscan, and at least they got that bastard White."

"Now let's see if they'll convict him."

"What? That's a lock, believe me."

"If he had shot only Harvey, I'm afraid you'd be wrong. Beating and killing gays isn't considered major crime."

"I think you're exaggerating, Jen. Proposition 6 went down by a million votes. Times have changed."

"Don't be too sure. Barbara's just as worried. You haven't lived our side of it."

"Barbara?"

"Yes, in the aftershock today we're talking again. Don't read anything into it. You know things are always better if people talk."

"Did you have an OK Thanksgiving?"

"Yes, I went to Tillingham's...the new lab director and his wife. They had a few of us stray ex-pats over. How about you?"

"I went to a restaurant with those married friends I've mentioned. Jim Jones was finally out of the headlines and things were starting to feel normal again."

"It doesn't feel close to normal now," Jenny added. "More like the end of something...something big."

"If this is the end, what was the beginning?"

"I don't know...maybe the Beatles. We weren't here then, but that's how it seems. Until now, however bad things got, you could hope it was temporary."

"You're right, that's how it does seem."

"Why do the haters have to kill people?" Jenny sighed.

"Listen, that guy...White...is strange. I saw him go berserk during a televised political rally the other night."

"That's why I think he'll get away with it. The more outrageous the violence, the more the lawyers use it as evidence that the perpetrator was insane."

"Yeah...definitely a circular problem. But changing the subject...if possible...do you know this other teaser, about the square root of a symmetrical number starting with 12 quadri...?"

She cut me off good humoredly. "111,111,111. A real chestnut, that one. You can multiply it out yourself. Does this mean Handy Andy is back in touch?"

"No...just curious. It did come from him, but I never tried to solve it."

"You've reminded me, though. At Thanksgiving I put your envelope problem to someone from the Philosophy Department...a logician, adept at maths...who came up with an alternate solution while pouring gravy. Inelegant, but no one could disprove it."

I felt a little stab, then hope. There might be more than one solution to my problem with Gomez as well, so nothing was final if my plea of City Hall intrigue didn't work out. "You know, Jen, I'm ready to show off my place and have you here for a drink."

"Oh, good, I'd like that."

"Maybe this weekend. How's Friday night?"

"Wide open."

"I'll call again tomorrow or Wednesday with specifics. We'll go to dinner after, but I want the restaurant to be a surprise and should check the reservation picture."

"OK. It's been too long since I've seen you even if there's nothing to celebrate these days."

Although I was still in my running shoes and sweats, and felt clammy, I decided to open a beer and turn the TV back on before I showered. I'm mainly a wine drinker, or have been since I moved to California, but I'd bought a six-pack of Anchor Steam on my last trip to the North Beach Safeway and was learning to like the stuff. I continued to be proud of the label, so why shy away from my own good work?

With the cold bottle against my sore knuckle, I walked across to the big living room window and let my eye follow the shape of the Transamerica Building narrowing and narrowing upward, some floors lit, some dark and some a checkerboard of both. Maybe, I thought, I'd put on some music instead of the TV. How much more could I relive the same horrifying story? Then I heard knocking on the door behind me. Having the doorbell ring was unusual enough, but a physical knock was completely unknown.

Another knock as I approached came with Jordan's voice. "Paul, it's me. Anybody home?"

I opened the door. He stood in the foreground, and largely hidden from view by his shoulder was Mad. "It's a dismal moment for the whole city," he said, "so I won't intrude, but this lovely creature has been wandering the halls looking for you. Since I owe some favors in that regard, here she is." He stepped aside, but acknowledging the wit of his reference to the times I'd escorted women from my door to his was beyond me.

Mad's lower lip quivered, her hair hung loose, her eye makeup was smudged, and the long black cape she wore made her look as dramatic as Maria Callas in the final act of *Medea*. "Will you let me in?" she asked helplessly, almost inhaling the words.

"Of course he will," Jordan said, pulling away and momentarily resting his hand on Mad's arm to urge her forward. I saw his head swivel so he could stare at her profile, then he pointed with his chin and silently mouthed to me the word, "Wow!" As she moved toward me, he continued his commentary by raising and wiggling the finger on which his wedding band would have been worn and

GOMEZ

mouthing, "It's...her!" His remaining gesture was to reach in and close the door.

With each step Mad took, I backed up. Why she'd picked me I couldn't fathom, but I thought I knew what she would say. It was more than the assassinations. Cancer had returned and killed her mother. "Would you like a beer?" I asked stupidly.

"Paul," she said, then drew a deep breath, "Gomez is dead."

From legs to torso, I was wracked by a jolting shudder. Mad took two more steps, threw her head onto my chest, hugged me and sobbed loudly. I held my open bottle away from us with one arm and placed the other over Mad's shoulders and against her beautiful hair. I felt a brief welling of tears, which I didn't try to hold back, but which never really came. We stood together like that, speechless, for several minutes.

She eased slowly away. "Sorry to burst in, but I had to see you. If beer is all there is, I'll take one...or anything."

"Are you sure?" I heard myself groan. "They only said Moscone and Milk."

"Completely sure. Just get me that drink."

"It's going to be brandy," I said, glad to have something to do. I dumped my beer down the sink, grabbed two water tumblers and a half-full bottle of VSOP, and mutely led Mad to the coffee table and couch.

"This place is *very* nice," she stated, looking around and dabbing her eyes with a tissue. "I should have made you bring me while I still could."

"Sit, for god's sake." I poured us three inches each and handed her a glass. My adrenaline began to kick in, along with denial. "Why wasn't it on the news?" I blurted.

She gulped half of what I'd given her, set down the glass and held the cape tightly to her body by wrapping her arms at her waist. "He wasn't shot," Mad said in a hoarse voice. "He was hit by a bus."

I gulped from my own drink, which filled my septum with upwelling fumes. "That ...that...seems almost worse." It was a struggle to get the words out.

"So sickening, so banal," she agreed dully. "There was a meeting with the mayor he'd been pushing for. He was late and parked behind Hayes Street Grill just before the first word of trouble came on the radio. He ran down the alley, must have seen a break in traffic on Van Ness and tried to dodge through.

"But a Muni bus pulled away from the curb just as he stepped off. It was chaos by then, people were screaming and shoving through the back doors of City Hall across the street. Gomez didn't see the bus, and the driver didn't see him."

I shuddered again. A meeting with the mayor had gotten him killed? A meeting for which I had likely set the agenda, and had pressured him into. "It's so unbelievable," I said, trying to rein in my disordered thoughts. "How do you know?" Yet that was Gomez to perfection, running toward what everyone else ran away from.

"People saw what happened and tried to revive him, but it was impossible to get an ambulance or even a cop. He was dead in ten minutes. Anyway, since he had City Hall ID, his secretary Elaine got the word. She notified the Centro and they called me. I called Susan, but Mimi Yost from Hayes Street had already heard and told her."

"Susan DeFeo?" I asked. "The artist?" It startled me that Mad knew Susan.

"You've met her?" Mad responded, drinking more brandy.

"No, seen her is all. But I heard she and Gomez might be an item."

"Well, they are…were. Susan's done props and sets at the Troupe for years to earn cash, and she was pretty open with me from early on. She's devastated now, poor thing, worse than us."

"So you and Gomez were back on good terms? He won't…" anguish rolled through my ribcage as I caught myself, "wouldn't…speak to me."

"I can't call it good terms, nothing like before, but I did him a big favor and he eased up a bit."

"I did everything I could to make him ease up in my direction."

"He would have eventually. Things were going really well for him. But you…both of you…have cost me a fortune in therapy since the summer."

"In all honesty, Mad, you had it coming."

"Fine…maybe…but there's a lot you didn't get. And some I didn't, either."

"The hardest thing," I said, "is why he even bothered with me. A guy like Gomez could have any friend he wanted. And why you had to do what you did."

GOMEZ

"You don't understand that?"

"No. None of it."

"We were both drawn to you for the same reason. Of course with him there were other factors, but my therapist says not so unusual for a dominant male. Gomez was the type who likes to go steady, to have one close friend at a time, and not somebody who'd be a rival. Also, the way he kept remaking his life...and finally his name...the fewer friends he had, the freer he was to do that. In a way, Susan replaced both you and me, but you were always closer to him than I was."

As good as it felt being told that, I was no nearer to understanding than before. "What do you mean 'drawn to me?' That's not the effect I have on people."

"You really don't know, do you? You've changed, so it's not as clear-cut now, but Gomez saw right away that you had an unclaimed heart. And at your age, such a rare thing. He couldn't pass it up. When I first heard, I didn't believe him, but he was right.

"There you were...polite, civilized," she went on, "with money, good taste and an unclaimed heart. Gomez wanted it, and I wanted it, too. And when he learned about *us* and the dossiers, it wasn't just that he'd lost his secret self...he thought I'd won. But he ended up winning, didn't he?"

"Yes, he did."

"The aspect I didn't see, that I've become aware of with my therapist, is how my side of it ties in with my family, and with Clark."

"Which is how?"

"A woman who marries a much older man is seeking an archetype of her father... partly to replicate him and partly to compensate for his failings...like mine, who was never around, who thought his money made up for that, and who rejected me physically the minute I hit puberty. In theory, once the woman possesses the archetype its power over her ceases, and she can deal the husband as an equal. That doesn't *always* work, but in my case it did.

"I got tired of Clark's complaining that he couldn't cope with all his travel, his nights alone in Indonesia without me, so I made him take on a mistress there. After he admitted to liking it, and said he felt guilty, I told him he shouldn't, because I'd do something similar while he was away."

GOMEZ

"Why didn't you just travel with him?"

"For what? To sit on the veranda drinking gin and tonics? I have a life, I have a job. Clark and I fought about it at first, but when he finally gave in, and when I met Gomez...everything fell into place."

"Did Gomez know that?"

"Never. He thought I was being wronged by Clark, which is how I had to make it sound for the sake of Gomez's damned scruples. Then you came along, and we found ourselves competing to influence what you read and thought, and Gomez has the brass to tell me about your father's...ah, penile complex...and your ex-wife, and say, 'Oh, flirt with Paul a bit, bring him around, he thinks he's been unmanned.'"

"Was that before or after Artichoke Joe's?"

"Both. But the whole male vanity thing was too much to take. Gomez believed Clark had all but assigned me to him, so now he had the right to assign me to you? No way. I wanted you, I went after you...just like Anaïs would...and too bad for both of them."

"What about me? You weren't what I'd call honest."

"Did I harm you? Would you want to erase what we had?"

I paused. She was right. "No. But investigating him and trying to deflate him in my eyes were part of the contest from early on, weren't they?"

"Of course, and you rejected me anyway. How do you think that feels?"

"I know how it feels."

"Well, Gomez needed to come down a peg. They say it builds character. Can I have more brandy? I'd like to get looped."

"What about your drive home?"

"I took BART. And if Clark were away, I wouldn't need to go home...or want to."

I poured another generous shot from the bottle for each of us, letting pass her remark about staying. "Where does he think you are?"

"At the prayer vigil in Civic Center Plaza."

"I didn't know there was one."

"It's what people always do. Listen, Paul, my new therapist is a Jungian. We met at Esalen, he's wonderful, and he's also my lover."

"I thought that violated professional ethics."

GOMEZ

"It does, and he was a hard sell, but I guess I love corrupting men. I'm also planning to get licensed as a therapist myself. Not an MD shrink, that's out of reach, but a counselor. Ira…the Jungian …says I'm a natural, that I'd be good at it. But I really don't want to give you up. Can't we be together like we used to?"

I looked at her. Although she was in no sense begging, she was serious. And with Gomez gone, it would be less wrong. My mind's ganglia and branching neurons still held a maze of desire for her, but I knew what came with venturing in. "No, Mad, we can't. I've decided to try again with Jenny…my ex. She's made the offer and I've really thought it over."

Mad was perceptibly surprised. "Wow, I didn't see that coming."

"It's for the best. I'm basically monogamous, and with you I'd always be sharing."

"I wouldn't mind sharing with Jenny, but if you'd rather I honor your wishes, I will."

"Thanks. Please."

"God," she grumbled, "monogamy. You and Gomez, what a pair."

I remembered his lecture to me in Berkeley on that subject, and had to smile at the thought of his lecturing Mad. "You were really right to come here," I said. "If what happened to him had to be, far better that I heard in person."

"It's helped me, too. No one else I know could grasp the full meaning. Oh, and another thing, there's a memorial service for him, seven o'clock Friday night at St. John's Chapel on 15th Street."

"I've done a lot of grieving over Gomez since July. Then Jonestown, then that fucking Dan White. I don't have energy for more."

"Come on, Paul, you have to. There'll be Centro people, City Hall people, Mime Troupe people, and Susan's friends. She'd been working for weeks on a fantasy portrait called *Andrés Gomez at Age 20*, showing him in a wild yellow-and-navy striped jacket. Now the unveiling will be part of the service."

"I don't think I could stand it…or the irony, since there was no Andrés until last summer."

"Which Susan probably knows, but I haven't said a thing. You need to put that aside and be there. Elaine is in charge of the arrangements, with Graciela and me as helpers. I'll even introduce you to Clark."

I let my expression tell Mad that I thought Clark was reason enough to stay home. "I'm still at no, and a room full of strangers would make things worse. Speaking of Graciela, did Gomez ever own up to lying about her?"

"It turns out he didn't. Graciela's uncle lied to him. Until I explained the facts, Gomez actually believed she'd fled Guatemalan death squads. Graciela isn't even her real name, which he didn't know either."

So, I thought joylessly, the guy was vindicated again. Beyond his having purloined Mad's gun, something entirely between them, and the trivial matter of his age, there had never been reason to distrust him. And now, because he'd been on his way to see the mayor with my career in his hands, Gomez's blood was on mine. "Whatever issues you two had, he never lied to *me* about anything important, and my feelings are too private to be prated about."

"Please. I'll make sure you're comfortable. His parents are so frail they can't leave Florida, and his brother in the army…he and Gomez were pretty much estranged for years…says he can't get here that soon. If you want to avoid Clark, fine, but it may be your only chance to meet June. She needs all the support we can give."

GOMEZ

CHAPTER 30

Thanks to the brandy, the shudder that went through me this time was warm. "Hold on a minute. Who *is* June?"

Mad blinked her eyes rapidly and leveled them on my face. "June," she said, "you know…Gomez's daughter."

"His what!"

"Oh, oh, I get it…you didn't read those pages of the dossier, did you?"

"No, Bonhof said there was nothing else that applied to what we'd asked."

"Paul, Gomez was married and had two kids. He hadn't lived with his wife since Alabama, but they never divorced. June's the oldest, just turned eighteen. The other is a severely retarded boy. He's institutionalized, but Gomez always helped maintain him and stayed married to…to…"

"Donna," I said.

"Yes, Donna…so she'd get his social security and life insurance if anything…" Mad's voice broke, "if anything happened to him."

"And something has…but I thought her parents were rich."

"Well off, but not rolling in it. She's been depressed and suicidal since the son was born. They help support the boy and her… earlier on, June too…but Gomez was such a hardhead he just had to stay aboard. I talked to a lawyer friend of Clark's about it after my big blowup with Gomez, and the lawyer said divorce per se would make no difference in the benefits Donna or her family could get."

"Is that why you were so pissed…because he was married?"

"Yes, a lot of it. The way he had to be so on top of everything, so superior. And that he would have kids, which I can't, and then deny them because they're defective."

"Huh? What's wrong with June?"

"She's gay, that's what, and it drove Gomez up the wall."

"Is this closet of his ever empty?" Not a time for humor, nor did I realize my words could be taken as a pun until I spoke them.

321

GOMEZ

Mad didn't notice. "Since you wouldn't read, I have to tell. Donna and Gomez were lovers in Greenwich Village, and June was born while he was in Argentina. When he returned to the US and found out, they married and came to Berkeley. She was pregnant again when they got to Alabama, and that's where Curt, the son, was born. He was in bad shape from day one, and neither of them could deal with it."

"I'm not sure I'd do any better."

"Well, the Gomez image didn't include a mentally ill wife, a retarded son and a gay daughter, so he started leaving them off his vitae."

"Not at first. His controversy with UC over married student housing probably means he tried to bring them back after Alabama."

"Only June, or that's what she says she remembers, but her mother's family wouldn't let her go. Then, last year, when she got involved with an older woman and said she was gay, her grandparents flipped out, called Gomez, he flipped out, and June ran away."

"Jesus," I interjected, "what a saga." Divorced and no children was what he'd told me, so plausible that I'd never questioned a word. Yet the reverse had been his big secrets.

Bonhof was convinced that Gomez would have opened up to me eventually — had I not betrayed him, that is, and had he not been heading for the Mayor's Office at the wrong time. The betrayal I'd been wrestling with for months. My culpability in launching him toward a fatal appointment was actively percolating through my consciousness like dye in a tissue sample.

Maybe, with everything else the same, if Gomez — or the *Chingados* — had beaten the crap out of me last summer and left me in the alley with Armando, facing people at the memorial service would have seemed possible. As it was, with neither source of guilt paid for, I knew I couldn't.

"Were you aware," I went on, dragging my thoughts back to Mad, "that he was connected with a program for teen runaways in the Tenderloin?"

"At the time, no," she answered. "I learned about it later, after June surfaced. He was terrified she would be roped into the sex industry. Street hustling is ugly, but the strip clubs, massage parlors and movie producers are no better. Remember his Mitchell

Brother's audition? That's why he really went. To get to know the porn world a bit, and put out feelers."

"Gay women are involved in that stuff?"

"Yes, of course. Not that they're all gay, but it's like a sisterhood. Good money, and whatever they earn reinforces their contempt for men."

"What makes you such an expert?"

"Pillow talk. God, Paul, do you think I haven't had sex with women? It would have been bad for your morale so I never brought it up, but Anaïs didn't turn her back on anything and neither do I."

On such a traumatic night, because I was already numb, I was better able to withstand this news. Not only had I become obsessed with someone who was AC/DC, but in recoiling from Jenny and Barbara I'd spent months in thrall to the physicality of other gay women, fueling my self-contempt with their contempt for me. Kara I didn't think was gay, but could her attitude toward her clients be that different? "Well, at least his strategy worked," I said, trying to sound collected. "Gomez and June found each other."

"No, he was barking up the wrong tree. That was the favor I did him."

"You found her?"

"More or less. It made sense that she'd come to SF. It's the gay Mecca, after all, and *he* was here. They were very close when she was younger, and spent time together every summer. By last spring he'd finally come to terms with her being lesbian, and was putting the word all over town that he understood and she should call him. For months he had a hidden answering machine and phone in his apartment. The ringer was turned off, but I discovered it just before we got serious with Bonhof."

"I'll be damned."

"The outgoing message identified him as Andrew Steentofter, so June would know she had the right place, but he couldn't face having us or anybody else in on it. I didn't tell you because you were so down on me for nosing around."

"Why do you suppose he changed his name? Bonhof couldn't figure out, and even asked me."

"My shrink says that after June came out as gay, he couldn't stand being Steentofter any more. There were so many contradic-

GOMEZ

tions, he had to become a different person. I still think it was more a joke than anything, like you first told me."

"I'd rather think that. And June you found how?"

"Through the Mime Troupe. She's a sweetheart, has her dad's charm and coloring, quite mature, with nice teeth and hair. There's a big lesbian community in Noe Valley, and they volunteer with the Troupe for this and that. In September I heard a rumor about a new girl from back east living with one of them, and hit the jackpot."

"Where is she now?"

"Still with her paramour, but she and Gomez were on track and doing pretty well. She was supposed to start college at SF State next semester, which he was paying for. Who knows what'll happen with that. I offered to tell June he was dead, but Susan wanted to."

"After tearing him down so much, why would you help trace his daughter?"

"Because I felt rotten. Not right away, but Gomez is…was…the most fabulous person I've known. I meant it when I said whatever answers Bonhof came up with would be OK. Gomez could be infuriating, and he hated my unraveling his cocoon, but the truth made him more fabulous in a way. I knew something was going sideways between us before I realized it was Susan, but I decided to bet the whole future on the dossiers. He'd either like not having to hide anymore, or he'd dump me and I'd have you."

"And Clark, and your shrink, and your friends from Noe Valley," I added quietly, with no reaction from her.

"But for that to work," she continued, "you couldn't be the one to tell him. Then, god, when I laid out what we'd discovered it was a disaster and I got carried away. I still think Hayes Street, with all of us there, would have gone better."

"Not based on the Gomez I knew. You may have danced with him and slept with him, but you never played racquetball."

As drained as Mad was, she managed a smile. And nothing she'd said tonight was at odds with what I'd heard outside Gomez's window. "I have to go, Paul," she sighed, "before I collapse. It felt good to walk here from BART, and the walk back will take care of the brandy, but I need to be awake when I get to Rockridge."

"I could drive you."

"No, I don't want that."

"Does having a gun in your purse make you feel safer?"

GOMEZ

"What gun? Clark is trying to push a new one on me, but I won't let him. They're too easy to misuse. No matter how crazy Dan White was…no gun, no murders."

"Gomez would be pleased."

"Fuck Gomez!" she laughed, standing up. "By the way," she continued, "do you still have my panties?"

"What do you mean?" I blushed, caught off guard.

"Paul, I saw you take them from under Gomez's pillow. I sort of thought you might. If you hadn't, they'd have been like others I used to leave sometimes as a tease when I popped in and he wasn't around."

I stood now, too. "Last spring I wasn't ready to believe women did that kind of thing. They were like a red flag for our having been in his bed. So yes, I've got them."

"Good," she said. "Keep them hidden from Jenny and think about what might have been."

"I'll do exactly that. It can add to my role in your diary…if I have one."

She smiled sadly. "Of course. All my men do."

I walked her to the door, and we hugged longingly, forlornly, for two full minutes. "You never took off your cape," I said when we separated, thankful to have been spared greater temptations.

"I forgot," she answered. "Maybe I'd have been more successful at ensorcelling you if I'd remembered."

"Tonight I was probably immune, and I don't see other chances on the horizon."

"Paul, really, you have to come to the memorial service. You owe it to him."

"What I owe would be better paid by staying home."

Once the door was locked, I felt woozy, punky with dried sweat, and still so jolted that I shuffled into the kitchen without knowing I was hungry, found some cold pizza and wolfed it down. Then I wandered into the bedroom with a fresh beer to turn on the TV. A large crowd, many holding candles, filled Civic Center Plaza, listening as Joan Baez sang *Swing Low, Sweet Chariot*. Gradually the whole crowd joined in, repeating and repeating verses because Joan didn't want to stop and neither did anybody else. I sat and watched, expecting to weep, but again I didn't, then or later during a ghastly and wretched night.

GOMEZ

What inexplicable mayhem. Three of the best people anyone watching on TV or there in person could possibly know had been snuffed out, permanently, forever, and long before their time. Being larger than life didn't mean they were larger than death—not even Gomez.

÷ ÷ ÷

It wasn't until 3:30 on Wednesday, at work, that I received the official word from Elaine, along with a second invitation to the memorial service. That done, she insisted on apologizing because she felt she was calling much later than she should have.

"Don't worry," I assured her. "Please. I heard on Monday. You're above and beyond to think of me at all. If it's hard being at my desk, how can you be at yours?"

"Until noon today, I wasn't. But there's people's phone numbers that I only have here, and this is a time to do things right."

"How're you holding up?"

"It's awful. Luckily, we're down the hall from where the shooting and the blood were, but it's still like working in the morgue."

"That part will fade, I suppose, but the end result won't."

"No, it won't. None of us could save the mayor or Supervisor Milk, and we heard about Andrés too late, but I *can* help with this. If you see me at St. John's, please do say hello."

"I don't know if I'll make the service."

"I understand. I should have gotten this letter out to you sooner, too, but I haven't."

"What letter?"

"From Andrés, saying he took care of your problem. He and the mayor met on it before Thanksgiving. There's a standard constituent letter which he was going to personalize..." Elaine's voice became high-pitched, stopped, then resumed, "...Sorry, I can't control myself. Anyway, now he never will, but I'll send it as soon as I can."

"No rush. I don't need anything in writing." With both my advocates—Gomez and Moscone—gone, what I'd done might have no effect at all on the C&T job. Or had a fair-play requirement already been handed down and Feinstein would enforce it? Either way a vast shadow over my life had lifted. "But if I am at the service," I said, "I'll find you for sure."

"There's going to be a wake for Andrés, too, Sunday at a bar near Bernal Heights. His artist friends are painting him into a mural there, and into another one on an outside wall up the hill. They'll announce it at St. John's when the portrait is unveiled. We're also trying to set up a fund to cover his daughter's college costs. Oh, sorry, I have to say goodbye and take another call." She hung up.

At last the tears came. I closed my door and rocked back in my chair. I didn't sob or choke, but salty moisture flowed silently down my face, dripping onto my collar and my tie. I couldn't have turned it off if I'd wanted to, nor did I try. Before Thanksgiving, Elaine had said. My issue had been dealt with before Thanksgiving, when all three of this week's dead were still alive. And as the tears kept coming, were they only for Gomez, or also for Paul—who had just been found not guilty on one of the counts against him?

I expected to cry again Friday night at the church, and I knew Jenny would let me modify our date to include an event as important as that. I needed her presence to discourage Mad, with whom I would never be friends. I didn't have the will power, nor could I trust her not to seduce Jenny on top of it all. But I wasn't going back to Jenny either. Being friends was my best offer. The line I fed Mad was for extra protection, and Kara was even less an answer to my lack of a relationship than Jenny or Mad would be.

Instead, if Elaine was as together as she sounded, and single, I'd ask her to attend the Hieronymus Boxx wake with me, and in coming weeks, the Mime Troupe show. If she was straight, wanted kids some day, and was maybe even cute, so much the better. It was exactly what Gomez would recommend. I couldn't keep striking out every time I went to bat. As for June, a college fund wasn't necessary. I would stake her to four years, no questions asked. That was a far more worthy use of my new raise than what I'd been doing.

And if Elaine wasn't a possibility, maybe the next step was finding a shrink. Unless I'd already been Mad's first therapy patient and she'd gotten the diagnosis right: you had to lay claim to your own heart before it could properly host anyone else.

SOLUTIONS TO THE $1,000 ENVELOPE PROBLEM

Enve-lope No.	Classic		Philosopher's		Yours	
	Amount	Cum. Amt.	Amount	Cum. Amt.	Amount	Cum. Am
1	$1	$1	$1	$1		
2	2	3	2	3		
3	4	7	4	7		
4	8	15	8	15		
5	16	31	16	31		
6	32	63	32	63		
7	64	127	63	126		
8	128	255	125	251		
9	256	511	250	501		
10	489	$1,000	499	$1,000		
Total	$1,000		$1,000			

As for Fibonacci Numbers, they describe everything from Bach fugues and the whorls of sunflowers to the proportions of the Parthenon and the breeding of rabbit pairs, depending on whom you talk to. They do not, however, solve the envelope problem.

Also, for non-believers 111,111,111 x 111,111,111 truly does = 12,345,678,987,654,321

Printed in the United States
217003BV00001B/10/A